The First Time

The First Time

ISBN 978-0692434949

The First Time

Bernadette Pajer

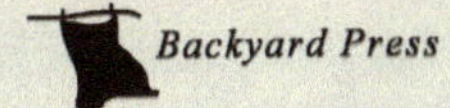

Also by Bernadette Pajer

A Spark of Death
Fatal Induction
Capacity for Murder
The Edison Effect

Dedicated to you, dear reader.
May you find magic in your own backyard.

1

"Paper or plastic?" Ivy O'Neal hadn't a clue that her life would completely change before she asked, in just a few short minutes, that dreary question again.

She'd asked it so many times, she'd begun forgetting to listen for an answer. Even worse, she'd begun asking the question at the wrong time, after she'd finished bagging the order, and she'd be left blushing and stammering an apology to her annoyed customer.

Most of the time she did listen, and she did try to be pleasant, to bring a bit of kindness into the day of those she waited on. But her customers at the Pig Palace Food Emporium on Highway 99 in Seattle had begun getting on her nerves with their constant and often obvious questions. *Where are your oranges?* Couldn't they think to look in Produce? *What time do you close?* What did they think *Open*

24 hours meant?

And her all-time most-hated question: *Are you open?*

Did they think she dressed in a white button-down collar shirt, a black bow tie, black polyester pants, black leather sneakers, and a neon-pink apron emblazoned with a cartoon pig face because she thought she looked cute? Did they think she stood smiling pleasantly in a grocery store checkstand, with an open sign brightly lit and barrier chain unhooked, just because she was a friendly sort of girl? How many clues did they need, for goodness' sake?

Maybe it was time for a change. Checking groceries was not exactly emotionally fulfilling, though it paid well and the benefits were good. There had to be more to life than beep, bag, and have a nice day. She'd never intended for this job to become her life's work, only something to fill the days until she knew what it was she really wanted to do. Something wonderful and fulfilling, something to make her feel complete. The days had accumulated into years, and now she was twenty-seven, still here, still waiting. Stagnating, really. She'd be here for the rest of her life if she didn't get proactive and find something else. But what? What else could she do that was any better? That paid as well but didn't get dull? If only she had a calling for something, a passion, a talent. But all she had was the ability to smile when bored and make accurate change.

These thoughts pestered her as the paper-or-plastic question hovered unanswered and she reached for the can of Folgers coffee on the conveyor belt. She mustered a cheerful smile as she scanned the coffee.

Her customer, a yoga mom wearing a Seahawks jersey,

handed over a bright pink canvas bag and replied, "Neither."

Today was the grand reopening of the Pig Palace after a major remodel. Ivy had thought it would be fun, at least for a little while, to work in fresh, gleaming surroundings. But nothing had really changed. Her job bored her as much as ever. Same questions, same responses. Same unending line of impatient customers who didn't realize how hard it was to keep smiling. Even the city-wide ban on plastic bags hadn't altered her routine. The Pig Palace simply switched to the thicker legal plastic bags and charged customers for the privilege of using them.

She sighed and hit the total button.

The checkstand scanners, new though they might be, were adding to Ivy's disgruntled mood. Instead of humming along quietly like the old ones, they emitted a faint high-pitched buzz. And the scanner in Ivy's checkstand, express lane four, had just this moment begun to squeal—an ear-piercing screech that surely could be heard all the way to the highway. Ivy pressed a hand to her temple where the sound hammered for entry. All down the long line of sparkling new checkstands, the other checkers, identical in their black bow ties and pink pig aprons, scanned groceries with efficient speed, seemingly oblivious to the noise.

"Sorry," Ivy said, but the yoga mom took her change without commenting on the horrible noise. The next customer approached, a small, smiling white-haired woman in a purple plaid pantsuit. A single cantaloupe sat waiting on the black conveyor belt. None of the other customers in line, all holding cartons of eggs because the twenty-five cent sale had just been announced, seemed to hear the horrible sound. How could they not?

Reaching for the cantaloupe, Ivy, a little disoriented by the squeal, wondered who she should call to report it, afraid that any minute the darn thing would blow up.

And then it happened.

Before she could even utter the dreaded paper-or-plastic question, the scanner's piercing squeal exploded and became, impossibly, visible.

There, above Ivy's conveyor belt, the sound had erupted into tiny little fireflies of light, swirling around and around, faster and faster, circling a black and seemingly endless void. Ivy stared up at it, too surprised to move.

Without warning, the void flashed with a light so bright that Ivy flinched and covered her eyes. Then just as suddenly, the void was no longer a void. As she peeked through her fingertips, Ivy found herself staring into another world—no, she saw another place, outdoors, a barren, brown field and a vast blue sky, and a man.

The man was dressed like an old-fashioned soldier. He stared back at her from that field, looking as shocked as she felt. His uniform was drab khaki with a diagonal black strap from shoulder to waist. On his head was a funny-shaped cowboy hat bent up on one side. He was tall and broad-shouldered like a poster soldier, his skin sunbaked to a golden brown. His eyes were the exact shade of the summer sky.

He will be your true love. The lyrics of the old song came to Ivy as she stared at the soldier. He hovered before her no more than a few seconds, yet every detail burned sharp and clear into her memory—the high forehead, the intense low brows, the carved cheekbones, the dimple, the full bottom lip. His startling blue eyes.

Ivy stood immobile, her pulse pounding, completely engrossed in the soldier hovering above her conveyor belt. Little pins of nervous anticipation prickled her skin. Her hand began to tingle, and she felt a tug, a pulling, and then the rough skin of the cantaloupe scraped her palm. Then it all vanished—the lights, the flashes, the soldier. Even the scanner squeal.

"Are you open? Miss, are you open?"

Ivy blinked, slowly becoming aware of her surroundings again. The white-haired old woman cocked her head, her face full of concern.

"Are you sick, dear?"

The long line of egg-buying customers had doubled, and all of them stared at her as if she were mad. Bob Evanston, the store manager, had opened the neighboring express lane.

Bob said curtly, "Would you please get back to work? Your line goes clear back to the bakery."

As manager, Bob wasn't required to wear a hideous pig apron, but his dark jacket lapel bore a pig emblem, and his tie had little pig faces. Only a man as good-looking as Bob could wear that tie and not look ridiculous. With blond hair, hazel eyes, and the physique and tan of a professional skier, he had the disgusting ability to rattle Ivy with a simple smile. The memory of their fling (could she call it a fling if they'd never had sex?) didn't help.

"My scanner gave off this horrible shriek and the lights exploded. You must have seen it." Her heart pounded so fiercely she felt it in her throat. Had somebody tinkered with the equipment—some computer-game genius? Was this a hoax? A YouTube prank? Part of the grand reopening hoopla?

"Is your scanner down?" Bob met her eyes, sending as always a flirtatious hello along with his question.

Ivy's back stiffened. "No. It's working, it—" She glanced up at the ceiling, looking for a camera or projection device, anything to reveal how the lights and seemingly real other-world had appeared. Nobody else was looking. The customers in line continued glaring at her as if she were nuts.

Bob's flirtatious eyes turned dismissive. "I'll take a look at it later, PJ. As long as it's working, just keep checking."

For a brief moment, irritation flared in Ivy. PJ! How she hated that nickname! But her annoyance was no match for the incredible soldier whose image valiantly burst her negative thoughts. Bob and his teasing eyes and horrible nick-naming could go to—she had seen—something!

Ivy, smiling hopefully, looked down her line of customers. "Oh, come on," she said. "Didn't any of you see that? The lights, the swirling, the flash, the soldier—" Her voice trailed off as she was met by stares and a few glares.

Bob turned around again and jerked his head, indicating for her to get back to her checking. She gave another glance down her line at the glaring faces, looked at the empty black conveyor belt, glanced up again at the empty air that had moments ago flashed and shone with the face of that blue-eyed soldier. Had she hallucinated? What in the world had just happened?

She reached for the customer's cantaloupe, but it wasn't

there. It had vanished, just like the swirling lights.

The customer harrumphed, gave her vinyl handbag a squeeze, then stormed away toward customer service, most likely to lodge a complaint.

The next customer approached.

"Paper or plastic," Ivy asked automatically.

She forgot to listen for the answer.

* * *

Transvaal, South Africa, May 1, 1901

"The Cap'n's down! 'is Lordship's down! Scully, get yer bleeding bum down 'ere!" Private Carter shouted in his thick cockney accent.

"I'm down, Carter. But I'm not deaf," said Harrison Darby, Lord of Wyndham, coughing from the effort. He was down all right, on his back. He'd fallen into a rocky ditch, not a hundred yards from the tin-roofed farmhouse that had been their objective. A few small jagged boulders forced his spine up, his shoulder askew, but he couldn't find the strength to move. It was as if communications between his mind and his muscles had been cut off, just like the snipping of a telegraph cable.

"Pardon, Cap'n. Scully'll be 'ere, soon as you can say Bob's yer uncle. Just lie still."

Since struggling proved futile, Harrison obeyed, closing his eyes against the blinding sun that was angled low on the horizon as it prepared to usher in the night.

He still felt the tingling of those confounding swirling

lights. What had he seen? Had the spray of bullets caught the sun's rays? Had the Boers developed some sort of artillery shell that exploded into mesmerizing bits of shrapnel?

He shivered, seeing again those lights and that face, hovering there for just an instant before he was struck down.

"It's bloomin' brass monkeys, Cap'n," Carter complained, his breath escaping in misty clouds.

Harrison felt the weight of a khaki jacket gently draped over him. Though the sun was blinding hot during the day, its warmth didn't reach into the shadows nor linger into night. It was almost winter here in South Africa, and dry as chalk dust. Far away, on the other side of the equator, it was spring, wet and green and lush. The leaves of the plane trees would be open by now, Harrison knew, but London seemed a lifetime away. And Wyndham in North Yorkshire might as well be on the moon.

Wyndham Manor beckoned, bittersweet. He loved the place, the town, the land, too dearly by far. It had become a dream to him, a place he would never see again. So much had happened since he set foot on the shores of Africa, so much horror. And death.

And Jeffrey. No. No, he mustn't think of his brother. He must try to think of England, of home. But the images would not come. They were the places of fairy tales, believed in by innocent children. Not men of war.

"Cap'n?"

"I'm still here," Harrison replied, bringing his thoughts painfully back to the cold rocky ditch and the chung-chung-

chung of an enemy Mauser, echoing in the evening air.

They'd been advancing on foot across the dry veldt, the autumn sky a deceptively peaceful blue, when the Boer commandos had opened fire. Early scouts had declared this desolate piece of earth safe. The farmhouse that was their destination was thought to be free of the enemy, though inhabited by two civilians—an old missionary and a small child.

Carter spoke again, but Harrison didn't hear him. He was thinking of that face in the lights. A face he'd never forget. He was sure he'd never seen her before and yet he knew her. His heart knew her. She'd looked right at him, right into his very soul. He'd stood transfixed, frozen before enemy fire.

But what had become of her? He was suddenly filled with alarm for her safety.

"Is she all right?"

"Cap'n?"

"The girl. The young woman."

"Wot? A gel? You're on the bat'lfield. Don't you 'member? Huh, well, never yer mind a bit. ’ad a wallop, din'ya? Wouldn't blame ya for seein’ a gel. Was she pretty, Cap'n?"

Harrison thought a moment. Her looks weren't of the sort he usually admired. Not worldly nor exotic nor particularly breathtaking. But something about her touched him. Dark-haired, brown-eyed, pale-skinned. Her sharp cheekbones and lionesque nose reminded him of an Irish-American he'd once met who was part Cherokee. She . . . glowed. Yes, that was it. She glowed with radiance from within, and her eyes held a warmth and gentleness of spirit.

"Yes," he said at last. "She's lovely," he added, for it seemed somehow disloyal to say otherwise. "But is she safe? You must find her and make sure she's not harmed."

"On me 'onor, Cap'n, there's not a duck in sight. Now, now, lie still, Your Lordship., I'll look about. Lie still. Scully!"

"I'm here, Carter. I had to fetch the stretcher, hadn't I? Gawd, he's lost a lot a blood."

"Shush your mouth, Scully, and git 'im on the stretcher."

The stretcher was in reality a fallen officer's greatcoat that had been tied between two wooden shafts pilfered from the wreckage of a transport rail car.

"The girl," Harrison said again. "Find the girl." He felt no pain, but a numbness crept into his chest and abdomen. He felt himself being lifted, and heard the grunts of his men's efforts. At thirteen stone and well over six feet, he was not an easy man to heft. He felt himself sink into the makeshift stretcher. Gunfire began to sound again, and then he was being jostled as Carter and Scully ran as best they could.

"Bloody beastly Boers!" Carter shouted above the gunfire.

Harrison grunted in pain as he was dropped to the earth in the dark shade of an outbuilding, and both Carter and Scully flung their bodies over him.

"Leave off, you two," Harrison demanded, but his voice held no strength. "Leave me here and go get those bastards. And find the girl. That's a direct order, now. She's out there somewhere. Find her!"

Private Scully obeyed without question.

Carter, bending low to avoid enemy fire, bolted from the safety of the outbuilding. He was back in a matter of minutes. "It's like I bin tellin' ya, Cap'n. Not a duck nor skirt nor ruffle within sight. Just two Boers got any fight left, and the rest a the blokes are after 'em now."

"For God's sake, Carter, get out there and do a proper search. Leave me here; I need no tending."

Harrison was used to having his orders obeyed fully and without question. Carter's insolence was not only unusual but frustrating.

"No, Your Lordship. Yer bleedin' somethin' awful. Say wot ya like. I won't go."

"I'll place you on report the moment we reach camp," Harrison growled. Carter's excessive devotion was leading him to disobey direct orders. The threat should have garnered Carter's reluctant obeyance; instead, his long face screwed up in fierce anger. He whipped a wicked Australian knife from his belt and flung it toward Harrison's head.

It happened so quickly, Harrison had no time to move nor react. He heard the blade whistle past his ear, but he felt no pain, no strike. He simply stared stupidly at Carter, whose face, in the growing darkness, collapsed with seeming relief.

"Snake," Carter said with a shake of his head, reaching for his knife. He held aloft the squirming skinny body of a very deadly night adder.

"Thank you," Harrison said as his pulse finally slowed.

Carter shrugged. "I hate them things, I do. Niver in me life 'ave I seen such spiders and snakes as wot I've seen in Africa. Makes me long fer the rats a Whitechapel, it does, and that's no lie."

Harrison gave a soft chuckle. Twice in five minutes he'd avoided sure death. He decided Carter's disobedience should be ignored, for now. "Where is Fleming?"

"Out behind the privy house, if I know him, sir. Waitin' for the all-clear."

As if summoned by the accusation, First Lieutenant Kyle Fleming slipped into the dark shelter of the outbuilding, crouched low and breathing hard. He was slightly built, Harrison's own age, and the son of an impoverished but politically powerful baron. He was handsome almost to the point of prettiness. The men of the company razzed him terribly, but Harrison had always been civil to the young man for he was certainly not cut out to be a soldier. He could better serve his country back in London, where his affinity for politics and society women would open many doors. But Fleming's father was also a retired general who insisted his son must prove himself a man by going to war.

"Captain? Are you seriously wounded?" Unlike Carter's rough and colorful speech, Fleming's words were soft and well-articulated.

"No, Fleming. I'll live. What of the farmhouse? Is it occupied? The scouts reported Dutch civilians, an old missionary and a young child. Are there any commandos?"

"I don't know, sir. I believe they've all been accounted for. Phillips has them on the other side of the field. Scully just shot another down by the well."

"I want you to check out the house. If the civilians are still there, tell them they are now under our protection and they are to remain indoors until we take them to the camp in Pretoria. And see if there is a young woman there as well. Be sure they are all unharmed."

"A young woman? Captain, the scouts said—."

Carter interjected, "You 'eard wot 'e said, Lef'tena. A gel."

Fleming retorted, "And you, Private, will do well to remember that I am your superior officer."

Harrison, irritated by his men's squabbling, ordered Fleming to carry out his order, but a rapid volley of gunfire delayed Fleming's departure from behind the outbuilding.

As Carter pressed a wad of cloth from his haversack onto Harrison's bleeding wound, Fleming stalled further, asking Harrison about the young woman.

"You actually saw a third civilian?"

"Yes. Actually. With my own eyes."

Carter glared at Fleming, but said nothing, turning kind eyes to his captain. "Couldya 'ave mistook her for the missionary?"

Harrison felt himself fading. It was a drifting feeling, as if the creeping night was taking him with it. Struggling to hold on to consciousness, he answered, "No, no. She had no beard, you fool. And she was too young. Didn't you see her? She was in the lights."

"Lights, Cap'n? No, sir, I dinna see no lights. Musta been the wallop, sir, wot brung the lights to your eyes."

"No, no. I saw the lights before I was shot. And the girl, she was in the lights."

"Wot she look like?"

"Oh, smiling, kind."

"Smiling, sir? Weren't no old Boer, then. Likely it were a

vision you had. Was it Lady Amalie?"

"No, no. She had dark hair."

"Dark hair, you say? Princess Philippa then? No? Lady Dover? Miss Simms, then, she's got dark hair, and nice big—no?"

"Carter, have I no secrets from you?"

"None, sir. This new gel. 'She the one you met at the Cape? On leave in Paris?"

"No. I've never met her before."

"An angel, sir? You seen an angel come to save yer life? Lucky devil, you are! Women all over Europe chasing to marry Your Lordship, and now the 'eavens' fairer sex after you as well. No bloody fair! My luck, I'd get a wallop and it'd be the scowling Queen Vicky, Gawd rest her soul, that'd come tell me to quit mucking about and get back to work."

Harrison's chuckle soon turned to a cough. When he could speak again, he looked at Fleming, who still hesitated though the gunfire had ceased.

"See to it," Harrison said. Reluctantly, Fleming obeyed, crouched and running, his rifle gripped with white knuckles.

"Lie still, now, sir—wot the bloody—" Carter flung himself protectively again over Harrison, as shots ricocheted off the wood planks above their heads. There was a shout that sounded like it came from Scully, and then a single shot sounded in the near distance. A moment later all was silent. Eerily silent.

Harrison listened to the silence, holding his breath. The sun chose that moment to hit the horizon in a blaze of red-gold and the sky surrendered to night. And with the night came the chilling and tender sound of a child crying.

* * *

It hadn't happened. It couldn't have happened.

Ivy downshifted for the red light on Highway 99 and pulled to a stop behind a BMW. Her own car, a 1980s Honda Civic, purred noisily but faithfully. On both sides of the highway, businesses flashed and winked with signs, competing for attention. *DVD Rentals—99 cents! Free Car Wash with Fill-up! Kung Fu lessons here! Checks cashed—no questions!*

Ivy rolled down her window, letting in the noise and smell of traffic and humanity that thankfully didn't completely drown the fresh breath of spring. Behind the corridor of businesses, homes and neighborhoods thrived. And rising in the distance, in nearly every direction, were forests and mountains, a constant smiling promise that civilization hadn't completely ruined the planet. Technology and modernization could be ugly in unpredictable ways.

Could technology be unpredictable in other ways? Go berserk? Turn a grocery scanner into a portal to another time and place?

It couldn't have happened. Already, after just seven hours of routine and boring checking, the incident was blurry in her mind. Like a dream. She began to blush with the memory of how she'd embarrassed herself asking Bob and all the customers if they had witnessed her hallucination.

The light changed. Ivy automatically shifted into first,

then second, as she passed through the intersection. She was shifting into third when she saw the billboard. Her foot slipped from the clutch and the gears ground. The little blue Honda choked, then died. Ivy sat dumbfounded, staring up at the billboard, while behind her a Volkswagen honked angrily.

Seattle Art Museum the billboard shouted in bold italic letters beneath an enormous reproduction of a painting. A green painting of ivy, nothing but ivy. Cleverly created within the delicate tendrils was the portrait of a woman with arched uneven brows, the right slightly higher than the left, high flat cheekbones with rounded cheeks, a long straight nose, a stubborn jaw.

The Volkswagen's driver had given up blowing his horn, had backed up and shot around her. Now a pickup truck pulled up behind her. The horn tapped politely.

But Ivy couldn't get her car started. She couldn't even remember how. She stared at the billboard. At the ivy. At her own image smiling down.

2

White sheets billowed softly on the parallel clotheslines. Ivy, in shorts and T-shirt, her feet bare, stepped between the sheets into the gleaming white world. She closed her eyes, her arms spread, her hands pressed into the wind-dried sheets. She began to walk forward, breathing the sweet scent of clean laundry, the freshness of the breeze, feeling the rough-cut grass beneath the soles of her feet. The crisp, nearly dry fabric snapped and fluttered.

Halfway down the line, the cherished memory came, and she saw her mother as she had once been, just twenty-four, with long black hair, her kind face glowing with a loving grin. She wore a shin-length floral dress that fluttered in the breeze. Ivy heard the soft echo of her mother's voice call out, *You can do it, Ivy. Run through. I'll catch you.*

As Ivy's memory unfolded, she felt her father's strong gentle hands on her shoulders, giving her an encouraging nudge. And now Ivy ran, as she had then at the age of four, arms outstretched into the sheets. She emerged into the open air of the huge, fenced-in backyard, her arms empty.

"There you are, Ivy," Aunt Daisy said from the back porch. She, too, was barefoot, but wearing a homemade cotton dress patterned with pale lilacs. Her white hair was teased and puffed; her makeup light and attractive. At seventy, Ivy's great-aunt was stiff in the joints but still young at heart.

Daisy said, "They're playing that show again—the one about life on Mars."

Ivy shrugged. It was too nice of a day to watch television. She dropped into a lawn chair, and Daisy settled gently into a chair beside her, squinting against the glare of the afternoon sun.

Resting in the shade beneath Ivy's chair was a 1970s AM radio—cantaloupe-orange and shaped like a lopsided donut—that had once belonged to her mother. Ivy felt for the ridged dial, turned up the volume, then settled back into her chair as Glen Miller's "A String of Pearls" drifted in from the oldies station.

Both Ivy and Daisy sighed. Ever since Ivy had seen the Jimmy Stewart movie about Glen Miller, this song made her so sad. Why did it seem all the great love stories ended tragically?

Audrey, a sleek black tailless cat, jumped up into Ivy's lap and stretched with a soft rattling purr.

"Life on Mars," Daisy said after "A String of Pearls" ended and "The Street Where You Live" began to play. "Can you imagine? When I was a little girl, we didn't think man would ever even make it to the moon, and now they've found life on another planet."

"Microscopic fossils," Ivy said with an indulgent smile. "From about a billion years ago."

"All the same, I hope they find something alive before I die. I'd really like to see that."

The television show was a repeat from nearly twenty

years ago. Nothing more had yet been discovered, but Ivy didn't want to ruin her aunt's enjoyment of the possibility. She said, "I suppose you'd like to be abducted by aliens."

"That depends. If they're like the aliens in Cocoon, I would. But if they're like the ones in those alien movies, I think I'd just as soon not."

Ivy stroked Audrey's sleek back, and the purring deepened. In the yard, the sheets ballooned with a gust of warm, pine-sweet wind, the slender leaves of the willow tree whispered, and a jet high overhead yawned, leaving a puffy white trail far, far away.

Ivy's foot tapped away at the scratchy grass. They never watered the backyard, but they kept the front yard green, the hydrangeas blue, the small house a cheerful white with mossy trim. This was home—this patch of earth on a dead-end block in Seattle—and had been all her life. Even when her parents had been alive.

"Daisy," Ivy said cautiously. "You believe in the possibility of life on other planets, right?"

"I think I just said that, Ivy dear."

"What about life in other dimensions?"

"You mean that soldier you saw the other day? The one who painted all those pictures that look like you?"

Ivy, careful not to topple Audrey, pulled a crumpled museum brochure from her pocket. She reread it for the thousandth time.

Edwardian painter, Harrison Darby, Earl of Wyndham, was born January 27, 1872. An Oxford graduate, in 1899 he joined the British army as a commissioned officer to fight the Boers in South Africa.

On May 1, 1901, Lord Wyndham, then serving with the Bushveldt Carbineers in the northern Transvaal, was injured. He claimed to have seen a vision of magical swirling lights and the face of an angel in their midst, just before he was shot. That particular battle later became the subject of a court-martial, but Lord Wyndham never stood trial. He was found incompetent by His Royal Majesty's Sanatorium, and on December 23, he died in hospital in South Africa, a haunted man.

His works were all inspired by the vision he'd experienced, and all were completed within an amazing six-month timespan, May through October, 1901.

A witness who could have testified on Lord Wyndham's behalf and perhaps saved him from his mental agony was Private Tom Carter. But Private Carter went missing from active duty, and foul play was suspected. Although he appeared in Johannesburg in June of 1901, he was subsequently killed—apparently the victim of a mugging—before he was able to testify. His private diary was recovered in 1989 by Lord Jason Pepper, historian and art promoter. In Carter's own words:

"His Lordship was enamored of the vision of the girl in the lights. She was real to him, an angel of loveliness and grace, he called her. I believe she was real, though I did not see her myself."

"It's just so bizarre," Ivy sighed. She'd gone to the museum downtown; she'd seen the eerie beautiful paintings in person. A dozen clean brochures sat neatly on her bedside table, and a dozen books on South Africa and the Boer War were piled on her dresser. Ivy had spent the past month completely immersed in South Africa and obsessed with Harrison Darby, Lord of Wyndham.

Daisy's chair creaked as she shifted to ease the pressure on her arthritic joints. "Well, all this newfangled technology is bound to set things off. The scientists and engineers don't really know all there is to know about such things, do they?"

"No, I guess not."

Ivy now knew she had not hallucinated Harrison Darby, though many people had said just that. She'd called CRC, the Cash Register Company—the makers of the new scanners—and they'd had no idea why she heard a squeal, nor did they think her vision, as they put it, had anything to do with their scanners. She'd called every computer and software company in Seattle—there were many—and they'd all said the same thing. Given the equipment, what she claimed had happened was impossible.

Daisy interrupted Ivy's fruitless thoughts. "Could be you saw that soldier in some other dimension. I once saw your great-grandma Rosie on television when the set wasn't even on. Plain as day, she was on the screen, smiling at me, like she was saying, 'Don't worry, everything will be okay.' That was right after the accident."

Daisy didn't need to specify which accident. Ivy knew she meant the car accident that had killed Ivy's parents when she was four, just two days after the magic summer afternoon when she ran through the sheets.

"Bob thinks I was hallucinating."

"Bob is an idiot. Why do you listen to a man who calls you PJ?"

"Oh, he doesn't mean to insult me," Ivy said, not sure

why she bothered defending him. "Anyway, I am a Plain Jane. I'm just like the plant I'm named after—ordinary and dull."

"Nonsense!" Daisy declared. Ivy believed Daisy hated Bob's nicknaming her more than she did. "PJ, indeed! You're beautiful, you're intelligent, you're kind. The man's crazy if he can't see that."

Ivy smiled into her aunt's determined, loving face. Basking in her aunt's fierce love, Ivy's plain looks mattered not at all to her.

"You need to go out more, Ivy. Go to the movies with a friend."

"Okay, friend. What do you want to see?"

Daisy shook her head, but a smile threatened to override her scowl. "You know what I mean, Ivy. It's been six months. You should be dating again."

"We've had this conversation a thousand times. I never dated much before I went out with Bob."

"I know, but at least you went out with friends. What about Fai and Marina? Why don't you call them up and go out to dinner or something?"

Ivy shrugged. She wasn't in the mood for seeing her friends. She hadn't told them anything about what had happened. All she wanted to do was sit in the sun, listen to Doris Day and Frank Sinatra, and think about Lord Wyndham and his blue eyes.

"I'm happy. Really, I am. I don't need anybody but you. Someday, when my Prince Charming comes along, maybe I'll consider making a change. Until then, I'm content."

Daisy opened her mouth to protest, so Ivy hastily

changed the subject. "Why do you think I saw him only once?"

"Him?" Daisy asked, her white brows lifting with interest.

"Him, the soldier in the lights, Harrison Darby."

Daisy sighed, settling back into her chair. "Oh. Well. I don't know. A fluke, I guess. A phenomenon. All the planets lined up or something."

"It must be something more than that. Something to do with the scanners. But what? What was so special about that day? That hour, that minute it happened?" It had been so busy because of the twenty-five-cent eggs sale. "Every checkstand was open," she said, sitting up straight so quickly that Audrey leapt to the grass with a chirp of protest. "That's it! I don't know why I didn't think of it before! Every checkstand was open, all fourteen of them, even lane one, which we rarely use because it's the backup for the main computer."

"There must've been times since then that all the lanes were open at the same time," Daisy protested.

"No, I don't think so. It happens only a few times a year. The day before Thanksgiving, the day before Christmas, the day before Easter. The Fourth of July. Customers are always complaining about it. They wonder why we have so many checkstands if we don't plan on using them. A few minutes after I saw him—Harrison, I mean—the special sale ended. Bob pulled his till and shut off his scanner. I don't think they've all been up and running since."

"Well, then, you'll just have to turn them all on and see what happens," Daisy said. "When's your next shift?"

* * *

Harrison shoved the clutter of reports to the edge of the writing table to better position the sheet of blank white paper before him. He stretched his arms, took a deep breath, rolled up his sleeves, then picked up the pencil.

The lead hovered for just a moment above the abyss of white before touching the page. He drew a curved line, added another, and another, and soon the delicate lines began to reveal a hauntingly familiar face. Without lifting the pencil, he surrounded the face with leafy tendrils until they were as one, the lady in the ivy.

He sat back and exhaled a long, contemplative breath.

His fingers itched. He touched the paper, skimmed his fingertips along the curve of the cheek. His skin craved texture, softness, warmth, not the unresponsive coldness of a sheet of writing paper.

He traced and retraced the lines until they blurred, leaving an image a hint closer to that which his mind sought. He squinted at the blur, trying to see her.

A moment later, he cursed, then shouted, "No, no!" It was wrong, all wrong! He crumpled the paper and slung it over his shoulder where, with a soft plop, it joined the growing pile.

He pulled forward another blank sheet, ran his fingers through his cropped hair, then tried again. This time, the result stared up at him, taunting him, so close, so very close. His palms began to sweat. Color. He needed color.

Where in the Officers Recovery House could he find

color? Were there still paints in the sitting room downstairs? Yes, he could remember Henderson toying with them last week while a talented lieutenant with a missing foot played the piano. Could he slip down there, steal the paints and a canvas or two, and return to his room without any of the other men seeing? His thoughts darted feverishly for a moment, planning the raid of paints. Then the absurdity of his eagerness, his nervousness, hit him.

Oh, what the hell was he doing?

He growled, snatched the sketch he'd just finished and wadded it viciously. The crumpled wad was in his hand and over his shoulder when he heard a clunking sound come from the adjoining bedroom.

He froze, listening intently. When no further sound came to him, he barked, "Jasper?"

There was no response. He rose, dropping the crumpled sketch onto the pile, and stepped out of the dressing room he was using as an office into the bedroom.

Jasper, one of the orderlies who served as batman to the twenty officers recuperating in this large modern Greek Revival farmhouse on the hill above Pretoria, was nowhere in sight, and everything appeared to be in place. Harrison began to feel foolish at his jumpiness.

He strained to listen, hearing only the night song of insects and the occasional low grumbling roar of a lion. The neighboring house, a quarter mile distant, kept a menagerie of animals in a sort of private zoo, and the recouping officers had all spent time watching the wild creatures.

But inside the house, not a sound issued.

His glance dropped to his feet. There, on the thick red

wool carpet, lay an odd clear flask filled with blue liquid. He bent to the carpet, wincing as he picked up the flask. His ribs still ached under the bandages; the stitches itched liked midges, but he resisted scratching.

The bottle was much lighter than he'd anticipated, and he gave it more heft than was needed, accidentally flinging it across the room. He braced for the crash of glass but it never came. Instead, the flask landed with a dull, bouncing thump-thump.

Curious now, he crossed to the flask and picked it up again. It wasn't glass at all but some sort of clear substance lighter and apparently less breakable than glass. He read the label. Jiffy Window Cleaner with ammonia. The back label listed ingredients and said, Made in the U.S.A.

Well, that figured. The Americans were always coming up with handy products, though he hadn't realized American goods were presently available in Pretoria. It was encouraging to know the supply trains from the Cape were getting through.

He squeezed the little trigger, and a spray of liquid shot out smelling like a perfumed antiseptic. Very clever indeed. He set the bottle near the door and stood for a moment, pondering the cleaning liquid.

Several native women from town came daily to clean the rooms. Had one of them left the flask behind? And if so, why had he heard it clatter to the floor just a moment ago? Where had it been before it fell? A glance around the room showed no likely place where the bottle might have sat in a precarious position, in imminent danger of falling.

A huge, stitch-pulling yawn overtook Harrison. He was

all at once bone-tired. He abandoned the idea of sneaking downstairs for paints.

He went about the room, turning off all the electric lamps with the flip of a switch, marveling that such modern conveniences were commonplace in Pretoria. It was the gold that had done it. The discovery of gold on the Witwatersrand had launched Pretoria overnight from paraffin to electricity, from leaking brick bungalows to Victorian mansions, for some. It was said, too, that gold and diamonds were behind this interminable war. Harrison was one to agree.

The light from his oil-fueled bedside lamp was refreshingly soft and golden. And the bed, with its feather mattress, was exceedingly comfortable to a man who'd spent the better part of the past two years sleeping on the ground. He mentally thanked the good homeowner, an English civilian with railroad interests, who'd donated his home for the wounded. This suite of rooms was indeed a luxury.

He thought of reading, but decided against the effort of choosing a selection, of making the words comprehensible to his still unsettled mind. Sleep, a good rest, was what he needed. He was reaching for the lamp when a skittering light danced across the sleeve of his nightshirt.

He didn't move. Reflections of playful fireflies winked from the shade of the lamp, against the taupe wallpaper. He was going mad. He knew it. He retracted his arm and slowly, carefully, turned in bed until the source of that reflective light was visible, there, across the room, about twelve feet away, just above the pomegranate rug. He knew that light. He'd seen it before, in battle, when he'd seen that angel with the lovely warm eyes. The angel whose face he'd been trying to capture on paper ever since. Only this time there was no spray of Boer fire, no setting sun to confuse his eyes. No explanation for this vision at all.

Around and around, faster and faster the lights went, forming an upright oval. In the center, in a black void, suddenly there was a flash. In the brief time it took him to flinch from the brightness, the lights vanished, completely gone, and something fell to the carpet with a thwap and bounced toward the bed.

Harrison sat immobile for a moment, barely breathing. Was this real, or was his mind playing tricks? Had the doctors been wrong, and was there still some piece of shrapnel buried within him, pressing on some vital nerve that led to his brain? He crawled stealthily over the bed cover, a pomegranate-red quilt with inlaid gold lions, to the edge of the bed. Cautiously, he peered over.

There on the rug lay a painted box, rectangular and narrow, the corners bashed in from its tumble. On the box was a caricature of a man in naval uniform and the words *Captain Sugar Cereal* in fat red script. Cereal? As in grains?

With a hand that shook more than it had when he'd been on the front lines at Mafeking, he reached out to the box. He tapped it with his fingertips, prepared for a shock or the lights to return or something. But nothing happened, so he picked up the box and sat in the center of the bed. He read front and back and both side panels, twice. Some of the ingredients were chemicals so scientific they were followed with a description. Sodium citrate (a flavoring agent). Mono and diglycerides (emulsifiers for uniform dispersion of oil).

Why were such things in a breakfast food?

A flap on the top of the box said, *To open, lift tab carefully.* There was also a stamp mark that said, *Best before June 2020.* Surely that didn't mean the year 2020. So did it mean the twentieth of June in the year 1920? That seemed equally preposterous. Or was that what the chemicals were for? To preserve the cereal for two decades? He lifted the flap and found inside a sealed bag of waxed paper. He pulled, but the bag resisted, as if attached inside. He pulled harder, and the waxed bag flew out and opened at the bottom, spilling little gold nuggets all over the red field of gold lions.

He bent and sniffed. Sweet. The picture on the box showed the yellow nuggets in a bowl, covered with milk, but he didn't want to go down to the kitchen. If he was going insane, he preferred no witnesses. He picked up a little pebble of the stuff. It was light. He squeezed, and it crumbled in his fingers. He sniffed his fingers, then licked them. Hmm. Not bad. He picked up another and bravely popped it into his mouth. Overwhelmingly sweet, but tasty.

He'd eaten several handfuls and was beginning to get a headache when the lights returned. He watched eagerly this time. If he was going mad, at least it was an entertaining state of mind.

This time, when the flash came and the lights disappeared, he was left with a smaller box, the size of his palm. *Ibuprofen,* the label said. *Pain Reliever/Fever Reducer.* This one showed a date of 2025. Maybe the date represented some new licensing system of the Americans. Perhaps they granted corporations rights to manufacture in hundred-year increments. It sounded foolish, but regulators of state were not known for their wisdom. He tore open the box and inside found a bottle of unusual material filled with pills. He could hear them clinking when he shook the bottle, but he couldn't manage to get the lid off. As he struggled, pushing and turning as the instructions said to do, with a palm sticky from cereal, the lights appeared again.

With a grunt of frustration, he tossed the bottle aside and waited. This time, a larger bottle appeared, without a box. A bottle made of an odd hard material like the cleaning fluid bottle, but opaque, not clear. The label declared it contained a floral-scented hair shampoo-plus-conditioner called Perky Shine.

For the next hour, he was entertained. In all, seven items fell from the flashing lights before the show ended. Besides the Captain Sugar, the ibuprofen, and the Perky Shine, there'd been a roll of Thirsty paper towels, a package of Chips Galore chocolate chip cookies, a packet of impossibly small electric batteries called High Voltage, and lastly, a bouquet of summer flowers in a transparent wrapping paper marked with a sticker and an astoundingly high price of seven dollars and ninety-nine cents.

He sat on the bed for several hours, staring at everything, reading all the labels, checking his pulse, going to the dresser mirror and putting himself through a number of sobriety and mental tests the army routinely gave during medical examinations. After a while, he gave up trying to make sense of it. His mind had grown numb with thinking and worrying. So he put the flowers in the water pitcher, and locked away the other items in the bottom drawer of the wardrobe.

He finally fell into a fitful sleep at dawn, the sweet perfume of summer flowers haunting his every breath.

3

Daisy, dressed in a thick purple robe, her white hair rolled into prickly curlers, sat upon the closed lid of the toilet watching Ivy at the sink put on her makeup. The radio clock on the shelf blinked 11:22 p.m.

"I still don't see why Bob is making you work graveyard. You ought to call the union."

"It's only for a couple of weeks. I don't mind." Ivy leaned toward the mirror, tilted her chin up, and carefully stroked mascara onto her lashes.

"You could nail him for sexual harassment," Daisy said.

Ivy gave her bottom lashes a final brush, then shoved the wand into the mascara bottle. "Daisy, you're making more of this than it is." Ivy's words were lightly spoken, but her stomach suddenly knotted. What could she possibly put on a harassment claim form? That he called her PJ? That six months ago he'd not pressed her into having sex with him? That he'd not protested when she'd timidly said she didn't think they should see each other anymore?

"You look lovely," Daisy said.

Ivy glanced at her reflection. Black hair temporarily held back with a plastic butterfly clip, unremarkable features adequately made up, the white collar of her starched blouse buttoned under her chin, she looked exactly what she was, a grocery checker. She sighed with resignation.

"Are you going to turn on those lights tonight?"

"Uh-huh," Ivy replied. She held her head upside down to fasten her hair into a black plastic clip-comb. Her scanner experiments had taught her two things. If all the scanners were turned on, the lights appeared. And the lights remained visible until an object was within a few inches. Then the object was sucked away, gone. The lights then also vanished. They reappeared twenty minutes later, if the scanners were left on.

"Do you think it's his bedroom you're seeing? Lord Wyndham's?"

"I don't know. The room always looks empty." Yet it didn't seem static, like a photograph. The angle of her view of the room often changed, though she'd never seen anything actually move. She'd seen only inanimate objects—a dark polished wardrobe, a matching dresser with a mirror on which sat a water pitcher with flowers, and a four-poster bed with a red quilt that was covered with small gold lions. Yet Ivy felt when she looked into the room as if time existed there. The room seemed alive. Three-dimensional. Real.

Her hair neatly pulled back, her face completed, Ivy strapped the black bow tie around the white collar of her shirt.

She turned, leaning against the sink as she faced Daisy.

"I was thinking I might try to send a message through. Like people stranded on desert islands used to do. A note in a bottle sort of thing."

"Wouldn't it be something if you got a reply?" Daisy's face glowed.

Ivy smiled broadly. No words were necessary between them as the idea percolated. It was a fantastic yet terrifying thought that somebody on the other side of the lights might respond.

Ivy chewed her lip thoughtfully. "Do you know what bothers me the most about all this?"

Daisy shook her head, her white brows lifted.

"My face in Harrison's artwork. He died haunted by my face. I feel so guilty about that."

"Ivy, you shouldn't. It wasn't your fault those lights came. You couldn't have helped it."

"I know," Ivy said, shrugging. "Still. It's how I feel."

"It may have been his fate to die in a mental hospital."

"Maybe. And maybe not. How do I know that he wasn't supposed to have some wonderful life? How do I know that it wasn't my face and only my face that messed him up?"

"Ivy, think about it. Do you blame him for appearing to you? No? Then why would he blame you for appearing to him?"

Ivy shrugged again. "Well, I guess I should get going."

Daisy followed her out into the cozy living room with its tidy worn furnishings, the overstuffed russet couch, Daisy's dusty blue rocking recliner, the old brass lamp with its cheerful white shade.

Leaving the house at nearly midnight felt decidedly wrong. In the corner of the living room, tucked between the lace beige curtains and the russet couch, sat her shiny new laptop computer on a wooden TV tray. On the floor beside it was a new printer. The computer called to her. *Try again, Ivy. Surf the great information highway.* She'd bought the darned thing on an impulse, hoping the Internet would lead to answers.

So far, it had only led her into debt.

She sighed with resignation. Work beckoned. She had a computer to pay for.

Daisy said, "You have a good night. Lock your car doors. Park up close to the store. I don't care what the rules are about employee parking. Anybody weird comes in, you call those stocker boys."

Ivy kissed her aunt on the cheek. Her skin was thin and soft, like pastry dough. "You get some sleep."

"I will. I'm going to that auction in Puyallup in the morning, and I want to get an early start. I'll be gone before you get home."

Ivy's glance crossed the room to the small glass curio cabinet. Inside, several dozen antique thimbles stood like pretty little soldiers arranged in rank and file.

"Good luck," Ivy said, knowing Daisy had her heart set on a 1920s gold-trimmed thimble that would be on silent bidding.

Ivy grabbed her apron, then was out the door. The night was cool, starless. A street light standing at the end of the short gravel driveway deposited a circle of light, revealing weeds that Ivy needed to pluck.

Under the open carport, her little blue Civic loyally waited for her beside Aunt Daisy's 1963 white Comet.

A sudden gust of wind struck Ivy, flapping her starched shirt. The sound was like freshly laundered sheets blowing on the line. Ivy thought of her mother, her father —that magical day before they died. Her mother's words—*Run through, Ivy.* Somewhere in the night, a cat howled. In the house, Audrey responded with a long maarrroooow. Ivy shivered and hurried to her car.

* * *

June 11, 1901
Pretoria, South Africa

"What is it, do you suppose?" whispered Lord Pepper.

"Cap'n, but it looks like a pig, dunnit?" came Private Carter's whispered reply.

Carter and Pepper had cautiously entered Harrison's bedroom after receiving no reply to their knock. Now they watched him from the doorway of the adjacent converted dressing room, as he stood at his easel before the open window, working on a painting . Though the day was chilly, the sky was clear, and the sun sent a shaft of heat into the room. The blue sky stretched endlessly toward the foothills of the Magaliesberg mountain range.

"Not a very real sort of pig." Pepper narrowed his eyes, but it didn't improve the art.

"It's one of them caricatures, innit? Like they 'ave in the newspapers."

Stacked against the wall were twenty-one completed canvasses, each an explosion of lush green ivy. Lovely though they were, they produced a rather unsettling effect. Faces appeared here and there, everywhere. Not faces, really. Just that same face appearing over and over again. In profile, straight on, with slim tendrils of ivy forming the lines of her face. A gentle, sweet face at that. But appearing so many times, it was overwhelming.

"Wyndham?" Pepper asked hesitantly.

"Hmm?" Harrison replied, without looking away from the pig caricature.

"Might we have a talk?"

Harrison looked up from his work and met his old friend's gaze. Joshua Pepper was dressed impeccably in his khaki and shining boots, holding his slouch hat, his head of black hair salted with gray, his full mustache trimmed and twisted just slightly on the ends.

"Private or official business?"

"Private," Pepper said, clicking his heels slightly and inclining his head.

"And you, Carter? Come to review my work, or have you personal matters to discuss with me as well?"

Carter smiled, twisting his own cap in his hands. "Oh, no, Cap'n. I mean ter say, Cap'n, nothin' pers'nal like. Your paintings is just swell, as I never seen." He hesitated a moment, glancing at Lord Pepper, who gave him a slight nod. "I, uh, if you don't mind Cap'n, I would like ter say, sir, I 'ave been given wot you call a summons."

"To the inquiry? You'd like to discuss your summons with me? For what purpose?"

"Aah, well, so I knows wot it is you want me to say, Cap'n."

"Private, you tell the truth. That will serve both of us quite well."

"But wot if they asks about the gel, Cap'n?"

"The truth in all matters, Private. I want you to relax,

speak the truth, and not worry about potential outcomes. Is that understood?"

Carter exhaled deeply, then smiled broadly again. "Yes, Cap'n. Thank you, Cap'n. I'll be clearin' off now, then. I've got twenty-four hours leave, dun' I? Time for a bit o' lark'n, ay?"

"Don't do anything I wouldn't do," Harrison warned jovially. Carter flushed to the tips of his ears, saluted both captains, then ducked out of the room.

Harrison found he was still holding the paintbrush. Wearily he set it down on the easel ledge and turned to face Pepper.

"So, what's this all about then?"

"Can't a man pay a visit to a childhood friend without suspicion?"

"Not in South Africa when one of the friends is half-mad and on the verge of court-martial."

Pepper did not smile. He twirled the end of his mustache thoughtfully.

"Tell me," Harrison said fondly. "What of you? Last I heard, you were in Kimberly, pushing papers around a polished desk."

"Now I'm in Pretoria. Same papers, different desk. Not so much polish." Joshua paced to the window. "You know, Pretoria reminds me a bit of home. The rolling grasslands, the craggy foothills. If only this damned place got some rain, it could be tolerable. I miss green as much as I miss my mother." He sighed. "Do you remember, Harry, when we were boys and our greatest challenge was to reach the peak of Kelsdale Hill just beyond Wyndham Woods?"

Harrison said nothing. He touched the ring he wore on the little finger of his right hand, the circle of gold with its engraved family crest, the center stone a half carat sapphire. Not an expensive ring, but meaningful.

Yes, he remembered the day they'd climbed Kelsdale. There'd been three of them—himself, Joshua, and Jeffrey, seven years their junior.

Joshua reminisced wistfully, "We reached that peak just before sunset on June 11, 1887. Fourteen years ago today, oddly enough. I'll never forget the view, the green of the valley, the town basking in the red glow of the setting sun, smoke rising from the chimneys, and the church bell tolling."

Harrison added with a soft chuckle, "I'll never forget the hour-long tongue lashing my mother delivered when we got back at four the next morning." She'd also given him the family crest ring that morning, and a lecture on being the eldest, on taking care of his brothers.

"Well," Joshua said, turning around with a lopsided grin. "We shouldn't have taken Jeffrey. He was just seven at the time."

Five years later, at the age of twelve, against English tradition but in keeping with family tradition, Jeffrey had been given an identical ring. Now Stuart, eighteen, had one as well, and even little Maggie, who'd turned twelve this year, wore one on a chain about her throat.

Harrison remembered how rambunctious Jeffrey had been as a child. So full of adventure. "We couldn't have stopped him. You know how stubborn he—" Harrison's tongue refused to utter the word *was*. Not about Jeffrey.

Jeffrey had never lost his taste for adventure. That's what had brought him to Africa. And Harrison had not looked after him as he should have. He'd not protected him.

And now, the image of his brother's dead and maliciously mutilated body haunted him. Six weeks had passed since he'd found Jeffrey's body, and there was no lessening of the pain. Six lifetimes could pass, and there would be no lessening.

Harrison looked down at the family ring. Somewhere out there, on some murderous Boer's hand, or in his pocket, was Jeffrey's ring. The very thought was a black cloud around his heart. He truly didn't care what the outcome of the court-martial was. His life meant nothing anymore; life itself seemed so very meaningless. He wanted to continue breathing for one reason alone—to find the Boer who had murdered his brother, put a bullet through his evil heart, and take back the family ring. Beyond that, tomorrow was a huge dark blank.

Joshua cleared his throat. "I'm sorry, Harry. I heard only last week what happened to Jeffrey."

A painful silence filled the room. Somewhere down in town, a band began to play, and the notes of a military march drifted up to them, heavy on the brass. The elephants in the menagerie down the road responded with a trumpeting complaint. They didn't seem to care for the tuba.

"Your letter arrived yesterday. Thank you for sending condolences on to my mother and family." Harrison spoke without a drop of emotion in his voice. He couldn't think of Jeffrey's death, or feel the pain of it. It was too much. He picked up the paintbrush again. The brush trembled in his hand as he continued working on the pig.

"I did come for another reason, actually," Pepper admitted. He folded his arms and rested himself against the windowsill. "To give you fair warning. There's a gentleman on his way here to see you. He'll be here shortly and will be seated at the table while you dine. You won't know who he is; he'll be introduced as Mr. Smythe-Child."

"I'm in no mood for company," Harrison said. "I'll dine in my room."

"It's in your best interest to dine downstairs, as usual."

"Why? What sort of influence could this gentleman have on me? Even if I am cleared of this false charge, even if I'm not shot at dawn on this damned African veldt, then I'll most likely die of internal injuries those butcher surgeons could not mend." The last wasn't true, he knew. He was healing well, physically if not mentally. He went to work again on the pig's lips.

"Harry, you're a pessimist—"

Harrison paused in his painting long enough to shout, "And you're a fool, Josh. Now leave me alone."

"If I'm the fool, then why are you painting lips onto a pig?" Joshua strode across the room. "Harry, I know it's been hell for you getting over Jeffrey, and now this injury. But really, you must come down today."

"And why today of all days?"

"Because Mr. Smythe-Child is a doctor from His Royal Majesty's Sanatorium. He's in Africa making a round of hospitals, and he'll be here, today, to evaluate you."

Harrison threw down the paintbrush. It stuck upright on the paint-speckled drop cloth. "Tell me you're joking."

"I wish I were. I've come to warn you. If you're found unfit, it will mean the asylum."

"A most unappetizing detour en route to court-martial," Harrison said bitterly.

Pepper was silent a moment. He seemed to purposefully let the silence grow between them until Harrison felt it surround him, cold and forbidding.

Very quietly, Pepper said, "Harry, I heard the details of Jeffrey's death. I want to kill the bastard who did it as much as you do. I've tried to get transferred into the Carbineers, but HQ won't let me free of my current assignment. So it's up to you. You must stay alive, out of the asylum, if you are to avenge his death. Are you listening to me? You must stop this mad behavior, now."

Harrison didn't give an answer, but it felt good to know he was understood. He'd not had to tell Pepper about this burning need to kill the man that had killed Jeffrey. Lord Pepper, Joshua, friend since childhood, had known.

Harrison stared at the pig painting, then looked toward the stack of ivy portraits.

Wearily, he said, "I don't know what it is. I don't know why I can't stop."

"Have you seen her again? Seen those lights?"

"Carter told you?"

"I'm afraid it's common knowledge down in town."

Should he confide in Josh? Show him what he had locked away in the wardrobe? The box of cereal, the medication?

His regiment already believed he was losing his mind. And maybe he was. But he preferred to bear his insanity alone. And his old friend was right. He needed to stop this behavior now, before it was too late. "I saw the lights only that once," he lied. "Just before I was shot."

"Battle can do strange things to a man."

"It wasn't the battle. I wish to heaven it had been."

"Then it was the injury. A blow to your head when you fell after being shot."

"Perhaps."

"And you did give that order to Fleming after you'd been wounded?"

Harrison's hands balled into fists. "My order was for Fleming to take the missionary into protective custody, not to shoot him!"

"No, no. Of course not. Say, look, Harry. Maybe you did see somebody, you know, your ideal woman, as it were. Some sort of wishful vision coming forth in a moment of battle-induced stress. It's not uncommon. It'd then been just two weeks since Jeffrey's death."

"What I saw had nothing to do with Jeffrey."

Joshua considered him silently a moment, again twirling his mustache. At last he said, "You must come down today and play Lord Wyndham to the old doctor and he'll go away. I'm only warning you because I'm hoping your dread of HRM's Sanatorium will snap you out of this. So, what do you say? Shall I tell Jasper to lay out your best drill? Shall we show this old fellow that the boys of North Yorkshire can't be so easily defeated?"

Harrison stared unseeingly out the window. A long minute passed. The sky was so very blue. It was a lovely autumn day. Too lovely to be indoors painting pig faces. He closed his eyes and nodded, and Pepper breathed with relief.

"I'll see you in the dining hall in one hour." Pepper hurried from the room as if afraid if he stayed any longer, Harrison would change his mind.

4

State laws concerning alcohol sales had evolved over the years in Washington State. As a grocery checker, Ivy was not allowed to sell alcohol between two and six a.m. The restriction did nothing to keep people from drinking, getting drunk, or even driving drunk. It just made them run into the Pig Palace five minutes before two to be sure they made the deadline.

It was nearly two a.m. when her boss and former boyfriend Bob Evanston, in tight black jeans and even tighter black T-shirt, waltzed through the automatic doors. On his arm was Mindy, the red-headed, long-legged mini-skirted and go-go booted bookkeeper from corporate office. They headed straight to the wine section, heads close, whispering and giggling.

Ivy, down on her knees to fill the bottom row of single pack cigarettes, swatted a loose strand of hair from her face and forced herself to stay at her task and not run to the restroom to freshen up. The knees of her black slacks were white with dust, her face felt shiny with exertion, and she knew her lipstick must have disappeared hours ago. She had a bad habit of chewing her lips when deep in thought.

It didn't matter that she looked a mess, she told herself. Why bother? Why care? Even at her best, she was no Mindy.

A few minutes later, Bob plunked two bottles of champagne onto the conveyor belt. Ivy slowly rose to her feet, stepped into the checkstand, and put a hand on one champagne bottle.

"How're you doing tonight, PJ?" Bob asked. His black clothes fit him well, defining his lean muscular shape, accenting his blond hair, his artificially golden skin. He dropped Ivy a seductive hazel wink, and at the same time, he gave Mindy's waist a tight squeeze.

Mindy said, "Hi, PJ. How are you? Bob says you went to Johnson High. Funny, I don't remember you."

Ivy had sat behind peppy popular cheerleader Mindy in three classes during senior year.

"It was a big school," Ivy said sweetly. "And my name is Ivy." She still didn't pick up the bottle of champagne.

"Oh. Ivy." Mindy's eyes went to Ivy's name badge, her pretty brow knit.

Bob explained with a shrug, "PJ's just my pet name for her. She wasn't involved in anything like you were, Min. She was sort of a quiet thing."

"Well, I was never quiet," Mindy laughed. "You don't get to be head cheerleader by being quiet." She tossed her red curls. Ivy didn't remember them being so vividly red in high school.

"Oh," Ivy said, her brows raised. "Were you a cheerleader? Funny, I don't remember."

Bob said, "Not just high school. Mindy was a Sea Gal for two years," he said, as if Ivy had been living in a vacuum and wouldn't know. How could Ivy avoid knowing? Bob went on, "I've been after her for ages to go out with me."

Even while you were dating me? Ivy wondered. What a creep. How had she ever liked him? How could she have thought he cared about her? That she cared about him? But the truth was, in private moments he had been tender, had said sweet things, had made her feel desirable. The truth was, his eyes still sparkled at her intimately, and his wink still hurt.

Bob pulled out his wallet and slid out his bank card.

"Two years, huh?" Ivy said to Mindy. "That must have been exciting."

"Oh, it was fun. A lot of work. We had to practice every day, and then there were dance classes, and the traveling, but it paid next to nothing. That's why I have to work at the Pig. I—"

Bob cut her off. "We really should get going. PJ?"

"Yes, Bobby?" Ivy asked sweetly.

He frowned. Nobody called him Bobby, at least, nobody who wasn't whispering in his ear. "Could you ring us up, please?"

"I'm sorry, I can't. It's two o'clock. You know the law."

Bob glanced at his watch, and his frown deepened. Then he shrugged with a sly smile. "We were here before two."

"Sorry, doesn't matter. The transaction must be completed before two, and it's now—" she made a display of checking her watch, "—thirty seconds after."

"Damn it, PJ!"

"Ivy. My name is Ivy."

Bob grunted, shrugging. "Fine. Be that way." He shoved his wallet into his back pocket. "You know, Ivy, you really ought to lighten up. You're about as dull as, well, a grocery checker. Come on, Mindy. I've got a bottle of Scotch at home."

They left the store, Mindy looking confused and sorry for Bob's rudeness.

Ivy stood in her checkstand for a long time, perfectly still except for the clenching of her jaw.

She had told Bob she loved him. They'd been dating for months. It had been secret and exciting. He'd catch her alone in the break room and kiss her. He'd call her on the intercom while she was checking and make her blush. They went to nice restaurants and sat huddled in back corners. Each date, each encounter, his kisses grew longer, his touches grew bolder. But when she said stop, he stopped.

She'd thought he was wonderful for that. Thought he was devoted, adoring. Loyal. One night, in his car, as he turned to kiss her, she'd blurted it out. The three words she'd never told a man before. I love you. And he'd smiled. He'd laughed. He'd reached over and ruffled her hair and said, "Aw, how sweet. My sweet PJ."

"PJ?" she'd asked, her heart dropping with a sickening thud to her stomach.

"You're my little Plain Jane, and it's flattering you feel that way about me." He ruffled her hair again.

"But, you don't love . . . ."

"Hey, look at the time. It's getting late, and I've got to be in early for inventory."

How many times had she relived that awful moment? PJ. The bastard.

When a single tear fell, she batted it away angrily.

She set the "Ring for Service" sign and bell at the end of

her checkstand, then for two hours she threw freight. Almost literally. The sound of soup cans hitting the shelf echoed down the tiled aisle. The harder she worked, the angrier she became.

She didn't want to be considered plain. She didn't want to be considered dull. She didn't want to be a lousy grocery checker! Oh! She had never been so frustrated in her life.

Ivy's such a sweet girl. Ivy's such a plain girl. Ivy's such a dull girl. The comments of a lifetime all came to prod her. Teachers and friends, coworkers and strangers in line. They ignored her, they neglected her, they didn't even realize she existed. Aagh!

A plan began to form. At first, it was a wild, crazy plan that she didn't seriously consider.

But by a quarter to four she had made up her mind.

Bob would never call her dull again.

It was crazy. She shouldn't do it. She couldn't do it.

But she was going to do it. Ivy O'Neal would show Bob Evanston—show the world—that she knew how to lighten up. Big time.

She abandoned the soup aisle and trod the black-and-white tiles to the front end, her gaze traveling down the row of gleaming checkstands.

There was nobody in the store except Ivy, the four night stockers, and a thin chalky-skinned man scuffling around in his bedroom slippers. He was a regular night shopper, and really a very nice man, though strange. Ivy tried not to judge him. At least he wasn't dull.

He always paid in cash so Ivy had never learned his name. He'd been nicknamed Shuffalong, because of the slippers he wore, and although Ivy didn't like the name, she found herself using it, only mentally, of course. She'd never dare say it aloud. He wore dark-rimmed glasses and a flannel robe, and he lived in the apartments across the street from the store. He'd been shopping for an hour, spending most of the time reading the personal ads in the magazines.

Should she call Aunt Daisy? Tell her what she planned to do? She debated for a few minutes on that. In the end, she decided against calling. Daisy believed in her, believed she'd seen the lights, that objects disappeared through them, that she had seen the painter named Harrison Darby, Lord of Wyndham, a captain in the Bushveldt Carbineers, a famous painter who'd gone mad and died too young.

But Daisy would never encourage Ivy to attempt to go through the lights herself. She would gently, kindly, guide Ivy toward rational behavior. And if that didn't work, she would get tough. Daisy was no pushover.

And normally, Ivy was. Funny, how that thought struck her just now. She was a pushover. No, no, she was a realist. She understood other people's needs. Yet, deep down, Ivy knew that in many ways she let people bowl her over because she didn't feel she deserved any different. No, that wasn't exactly right either. It was just that she'd never really found anything to care about enough to fight for.

Until now.

Ivy O'Neal was going to do something bold and brash and brave and possibly insane. What had she to lose? Her job? Her social life? Who would care if anything happened to her, besides Daisy?

Nobody.

Don't think about Daisy.

She wasn't exactly feeling suicidal, only reckless. Dangerously reckless. The feeling was new and exciting. Her palms began to sweat. She felt alive. As if she'd been in a fog all her life until now.

Lighten up? Bob would think twice about using that phrase ever again.

She ducked quickly into the restroom, powdered her face, put on fresh lipstick, removed the plastic headband, and ran her fingers through her hair. Then before she could talk herself out of it, she popped a breath mint into her mouth and returned to the front end of the store.

She picked up the intercom and announced, "Hey guys, I'm going to lunch."

Shouts of acknowledgment carried from four corners of the store. Slowly, she replaced the intercom.

The scanners buzzed; her temple throbbed. She was anxious and terrified. She must do it now, before she lost her nerve. She didn't know what would happen to her or even if she could find her way back. But she was going.

She might be trapping herself in some bizarre otherworld, but her fears were nothing compared with her need to go. Her need to do something so un-Ivy.

And if Harrison Darby was there, through those lights? So what? Lord Wyndham, wherever he was, whoever he was, most probably was just another handsome face, a gorgeous man with bedroom eyes who winked at one girl while squeezing another. What did it matter that she felt as if he had touched her heart? If she thought of foolish love songs, that was her fault.

She wasn't about to leap into the experiment of the millennium for a man; she was doing it for herself. Because she was tired of being the Plain Jane checker.

Ivy O'Neal was taking a chance.

She flipped on the final scanner, and her pulse soared as the lights materialized, swirling and sparkling and inviting.

Wringing her hands, she approached express lane four. *Ten Items or Less,* the sign said. Her excited mind read it as *Ten Items or Else.*

Now she was at the belt, staring up at the humming lights. They seemed to welcome her, to encourage her.

Then she heard that shuff-shuff-shuff of slippers on tile. "Excuse me, are you open?"

The old standard and often hated question caught her unprepared. She didn't want to be rude, but if just one more person asked her that question, she was going to scream! No, she was not open!

Aloud, she pleaded, "Not now. Please. Not now!"

Then, before Shuffalong's dumbfounded dark-rimmed eyes, she climbed up onto the conveyor belt. She stood for an eternally long three seconds before the swirling, buzzing lights, thought briefly and apologetically of doing this without telling Daisy, and when the black center void flashed and she saw a glimpse of red, she closed her eyes.

And jumped.

5

The lights appeared as Harrison sat on the edge of the bed, waiting for Jasper and pondering his obsession. He looked at them with a sort of forlorn helplessness.

When a girl fell to the floor, he knew it was over. Somehow fitting, really. Insanity. Perhaps it wouldn't be so bad after all.

Then the girl lifted her face, and all thoughts fled but one. She was real.

At first he couldn't move. He stared at her just as she stared at him, there on her knees on the thick red carpet, as if she were as confused and alarmed and thrilled as he.

When at last he found the strength to move, he rose, took two staggering steps, then dropped to his knees before her—the girl of his vision. Like a blind man, he reached out to her, traced her so-familiar features. He skimmed her cheekbones, her square stubborn chin. His hands trembled as he traced her uneven brows, her straight nose, and then came to rest cupping her face gently, to look at her completely. Every curve and line of her was exactly how he'd drawn her time and time again. Those warm gentle brown eyes with their fringe of dark lashes gazed directly into his.

Warming him. Filling him.

And he could feel her, really and truly feel her.

If this were insanity, then let it be so.

To hold her face was such a relief. He felt as if a thousand pounds had been lifted from his heart. She was real, and he was touching her.

He must kiss her. He didn't stop to think if this was a wise thing to do. He didn't even pause. He simply bent to her, brought his lips to hers, felt the silkiness of her mouth, inhaled her sweet minty breath. And then he pulled away and became lost once again in her gentle brown eyes.

He took a deep, unsteady breath.

Well.

Carefully, he rose, taking her arm, helping her to her feet. He gently eased her into a chair, and it was then he saw the smiling pink pig face on her apron.

He stood above her, not smiling nor masking his onslaught of emotions. He was most definitely experiencing shock.

Slowly, his mind began to work again. He began to think.

What was happening?

She'd come to him, just like the box of cereal and the medicine, falling through those crazy lights. Impossibly, his vision was a real flesh-and-blood woman, and she was sitting before him, staring up at him. Dear God, he had even kissed her. He put his hand to his lips, not to erase the memory but to keep it safe. His fingers came away with a slight reddish stain, and he was startled to realize he hadn't noticed she wore lip rouge.

He glanced at her to see that she also wore rouge on her

cheeks and blacking on her eyes. Yet the paint could not mask nor mar the sweetness of her expression. Yes, her presence brought him relief, but her presence also brought him such confusion!

Movement would help. Yes. Action.

He began to pace back and forth before her, his bare feet silent on the thick carpet. Silently, she regarded him with those big brown eyes. He walked faster. It didn't help.

As he paced, he grew more agitated, not less. Who in heaven's name was she? How had she gotten inside his head? Why had he first seen her in battle? How could she possibly be here now, her face so exactly like his haunted visions, yet wearing that ridiculous and somehow familiar costume? Had somebody planted her here? Was somebody taunting him?

And why did he feel so ridiculously happy?

He turned on his heel and faced her, setting his expression hard to control his inner giddiness. She flinched, and she swallowed nervously. Tears threatened to spill.

My God, she was so real. He wanted to scoop her up in his arms and hold her tightly, but he felt he should attempt to curb his outlandish desire to touch her. He maintained a decent distance from her and spoke, his voice emerging as a growl from emotional constraint. "Now, now, just sit. Don't start crying or anything foolish. Can I get you a glass of water?"

She—this vision—shook her head slowly.

He pulled another chair before her and sat, leaning forward. Uncanny. Every inch of her face so right, so familiar. She attempted a shaky smile, and it transformed her whole face, rounding her cheeks, lifting her brows. She was, in every sense of the word, exquisite. Despite the face paint, despite the man's bow tie and white shirt, despite the hideous pink pig apron.

Her gaze dropped to her wrist, and he followed her lead.

He reached out to her, gripped her arm firmly yet gently, pulling the object of her attention toward him. It was a wrist watch, very modern and incredibly small. It had an oval face with delicate numbers and a slim leather band.

He asked, "Where did you get this?"

"Online. At Amazon. Haven't you ever seen a wrist watch before?" Her voice was soft, quavering, American accented.

"Of course. All officers have a campaign watch, but it's far larger than this. How did they make the clockworks so small?" He narrowed his eyes onto the small print. "Japan? Since when do the Japanese have such skills? It doesn't work well, does it? The time is incorrect. It's one, not four."

"One? In the morning? Or afternoon? What day is it? Is it still June? June 11th?"

Was she really as confused as he? How could she be here, matching his visions even down to that pig? What did it all mean? Was this a hoax? A trick? Had she heard of his vision and come here to taunt him?

Common knowledge. That's what Pepper had said, that his visions were common knowledge. Had she been hired to bring his vision alive? Why? For what purpose? Who hated him so much they wanted to drive him mad?

She asked, "What day is it? What year? Where am I?"

"What year? A ploy of amnesia will not win my confidence. Who hired you?"

"What year is it?"

He brought his face closer, his eyes level with hers, forcing her back into the chair. "The eleventh of June, nineteen hundred and one. It's one o'clock in the afternoon. And you're in Pretoria. Does that bring back your memory? Now, how did you get in my room? Where did you come from?"

His demonstration of authority didn't daunt her in the least. She actually smiled. "Pretoria? As in South Africa? And it really is 1901?"

Her smile broadened, transforming her, unnerving him.

She asked him excitedly, "How many hours is it between here and Seattle? You know, Washington. In the United States."

"Would you stop answering my questions with ridiculous ones of your own!"

Her smile vanished, and she produced a scowl surely as grim as his own. "I can't answer your stupid questions until you answer mine. Stop shouting at me!"

He leaned even closer, and she didn't shrink away. "And what, dear lady, does Seattle, you know, Washington, in the United States, have anything to do with your being here?"

Her eyes suddenly misted. "Your eyes are very deceiving," she snapped. "I thought they belonged to a warm and gentle man, but now I see they belong to an arrogant turn-of-the century jerk. A hundred years makes no difference in the evolution of men. Do you know the answer or not? If it's one here, what time would it be in Seattle?"

The disappointment in her eyes tightened his stomach.

He knew he was behaving abominably, but it was either rudeness or dissolve into a puddle at her feet and beg for another kiss. He most certainly would not do that.

He pulled away. "Do I look like a bloody timekeeper? I don't know. There's probably nine, maybe ten, hours difference between here and the American West."

The girl blinked away her tears and counted on her fingers. "Nine. It was four in the morning when I jumped. If it's one in the afternoon here, then nothing's changed. I mean the time of day didn't change. Neither did the day. The only difference is the year. And you. You are the painter? Harrison Darby?"

"Yes, of course I'm Harrison Darby. Lord Wyndham. You must know that. You came to me. But I'm a soldier, not a painter. At least, I'm not meant to be. Now tell me. What have you to do with those ridiculous magic lights? Bloody hell and bilge water, it makes no sense, no sense at all! And why, in heavens name, are you wearing that ridiculous apron? How did you know about the pig? I only began painting it this morning?"

She toyed with the apron strings at her waist with nervous fingers. "It's part of my uniform. I work at the Pig Palace."

Harrison studied the patch on her apron with the silly smiling cartoon pig face, and the words *Pig Palace, Open 24 hours.*

"And what sort of establishment is the Pig Palace, pray tell? A butcher's? And what does *Open 24 hours* mean?"

"The Pig Palace is a grocery store. You have grocery stores, don't you? We sell meat and vegetables and canned food and frozen food. And *Open 24 hours* means we never close. We're open 24 hours day, 364 days a year. We only close on Christmas."

He laughed softly, shaking his head. What sort of game was she playing? What sort of insanity created such hallucinations? He'd abandoned the idea that some unknown enemy had hired her to torture him. This was too mad to be believed.

She said softly, "I'm telling the truth."

He smiled. "If so, why did this Pig Palace send you to me? Am I being recruited, perhaps, for an advertisement? To lend the Wyndham name to the cause?"

She smiled again, shyly, her eyes sparkling with humor, and he was glad of it. Her smile made him feel better, untied that knot her disappointment had tangled. He began to feel ridiculously happy again, gazing into her smiling eyes.

"The Pig has no idea where I've disappeared to."

"Aah, I see. You're acting on your own then. Tell me," he said gently. "What is your name?"

"Ivy. Ivy O'Neal."

He nodded. "Of course. I should have known. Not original, but it fits in nicely with my obsession. But how—" He was interrupted from asking Miss O'Neal how she knew of his ivy paintings, how she had managed to look in every detail like the woman he'd envisioned, when across the room, the door opened, and Jasper stepped in, holding Harrison's coat.

For a startled moment, Jasper stared uncomprehendingly, then he dropped his eyes, saying, "Pardon, Captain. I'll be, uh, out in the hall, when you're ready."

Miss O'Neal spoke up then with her energetic American accent. "What's he called? A manservant? A valet?"

"He's called a batman, a private in the British army, only posing as a manservant. Oh, good heavens," Harrison cursed, glancing down at himself, realizing that he was in his underclothes. He grabbed the robe of red flannel that was draped over the foot of the bed, put it on, and sank again into the chair before Miss Ivy O'Neal, his long legs stretched beside her as he contemplated her seriously. He must get this sorted.

"Now, tell me how you got into my room. Tell me how those bloody lights work. How the devil did you get here?"

Her explanation only muddled things worse. "I-I don't know," she began. "I came from my checkstand, from Seattle, from the year 2015. I just jumped into the lights and landed here. It must be the new scanners. At first I didn't believe it. I'm not sure I believe it now. I might just be having a really weird dream. I mean, it's not possible. That's what all the computer companies said."

How could she speak such nonsense with such seeming honesty?"From 2015? Are you saying you are a time traveler like a character from H.G. Wells' novel? And what is a computer supposed to be?"

"A sort of thinking machine. They must be controlling the lights, but nobody could see them or hear them but me. I called everybody, but they all said it was impossible. I mean, even if someone had hooked up the scanners to some giant Xbox or a virtual reality program, it couldn't happen. But it did, didn't it? I'm here. I've traveled over a hundred years into the past. I did travel through time. It's fantastic, isn't it? And you're here. Somehow, I knew you would be. Did all that other stuff land here, too? The window cleaner and cereal?"

Her brown eyes pleaded for understanding. She'd wrung her apron ties into a tight knot.

Her ridiculous tale of coming from some future world was completely ludicrous and yet Harrison was actually considering the possibility. He didn't understand the meaning of half the words she spoke, and yet there was an uncanny ring of truth in her voice.

He shook his head and took a deep cleansing breath. He felt he ought to at least give sanity one more shot. There must be a logical explanation for her, for the lights, for all the things that had come to him.

"Gibberish," he barked, more for his own benefit than for hers. "An actress well-versed in the nonsensical. What are you, a vaudeville comedienne?"

"Well, how do you explain those?" she said, and she pointed across the room.

He turned.

They were there again, those lights, sparkling, swirling, mocking. He sensed Ivy O'Neal rise from the chair, and he spun on his heel so quickly, she dropped back onto the seat with a thump.

"Just where do you think you're going?"

"Back?"

"You're not going anywhere until I get this sorted out. There must be a logical explanation for those, for you, for everything."

"I'll stay a little longer, but I'll be in big trouble if I don't get back soon. Toss something and see if it goes away."

"Toss?"

"The lights stay until something gets pulled into them, at least, that's how they work from the other side. Throw something."

"What?"

"Anything."

He grabbed the first thing to hand, something large because he believed it would be harder for her to make it disappear—a feather pillow from the bed. The center void gave a flash as it often did, and he had a glimpse of some strange place, black wire racks of colorful periodicals, or so it seemed to him in the brief moment he glimpsed it. He gave the pillow a great toss straight into the center of the lights, and with a *schwoop* it disappeared and the lights vanished, and there was nothing there any longer.

He turned around slowly, facing Ivy O'Neal.

Before she could respond with more than another adorable grin, a rapid knock at the door made them both start. Miss O'Neal's brown eyes opened wide in panic, and Harrison's reflexes kicked in. He reached automatically for his rifle, which of course he didn't have and didn't need in any case.

"Wyndham? It's me. Pepper."

Harrison moaned. That's all he needed. How could he possibly explain Ivy O'Neal to Joshua?

The door reverberated with another pounding. There was no time to waste.

"Go into the bath and change out of that costume. Go quickly."

"What am I supposed to put on?"

"A dress, a gown, anything but that. Surely you didn't walk the streets of Pretoria in that."

"I told you, I came from the future. I didn't bring any clothes. This is all I have."

What next? Explaining her presence would be bad enough. He wasn't about to explain her clothing as well.

"Then get into bed," he demanded suddenly. Wherever she had come from, by God he would use this Ivy person to his advantage. When she didn't move from where she stood, he picked her up and dumped her on the bed. In one swift movement, he tore the red and gold lion quilt from under her, like a waiter displaying his talents by removing a table cloth from beneath a china setting. He tossed the quilt over her legs. "Take off your shirt," he demanded in a whisper, reaching for the buttons of her blouse. She batted his hands away.

He whipped his handkerchief from his robe pocket, and before she could stop him, he wiped her cheeks and lips, removing most of the paint.

"Now the shirt. Oh, heavens, Miss O'Neal," he said, as she began batting him away again. "Don't fight me; just do as I say. Oh, for heaven's sake, get under the covers and do it. We have no time to argue."

She shot him a look of defiance, but under the red and gold lion quilt she dove.

"Hurry!" he whispered. She emerged, clutching the quilt to her chest, her hair all tousled and tangled, her shoulders bare but for narrow little straps of some sort.

"Wyndham," Joshua called again through the door.

Harrison snatched the quilt from Ivy's hands. Her face inflamed with embarrassment, and for good reason. The little straps at her shoulders were connected to some sort of female undergarment. It was white and lacy and very small, cupping and holding and lifting her breasts.

"My, God, what's that? Take it off."

"It's a bra, you idiot, and I won't—"

The door shook with Joshua's pounding.

"Now is not the time to display American ingenuity. Ladies do not wear such things."

"How do you know? Are you such an expert on female underwear?"

"Miss O'Neal," he begged, feeling his face flush to match hers. He was not in the habit of begging women to strip for him. They usually did so willingly enough and of their own volition. "Please, just do as I ask."

She growled, but she obeyed, diving again. She resurfaced flushed and angry, her eyes shooting proverbial daggers. But her shoulders were now completely bare, and her hair a disheveled mess and she looked like a woman who'd just been made love to. He had a sudden irrational need to turn that appearance into reality. Another knock at the door burst into his rash, lustful thoughts.

He fairly growled, "Now, you stay silent. Let me do the talking."

6

Ivy had known Harrison Darby was handsome and tall, but the reality of him was too much. He was broad-shouldered, long-legged, every inch of him rippling with muscle. Built like Michelangelo's David, only leaner, his face that of a man, not a boy, and carved of bronzed flesh. Well, partially bronzed, for he had a farmer's tan—no, a soldier's tan—that stopped at the neck and wrists.

The only soft part of him was that sexy dimple in one cheek that flashed when he smiled, turning her knees turn to jelly. And his lips. Yes, his lips were soft.

He'd kissed her.

He stared down at her now as if he might kiss her again.

The knocking intruded, rapid and insistent.

A muffled voice came through the door. "Harry, I know you're in there, so open the door or I'll break it down. Are you all right? I'm going to summon help if you don't open this door immediately!" Harrison strode to the door with three long, powerful strides, and threw it open.

The voice abruptly changed. "Oh, hallo there. Nice of you to open up. I say, why aren't you dressed?"

Ivy tightened her grip on the quilt as a stout officer in khaki uniform, carefully holding another khaki jacket by a crooked finger, entered the room. He was short in comparison to Harrison, and he was more squarely built. But he was handsome in a quirky sort of way with a broad tanned face and a dark mustache and prematurely graying hair. His gaze hadn't yet discovered her, but she became keenly aware of her partial nakedness under the quilt.

Harrison shut the door.

"Harry, the doctor's arrived. You really should get a move on."

But Harrison only took the jacket from the soldier and tossed it over a chair.

The stout officer's eyes suddenly lighted on Ivy. His mouth gaped in complete astonishment. Ivy shot a glance at Harrison and his stern expression begged, no demanded, she play along.

The stout officer continued to stare at her in bewilderment.

Harrison came up behind him and cuffed him on the back of the head. "Lord Pepper, quit ogling my wife."

"Your wife?" Lord Pepper choked.

Ivy squeaked on her own gasp of surprise. His wife! She would have echoed Lord Pepper's protest aloud, were it not for Harrison's continued stern silent command.

Lord Pepper seemed to recover then. He closed his mouth and his eyes dashed politely away from her to Harrison.

She wanted to hide under the quilt. What must he be thinking of her?

"If this is a joke, Harry, I do wish you'd tell me so."

Yes, Ivy thought, looking for a cue from Harrison to laugh or explain or something. But apparently, he wanted

Lord Pepper to seriously believe she was his wife. He said, after clearing his throat and jutting his chin like a man about to swallow a spoonful of cod liver oil, "Let me introduce you. Lord Pepper, this is Lady Wyndham, formerly Ivy O'Neal. My bride."

Lord Pepper gaped again, then bowed stiffly. "A pleasure to meet you, milady."

Harrison's stern awkwardness vanished for a moment as a smile picked up the corner of his mouth. He chuckled softly, "You see, Joshua, that I have no need of a doctor after all."

Lord Pepper—Joshua—shook his head, then he switched to nodding it. He looked again at Ivy. She tightened her hold on the quilt. He said, "Well. I'll be. Your bride. But when you painted her, you said you had no idea who she was. You said she just appeared. She was real after all?"

"Yes," Harrison said, his amazing blue eyes turning to Ivy. "She's real."

"And you'd met her before?"

"No, I mean, yes." His eyes dropped, and he cleared his throat, and looked a bit queasy. Lying didn't come naturally to him, Ivy realized. "Not that I remembered. The battle must have damaged my memory temporarily. I'd forgotten that I'd met her during my leave in Paris. We were married there."

Paris! She'd never been to Paris. How was she supposed to fake Paris?

Joshua exclaimed, "Harry, you are mad. You got married and told no one, not even me, your oldest friend?"

"We had very little time. And, well, it seemed wrong to speak of it here in Africa. Men were dying. It seemed wrong to speak of marriage. Besides, I didn't want to take the chance of rumor getting back home to England. You know how my mother is. I was going to break the news when I next got leave, but then I was injured and lost my memory." Harrison rubbed his jaw now, his eyes lifting to the ceiling. Ivy felt sure he was asking for mercy, or maybe help.

"Well, your paintbrush had no memory problem. She's as sweet as you painted her." Joshua's eyes were on her again. "Doesn't she speak, this angel of ivy?"

Harrison sighed heavily. "Of course she speaks. Say hallo, Ivy."

Ivy smiled nervously and croaked, "Hello."

"American?" Joshua asked in astonishment. "Good Lord. And how the devil did she get here? Didn't you leave her safely in Paris? Don't tell me you packed her in your bags and she's been hiding out in Pretoria all this time."

"Of course not. She's only just arrived."

Joshua looked at Ivy now. "How did you manage it?"

Ivy shrugged. "Boat? Train?"

Joshua frowned for a moment, then a broad smile broke. "A boat, she says. A train. What a clever girl. Not going to let something so small as the African continent keep you from your new husband, eh? By Jove, you Americans are adventurous."

If only he knew just how far she'd really come.

Harrison took Pepper's elbow. "Josh, I want you to go downstairs and inform the good doctor that I am not mad—only in love."

The words were delivered as an order. There was no tenderness when he said *only in love.* Ivy felt foolishly offended.

Joshua was not to be so easily sent away. He ducked from Harrison's grasp and crossed to the chair, where he dropped down, prepared to stay.

"Harry, you've not thought this through. I can't just waltz downstairs and make that sort of announcement. First of all, they'll want to know where this wife of yours is, and then they'll wonder what she's doing up here, in your bed, in a military recovery house."

"She snuck in," Harrison replied vaguely.

"Past the armed sentry? Past the men on the porch, in the sitting room. One doesn't sneak into a house full of veteran officers, Harry. And how in heaven's name did she find you?"

"She read of my whereabouts, my obsession, in the French newspapers and so came to me. But never mind the details of her arrival, Josh. How do you propose I make the announcement of her arrival?"

"Bringing her in the front door would be a help. Tell them your memory has come back. Bring her in properly. You could be fined for having her here without authorization."

Harrison paced. Ivy clutched the quilt. Joshua's polite gaze returned to Ivy, full of amazement.

Harrison stopped pacing and turned to Joshua. "I need you to do me a favor."

"Anything."

"I need you to buy her—buy my wife—some clothing."

Joshua's brow narrowed. "And what has happened to her clothing?"

"Lost," Harrison explained simply. "She'll need complete walking-out attire, and I mean complete. Underthings and all."

Joshua's eyebrows raised higher, and he began to twirl the end of his mustache into a neat, dark pencil.

Harrison ignored his friend's curiosity. "Bring them yourself, will you? No one else need know she is here until I bring her in properly, as you suggest."

Joshua rose reluctantly and stood beside Harrison, gazing thoughtfully at Ivy. She had to smother a laugh. With one side of his mustache twirled, and the other fluffy, he looked like a half-groomed poodle.

"But what size shall I get? I can't tell from what little is showing of her. She is an attractive girl, by the way."

Harrison looked at Ivy with assessing yet kind eyes. She'd felt several times since she'd arrived here that his natural politeness was being overwhelmed by curiosity and confusion. He'd growled at her, he'd glared at her, but not with cruelty, only frustration. She hadn't meant it earlier when she'd called him a jerk. Despite his size and strength, she wasn't the least bit frightened of him. She didn't mind his looking at her now with such intensity, but she did feel her skin flush.

"Yes," Harrison agreed solemnly. "She's beautiful."

Joshua scratched his head thoughtfully. "I can see why she stayed in your mind after your injury. I mean, she's plain of feature and yet somehow memorable. Something in her eyes, or is it her lips?"

Ivy prickled. Even in another century she was ordinary. But Harrison's steady, thoughtful gaze brought a deeper flush to Ivy's entire being.

"Plain? I don't see that at all. And I believe it's the combination of her eyes and her rather regal nose, and the way her brows arch and her mouth ribbons. An overall sweetness that transcends mere physical attributes. You can see why I thought she was an angel." His voice held no sarcasm, only a strange awe. He didn't see her as plain!

"Your mother will like her."

"Do you think so?"

"Oh, sure. But it'll be rough going. You know what a stickler she is for proper society and all that rot. She's not titled nor wealthy, I suppose?"

Ivy answered Harrison with her eyes and the slightest movement of her head.

"No," he said.

"And of course she's American. Your mother won't like that. But with that sweet face, she'll likely win her over. You know, Harry, I always thought it would be me who married some ravishing commoner. I never thought it would be you who—well, it is a new century. Perhaps it is time to move beyond such considerations as title and family honor."

Their curious gazes were one thing, but this continued description of her as if she were another of Harrison's paintings was too much. Ivy looked from one to the other. Her brows lifted, but their studied expressions didn't change. Apparently they'd forgotten she could hear.

"Hel-lo," she said. "I'm in the room."

Harrison, the wonderful man, was startled out of his

reverie and smiled an apology. Joshua turned a deep scarlet, apparently realizing for the first time that ever since he'd walked into the room he'd been gaping at another man's nearly naked wife in bed.

"I take a size six," Ivy said.

Joshua looked puzzled. "What is a size six? An American measurement?"

"Yes," Harrison said quickly. "And it means she's the size of your friend Diana. Just make your selections as if for her, and that will do."

"Ah," was all Joshua said, with a definite appreciation, a quick glance shooting to where she clutched the quilt to her breast.

"Not Diana from the inn, you fool. Diana of Manchester. The daughter of Sir Guy."

"Oh," said Joshua, this time with definite disappointment. "Well. She does have a sweet face."

"And tell the doctor that I won't be down. You may give my apologies."

"Whatever you say, Harry. I'll be quick as I can." And with that, Joshua was gone.

7

Ivy tucked the quilt more securely under her arms as Harrison perched on the edge of the bed. They looked at one another for several long minutes. Like two lost friends, so familiar was his face to her and hers to him. They were, of course, strangers—and yet, not. She knew his history, the names of his mother and brothers and sister.

Your mother will like her. Lord Pepper's words came rushing back. Lady Wyndham, Harrison's mother. Louisa. A lovely, full-figured, white-haired woman with breeding and poise. Ivy had seen several portraits of her. Would his mother like her? She doubted it, and what could it possibly matter? They would never meet. Still, it wasn't pleasant thinking that this man's own mother would find her lacking.

With a sigh, her mind wandered to other thoughts of him as she continued examining those chiseled features. Bits of his life came to mind—his birthday, where he'd gone to school. Even the name of his house in London—Darby House—where his family lived when they weren't in North Yorkshire at the beautiful Wyndham Manor. She knew those sort of details, but of him—who he was on the inside—she had only the anxious feeling in her stomach to go by. And the feeling in her heart that he was somebody very special.

Good grief, he was beautiful. Even dressed in a bathrobe, he really looked like a lord and captain, an officer and a gentleman. And she felt every inch a humble grocery checker.

At last he said, politely interrupting her silent examination, "Miss O'Neal, I say we come to some sort of agreement."

"What do you mean?"

"I mean, your arrival may benefit me. I can make it worth your while, if you behave and play the part."

"You mean pretend to be your wife?"

"Yes, to keep the army from trying to have me committed to a home for the insane. To give the gossips a rest. I don't enjoy having the Darby name dragged through the mud because of my visions."

So that was it. The purpose of her being here, if her being here had a purpose. To keep Harrison Darby from dying of post-traumatic stress disorder, or whatever it was called at the turn of the century, which no doubt was brought about, not by battle, but by her appearance to him on the battlefield.

She said, "You can't explain that, can you? How I look exactly like your visions?"

"No. I can't. And neither can you without some tale of time travel. I've read Wells' little novel, too, Miss O'Neal. And I found it completely unbelievable. You, however, and those lights, I'm finding more difficult to dismiss."

She shrugged, smiling. It was hard not to smile while looking at him.

"Sticking to your story?"

"Yes," she said. "Because it's true." He would need time to adjust to the idea of time travel. She hardly believed it herself, and yet here she was. But she couldn't just sit here, half-naked, waiting for him to believe her. She wanted to know if she'd done her job and changed his fate. She pinned the quilt under her arms, tugged her apron out from under, then dug into the apron pocket. She found a key to the cigarette case, a few quarters and dimes, which she'd planned to spend on a discounted employee coffee and a maple bar during her break, half a roll of mints, and the crumpled brochure from the Seattle Art Museum.

Harrison palmed the coins, and Ivy noticed how large his hands were, how long and strong and bronze his fingers. When he'd cupped her face, those hands had nearly surrounded her.

He studied the coins carefully. "1976," he said with a laugh, "2014, 1988. Miss O'Neal, putting false dates on coins will not convince anyone that you've come from the future. You should at least have had them made out of silver instead of this cheap plate. Who is this supposed to be?" He held out the dime.

"Franklin Roosevelt. American President until 1945, I think."

Harrison's shoulders shook as he laughed. "A descendant of your current vice president, no doubt."

"Current? Oh, you mean Teddy Roosevelt. He's vice president now? So the president would then be, gee, I can't remember."

"William McKinley?"

"Yes, that's right. Uh-oh." She suddenly remembered

her history. William McKinley was assassinated in 1901. Just a few months from now. Could she do anything to prevent that? Should she? It was with great relief she realized the answer was no. A lifetime of watching movies and television shows had taught her the dangers of time travelers changing history. She needed to undo the damage her face had brought to Harrison, not try to change the history of the world.

"Uh-oh?" he mimicked her.

"Nothing. Never mind."

"And what's this key?"

She returned his grin. "It's for the cigarettes. We keep the cartons locked up because of shoplifters. At fifty bucks a pop, they get expensive to lose."

"Fifty bucks?"

"Dollars. American money."

"For tobacco cigarettes? That's insane. Is there a shortage or blight or drought or something in 2015?"

"No, just a lot of taxes intended to keep people from smoking. It causes cancer, you know. And does this mean you believe me?"

"I have no idea what I believe. I may be hallucinating this entire conversation. But, for the sake of argument, if you insist on describing this future world of yours, I am going to challenge you at every detail."

"And then what? I mean, if I agree to stick around and play your wife, how will you explain my absence when I leave?"

"Good heavens," he said, "I hadn't thought beyond proving to those who would lock me up that I'm not insane."

He no longer smiled, but his lips twitched as if he were about to laugh.

"What are you thinking now?" she demanded.

He shrugged, the sly smile still threatening. "I've created quite a pickle, haven't I? Strapped myself with a wife who doesn't actually exist, at least not in my lifetime, or so she claims. So what do I do? Heavens, my mother is going to throw a fit when she hears I've married without her knowledge. This ruse will be with me the rest of my life, however long that shall be." He tugged an ear thoughtfully, then sighed. "I guess there's no way round it. You'll have to die."

Her mouth fell open, and his breaking grin told her he was joking. But he continued saying, "I don't know how. We'll think of something. Perhaps you'll be called back to the states by a family emergency or something, and your ship will sink on the way. Poor me, sad widower." His blue eyes filled with a wicked gleam. "And in a year I'll be free to marry again."

He may be joking, but Ivy was disappointed all the same. She blew out a long, weary breath. Time travel felt suddenly too much like real life. This era was like all others—unfair to ordinary people. Here was a handsome lord willing to conveniently fake her death. He was looking her in the eye and saying, albeit with a teasing smirk, that he'd be glad to see her go. What she needed was a fairy-tale world where the prince or earl couldn't live without her and would sweep her into his arms and kiss her passionately.

Come to think of it, he had kissed her. Very tenderly, as if she were some fragile exotic thing. He'd touched her with such reverence, such trembling joy, she'd felt more cherished than she ever had in her life. If only he would do that again.

"Pleasant thoughts, Miss O'Neal?"

"Oh," she said, feeling a flush heat her neck and cheeks. She dropped her gaze to the brochure in her hands and opened it, skimming the text. Everything read the same, except two things. Now there were just twenty-one canvasses on display at the art museum, instead of the hundred Ivy had seen. And the cause and date of Harrison's death had changed.

She couldn't stop the sharp intake of breath, and her flushed face instantly drained.

"May I?" Harrison asked, politely easing the brochure from her numb fingers. She watched him as he glanced over his artwork on the cover page. He opened the brochure, at first looking at the thing as a whole, at the color photographs of his work, remarking on the amazing quality and color of the small reproductions. Then he began to read, and Ivy waited, cold fingers pressed to her mouth as she watched every nuance of his facial expression.

"I am to be executed?" he asked softly. "July the 20th? I've just a bit more than a month to live?"

"No, maybe not," she hastily assured him. "Probably you've got years and years to live. It could change. Your date of death, I mean. I have no idea what this brochure said before that day I saw you, or even if the brochure existed before that day, so I don't know what the original outcome of your life was supposed to be, but I'm sure this wasn't it." She took a breath as she realized that she was rambling.

"Anyway, before I jumped through the lights, the brochure was different. My face was there on the cover of that brochure and your paintings were inside, but it said that you'd died in a hospital, in December, with the military charge dropped because you weren't competent to stand trial. It doesn't say that anymore. It's changed. And now there's no mention of a Private Carter and his diary or his death in Johannesburg."

"Carter's diary? His death? Who made this for you?" He indicated the brochure.

"It wasn't made for me. It was made for the museum."

"Miss O'Neal, I don't find this at all kind nor amusing. Telling a man he may be executed, when the possibility is so very real, is not a laughing matter."

"I came here to help you, honestly. I think it might be important for you to prevent Carter from being killed in Johannesburg."

"Do you know what you're saying?"

"Not really," she said. "Do you know what I'm saying?"

Harrison handed the brochure back to her and rose with a grunt. The release of his substantial weight from the mattress nearly knocked Ivy off balance. Tired of clinging to the quilt, Ivy pulled it over her head and struggled to get dressed.

She heard his muffled words as he set up pacing again. "You are suggesting that Private Carter, a good and faithful soldier, would abandon his company, his captain, the British army, and go traipsing off to Johannesburg and get himself killed? Good heavens, Miss O'Neal!"

"I only know what I read," she said, raising her voice to

be heard through the quilt.

"Private Carter is here, in Pretoria, under orders to remain here to give testimony. He is currently enjoying twenty-four hours leave, most likely eating and drinking himself silly. Why do you believe he will suddenly abandon his senses?"

"I don't. It was in the brochure. Someone found his diary in 1989. Oh, I know his name. It was a cute name, peppy, Pepper!" She pointed at the closed door. "The man who was just here!"

Harrison laughed. "Pepper? Joshua Pepper—at more than one hundred years of age—will find Private Carter's diary?"

Ivy threw the covers off her head and emerged with a breath of relief, her hair full of static, her shirt askew and miss-buttoned. "Not him, silly. His grandson."

Harrison did not look convinced, but joy began to seep into Ivy's blood as bits and pieces of her research became real-life entities. Perhaps she could help Harrison after all. It was like a puzzle, and she had to find the pieces and put them back the way they belonged. The way they were before Harrison ever saw her, that is. Of course she didn't know what that version of his fate entailed. She would have to take the chance that before the scanner lights had altered his fate, he had lived a long and healthy life.

She smiled up at him, but he did not return the grin. He looked as if he might like to toss her out the window. Instead, he stormed to his wardrobe, and stared at his neatly hanging clothes: two pairs of khaki pants, a khaki coat, and a regular suit of pale gray wool.

Ivy climbed from the bed and followed him to the wardrobe. She forced her voice to sound calm. "I wish you could believe me. It would make this a whole lot easier for both of us." She studied his profile, the carved line of his jaw. A pulse throbbed just below his ear. Shot at dawn. Her stomach sank like a rock.

"Why are you in trouble? What did you do?"

"I did nothing," he snapped, then quickly apologized. "Forgive me; it's just that your presence has me unnerved. My manners are not what they should be." He snatched the trousers from the peg inside the wardrobe door.

His honesty was refreshing. No macho stand for Harrison Darby. He was unnerved and admitted it. He was also sorry for not being more of a gentleman, and for that Ivy wanted to laugh out loud. Even unnerved he had better manners than any man she'd ever met of her generation.

"Then why are they going to court-martial you?"

"Because Fleming's lying."

"Who's Fleming?"

"First Lieutenant Kyle Fleming, son of retired general Lord Fleming."

"Oh," she said, though this information cleared the matter not at all. She reached past him, stretching up on her tiptoes to the top shelf and took down a rugged sloping helmet. "What's this for?"

"It's part of the uniform."

"It looks new. Have you ever worn it?" She placed it on her head. It was heavy, and too large, and rode low on her forehead.

"I prefer the slouch hat."

Another hat sat on the shelf, a broad-brimmed felt that was tacked up on one side. "Is that a slouch hat? I've seen them in the movies. Isn't it Australian? When do you wear it?"

"When fighting the enemy. Now please," he said, talking to her as if she were a troublesome child. "Leave things be." He gingerly lifted the helmet from her head and returned it to its place. She smiled and put on the slouch hat. Too large again, but being of softer stuff, it didn't ride so low.

His gaze darted over her, touching her eyes. The smile he'd been suppressing won, and brightened his whole face. He turned away as he said, "If you'll pardon me," and he ducked behind a plain white privacy screen to change. Ivy sat on the edge of the rumpled bed.

She tried not to imagine him disrobing down to those boxers again.

"So tell me what happened with Lieutenant Fleming?"

For a moment, it seemed he wouldn't answer her. She began to think he wouldn't trust her with the details. But then, he began to speak, his voice deep and earnest. As he dressed behind the screen, he told her everything about that day. How cold it had been, and windy. The sky a never-ending autumn blue. How he and his men, Fleming included, had been beyond tired and hungry and filthy. How the war had degenerated into uncivilized guerrilla attacks, the burning of farms and land, the incarceration of Boer women and children in concentration camps. How, while looking for shelter for the night, they'd been ambushed outside a farmhouse where a missionary and recently orphaned child had found temporary refuge.

"That's when I first saw you and your magician lights," he said accusingly. "And then I was shot. In the skirmish that followed, a missionary named Reverend Schmidt was also shot and killed. Do you know what I ate for supper that night?"

Ivy had stepped into his adjoining office and snatched a pencil from his writing table. It was the prettiest pencil she'd ever seen, made of red cedar, the point looking pitch black.

"Miss O'Neal?"

"Hmm? Oh, for dinner. What did you have?" she asked from the office doorway.

He poked his head around the screen, frowning at her. She held up the pencil and resumed her seat in the arm chair.

He disappeared behind the screen again. "Three guesses."

"Three—oh, you mean cantaloupe?" She'd forgotten about that melon. So it had traveled in time, too!

"Right on the first try. A ripe melon, sweet and tasty. Care to explain how you know?"

"It was on the belt when the lights appeared," she said.

Harrison's weary sigh filled the room. "Three days after the incident," he went on, "here in Pretoria, Fleming came to me in hospital and confessed that he might be responsible for the shooting of Reverend Schmidt. There was so much gunfire, he said, he became frightened, had panicked. He was terrified of recrimination. He said over and over again that he hadn't meant to shoot the missionary, that he'd only approached the farmhouse according to my orders. Fleming had been adamant about that, asking me several times to agree with him about the orders."

"And did you give him orders?"

"To approach the farmhouse? Yes. To shoot the missionary? No."

"And Private Carter, he was there?"

"Yes, and he's now here, in Pretoria. He'll testify on my behalf day after tomorrow."

"You're sure he's not in Johannesburg?"

"Positive."

"Good. Maybe things changed. Go on with what you were saying, about Fleming coming to you in the hospital."

"He was in a state of delayed shock when he confessed to the shooting. He was quite plainly terrified. I told him it would be all right, that I understood how the shooting had happened. I promised that my report to Head Office would say simply that the Boer missionary was caught in the crossfire, that it was an accident. But apparently the report hasn't satisfied high command, and an inquiry has been made. And Fleming has given an accounting that puts the responsibility directly upon my head. Now there is to be a hearing the day after tomorrow. To see if there is to be a court-martial."

Ivy scribbled on the back of the brochure: Kyle Fleming, Reverend Schmidt . . . .

"Is Schmidt spelled with a d, or without?" Harrison suddenly stepped out from behind the screen. He looked wonderful in the light wool khaki uniform. Just like a cover model.

"With." He buttoned the khaki coat up to his throat, watching her as if waiting for her to respond, to explain about the lights, his vision. She didn't want to repeat herself; he still wouldn't believe her. So instead, she asked about Fleming.

"Have you known him a long time? Are you friends?"

"I wouldn't call us friends. But I looked after him. We attended Oxford together, and when the war started, we were assigned to the same regiment. He wasn't cut out for military service. His father is a very powerful baron and a retired general. Not wealthy any longer, he lost nearly everything a decade ago to bad investments and has barely managed to hold on to his estate. But he remains influential. I'm sure it was the baron's idea for Kyle to join the army. He was in my company because I felt sorry for him. I thought I could protect him until he'd done his duty, in his father's eyes anyway. It seems I shouldn't have wasted my time. I should have been protecting somebody else altogether. And I honestly don't know why I'm telling you all this."

Ivy smiled up at him. "Because you trust me. Did Kyle Fleming know that you were protecting him?"

He regarded her thoughtfully before answering. "I suppose. He must have. Why do I trust you?"

He looked at her gravely, his face quite still, his eyes consuming hers as if looking for answers. She desperately wanted to help him. She bit her lip in contemplation.

"Well," she began, "Because I trust you. And because we both saw the scanner lights. Now, when Kyle confessed to you, he might have been sure he'd done it, but was trying to convince himself that maybe he hadn't. You know, creating his own version of reality. When did he change his story?"

"Near as I can tell, it was at the inquiry."

"Are there always inquiries when a civilian is shot?"

"No, not if the reports are in order. I'm told my reports were questioned when Fleming went to my superiors with a contradicting claim." Harrison's brow creased and his blue eyes narrowed.

"Tell me," Ivy demanded, seeing his mind race, and wanting every scrap of detail.

He shrugged, shaking his head. But then he frowned again. "My reports never stated that we shot that missionary, only that his death had been accidental during an exchange of gunfire. I didn't mention Fleming's fear. There was no need. He had no need to say another word about the matter to anybody."

"Then why did he?"

He stood before her, staring into her eyes again. As his gaze remained on her, thoughts became impossible. Her cheeks grew warm, her pulse quickened, and she heard the faint echo of an old romantic love song.

Those broad shoulders, that dimple, those boyish ears and incredible eyes—he was too handsome for her own good. She didn't know how to behave with him. *Face it, Ivy,* she told herself. *He's an earl, you're a grocery checker. He's from the romantic turn-of-the-century. You're from post-modern turn-of-the-millennium. He's gorgeous, you're not. He will never see you romantically, so just relax. Enjoy this fantastic adventure.*

With those thoughts, Ivy felt considerably better. She was here to save his life. She was not here to be swept off her feet. And with those shoulders, boy, could he ever sweep.

She eyed Harrison with a new perspective, that of scientist, historian, adventurer. Unfortunately, now she remembered the words to another old love song—about fairy tales coming true.

"Oh, shut up," she muttered. She watched the classic movie channel far too much.

"Pardon me?" Harrison asked.

"Nothing."

She struggled for something to say, finally asking, "What happened to the child? The one with Reverend Schmidt?"

"Hmm?" he asked, blinking. Had he been lost in her eyes, too? No. Wishful thinking. He'd been merely lost in thought. "We turned the child over to the care of the camp minister here in Pretoria. I believe he was placed in an orphanage."

She exhaled a long soft sigh, then looked at the SAM brochure again, hoping to find some answers. Nothing came to her.

"If you'll excuse me a moment," he said politely. He opened a door, and she caught a glimpse of a black-and-white tiled floor and a claw-footed white tub before he stepped inside and closed the door behind him.

Before Ivy even had a moment to think, the sparkling scanner lights suddenly and silently appeared at the side of the bed. Had another twenty minutes passed already?

She glanced at the closed bathroom door. She hated to leave him, but she needed more information. She turned to the lights.

This was her chance. Her chance to test the lights and see if they would take her back. And she really did need to go back before she lost her job. It would be hard enough explaining her absence as it was. She was already late from her lunch break. And she had to tell Daisy. Oh, Daisy was going to flip.

More importantly, Ivy had so much to research about the Flemings and Private Carter and the court-martial. There must be some other place to research, some other library, some other website she'd missed, somewhere the answers just sat waiting to be found.

She didn't want to leave Harrison and this wonderful adventure, but she couldn't stay any longer without telling Daisy. And if she were going to help, if she were going to save Lord Wyndham from an execution that was surely a direct result of her arrival, then she must go find some answers. She would return to him as soon as she could. She had to. She'd agreed to pretend to be his wife to save him from the insane asylum. But surely being away a day or so wouldn't be too bad. Lord Pepper had seen her; he could vouch for Harrison's story of having a new bride.

She scrambled from the bed, grabbed her apron, and when the center void flashed, revealing express lane four, she leapt into the lights.

8

Ivy opened her eyes, knowing immediately she was back at the Pig. The feel of the rubber conveyor belt beneath her, the blast of rock-n-roll music, the exhaust smell of the floor buffer, were all familiar store sensations. And there, a few feet away on the black-and-white tile floor was Harrison's feather pillow. She scrambled down from the checkstand and grabbed the pillow. Unsure where to hide it, she finally stuffed it into a plastic shopping bag and hid it under her checkstand.

She hastily donned her apron, glancing around. The checkstands were empty, no customers in sight. She cocked an ear and heard male voices nearby and the thunk of cans onto metal shelves. Everything seemed normal. Nobody had even missed her.

She checked her watch. Twenty minutes to five. The same amount of time had passed here that had passed in 1901.

"Aaaaah!"

The scream of pure terror had come from the other side of the express lane. It brought the stockers running to the front, holding their box knives like street thugs ready to pounce.

"What's up? Who screamed?" Paul asked.

Ivy cautiously went around the end of the checkstand, craning her neck, ready to jump back if she should find something—or somebody—gruesome.

What she found wasn't gruesome, but it was pathetic. She bit her lip to hold back an apology that threatened to burst from her. Huddled on the floor was poor Shuffalong, his white hands clasped to his chest, his knees drawn up. When he saw her, he let out another terrified howl.

"What's gotten into him?" Paul asked.

"I don't know," Ivy lied, hating herself for it.

"You vanished!" Shuffalong shouted, pointing a trembling white finger at Ivy. "You jumped and vanished!"

Ivy hunkered down before the poor man. "I'm right here, see?"

"Where'd they take you?"

"Where'd who take me?" Did he know something about the scanners? Was he a mad scientist-engineer in disguise? Had he been secretly coming into the store to tamper with the equipment?

"You don't remember," he wailed. "Oh, God! They took you up to their ship and now you don't remember!"

Paul stepped up beside Ivy. "Who took her?"

"The aliens! I watched The X-Files; I know about abductions." Shuffalong suddenly gasped. He scrambled to his feet. "I have to go. I have valuable knowledge. They'd suck me dry. Oh, God, maybe they already did, only I don't remember. What's the square root of 47? I don't know, I don't know. Aaaah!" He ran toward the doors and hurtled himself through them. His scream echoed across the dark parking lot.

"What a nut," Paul said.

"Psycho, man," said Craig.

"You okay, Ivy? You look a bit shaken. Did he hurt you?"

"No, no. I'm fine."

Paul patted her arm, then, with the other stockers, headed back to work. The rock-n-roll music cut off suddenly, and the softer instrumentals of Muzak began to play—the signal that night shift was ending and soon the day shift workers and regular morning customers would be coming in. Ivy could hear the stockers reviewing X-Files episodes.

She exhaled a long breath.

She needed a moment to compose her thoughts. She had chores to do, of course; she was still on the clock. She had cigarettes to fill and a pallet load of candy to deal with. But that would have to wait. She leaned back against the checkstand and tried to sort things out.

As she stood thinking, the whine of the scanners began to grow. It wouldn't be long before the lights returned and she had no idea what she should do. She dug into her apron pocket for the SAM brochure and hurried to the bit about Harrison's death. The brochure had changed again.

While recuperating in Pretoria, Lord Wyndham claimed his obsession was simply his mind struggling to recall his wife, one Ivy O'Neal, an American woman he met and married in Paris.

Lord Joshua Pepper, lifelong friend of Lord Wyndham, claims he met the woman in Pretoria, but she vanished the same day she appeared. No record of the woman or the marriage exists.

Despite Lord Pepper's protests, Lord Wyndham was involuntarily admitted to a sanatorium in Cape Town. In December of 1901, Lord Wyndham died of an allergic reaction to an experimental drug administered by Dr. Smythe-Child, a leading pioneer in psychotherapy.

Oh, for crying out loud, what had she done? Jumping into those lights had not only been brainless, it had messed up everything. Again. Harrison's fate was being tossed back and forth from one horrible demise to another.

His words echoed back to her. As he spoke to Pepper, he'd said, "Josh, I want you to go downstairs and inform the good doctor that I am not mad—only in love."

The good doctor—had Harrison meant Dr. Smythe-Child? Was he the doctor—downstairs right now—that Joshua was attempting to convince of Ivy's existence?

This meant, of course, that she would have to go back very soon. She couldn't let Harrison be put into that man's lethal care. She would go back. But not yet. She would first talk everything over with Daisy. And then she would find out all she could about the Flemings. And Carter. And Dr. Smythe-Child. With a sudden gasp of fear, she turned the brochure over. Yes, her scribbled notes were still there.

She breathed a heavy sigh. She thought of Harrison, in his room, alone and not knowing where she'd gone. He was probably thinking he really had lost his mind. And that the doctor might not believe Joshua, and might very well be on his way upstairs to investigate things in person.

She pulled out a length of receipt paper from the printer and hastily scribbled a note.

Harrison,

I'll be back after I get more information. You're not insane. Don't let Dr. Smythe-Child near you.

Before she could write anything more, the whining scanners peaked and the sound circled Ivy's ears. She hastily signed the note, scrambled on top of the conveyor belt and stood before the swirling humming lights. She folded the note as tightly as possible to make it a better projectile. When the void flashed, she saw not only the red bedroom, but Harrison himself, so handsome in his uniform, staring at her with a mixture of anger and sadness. She threw the note to him with a look of apology. The bit of paper swooshed away, and the lights vanished.

* * *

Home, with its cheery white paint and boldly blue hydrangeas, welcomed Ivy. It seemed strange she'd been gone only eight hours. Perhaps because for a while she'd been more than a hundred years away.

Clutching Harrison's pillow in the plastic bag, she kicked off her shoes, then opened blinds and drapes to let in the morning sun. After placing Harrison's pillow tenderly on her narrow bed, she set a pot of coffee brewing, then fed a complaining Audrey.

Then she gathered her library books on the kitchen table and sat in the warmth of the morning sun, searching indexes over coffee and sourdough toast. Harrison's cause of death was consistently recorded as mental illness. She looked for the names Kyle Fleming, Joshua Pepper, Tom Carter, Reverend Schmidt, and Dr. Smythe-Child.

Carter's name appeared just once. He was again mentioned as the witness who had turned up dead in Johannesburg before the inquiry hearing. Only this time his death had not been blamed on a mugging but on the Boers. It was now recorded that Private Tom Carter had been captured by the Boers and his body had been found near a gold mine, Amalgamated Mines to be exact, just outside Johannesburg.

Reverend Schmidt's name appeared only in connection to the court-martial, though Ivy did stumble into a website for his church, South Africa's Dutch Reformed Church, which was still in existence. Reverend Schmidt was listed among those buried in the historic church cemetery.

The name Fleming popped up several dozen times, but just once in connection to Harrison. It simply said that First Lieutenant Kyle Fleming had given opposing testimony at the inquiry. But the Flemings had a surprising connection with Private Carter. Kyle's dad, Lord Fleming, owned Amalgamated Mines, where Carter's body was found.

There must have been two dozen references to the Flemings, their gold and diamonds, the Amalgamated Mining Company, and the baron's abrupt turn of fortune—from impoverished nobility to mighty capitalist—all within the timespan of the Boer War.

By the time Ivy finished reading, her coffee had grown cold and her lap had grown hot because Audrey had curled herself into a tight ball, paws kneading, claws piercing Ivy's uniform slacks.

"Ouch, ouch, ouch," Ivy whispered, gently easing the claws from her skin. "I need to move to the computer, Audrey. Do you want to get down or shall I carry you?"

Audrey's reply was to dig her claws. Ivy braced the cat, stood in a crouch, and waddled into the living room. She settled herself before the computer, and Audrey purred contentedly.

As birds chirped outside, and the playful shouts of the neighborhood children drifted in through the open window, Ivy checked her email. Until lately, she'd never spent much time on a computer. She had no Facebook page, no Twitter account, not even a Pinterest page. When it came to technology, she was a dinosaur. She didn't own a smart phone or any sort of pad or pod. She wasn't against them; she just never saw a use for them in her life. She only now checked her email to see if Daisy had sent her one. Daisy was a modern senior. She emailed and texted and pinned like a pro.

There was nothing from Daisy, but amidst the spam, one email leapt out. The subject line read: Harrison Darby, Lord of Wyndham.

Ivy's pulse quickened as she clicked open the message.

Thank you for your interest in our website. We invite you to browse our updated page: An American in Paris. Our web address is: http://www . . .

The web address was highlighted. She clicked on it, fidgeting anxiously as her browser launched. Audrey opened one eye, and Ivy lifted the cat down with an apology.

When had she expressed an interest in this website? Had her earlier searches triggered this email? Or had her trip to the past?

An American in Paris? She remembered Harrison's fabricated tale of how they'd met in Paris. Could this be related somehow? She had a vivid image of him now, standing in that bedroom, dressed only in his boxers, staring at her with awe and wonder, dropping to his knees, touching her face, bringing her lips to his.

The computer screen went completely blank for a frightening half-second, jolting Ivy completely out of her thoughts.

Then, *Welcome to the Wyndham Mystery Home Page* appeared, and Harrison's art began to slowly fill the screen.

Three hours later, eyes numb with exhaustion, Ivy closed the browser and gathered the pages she'd printed. Immediately, the telephone rang. She dashed into the kitchen where the old-fashioned corded phone jangled on the wall.

"I hope I didn't wake you," Daisy said apologetically.

"No, I haven't gone to bed yet. I've been researching."

"Did you find anything?"

Ivy glanced at the pages of text clutched in her hand. "Actually, a lot of personal stuff about his family. Nothing yet that will save him."

"Save him? What are you talking about, Ivy?"

"It can wait until you get here. When will you be home?"

"I won't be home tonight. The girls and I found an auction in Portland."

The girls, Ivy knew, meant Daisy's walking group, five seniors with an attitude.

"We're going to drive down and see what we can find. It'll be late by the time we're done, so we'll spend the night and come home first thing in the morning. We'll be at the Best Western if you need me. Will you be all right?"

"Of course. I have to work tonight anyway."

"Be careful. Lock your doors. Be sure the stove's off before you leave the house."

"I will. You girls have fun." Ivy slowly replaced the receiver. Audrey began purring, twining herself around Ivy's ankles. This was the first time in her life she had ever kept a secret from Daisy. Still, she couldn't have told her over the phone. Not this. Daisy would have gotten upset, come home, missed her auction.

"I'll tell her tomorrow, Audrey. I couldn't spoil her fun, could I?"

Audrey chirped her agreement.

Ivy heaved a heavy sigh. She glanced again at the text she'd downloaded from the website. Tonight she had a lot of questions for Harrison.

She lifted her eyes to the kitchen window. The clotheslines stood empty in the sunshine; the grass needed mowing again. The fir trees in the far back stood still and straight. Not a breeze stirred them. It felt so strange to be here, now. Home. More than a hundred years away from him. He wasn't even alive now. He'd been dead and buried decades ago. That vital, healthy, polite, handsome man. Gone.

She would never be able to sleep. Still, she had to try. She gave Audrey a treat, then went to her bedroom. She turned the blinds to darkness, blocking the late afternoon sun, then stripped out of her uniform. When Audrey came padding in an hour later, Ivy was still awake, hugging Harrison's feather pillow. Worrying, wondering, lost in the memory of Harrison's eyes.

9

Wyndham, is this your blushing bride?"

Ivy slowly turned around. Her leap through the lights hadn't landed her in Harrison's bedroom as she'd foolishly assumed. This sunshine-bright room had golden paneling, nearly white wood floors, blue velvet chairs and couches, a white marble fireplace. And Harrison, in khaki uniform, storming toward her, his face ablaze with pure anger.

"Take off that hideous apron," he whispered. There were men in the room behind him, near an open doorway, but he stood blocking her view of them as she fumbled with the ties, tore off the pink pig apron and wadded it into a ball.

"I can't stay," she whispered.

"Just smile, and play along," Harrison hissed. He stepped aside.

Standing across the room in an astonished cluster were three uniformed men and one civilian, an obese man dressed in a brown wool suit.

"Oh, sh—" The expletive was nearly out of her mouth before she could stop it.

Harrison gave her arm a painful squeeze, halting her speech mid-word.

"Gentlemen, let me introduce my wife, Lady Wyndham."

The men stared at her in disbelief, all but Lord Pepper, who smiled with relief and friendly support.

"Ivy, dear, this is Major Walton, my defense attorney; Captain Reed, Intelligence Officer; Dr. Smythe-Child of His Royal Majesty's Sanatorium; and Lord Pepper, whom you met yesterday."

All four men bowed their heads and murmured greetings. Ivy mumbled her own responses, her mind reeling with the knowledge that the obese civilian, Dr. Smythe-Child—a red-faced and jowly man bursting from his yellow silk vest—had, in one alternate recording of history, killed Harrison with an experimental drug.

The doctor, Major Walton, and Captain Reed all continued staring at her as if she were an alien.

Harrison explained with wry humor, "Please forgive their rudeness, my dear. They've just been studying your portraits and were under the understandable but quite inaccurate belief that you were a product of my imagination."

Ivy smiled so broadly her face hurt.

"Shall we all have a seat then?" Harrison said, and led Ivy to one of the blue velvet couches that glowed in the striped sunlight streaming in through the wooden venetian blinds. She clutched her balled up apron in her lap. Harrison sat beside her.

Somewhere in the house, a window was open, letting in a sweet-scented cool breeze and faint unidentifiable sounds. Ivy could have sworn she heard the distant roar of a lion.

Captain Reed, a silent, speculative man, sat opposite them on the other velvet couch. He wore wire glasses over small dark eyes, and a very thick brown mustache quivered like a little mouse whenever he pursed his lips, which he did often. Beside him sat the doctor, who regarded Ivy closely, his perspiring face revealing distinct disappointment. *Well, let him be disappointed*, she thought. He would not use Harrison as a guinea pig for his lethal drugs.

In one velvet armchair sat Major Walton, a large man with a broad clean-shaven face and a kind smile. And Lord Pepper, stout and friendly, took the armchair nearest Ivy, as if trying to support her and Harrison with his nearness.

The silence in the room was so deep that Ivy could hear a clock ticking. And the faint sound of a brass band. This time she was sure she heard the shrill trumpet of an elephant echoing on the breeze. An elephant!

How she longed to go outside and see Africa. But she didn't have time. This trip had to be a fast one. She hadn't yet told Daisy what was happening, and she hadn't figured out how to explain her absence at work.

She checked her watch, aware that five men saw her do it. She had maybe fifteen minutes. No more. Then the lights would return, and she couldn't be back late from lunch again.

Harrison's deep voice suddenly broke the awkward silence. "You must be wondering why my wife is dressed as she is."

Polite smiles and curious eyes looked Ivy up and down.

"It's the new American bicycling costume, "Harrison explained. "All the rage now among the ladies. I dare say it's a bit modern for Pretoria, but my wife is stubborn when it comes to such things."

"Americans do have a reputation for stubbornness and invention, both," said the broad-faced Major Walton. "And I hope the trend catches on at home. I find the costume most becoming." He smiled at Ivy, and she felt she should respond.

"Thank you."

"Tell us, Lady Wyndham," continued Major Walton, "how you come to be in South Africa. It's quite extraordinary. How did you find passage through enemy lines?"

Major Walton, and Captain Reed, and Dr. Smythe-Child, sat a bit forward, seeming eager to hear a story of adventure and daring. Apparently a man's wife visiting her husband in wartime South Africa was not commonplace.

"Oh, well," she faltered, looking to Harrison for help, but he gave her none. He looked as stumped as she for an answer.

"It was nothing, really," she said feebly. "The journey was unremarkable."

"No trouble with the Boers?"

Ivy shook her head and shrugged and smiled all at once. "Not a bit."

They settled back in their chairs, looking disappointed but not skeptical.

"Your husband tells us you met in Paris."

"Yes. Paris."

The doctor cocked his head. His jowls puffed out a bit, and a gleam of excitement touched his small dark eyes. He looked at Harrison with something like hunger. "Your lovely wife here explains your ivy paintings, Lord Wyndham. However, it does not explain that pig you were compelled to draw yesterday."

Harrison shook his head. "Oh, that. You know, I still don't recall a thing about that."

The doctor seemed hardly able to control his glee, and Ivy wanted to smack him. "So there are spaces of your memory which are still blank?" the doctor asked, accusingly. Glances were exchanged.

Ivy knew exactly what the doctor was getting at. A blank memory was a damaged memory and needed medical evaluation, maybe even a dose of his deadly experimental drug.

As if the doctor's threat wasn't enough, Captain Reed and his mustache now seemed interested, too.

"Lord Wyndham," Captain Reed said very quietly, "If you've forgotten the details of meeting your own wife, might you not have forgotten an order given in battle?"

"No!" Ivy blurted, a thought forming even as she spoke. "Harrison remembers his orders perfectly, don't you? And the pig? You remember that, too. It's from the book, you know, *The Three Little Pigs.* I was reading it in Paris when we met. It's a children's book." She looked around at them all. “Do you know it?”

Harrison clutched her arm gratefully, giving her a squeeze of thankfulness. "Yes, of course. The book of fairy tales with illustrations. How could I forget that? I shall never forget the moment we first met." He looked into her eyes, and his hidden meaning sparkled at her. "Not ever."

Lord Pepper cleared his throat. "It looks as though your case shall go smoothly tomorrow then, Wyndham. Do you agree, Major Walton?"

"Certainly, yes. Now that his paintings and vision on the battlefield can be so readily explained, I don't see how we can do anything but have the matter dropped. We've Carter as witness. Fleming has nothing but his father's name to back him up, and that's certainly not enough to bring charges. And you, doctor, have we your support as well?"

"Mmmm," said the doctor grudgingly. "I shall give evidence as to Lord Wyndham's fitness and recovering mental stability. You do need continued rest, though, my lord. Memory loss is serious and unpredictable."

Captain Reed said nothing. His mousy mustache danced a bit, but Ivy couldn't see his eyes behind the glare of his glasses. Just exactly what an Intelligence Officer did, she didn't know. But the little man gave her the creeps, and she certainly didn't like his suggestion that Harrison could possibly have given Kyle Fleming an order to shoot that missionary.

Major Walton said enthusiastically, "Might I suggest, Lord Wyndham, that you and your wife attend the dinner party at General Milner's tonight? The members of the court are sure to attend. It would be a good chance for everyone to see your bride in person, and thus lay to rest all the gossip."

"Excellent idea," Harrison agreed, turning the full of his gaze on Ivy. "We shall be there." His eyes held a demand.

He could demand all he wanted, but she couldn't stay that long, not this time. Not until she talked to Daisy, and not until she came up with some sort of cover story so she wouldn't be missed at work. If she lost her job, she lost access to the scanners. She checked her watch. She had just ten minutes, at the most.

It would be impossible to leap through the lights before the eyes of all these men who meant so much to Harrison's future.

"It was nice meeting all of you," she said as she rose to her feet, clutching her apron, hoping Harrison would follow her lead.

She underestimated the manners of turn-of-the-century officers. They all stood, even the doctor, huffing and puffing as he did so.

And then she didn't know what to do. She didn't know where she was. In Pretoria, certainly. But whose house was this? Where did they think she was staying? Where should she claim to be going?

Harrison came to her rescue.

"While you were out," he said, "I spoke with regimental command about our situation. You've been granted permission to stay here with me at Recovery House until I return to my unit."

"Great," she said with relief.

The doctor bowed to her, Major Walton shook her hand, and Captain Reed clicked his heels and gave her a military nod. Joshua kissed her cheek. They all said they looked forward to seeing her again that night.

Harrison took her elbow, and Ivy, still clutching her apron, gladly followed him out of the plush sitting room into a cool hall, and up two flights of stairs, and finally into the familiar bedroom with the red and gold lion quilt. When the door was firmly closed behind them, Ivy sank against it with relief. Here, out of sight of all but Harrison, she could safely wait for the lights. Or could she? Would the lights appear up here in Harrison's room? Or downstairs? Or in some other part of the house? Some other part of Africa?

At home in her own time, the lights only appeared at the Pig Palace, and only above express lane four. Where did they appear on Harrison's side? She studied his back thoughtfully as he stood staring out the window. The lights only appeared somewhere near him. Always near him. On the battlefield. In this room. Downstairs. At a distance of about, what? Ten or twelve feet? Yes. So far, the lights had always appeared near him.

"Har—" she began, intending to broach the subject of the lights, but he turned on his heel suddenly, with military grace, and exploded.

"Where the hell were you!" He threw up his hands in disgust. "Look what you've made of me! You've driven me to obscenities. I don't usually use such language in the company of a woman, but Miss Ivy O'Neal, you are driving me mad!"

She attempted an apologetic smile.

"Where were you!" He demanded again, this time not with so much volume as fury. He took four long angry strides in her direction, and she involuntarily pressed back against the door. He towered over her, his broad shoulders blocking the sunlight, hands on his hips, gorgeous blue eyes narrowed, lean jaw set as hard as a statue.

Before she could even open her mouth to respond, he continued in a harsh lowered voice. "We agreed you would play my wife. Lord Pepper met you, Jasper saw you, and then you go and disappear! Damn it all to pieces, woman, stop tormenting me!"

"I'm sorry, Harrison. But I couldn't help it. I had to go. And I can't stay. The lights will return any minute, and I'll have to go. But I have questions. First of all, can you get Joshua interested in your vision of me again?"

He stood breathing heavily for a moment, scowling. And she stood, trying not to think about how his nearness, his size, even his clean spicy scent, made every nerve in her body quiver.

Finally he asked, "Can I what?"

She had to swallow before she could speak. "Get Joshua interested in your visions again. He used to be, before I arrived the last time and turned out to be real. You remember I told you about his grandson? But now that your vision has a logical explanation, he's lost interest in your obsessive painting, and so his grandson never gains interest and never goes searching for Tom Carter's diary."

"You're not making any bloody sense! And would you please get out of those clothes!" He got down on the floor, reached under the poster bed, and pulled out several white boxes. He tossed them on the lion quilt and ripped off their lids.

Inside were yards of frilly, feminine underclothes, a pair of black leather button boots with clunky wide heels, a long skirt with a matching short-waisted jacket in the softest, prettiest checked gray wool Ivy had ever seen. There was also a starched white blouse with a high tight collar and puffy long sleeves. She touched the clothes reverently. It would be so fun to try them all on.

"Your friend bought all this yesterday?"

"It was the best he could find on short notice," he said,

as if apologizing. "You may go behind the screen and change."

She wished she could do as he asked. The clothes were so pretty. Instead, with a wistful sigh, she abandoned the clothes and looked again at her list. "Do you know anything about Amalgamated Mines or a company called Provisions Corp? I don't know if they have anything at all to do with helping you, it's just that whenever I googled Boer War, besides the usual websites, it came up with these company names. I know Lord Fleming owns Amalgamated Mines, but I have no idea who owns Provisions Corp or why it kept showing up."

He stared at her as if she'd just spoken Zulu or something, and he'd not understood a single word.

She dove back into her list. "And we really need Joshua's grandson to find Carter's diary. I'm afraid there might be something very important I'm missing, since he's your only witness. Did I tell you that now history shows that Carter is taken prisoner by the Boers and is killed near a gold mine outside Johannesburg? A mine called Amalgamated, which Fleming owns?"

He answered her with a silent glare.

"Is Carter still here in Pretoria?"

"Yes," he barked. He ran a hand over his face, and she had the sudden desire to follow the same course with her lips.

Instead, she returned to her notes. "As far as your family goes, it wouldn't hurt for your brother Stuart to take a few business classes to learn how to run your family estate, just in case. And you must tell your sister Maggie to follow her heart and not marry for money. I don't know what to do about your mother. Has aspirin been invented yet? At least tell her she must watch her diet, cut out all the gravy and white flour and sweets. Vitamin B is supposed to help in times of stress. Tell her to eat more beans and leafy greens, and not keep her emotions all bottled up inside."

There. That was everything the website had told her about the fate of Harrison's family. She reread her list. His immediate family consisted of his mother, Louisa, a beautiful, plump, kind woman, who worried about her children and was a heart attack just waiting to happen; a younger brother, Stuart, eighteen and shy and a budding poet but completely incompetent businessman; and a younger sister, Margaret, who was called Maggie, and was just twelve and a feisty young thing but with a heart of gold, and who would sacrifice her own happiness for her family, if she felt it would help.

Harrison's father, also a British officer, had been killed ten years ago while serving in India; Harrison's brother Jeffrey died just six weeks ago. He'd been only twenty-three, serving in the northern Transvaal. When he was reported missing, Harrison had joined the search party. He'd been the one who'd found Jeffrey's body out on the veldt, in the most rugged and desolate area of the northern country.

She wasn't sure she could help Harrison, and she couldn't save Jeffrey, but maybe she could help the rest of his family if she gave them sufficient warning. She looked up.

Harrison glowered at her and a muscle pulsed near his clenched jaw. "I told you to change behind the screen."

"Haven't you been listening to me? Any minute now the

lights are going to come back and I'll have to go. If I'm going to help you, I need some information and your cooperation."

"Get dressed."

"Get stuffed!"

He stormed to the small table by the door, snatched up the heavy, leather-bound book as if it were as light as a paperback, and thrust it at her. "This is a gift from Lord Pepper. I believe you'll find an entire chapter on appropriate language. Read it."

She staggered under the weight of the book as he dropped it in her hands. He turned on his heel and stormed out.

She followed him into his study. Like the bedroom and the rest of the house, the floors were of a nearly white wood, the furniture dark and heavy, the walls papered in a pale taupe. A window with drawn white sheers let in a glowing light. Beneath them, a cozy cushioned window seat was covered in the same red-with-gold-lions cloth as the quilt on the bed.

Harrison dropped into the chair before a small table and opened a leather-bound journal. He picked up a pen, and opened the lid to a crystal ink well, but he didn't dip.

Ivy spied a stack of canvasses propped against the wall beside the table. She went to them, tipping them back one at a time to peer at the oils of ivy, of herself, which she had seen at the Seattle Art Museum. Her arms tingled with goose bumps.

She carefully returned the canvasses to their original positions. Still hugging the heavy compendium, she began to pace the room.

"I must have been out of my mind to attempt this charade!"

Harrison's outburst came so suddenly, Ivy jumped. He turned in his chair and faced her. "I should have told Joshua you were my mistress, not my wife. But it's too late now. It's done and begun and we must see it through. Your contrived death will be a blessing, the sooner the better. Meanwhile, you'll find that compendium useful. I expect you to read it, cover to cover."

Ivy, mouth agape and speechless, could only stare at him as he spoke for the second time of faking her death. But he was right of course. So right. She would be leaving any minute, and though she knew she would have to return, maybe several times, to get him through this mess, eventually she would leave him for good. And then he would have to explain her disappearance. And if she could somehow stay, which was ridiculous to even think about, she was all wrong for him. She knew it. She'd been telling herself that ever since she jumped through the lights. She was here to save his life, not to win his love.

A glance at the crumpled SAM brochure told her what she expected. She'd saved him from the doctor's needle, but not from court-martial. He'd been shot at dawn. Again.

"Listen, please. I need you to give me more information. I'm pretty sure you won't be killed by that horrible doctor any longer, but there is still this court-martial to worry about. You have to try to figure out why Kyle Fleming is lying about the order you gave. I can't help you until you do."

"The only help I need from you is your presence. Your silent presence. Now quit annoying me with your nonsense about Joshua and vitamins and my mother eating beans." His eyes turned warmer, apologetic. "Please, Miss O'Neal. Sit down and study."

He turned around, picked up his pen, and dipped the nib into the inkwell.

Ivy sighed with exasperation. Where were those lights? Twenty minutes had passed. Had she missed them somehow? Had they appeared while her back was turned? Now she'd have to wait another twenty minutes. She'd be back late from lunch, and this time she might not get away with it. What excuse could she possibly give?

She turned her gaze out the window, and for a moment forgot all else. The heavy compendium sunk onto her lap as she pressed her face to the warm glass. Out there was Africa—Africa of 1901.

The day was sunny and bright, not a single cloud to mar the deep blue. And the sky looked so huge and the blue of—of Harrison's eyes—above the jagged barren hills.

In the valley, Pretoria was much larger than she'd imagined. There were church spires, and large impressive white stone buildings, a few smoke stacks of industry at the edge of town, and neighborhoods of red and blue roofed houses at the center. Hundreds of patches of green gardens stood out boldly against the otherwise brown and treeless landscape, giving the city a thriving oasis charm.

There was something vaguely familiar about the scene down there, something nostalgic. It took her a moment to figure out just what it was. And then she knew. There were telephone and telegraph poles crisscrossing the streets, and a line of them stretching through the town and out toward the hill along the railroad tracks. That's what most gave the place the old town look. It reminded Ivy of photos of her parents' childhood, before the days when most of Seattle's suburban phone and power lines were buried underground.

A road leading into Pretoria wound its way past the Recovery House, and along this road a farmer with a thick beard and stove-top hat pedaled an old-fashioned heavy-framed bicycle.

Fascinated now, Ivy forgot all about the book on her lap. She continued to watch the road, and soon a native African came along, a huge woman in a multicolored skirt that hung down to her bare ankles. Her ample bosom was covered in a bright green scarf. There were ropes of beads around her neck and wrists, and on her head was a tapestry hat shaped like a huge donut. Behind her, three nearly naked little boys scampered playfully as they hurried along beside a small and delicate giraffe. The giraffe moved at its own pace, despite the children, gracefully picking up her skinny, knobby-kneed legs, like a ballerina picking her way through broken glass.

Ivy smiled eagerly to herself. This sure beat checking groceries.

"Read!" Harrison commanded, and Ivy jumped, startled out of her fascination.

Here she was, behaving as if this were a Disneyland ride, when Harrison's life was at stake. She studied his chiseled profile, recalling his detailed biography on the Wyndham Mystery website, and the many photographs of him as a child and young man posing with his family in the lovely English village.

"You knew even as a child, didn't you? That you would be earl one day. Little Lord Darby."

"Lord Wyndham. I know Americans are confused by our titles. My name is Harrison Darby, Lord of Wyndham. Everyone calls me Wyndham. I was the firstborn male. One must start preparing at a very young age for the title."

"Why is it that your last name is Darby and they call you Lord Wyndham, but Joshua Pepper is called Lord Pepper? Doesn't he have an estate, too?"

"Lord Pepper is a baron, and thus has no geographical location attached to his title. Peerage can be confusing, I'll admit. But it's all explained in that book."

He dipped the pen again, and the scratching continued. Ivy thought about her own carefree, happy childhood with Daisy. The big backyard, games of Kick-the-Can and Red Rover. Running through the sheets on the clotheslines.

"Did you ever get to have any fun? Did you ever get to play? Did you ever just lie in the grass and stare at the clouds and pick out shapes and make up dreams?"

His pen hesitated a moment. When he spoke, his voice was solemn. "There were a few occasions. But for the most part, I was preoccupied with lessons and the responsibilities of being the eldest. I do remember Jeffrey wandering off and returning home full of sighs and daydreams. But as second born, he is entitled to such moments of leisure."

Ivy recalled Jeffrey. The brother seven years younger who'd died here, in Africa. And yet Harrison was speaking of him as if he were still alive. He'd said *is*, not *was*.

She said softly, "I'm very sorry about Jeffrey."

Harrison's pen didn't stop, and Ivy wondered if the historical information she'd read had been wrong.

"He was a soldier?" she asked, probing gently.

Harrison continued writing. Ivy asked no more about him. It certainly wasn't kind to pry into the death of a loved one.

"If we had a son," she began, and then screeched to a halt, her mouth open, her cheeks burning, as in her mind the image of herself in bed with Lord Wyndham came all too vividly. "I mean, when you someday have a son, will he inherit the title of Lord Wyndham?"

"Yes."

"Will you raise a son the way you were raised?"

"I had an excellent education and very happy childhood."

Ivy recalled one particular photograph of Harrison as a serious little boy on the steps of a massive stone castle-like place with turrets. "I guess it's just as well that this isn't a real marriage then."

He shot her a glance. "And why is that?"

"Because when I have a child, I want him to have a wonderful, carefree childhood. Full of dreams and happy times. Believing the world a magical place and that anything is possible."

His pen hovered. "Spend much more time in South Africa, and I assure you those dreams will die."

"Has it been that bad?"

"Do you know anything of war, Miss O'Neal?"

"Not firsthand."

"Keep it that way." He set down the pen and, with tense and trembling fingers, touched a jeweled ring he wore on the little finger of his right hand. The family crest ring. She'd seen a photograph of it on the website. Each member of the family wore one, even the women. Jeffrey's had been stolen by the Boers who had killed him. It had never been recovered.

Suddenly, Harrison slid the ring from his finger and held it out to her.

"What do you want me to do with that?" she asked, dumbfounded.

"Put it on. You must have a wedding ring to go along with our charade."

She shook her head firmly. "No, I can't. It means too much to you. What if I lose it?"

"Please, do as I ask."

She took the ring, their fingers touching in the exchange.

He picked up his pen again, but his hand still shook. She found she couldn't watch him. Her hands were unsteady as she slid his family crest ring onto her wedding finger.

"It's too big," she said, holding her hand up to show him the gap.

He stared thoughtfully for minute, then rummaged in the desk drawer until he pulled forth a length of string. This he wound tightly around the bottom of the band, and when he slid it onto her wedding finger, it fit snugly.

She stared at it for a very long time, her emotions tumbling, before turning her attention to the book on her lap. *A Colonist's Guide to English Ways.* Joshua Pepper, the kind man, had seen how desperately she needed this.

"Aah, hang it all!"

Ivy looked up. Harrison had flung down his pen and turned to her.

"Get dressed," he demanded.

"Why?"

"Because, Miss O'Neal, we're going out, that's why. Get out of those trousers and into proper clothing. Please."

Going out? Into Pretoria? Out there? She couldn't—could she?

Why not? The lights seemed to follow him. They would appear wherever he was. If he wanted to go out, she must go out with him or risk missing the return of the lights.

She glanced again at her watch. She'd been staring out the window much longer than she'd realized. Another twenty minutes had long passed. The lights had never taken this long to return before, not when she left them all on.

Had somebody turned off a scanner?

If so, when would they all be turned on again? The next holiday? But that wasn't until this summer, the Fourth of July! What would everyone think happened to her? She gasped. What would Daisy think?

Her mind whirled with thoughts, with fears, with imaginary scenarios of what was happening back home. She could see the night stockers scratching their heads, searching for her, considering calling the police. She didn't protest when Harrison gently took the book from her hands, or when he led her into his bedroom and loaded her arms with lacy white drawers and voluminous underskirts, a girdle-like thing that turned out to be a "modern" corset, silk stockings, and a camisole. On top of that he pressed the beautiful gray summer wool skirt and the matching jacket, then the crisp white blouse with tiny pearl buttons.

Barely able to see over the pile of clothing, she could only obey as he gently turned her around and pressed her behind the changing screen.

It was all too much. Her mind was numb. Like it or not, she was here. And she was going out into Africa.

10

They stood between tall white columns on the wide verandah of the Officers Recovery House. In the distance, Pretoria was a city of multi-colored roofs and gleaming majestic white buildings. The air was crisp and clear and clean but for the ever-present hint of burnt grass.

Harrison turned from the view and eyed Miss Ivy O'Neal with a mixture of relief and wariness. In the attire Joshua had provided, with her dark hair tied back in a ribbon, she looked not only respectable but lovely. Quite lovely. The Midway straw hat riding low on her head gave her an American cowboy charm Her warm gentle eyes smiled up at him from the shadow of the brim, touching his heart.

Her very existence defied the laws of nature, and he wished he could arrive at some explanation other than time travel for her being here, for the sparkling lights, for all those strange objects. But he couldn't.

She glanced for the hundredth time at her wrist watch.

"Are you late for an appointment, Miss O'Neal?"

"I'm going to be in so much trouble when I get back. They'll think I abandoned my job. And you'd better call me Ivy. Or are you supposed to call me something more formal?"

"Ivy will do nicely."

"Can I call you Harrison? Or must I say Wyndham like everyone else. Or, my lord?"

"Harrison will do. Shall we?" He offered his arm.

"Where are we going?"

"To see my company. They're camped with a regiment just outside town." He pointed, and together they looked across the roofs and spires of Pretoria to the outskirts, where a sea of white dots showed the pitched tents of the British army.

"Okay," she agreed eagerly.

"How are the shoes? It's a short distance. Are you up to walking?"

She looked down at the button boots. "They're a little stiff, but I should be all right. It's this stupid corset I'm worried about. Are you sure I have to wear it?"

"Very sure. And are you warm enough? The sun can be deceptive here in wintertime. There's a chill wind blowing."

"I'm fine. Hot, actually, in all these layers."

They descended the porch stairs, and began to walk down the sandy rutted road toward town. She gaped like a child at the open space and enormous sky, enchanted by every blade of grass, clump of bracken, and chirp of bird.

When they came to the neighbor's small zoo, Miss O'Neal rushed to the fenced enclosure. Together they stood peering through the wire at the animals who roamed freely within the one acre grassy enclosure. Monkeys lazed in the limbs of several broad-crowned blue gum trees, and exotic birds with colorful plumage perched in native bushes. A mother elephant with her baby stood in the shade of a

Jacaranda tree, their huge ears fanning gently, and a half dozen zebra nibbled at a stack of dried grass near a petite springbok, their tails flicking at ever-present flies.

Only the lion was caged, a great huge male with a magnificent mane, who now slept like a harmless house cat, his belly up, enormous paws hanging bent in the air.

The smell was earthy, slightly musky, but the animals were relatively quiet just now, in the warmth of late afternoon. Only an occasional twitter and grumble disturbed the peaceful setting.

"There's the baby giraffe," Ivy exclaimed as the delicate long-necked creature strode slowly across the yard. "I saw her going down the road with a native woman and three little boys."

So that's what had her gaping out the window earlier. "Her name is Lulu, and she likes to take a walk every day. The woman is employed by the owner, Mr. Harvey, and the boys are hers."

They stood for a moment silently enjoying Lulu's dignified and delicate saunter across the compound.

"Do all these animals live in the wild here—in Pretoria, I mean?"

"All the big game are here in South Africa, but not so near the cities. You have to go out into lion country to the north and east, or west to the Limpopo River, to find them. Here, we get the occasional zebra or antelope wandering by in search of food. And I once spotted a cheetah over to the east, just outside town. But the real dangers of South Africa are disease. Enteric fever is not uncommon, and neither are cholera and malaria. More men in my regiment have died of fever than from enemy fire. This is not a healthy place for a young woman. I must ask you to touch nothing that hasn't been sterilized. And don't drink the water unless it's been boiled. This time of year, it's very dry, and the water can harbor all sorts of disease."

She only smiled as if he'd told her to look twice before crossing the road. She asked eagerly, "Have you ever seen a gorilla?"

"No, I'm afraid I haven't. They live in the jungles, I believe, not in the grasslands. And Mr. Harvey has no gorilla."

She sighed as if he'd missed out on something tremendous.

"But I've been to Piccadilly Circus during the rush of tea-time traffic, and I tell you, that is the place to go to see wild animals."

She laughed at that, and the sound was sweet, refreshing, as it echoed across the valley. They walked on in companionable silence.

She took a deep breath of the cool air. Surprisingly, her mind was not on Africa any longer, for her next words were, "I've always wanted to go to England."

"Perhaps someday you shall." He took her arm and led her away from the enticing zoo.

"Where's your home? Tell me what it's like."

Her request, so carelessly voiced, should have presented no problem. He knew North Yorkshire—hills and vales, the rivers and small villages—far better than he knew this land here. Yet it would not come to him, not in his mind's eye nor in words. Home had been lost to him the day he found Jeffrey's body. He replied simply, "It's very far away, Ivy. So far, I don't know if I shall ever return."

She stopped then, frowning up at him. "What do you mean, you'll never return? Why do you say that?"

He looked into her eyes thoughtfully, trying to figure out how to best explain, not sure why he felt the need. "I suppose I'm just being morbid and cynical. War has that effect. England and the life I had there are like a dream. I don't see how I shall ever return to it, not with the same lightness of heart and joy that I once felt. I've seen too much, Ivy. Nothing will ever be the same again."

"I'm sorry," she said softly. A gust of wind tugged at her hat. She held it firmly as she looked up at him. From somewhere nearby came the melancholy song of a native bird.

"What is that?" Ivy asked. "It sounds very sad."

"It's called a titihoya, and I agree. It seems to cry for all this nonsense and fighting to come to end, doesn't it?"

He took Ivy's arm again, and they continued on their way, their easy bantering mood completely gone.

They followed a more or less direct course toward the army encampment, passing modest bungalows of pale unburnt brick covered with thatched roofs and surrounded by green gardens of fig trees and fruit trees. Young Jacaranda trees lined the wide sandy streets; their canopies of green fern-like leaves rattled softly in the wind, revealing their parched condition.

At a small produce stand, a native boy of perhaps twelve years sold Harrison two perfect oranges, that, though non-native to Africa, grew well in pampered gardens. The boy asked the hideous price of a shilling for each, and Harrison brought them to Ivy like treasures.

They continued walking out of town, peeling the oranges and leaving the peels like a trail to find their way home. The houses gave way to small farms and fields of corn, grazing sheep and Jersey cows.

After swallowing her last bite of orange, Ivy asked him very thoughtfully, "What's the war about, exactly?"

"I thought you said you'd done your research."

"I did, but nobody seemed to agree on what really started it."

"I suppose that's fair enough. War is about many things, including an accumulation of disagreements, resentments, and even desires. I suppose the main reason we're fighting is for representation in the Transvaal government. Most of the industry here is owned by the English, but the Dutch refuse to allow our participation in political matters."

"And everyone wants control over the diamonds and gold, right?"

"One can't discount greed as a factor in war. But there are other more noble factors as well. For each side, there are reasons to fight. For each man, there are yet more."

"What about you? Why did you join?"

"I wanted to do my duty—fight for the Empire. Defeat the Boers who would have every white man in South Africa praying in his Calvinistic ways, and every black man a slave."

She was silent for a few moments, checking her watch several times. Her pretty features became increasingly troubled.

Finally, she heaved a heavy sigh, as if resigning herself

to something. And then she grew thoughtful. They were nearly to the encampment, after walking more than an hour. It felt good to get the air into his lungs and move his legs. He'd been idle far too long.

"Harrison, does the word *apartheid* mean anything to you?"

"No. Should it?"

She stopped, and so did he, turning to face her. She looked deeply sad. "I wish I didn't know," she said softly.

"About what?"

"Anything about the future."

He gave her arm a nudge and they began walking again. "Come now; it can't be as bad as all that. You must foresee something good. Tell me more about this Pig Palace you work for."

"Oh, please. I'm having the adventure of a lifetime and you want me to talk about my job?"

"Then you choose something. Tell me something to convince me you came from the future."

"All right. Airplanes. Flight. In 1903, the Wright Brothers in Kitty Hawk, North Carolina, will be the first to fly."

Harrison threw back his head and laughed. "Americans, of course."

"Of course."

"In just two years? Preposterous."

"It's true. You'll see."

He eyed her. "Will I? You predict that too, do you?"

"I'm trying my hardest to make it so. You really should be more cooperative. Do you want to hear more?"

"Oh, yes. Please."

"Well, I don't know the exact progression of things, but the airplanes will grow more sophisticated and larger every year."

She went on and on, explaining about propellers on wings, jet engines, and something she called a seven-forty-seven. "And then there's space travel. In 1969, the first man will walk on the moon."

He continued to laugh until tears came to his eyes. He realized it had been a very long time since he'd laughed so much—not since he was a child. And he'd gone an entire half hour without once thinking of Jeffrey.

"So, do you believe me now?"

It was he who stopped this time, in the middle of the road, at the top of a rise, with the white tents and corrals of the encampment just below them.

His hands itched to touch Ivy O'Neal's familiar face, and so he let them, skimming over those cheekbones, along her stubborn chin, to her full lips. Her eyes fluttered closed; she pursed her lips, so untouched by the horrors of war that she showed no hesitation in wishing to be kissed, here and now. He wished her always to remain so.

He kissed her forehead platonically. Her eyes snapped open, and she glared at him, her face growing pink.

"Well, then, Harrison Darby. If I didn't come from the future, where did I come from?"

He considered this a moment as the wind brought the scent of burnt grass, and a pleasant songbird sang, and in the distance, the whistle of the Delagoa Bay Railway echoed over the foothills.

"From heaven?" he murmured, then cupped her face

and drew her nearer, bringing his mouth down on hers.

She melted into him, her arms encircling him, and nothing in the world had ever felt so perfect. He kissed her tenderly, and she returned the kiss with trembling honesty and hunger. No man had ever been kissed with such feeling.

That kiss might have gone on for some time had it not been for the sudden blast of gunfire that shattered the peaceful afternoon. Harrison abruptly looked up, pulling Ivy protectively against him.

Smoke rose from beyond the foothills, while in the encampment below, brown-clad soldiers dashed among the small white tents in disorderly confusion.

"Ivy, you must go back to Recovery House."

She struggled free of his tight hold. "No, no. I have to stay with you."

"Just do as I say and return at once. I'll follow just as soon as I see what has happened."

"No. I'm staying with you, and that's final." That stubborn jaw of hers, which he'd painted so many times, set, and he could see there was no changing her mind.

He stood tense and indecisive, his hands balled into fists while she stared at him with steely determination.

If he truly believed the Boers would risk attacking the camp itself, he would have carried her bodily back to the house. But Pretoria was well secured. They dared not come any closer than the far side of the foothills. "Very well then, but mind you stick with me. You run when I say run, and you duck when I say duck."

"I will," she said earnestly. The tremble in her voice revealed she understood the true danger they were in. He grabbed her hand and pulled her into a run.

He led her off the sandy road, plunging them down the hillside on a more direct route to the camp. She kept up with him with no complaint, dodging jagged rocks and prickly cactus-like shrubs, and soon they were on level ground, racing toward the encampment.

As they ran, they witnessed a great scrambling in the camp—horses being mounted, orders shouted. By the time they came to the narrow tin sentry hut, all was quiet, and a dust cloud rose behind the departing mounted unit.

"Is that you, Kelly?" called Harrison to the sentry on guard.

"Aye, Captain," acknowledged the Irish sentry. "We had word of a Boer attack, just the other side a the hill. They ambushed a scouting party. One dead, one injured, and one prisoner."

"Who, Kelly?"

"Captain, it's not good, sir. Goodman's the dead man; my cousin's the wounded. And sir, it's Private Carter they took prisoner."

11

"Carter?" Harrison gasped.

Ivy choked. No, no, it couldn't be coming true.

"There's a party gone after them, Captain. They'll do their best. They know what Carter means to your case, and they're all behind you."

Harrison held on firmly to Ivy. "Thank you, Kelly. Where's Major Hancock?"

"In the wee house, Captain," Kelly said, pointing to a small porchless plank house that stood in the shade of a majestic blue gum at the head of the rows of conical white tents. "Camp headquarters."

Harrison nodded. "Kelly, this is my wife, Lady Wyndham."

Kelly's eyes grew wide, and he smiled awkwardly at Ivy. "How do, milady."

"Hi," she said; despite her anxiety, she enjoyed the way Kelly looked as if he was seeing a ghost.

They crossed the brown grass at a fast pace, but not a run. Ivy was glad for the lesser pace, for somewhere along their plunge down the hill she'd gotten a rock in her shoe, and it stabbed the arch of her foot with each step. A few yards later, she stumbled beside Harrison, and he turned to look at her with worry creasing his brow.

"Just a rock in my boot," she said.

"I do wish you'd returned to the safety of town, Ivy."

"It's just a rock," she said. "I'm fine."

He went inside the small house, leaving her seated on a crate outside the door so she could remove the painful rock.

"Now, stay put," he told her firmly. "I won't be long."

From beneath her broad-brimmed hat, she smiled up at him in a way she hoped was beguiling.

"Behave," he demanded, "Those eyes of yours hold a glimmer that doesn't bode well. You'd best be here when I come out." Then he marched inside to find out why Carter had been on patrol when he, as Harrison had worded it, was meant to be on leave.

Ivy was glad to obey. She unbuttoned a stiff and now dusty boot and carefully pried it from her aching foot. "A *short* walk," he'd said. They'd walked at least three miles! The leather chafed the top of her foot and the back of her ankle, and her toes felt like they'd been twisted in a vise. She wiggled them to be sure they still moved.

She heard male voices inside the house, but couldn't make out what was being said. She turned the boot upside down and shook until the culprit, a tiny sharp pebble, tumbled out onto the dead grass. While leaning over to tie her boot, she noticed the upside-down black lettering on the crate beneath her.

She leaned further to be sure she had read it right. *Provisions Corp.*

Provisions Corp? The same company the Internet kept plucking from the electronic masses? Was this one more link in the complicated chain of events that seemed to trap

Harrison in a final fate here in Africa?

She took a deep breath, trying to focus her thoughts. The air was heavy with the aroma of the blue gum, a eucalyptus scent, and tinged with other odors: horse, hay, smoke, and cooking meat. Deep breathing didn't help. She was so frustrated with her inability to help Harrison, she could just spit!

Carter taken prisoner by the Boers. Was that part of the original unfolding of events? Or was that something her appearance had triggered? And this crate underneath her from Provisions Corp—what did it have to do with anything?

Would the Boers bring Carter to the Amalgamated Mine as the history books recorded? Even she knew the British were in control of Johannesburg, Mafeking, Pietersburg—all the towns and villages. At this stage, the Boers held nothing but a few nearby hills and the roughest land in the northern parts, but their guerrilla attacks were enough to keep the war from ending. Who held the mines?

She scanned the beautiful blue horizon beyond the sea of white tents. All was quiet now. The black plume of an approaching train was followed a moment later by the whistle and grumble of its approach. The sun was sinking lower, and huge puffy white clouds had appeared, drawing nearer across the valley. Their shadows moved along the brown undulating veldt like stealthy animals.

Boot steps clomped behind Ivy, and the Intelligence Officer, Captain Reed, came out of the house. He didn't seem to notice her where she sat on the crate. He marched past her, his mouse mustache doing a little dance, and hurried away around the house, toward another grouping of white tents.

Ivy leaned over, peering in through the open doorway. She saw nothing but a dark short hallway. The sound of male conversation continued, and she identified Harrison in the mix.

Stay put, he'd said. But what harm could there be in just peeking around a little?

She got up and followed in Captain Reed's footsteps around the house. She saw him marching stiffly down the tent rows. He came to an abrupt halt in front of the farthest tent, said something Ivy couldn't hear, then ducked inside.

Something about that man bothered her. She didn't like him, and she didn't know why. She hadn't liked his silence when she'd met him this afternoon. She hadn't like the way he'd stared at Harrison, his mustache twitching. She hadn't liked his accusation that maybe Harrison had forgotten he'd given Fleming an order he would never have given.

She turned, intending to return to the front of the house and her crate, but Harrison rounded the corner before she could take a step, his brow furrowed. He stopped abruptly when he saw her, as if he'd expected she'd be much more difficult to find.

"Did you find your rock?" he asked, seeming annoyed with her for leaving her post, and yet relieved he'd found her.

"All gone. What about you? Did you learn anything?"

"Only that it was Reed who terminated Carter's leave and had him sent on patrol."

"Why would he do that?"

"That's what I'd like to know. He didn't seem inclined to justify his order to me. Did you see where he went?"

Ivy pointed. "That last tent down there."

A puffy white cloud scudded across the sun, and its shadow raced along the row of tents, making them wink, one after the other. Just as the shadow passed over the farthest tent, Captain Reed and a young soldier stepped out of the tent.

"I don't believe it," Harrison breathed.

"Who is it?"

"Fleming."

Ivy looked at the young soldier with renewed interest. Pale skin, red hair, slim build.

"You didn't know he was here?"

"No. He'd managed to pull a post in town until the hearing was over. For his own protection, really. The men had been giving him a hard time. I'm very surprised he's back."

"Maybe Captain Reed changed that, too."

"Yes. Maybe. But why?"

As they watched, Reed and Fleming shook hands; then Fleming disappeared inside the tent again. Reed turned around, and seeing Harrison and Ivy, hesitated, his step jerking slightly. His mustache leapt up a storm over his thin puckered mouth; then he marched away, across the compound and up toward a long dark stone building.

"What's up there?"

"Used to be an ostrich farm. Now it's a military court and prison. For our men; not the Boers. My hearing is scheduled to take place there tomorrow."

She met Harrison's eye.

He said, "I'm not going without a fight. Come along. We must find Major Walton and get him to delay the hearing."

They rounded the small house again, and Ivy pulled on Harrison's arm. "Wait a minute; I want to show you something."

She lifted the crate on which she'd sat, finding it heavier than she'd anticipated, and turned it right-side-up to show him the lettering. "I asked you about this Provisions Corp earlier."

"So you did," he said very slowly, the blood draining from his features before her very eyes.

"You know something," she said accusingly. "Is it important? Will it help you?"

He swallowed hard, and moved very carefully to take the crate from her. He turned it upside down again and gently set it on the ground.

"Did I," he asked, taking her arm firmly and pulling her away from the crate, "forget to mention the snakes?"

"What snakes?"

"African snakes."

"No, you didn't mention any snakes."

"So sorry. I should have. They're quite deadly, you know. Many of them. Don't touch any spiders either. And if you see a red ant, step on it. Get more than a dozen of those things on you, they'll eat the clothes right off your body."

They stood a healthy three yards distant now from the crate, and Ivy felt her own features grow pale. She'd been sitting on that crate. She'd examined it, lifted it, shoved it at Harrison.

His talk of red ants made her itch, but she was afraid to

move, let alone scratch.

"What do we do?" she whispered.

"Well, you do nothing," he whispered back. "I, being a captain, order the nearest private to dispose of it, pronto."

"Isn't that a cowardly thing to do?"

"Would you rather I attempt to kill it myself? I thought you wanted to save my life."

"I do."

"Then stop calling me a coward for harboring a healthy dislike of deadly snakes, or I'll most likely get myself bitten attempting to prove my manhood."

"You'd do that for me?" she asked, braving a look away from the crate. Harrison grinned, and she was glad to see he was no longer pale.

"I could, but I'd rather not. Perhaps later. Aah, Private," Harrison called, his voice rising to normal as a dusty soldier approached and saluted. "There's a six-foot black mamba underneath that crate. Be a good chap and get rid of it, will you?"

The soldier's salute drooped as his mouth fell open.

Ivy and Harrison turned swiftly and fled like guilty children, abandoning the poor private to his duty.

12

Ivy found herself again waiting for Harrison, this time in the huge polished stone hall of the majestic Raadzaal—the Parliament Building in Church Square—which the British had seized from the Dutch. According to Harrison, just prior to British occupation nearly a year ago, the Boer President Paul Kruger had managed to escape Pretoria with a million pounds in gold that had been stored in the bowels of this building. He'd also taken with him the gold hands from the town clock.

Provisions Corp, she'd also learned from Harrison as they'd made the long walk back into town, was an arms supplier run by a Turk named Mahmud who was becoming very rich off the war.

"And what about Amalgamated Mines—the company Fleming owns," she'd asked, hoping to find some link to connect the disjointed information her research had unearthed.

But Harrison had replied, "Ivy, I'm sure you must be mistaken. Or the history books are. Fleming is stone broke. He can't afford to buy so much as a shovel. He could not finance an entire mining operation."

Ivy hadn't argued, but as she sat now in the Raadzaal's ambiance of power and wealth, with its polished decor and simple elegance, she thought about gold and diamonds, and of their lure. She thought of young red-headed Kyle Fleming and his impoverished father, the baron, and she knew that the history books hadn't been mistaken. The Flemings had found, —or rather would find—wealth in South Africa, deep in the earth. How the baron would afford to begin mining, and whether his newfound wealth had anything at all to do with his son getting Harrison into trouble, she didn't know. She'd have to try to find answers to those questions when she got home.

Home.

She checked her watch again. Back home, it was five minutes before eight in the morning. She felt her enthusiasm for her adventure plummeting as she finally faced the unavoidable conclusion she'd been denying.

She was stuck.

Somebody had turned off a scanner. The lights wouldn't return until they were all on again. Her absence would have been noticed hours ago. Would they have called the police? Called the house? Thank heavens Daisy was in Portland, although she had said she'd be home first thing in the morning—which meant she would be getting home any minute.

Ivy sighed heavily, leaning her head back against the polished paneled wall. It was very quiet in the building. The thick walls muffled even the sound of the band playing in the square outside. Her breathing carried in the vast hallway like a ghostly echo.

She imagined Daisy pulling into the driveway, not seeing Ivy's car under the carport. Daisy would frown, hurry inside, and not find Ivy there, not even a note explaining where she was. Thank goodness they had no answering machine or a message would surely be waiting from the Pig, or maybe even the police.

But Daisy would be worried all the same, because Ivy never came home late, not without calling. Daisy would call the Pig. She'd be told that Ivy had disappeared, left the store without a trace, without a word.

Ivy opened her eyes, not wanting to imagine the shock and fright that would make her dear aunt weak, a pale wrinkled hand fluttering to her heart.

She had to get a message to Daisy that she was all right. She just had to. Now. But how?

There were telephones here in Pretoria, and telegraphs. And communication with England was possible, she knew, because the newspapers all wrote of messages passing back and forth. But what about America? And what good would it do to phone or wire Seattle now, when Aunt Daisy wouldn't even be born for another forty years?

A delayed message was what she needed. Something she could send now, yet be delivered to Daisy later. A letter? But who could she possibly send it to?

Who in her family was alive in 1901? Great-grandma Rosie?

Yes! Her dear, late, great-grandmother who had moved to Seattle in the 1890s during Alaska's gold rush. Rosie, who'd shocked Seattleites by marrying a Cherokee Indian who dressed half the week like a businessman, and the other half like a native American. Rosie, who'd made a ghostly appearance on Daisy's switched-off television to send a message of hopefulness.

Yes. Eccentric and wonderful Grandma Rosie.

Ivy jumped up, the sound of her boots echoing in the massive hall. Harrison could be minutes or hours longer. She'd simply been ordered to wait. He liked to give orders. She imagined most people liked to obey his orders. Or were afraid not to. But she couldn't wait any longer. Every minute that passed meant a greater chance her absence was giving Aunt Daisy a heart attack.

Ivy hurried down the hall, bursting out of the building into the bright sunshine just as the clock tower began to toll the hour. Bong, bong, bong. She glanced at her watch again. Eight o'clock, to the second, back home. Here it was five in the afternoon. Even without its gold hands, that tower clock was accurate.

The puffy white clouds were gone now, the sky a dark but clear blue as evening approached. The wind had kicked up and brought a biting icy chill Ivy would never have thought to feel in Africa.

Before her in the large Church Square, a steady unhurried stream of citizens in various attire, and soldiers in various uniforms, crisscrossed the bleached stone pathways. Church Square lay in the heart of Pretoria. To get just about anywhere in the city from one side to the other, one had to cross it.

Ivy crossed at a near run, in the direction of a busy street where dusty black carriages and bulky slow ox carts rolled with a muffled grinding sound along the sandy red earth. Once on the paved sidewalk, she stopped to get her bearings, looking up and down the wide, Jacaranda-lined avenue. She allowed herself to gape a bit as she began to make her way down the street—at the women with their bustles and parasols, the men in their dark suits. Black nurses in starched black uniforms strolled their little white charges in frilly baby carriages.

Men and boys on bicycles darted around the slower moving ox carts, and several lean and muscled black men in diaper-like shorts and huge feather headdresses loped easily as they pulled rickshaws, not even sweating under their heavy burdens.

By far the most numerous of the pedestrians were soldiers—Scottish Highland Guards in their kilts, Australians with their swaggering walk and slouch hats, which Harrison himself preferred to wear.

Mostly, there were English soldiers, seeming glad for a day of leave to stroll, shop, smoke, and whistle at the few unattended females.

Being unattended, Ivy heard many whistles aimed her way. And although as a feminist she knew she should hate the objectifying of her person, she enjoyed each and every whistle. The trick, it seemed, to getting noticed when one was plain, was to put oneself smack dab in the middle of a city filled with war-weary soldiers.

The shop windows bore advertisements in both English and the language of Afrikaans, a language mainly Dutch in origin but enriched with Malay, Portuguese, English, French and German. The words all seemed to contain far too many k's and a's and r's. The bakery, with its tempting displays, permeated the air with the mouthwatering scents of treats that their signs called *koeksisters* and *rusk* and *vetkoek*.

But it was before the next shop, a dress shop, that Ivy stood the longest. Inside the window, beneath gowns of shimmering silks, tucked between ivory hair brushes and beaded purses, were nestled a half-dozen vintage thimbles beautifully painted and trimmed with real gold.

Ivy chewed her lip. Daisy would absolutely love to possess those thimbles. If they were vintage in 1901, they would surely be antiques in the future. She turned away with deep regret. The next time she made a trip into the past, she was bringing money with her.

After walking several blocks, she found a post office located on the lower floor of a three-story brick office. The signs were thankfully in English, and the place was run by a small Portuguese man who spoke fluent English. Ivy told him she needed paper and two envelopes and sufficient postage to get a letter to the United States. He quoted her a price in pounds that meant nothing to her. She held out her wrist watch.

"Will you take this in trade?"

* * *

Daisy pulled into the carport, frowning. Ivy's blue Honda was not there. The girl should be sleeping after working all night. Where on earth could she be?

She gathered her small package of thimbles (three of them from the 1920s and such bargains!), and eased herself out of her old Comet. Inside the house, Audrey greeted her with howls of complaint and an empty food bowl.

"Didn't Ivy feed you yet this morning? Poor little

Audrey. Did she phone? Where is she?" Daisy went on talking to the cat as she fed her and filled her water bowl. She then carefully tucked her new antique thimbles into her curio, gave them a long appreciative look, then put on a pot of water for tea. A nice cup, and then a little nap. They'd gotten up at four a.m. to hit the road before traffic got too bad.

Where was Ivy? Darn that girl. Her shift ended at seven, and it didn't take more than fifteen minutes for her to drive home. Daisy stared at the phone. She hated to call and sound like a foolish old woman. She'd ask, *Where's Ivy?* and they'd answer, *How are we supposed to know?* Ivy wasn't really too terribly late yet. Perhaps they had asked her to work an extra hour.

Or she could have stopped somewhere on the way home. Gone shopping. But that didn't seem likely. Ivy hated shopping. And the mall wasn't open yet.

She reached for the phone, then stopped. The calendar caught her eye. It was one of those pretty sunflower calendars by some famous artist, and on today's date, June the 14th, a huge red circle surrounded the numbers.

The letter! Good heavens, how had she forgotten?

She'd really wanted Ivy to be here for this, but her excitement was all at once too much. She forgot the telephone and quickly hurried into her bedroom. She opened the drawer of her nightstand and took out the old family Bible.

Reverently she carried the Bible out to the living room and set it beside her favorite chair. She'd make herself wait. She'd give Ivy another half hour.

But after making herself a cup of tea and settling down

into the chair, Daisy could wait no longer. She pulled the yellowed envelope from between the Bible's pages. Written in a handsome script was the command:

To be opened by Daisy, the granddaughter of Rosie Tall Chief, on June 14, 2015.

At last, the day had come. All her life, Daisy had wanted to open up this letter and see what was inside. Her late grandmother Rosie had said it had come from South Africa in 1901, addressed to Rosie herself, in care of the general post office in Seattle. Rosie, at the time being newly wed to the handsome Indian, had thought it an omen of immense portent. Being superstitious to the point of hysteria, Rosie had refused to let anyone even touch the envelope. Fifteen years passed before Rosie gave birth to a girl, who she named Orchid. When Orchid gave birth some twenty-five years later, she named the child Daisy, as a sort of fulfillment of the letter's prophecy.

And now Daisy was past seventy, and it was time. She laughed aloud, and Audrey came to sit on her haunches and watch her with narrowed yellow eyes. Carefully, she opened the envelope.

The writing on the note paper inside was different from that on the envelope. This writing was modern and round and a mixture of printing and cursive.

Daisy's heart plummeted a bit. She was so disappointed that the letter was not authentic and from her grandmother's time she nearly tore it up. Then it struck her that the writing was not only modern but familiar. The writing was Ivy's.

"Dear Aunt Daisy,

Those three words made her gasp. How had she not put the two together before? South Africa. 1901. That's where Ivy's blue-eyed soldier was—that earl, Lord Wyndham, on the other side of those swirling scanner lights. Good gracious, Ivy hadn't gone and done anything stupid, had she? Oh, dear.

Please don't panic and don't get upset. Take a deep breath, then make yourself a cup of tea. This is going to sound unbelievable, but I need you to believe me. And I need your help . . ."

13

Ivy shivered uncontrollably as the letter slipped from her fingers and into the postman's possession. A wave of goose bumps prickled her skin. Then instantly, she remembered the old letter Daisy had talked about her whole life, remembered the circled date on the kitchen calendar. Ivy was positive she'd not possessed these memories until the letter had passed from her hand to the smiling Portuguese man.

"Are you ill, Madam?"

"No. Thanks. I just had a glimpse of the future."

"Is it a tradition in your family to send off time-capsule letters, as you called it?"

"No, this is a first. Thanks for addressing those envelopes for me."

"Glad to be of service, Madam. This wrist watch—you say it needs no winding? But the time is all wrong."

"Oh, here, I'll show you. I have it set for the time back home." She showed him how to move the hands to the correct time. "There's a fresh battery in there. It should run for five years."

His small dark eyes narrowed on the tiny moving hands, his dark face full of wonder and a trace of doubt.

"Oh, and I forgot. When you press this," she said, pressing the tiny button to activate the light that flooded the watch face in a glowing blue, "you can see the time at night."

His mouth fell open. He snatched the watch from her, as if afraid she might change her mind and want it back. "What will you Americans think of next?"

"You never know," Ivy replied, resisting the urge to tell him more, and hurried out onto the street.

Harrison was waiting for her on the steps of the Parliament Building, his uniform buffeted by the gusting wind. She approached him as if approaching a stormy mountain, stepping into the shadow of his broad shoulders, not exactly fearful, but with a good measure of caution.

He took her arm firmly, and they headed across Church Square in the direction she'd just come.

"Do you never obey orders, Ivy O'Neal?"

"I had something important to do."

"You couldn't have waited for me? Or do you simply enjoy striking fear into my heart?"

She smiled up at him. "You were afraid?"

"You've left me in awkward positions."

He scowled all the harder, as if trying to mask his emotions. He'd been afraid she'd left him for good, and she felt inexplicably pleased. "I'm sorry," she said, not meaning it. "Did you get an extension?"

"A few days. It's set for the eighteenth."

Today was the fourteenth, Friday. That meant they had the whole weekend. "We might have time, then, to get to Johannesburg and find Carter before he's killed."

"Carter has been captured by the Boers. They are not in the habit of delivering their enemy to occupied cities, not even for the convenience of time travelers."

She skidded to a halt, and he took a step back to her.

"You believe that I came from the future?"

"I believe you came to torment and save me both. From where, heaven only knows."

"Well, could you trust me on this then? Tell the army that the Boers might have taken Carter to Johannesburg. Or couldn't we go to Johannesburg and look ourselves? He's at Amalgamated, or he will be. I wish I knew the exact date of his death, and where. I only know that his body will be found near the mine."

"I've been accused of a crime and am lucky not to be under close arrest. I certainly cannot leave Pretoria before the hearing. And I tell you, Miss Ivy O'Neal, Private Carter is not in Johannesburg. He's not near any gold mine, and Fleming owns no gold mine. He barely owns the shirt on his back."

"But—"

"No. That's an end to it. Carter was taken northeast, into the bush. A hundred mounted men are in pursuit."

A whistle carried from across the street. Harrison's head lifted. "Have they no manners?" he said, and then shouted to the soldier who'd whistled, "Behave yourself! She's my wife!"

He turned again to her, his eye traveling the length of her as he continued to glare. "One would think they'd never seen a pretty girl in their lives. I'll buy you a veil, if that's what it takes to protect you."

The warm giddy feelings were back in droves. "I don't mind the whistles."

"Well, I do. You're my—I mean, they don't know that

you're not my wife. They ought to behave themselves."

She couldn't feel her feet touching the ground; his words left her so happy. He'd called her pretty. Her. Ivy O'Neal, the Plain Jane grocery checker. Pretty.

"And just what are you smiling about? I have not changed my mind."

"Hmm?" she asked dreamily, trying to bring her mind back down to earth. Oh, yes. Carter. Johannesburg.

"But couldn't somebody just go look near Amalgamated? What harm would it do?"

"The very suggestion would cast doubt again as to my sanity. Carter has been taken prisoner, taken north toward enemy territory. We have witnesses to that. I hope to God he is alive and unharmed. I hope he is returned to us or exchanged or rescued in time for the hearing. Now, please, let's hear no more about it."

He took her arm again and led her, not toward the Officers Recovery House on the hill, but down Church Street and to the very dress shop she'd passed on her way to the post office. The shop with the thimbles.

He pressed open the door, causing a little bell above it to ring, then ushered Ivy in.

The shop was low-ceilinged and intimate, carpeted in scarlet, smelling subtly like perfume and new fabric. A very elegant woman of about fifty emerged from the back and greeted them. Her voice was French accented, but she wore a narrow-cut red silk dress that was very Asian in style. She called herself Madame Georgina.

"A dinner tonight with the officers, you say? Very well, I can find something suitable. Have a seat, Lord Wyndham, and make yourself comfortable. Lady Wyndham, please come with me."

Madame escorted Ivy to a bright fitting room. "Undress behind the screen please, milady. Then come stand up here so I may properly fit you."

Behind the white screen, Ivy stripped down to the cotton chemise, then obediently padded barefoot to the small elevated platform.

Dressmaker dummies in various costumes lined the walls. Gowns of yellow silk, gowns of black linen, light frilly gowns of pale cotton. And one gown and jacket combination that looked just like a safari costume from the old Tarzan movies. The sight of it niggled an idea at the back of Ivy's mind, and it had to do with being brave and probably stupid and poking around a gold mine all by herself. She'd seen enough of Africa this afternoon to know she couldn't attempt such a thing wearing the clothes she'd had on today. That safari outfit looked as if it would give her a bit more protection against the dreaded three: spiders, snakes, and ants. Madame, however, gave her no time to scheme any further.

"Face the mirror, now. We shall see what we have."

A delightful half hour passed. While Harrison drank strong sweet tea as he waited in the plush pink drawing room, in the fitting room, Ivy stood atop the short pedestal before a trio of gilt mirrors to be pampered and pinned and draped with exquisite fabrics and lovely gowns and suits, frilly underclothes and trim hats. She felt like a queen.

A young black girl of maybe eleven years, dressed simply in a black silk pantsuit, assisted Madame. She was a quiet and watchful girl, ready with the required needle or thread or scissors, with a very round, very dark face, a slightly flattened nose and dark intelligent eyes. Madame addressed her as Titi, and spoke to her in a language that sounded like a mixture of many.

When Ivy asked, Madame explained that Titi was short for Titihoya. The girl had been named after the sad bird of the veldt that Ivy had heard that afternoon. Titi was an orphan, and Madame had been her employer for the past five years.

"She speaks Fanakalo. It's a blend of Zulu, English and Afrikaans. Her father worked in the mines. It was there he was killed. But I am teaching her French. I may take her home with me someday. For now, we stay. The money is good, and the war should be ending soon with the English the victors, so my little Titi should have a good life. The gold diggers will return and prosperity will abound."

Ivy had to bite her tongue to keep from spouting about the future of South Africa, even with English victory. Little Titi's future was not so bright. But then again, perhaps little Titi would be one of those who would help bring about eventual change. She could be a future relative of Nelson Mandela, for all Ivy knew.

Madame smiled hopefully, saying, "You see, the fabrics I have been able to get are the very best, even now. You like? This one, yes?"

Ivy answered "Oh, yes" to all Madame Georgina's inquiries until the poor woman directly asked her, "But which do you like best, milady?"

"I don't know. I can't decide. Will you choose for me?"

"I'd be delighted."

And so Madame chose a lovely silk apricot gown that was both demure and sensual.

"Are you sure I won't be overdressed? I look like I'm going to a ball."

"You will be perfection itself, I am sure. You will outshine the moon with your youthful beauty."

For the second time in a matter of an hour, Ivy was shocked at a compliment. Youthful beauty? She looked up and examined her reflection in the mirror. She studied—not the gown, as she'd done up until now—but herself in it, and she barely recognized herself. Her normally pale skin glowed with a sun-kissed radiance; her dull brown eyes weren't dull at all, but sparkled as if with joyful secrets; her lips even bloomed with natural color and still looked slightly swollen from Harrison's wonderful kiss. It was like a good fairy had waved a magic wand over her. And the apricot silk gown highlighted these changes, revealing a long slender neck, rounded soft shoulders, and more cleavage than she realized she possessed. Never in her life had she looked so feminine, so pretty.

This truly did beat checking groceries.

She smiled broadly at Madame, at little Titi, and then her eye swept the fitting room.

She noticed again that safari costume, and she felt her eager joy drain into foreboding. Her purpose in being here wasn't to become Cinderella, but to save Harrison's life.

"What is it, milady? You see something you desire?"

"Yes, Madame, that costume over there. Does that belong to anybody?"

"You mean the trekking costume? No, it does not belong to anybody. I made it for the wife of an Englishman, but she has been taken with fever and decided to return to England. Do you like it?"

"Is it expensive?" Harrison would be the one paying for it, though she had no intention of telling him.

"Not for the quality, milady. Here, let me show you. Titi?"

Little Titi circled the dummy with her arms and carefully carried it, costume and all, over to where Ivy stood on the pedestal.

"The fabric," Madame explained, "is heavy twill. It will wear well, and protect from the sun, thorns, and bush. The skirt is short, just to the boot tops, so it will not trip you. The collar and sleeves are both fitted with leather that straps securely so no insects or snakes can wriggle their way in."

Ivy gave an involuntary shudder. What in the world made her even consider this insane plan?

"And there is a matching hat, here, you see? An American Stetson with snaps to secure a mesh veil, and soft leather gloves to protect the hands. Even laced knee-high boots. A bit too large for you, I believe. The English lady this was intended for, she was a big girl. But an extra pair of socks in the boots and a stitch here and there, and it would fit you nicely."

"I'll take it," Ivy said, before she could change her mind. "But never mind the alterations. And could you wrap it up with my other things so my husband doesn't see them. I want to surprise him."

"Of course, I understand. But first, we must finish with

your gown for tonight. Up, up," Madame Georgina commanded.

The trekking costume was whisked away to be packed, and Ivy straightened her spine and pushed back her shoulders, pressing away thoughts of spiders and snakes, as well as terrifying thoughts of a solo journey to Johannesburg to look for Carter. She focused instead on Daisy. Surely, that ominous chill she'd felt when mailing that letter had meant her plan had worked and that Daisy would do her best to help.

"Just don't get too upset," Ivy whispered softly. "I'm all right." She caught her own reflection, and smiled. Giddy again. "More than all right."

"What's that Lady Wyndham?"

"Nothing. This is really beautiful."

"I'm very glad you like it. It suits you well. If I may ask, how will you wear your hair tonight?"

"My hair?" Ivy touched the strand that had escaped Madame's pins. "Like this?"

Madame Georgina gasped with shock.

"No good?" Ivy asked.

"Oh, you look lovely, milady, even with my hasty pinning, but surely you will do it up properly. Surely, your maid will pile it artfully."

"I don't have a maid."

Another gasp issued from Madame. "If I may boast, I am very good with the coiffure. May I style you, before you go? I would consider it an honor."

"You're sure it wouldn't be any trouble?"

"No trouble at all."

"Will it take long? I don't want to keep Har—my husband—waiting."

"I checked on him a moment ago. He is comfortable with his tea and content to wait. He knows, I believe, how long these things take."

It took two hours.

Finally, Ivy, dressed in the apricot silk, her hair piled artfully atop her head with little curls dangling about her neck, the Wyndham ring on her wedding finger her only jewelry, was presented to Harrison.

He rose from the pink chair as soon as he saw her, picking up his slouch hat. He stared for a flattering silent minute before finally muttering, "I'll see to a ride." But he didn't move; he just stood staring, worrying the brim of his hat.

Ivy grew increasingly warm under his gaze. What was he thinking? Why didn't he say anything else?

"Where shall we have Lady Wyndham's other things sent?" Madame asked softly.

"Oh, to the Officers Recovery House, please."

Ivy watched several large parcels leave Madame's shop in the hands of a courier, but luckily, Harrison didn't notice. In fact, he'd not yet taken his eyes from her.

In for penny, in for a pound, Aunt Daisy always said, surprisingly, for it was an English saying. At any rate, Harrison had paid for three outfits for her already; how much more could those half dozen thimbles in the window cost?

She said, "Could I ask you a favor?"

"Anything," he answered huskily. "Anything at all."

14

Daisy entered the Pig Palace cautiously, feeling like a criminal about to rob a bank. She gripped her pocketbook with nervous fingers as she looked down the long line of gleaming new checkstands.

Oh, dear.

This was absolutely crazy. She'd hoped to arrive to find Ivy standing at her post, working overtime, this entire thing just one huge misunderstanding. But Ivy was not here. Instead, she found Dee, a very friendly and talkative checker with bouncy brown curls, who'd just had a baby and was always prepared with photographs.

"Hi, Aunt Daisy," Dee called, bouncing over in her pink pig apron. "How's Ivy? I hear she went home with the flu last night. Bob said you called just a bit ago. Is she okay?"

My, how that girl did rattle on!

"Yes, my dear," Daisy said, smiling pleasantly. "Thank you for asking. Actually, I'm here to look for something Ivy may have lost. Would it be all right if I just peeked in the checkstands?"

"Oh, sure. What is it? I can help you look. Was it an earring? I'm always losing my earrings because I wear these French hooks and my hair is always pushing them up, but I really shouldn't wear earrings at all anymore with the little guy now getting so active. Have you seen his pictures? He's three months old now. Do you want to see?"

Daisy didn't want to see. The child was not in the least bit extraordinary. Now, Ivy had been a charming baby. But Dee had the pictures out of her pocket, and so Daisy looked and smiled and nodded until, thankfully, a customer arrived with an enormous cart of groceries to be checked.

"You do your job, dear. I'll just have a quick peek."

Daisy glanced about hurriedly, but there was no sign of that nasty Bob, nor anybody else. The place was as quiet as a church.

She hurried down to the last checkstand and stepped into the tiny checking area. She faced the scanner as Ivy had said to do in her letter, looked down, and there was the black switch. She flipped it up, and a soft faint spinning sound whined, and a narrow beam of red light glowed underneath the glass.

Daisy moved on to the next checkstand scanner, then the next.

It proved to be much easier than she'd anticipated, though her poor old heart was beating so hard she just knew her blood pressure was not a pretty number.

When she had them all on, she looked at lane four, the express lane where Ivy said the swirling lights would appear. There was nothing there. Nothing abnormal at all.

Dee, checking and gabbing away in checkstand seven, was only halfway through the huge order.

Trying to look nonchalant, Daisy made her way to checkstand four, pretending to examine the tabloid headlines.

Bigfoot Seen on White House Lawn! Two-Headed Alligator Boy Attacks Himself!

Daisy could top that. Her niece had traveled through time! But where were those magic lights of hers? Ivy had warned her that she might not see them. Nobody but Ivy and Harrison had so far. But how could she know for sure they were there? Toss something up there, into the seemingly empty space above the belt of lane four?

Whatever she threw, she didn't want it to get Ivy into any sort of trouble. And she certainly didn't want to send across any messages until she'd alerted Ivy in some way to watch for them.

So what existed in Africa that she could reasonably toss?

What did she know about Africa? They had elephants and tigers and monkeys. Monkeys. And what did monkeys eat?

Bananas.

Daisy hurried off to Produce.

15

Ivy felt like the belle of a very strange ball.

The officers' dinner was held in a huge red-tile-roofed Victorian home near the outskirts of town, surrounded by rose gardens and citrus trees, and protected by a rough stone wall seven feet high. The dining room opened onto a brick terrace, but tonight the glass doors were closed tightly against the cold. Wall-mounted electric lights glowed in white globes, an electric chandelier shone, and candles flickered on the massive dining table.

There were twenty men present, all of them officers wearing what Harrison called their best drill: wool khaki, medals and insignia visibly displayed, black boots shining, hair and sideburns and mustaches all slick with hair oil. Ivy recognized only two of them: Lord Pepper, Harrison's childhood friend and the man whose grandson would, maybe, find Carter's diary. And Major Walton, the large, broad-faced man with the kind smile who was Harrison's defense attorney.

As the only woman present, Ivy was the center of attention. Harrison had paraded her before the officers, most of them senior to himself, and they'd eyed her appreciatively. They'd shaken her hand and kissed her cheek and made her feel utterly beautiful.

Then somebody had demanded to see her portraits, and the rest of them had said, "Hear, hear," and a half hour later, a junior officer arrived with a half dozen of Harrison's paintings. They were each in turn held up next to Ivy, and then scrutinized and praised, and finally Ivy was declared a vision of loveliness and not imagination.

A vision of loveliness. *Eat that, Bob,* she thought giddily. She was a vision. How bizarre, and how wonderful.

Then Harrison indulged her by very earnestly asking Lord Pepper to promise that he would one day ask his grandson to find Private Carter's diary.

"An odd request, Harry? Why on earth?"

"I'd prefer not to answer that, at least not now."

"Well, I'm a sport. My grandson, you say? Am I to have a grandson? I haven't produced a son yet. Nor a wife."

"My wife is certain you'll produce all three."

Pepper graced Ivy with a lavish smile. "Well then, why not save my grandson the trouble and go and fetch Carter's diary now. It's in his tent, surely."

"No," Harrison said, "it's on his person. He carries it always."

"Oh, well. If I could find the diary now, I suppose I'd solve all your problems, wouldn't I, Harry?"

"Indeed. Would you be so kind? I'm sure the Boers would be terrified at the sight of you and gladly hand him over."

"If I but could, my friend, you know I would."

"Say, Pepper," said Major Walton, approaching with a small box-shaped object Ivy recognized as an old-fashioned camera. "Have you any idea how to operate these things?"

"Is that a new Brownie?" Pepper exclaimed. "Good show! Is there flash paper? Hand it over, and I'll make a record of the happy couple." With practiced efficiency, Pepper positioned Ivy and Harrison with their backs to the piano, positioned the Brownie on the edge of the dining table, and mounted a black sheet of paper to a holder that he instructed Major Walton to hold at arm's length.

"Hold still now, and try not to flinch when it flashes," he instructed as he opened the camera shutter, then struck a match. The paper erupted into a blinding white light, then went dark. Lord Pepper grinned. "Let's do another!"

Dinner was soon announced, and Ivy took her seat at the long gleaming dining table beside Harrison. He squeezed her hand gently and whispered, "You're doing well. Thank you."

"That's why I'm here," she whispered. She became lost in his eyes for a moment, her heart doing little leaps of joy, her skin tingling under the warmth he transmitted. So kind he was, so proper, so strong, so confident. So bold, and yet so tender.

She would have liked, then and there, to kiss every inch of him.

He leaned closer and whispered in her ear, "For such a sweet girl, you can certainly deliver a most wanton look." He nuzzled her earlobe with the tip of his nose as he drew away, and his warm breath sent a chill shuddering through her.

He turned, with seeming reluctance, to the other dinner guests, letting go of her hand after giving it a final, suggestive squeeze.

Small conversations started up around the table, all talk

of war. Ivy listened silently, slowly drifting back to earth as the tone grew more serious.

Wine was served, a pale and very dry white wine poured by the butler with great ceremony. Ivy didn't like it much until the soup was served, a sauerkraut soup with pork and onions. It was surprisingly delicious, and balanced the wine so well, she finished her entire glass.

She felt warm and glowing from the inside out. She wasn't used to drinking much, just the occasional glass of wine with Aunt Daisy at the holidays, or when Daisy made homemade spaghetti pie. She didn't recall ever feeling this giddy after a single glass. But of course, she'd never before dined under the simmering blue gaze of a perfectly chiseled English god either. She smiled dreamily at Harrison, forgetting they weren't alone. He smiled back, his blue eyes traveling over her with distinct appreciation, as if he found not a single inch of her plain or dull.

"Lord Fleming's been nosing around Whitehall, from what I hear," said Lord Pepper to no one in particular when there was a lull in conversation. The words came like shattering glass to Ivy's dreamy happiness. She tore her gaze from Harrison's.

Major Cheltondon, a gray and dignified officer at the far end of the table, gave a grunt. "Fleming's more active now than before he retired. Once more, he goes where he wants. Without military ties and commands, he's free to travel to see his blasted mines."

"His mines?" Harrison gasped, choking on his wine. The butler, a thin little man in a tuxedo, scurried over with a glass of water.

Ivy had to bite her tongue to contain her own gasp.

"Yes, didn't you know? Fleming is chief stockholder in Amalgamated, those new mines that popped up in Jo'burg and Kimberly, and which, by the way, have begun operations despite the war. I hear Cecil Rhodes, Barney Barnato—the lot of them—are furious. Fleming's hired Chinese workers, brought them in when the local laborers refused to work after war broke out."

Ivy caught Harrison's eye again, and he gave her a shrug of apology for not believing her.

He asked of Major Cheltondon, "But how can he afford it? I was under the impression he was bankrupt."

"Nobody knows how he's financing the operation, but there he is, digging away. And he suddenly has the money to travel, don't you know. Named himself honorary diplomat. Claims he'll be the one to bring both sides to the table. He visits Whitehall; he visits South Africa. He dines with Kitchener one night; then a fortnight later he dines with Kruger."

"All the while," Joshua Pepper put in, "he manages to keep a tight leash on young Kyle. Is it true, Wyndham, that young Fleming cables his father every week, even in the heart of battle?"

"When possible, yes. Sometimes twice a week. There were a few times his wires saved our hides, so don't judge him too harshly for that. Kyle's fear of his father drove him to extremes at times to get a message out. He became quite skilled in repairing downed lines."

"Skilled he may be," Joshua Pepper countered. "But you'll never get me to thank him for anything. To accuse you of such an order, Harry! How can anyone possibly believe him? You know what the soldiers call him? Kyle Kipper. He's a joke amongst the ranks. Nobody believes him, surely, when he says you ordered him to shoot a civilian."

Harrison shrugged. "His accusation is too serious to be ignored. And apparently his father's Whitehall connections are bolstering his image to the inquiry board. The proper investigations will have to be done, but even so, Fleming must know he can't prove his lie."

Major Cheltondon remarked soberly, "It would be better if Private Carter hadn't been captured."

The table became very quiet then, and everyone seemed grateful when the next course arrived with a red wine.

Harrison ladled a modest spoonful of the dish onto Ivy's plate. Savory steam rose from the serving of minced meat that was covered in a thick golden egg custard.

This, too, Ivy devoured with an entire glass of wine. She thought she might be becoming a little tipsy. She probably should not touch the wine served with the next course. But then again, it might be nice to get just a little drunk. It might be very nice to lose some of her inhibitions once they returned to Harrison's room and were again alone, just the two of them.

She sighed, resting her chin in her hand to better study him as he spoke with the other officers. That dimple of his winked whenever his smile flashed. It flashed often. He was very animated in speech. His gestures were as large and generous as he was, and as refined and graceful. His voice was male music, deep and stirring like an instrument. She could feel his voice on her skin. Almost taste it on her tongue.

Yes, she was most definitely tipsy.

Harrison looked at her as she pondered him. He smiled, and she smiled, her chin wobbling on her hand. He carefully took that hand, which made her sit up straight, and the room became very quiet. Ivy realized she had missed an important change in the conversation.

He said to the others, while looking deeply into her eyes, "Finding Ivy was the best thing that ever happened to me."

A murmuring of approval sounded around the table, and Ivy felt heat rise to her neck and cheeks.

"Now here's a fitting subject for the dining table," Major Cheltondon exclaimed. "You met in Paris, I hear."

Harrison launched into the fabricated tale of how they'd met in Paris while he was on leave in the spring, and how she'd been reading an illustrated edition of a children's book, *The Three Little Pigs*, when he first saw her. All the while, he held her hand in his, cradling it, stroking it with his thumb, entwining his fingers with hers.

The men all seemed pleased by the tale, by their hand-holding, eyeing the two of them with knowing winks and cheers of congratulations.

Finally, dessert came, and the end was in sight. Ivy felt a draining sense of relief blend with her floating euphoria.

They'd done it. She'd been introduced, and all had gone well. Nobody believed him crazy any longer. She'd learned that Kyle's father truly did own Amalgamated Mines, though she still didn't understand what that meant to Harrison. But she'd also learned that every one of these knowledgeable men agreed Carter was crucial to his case. Carter must be found.

But not tonight. Tonight, she was going to continue to enjoy herself. The food was delicious, the wine intoxicating, and Harrison's nearness heartachingly wonderful. She'd not said anything majorly stupid, not done anything socially appalling, that she knew of. Harrison looked pleased and relaxed, giving her indulgent smiles.

Champagne was poured, and as Ivy lifted her glass, she was surprised to see the light of the chandelier captured in the bubbles. A pleasant dance of light winked at her. She sipped the bubbly cold champagne, set the glass down, and to her horror saw that the winking lights remained.

Her mind sobered so quickly, it hurt.

Above the floral centerpiece of the table, the swirling lights hovered. For a split second, she actually contemplated climbing up on the table and throwing herself through them. Then she felt Harrison grip her thigh.

She braved a look at him and recognized in his quick angry glance that he, too, saw the lights, and that he thought her directly responsible for them.

But conversation about the table was flowing normally. Ices were being eaten, champagne consumed. As before, only Ivy and Harrison were witness to the spectacle.

When the black central void of the swirling lights flashed, Ivy glimpsed express lane four, the magazine racks with the National Intruder headlines, and Daisy—dear, sweet, wonderful Daisy, in her favorite pale pink polyester, holding a banana, bringing her arm back as if to throw.

"Ivy," Harrison prompted, with a squeezing of her thigh

to shake her attention. "The Major asked if you heard much of the Klondike. Seattle is said to be getting rich off the miners heading north."

Ivy glanced down the table, but her view of Major Cheltondon was obscured by the lights of the open time-window.

"I uh—"

A hand over his mouth, Harrison whispered, "Stop it, Ivy! Stop it!"

"I'm not doing it," she whispered back.

Daisy let the banana fly, and it dropped from the lights onto the floral centerpiece as the time-window slammed shut and the lights vanished.

All the dinner guests gasped and jumped, except Ivy and Harrison, who'd seen it coming.

Chairs were scooted back, shoulders turned, legs tensed and ready to flee, while all eyes stayed glued to that centerpiece where a lily still trembled from the disturbance. A few of the officers drew their weapons.

The butler approached the table with a long knife, his slight form braced, his narrow chin thrust forward. Lord Pepper scooted his chair aside to allow the butler closer access to the trembling centerpiece.

Ivy held her breath as the butler plunged the knife into the arranged flowers, then slowly retracted his arm to hold the pierced banana aloft.

"How on earth!"

"My word."

"A banana?"

"But where on earth did it come from?"

16

The train to Johannesburg eased out of the station, and Ivy settled back into her seat, trying to catch her breath. She'd run nearly all the way to the station, managing to catch a lift from a kind farmer in his wagon the last half-mile.

The train was more comfortable than an airline's first class. The seat was a plush scarlet trimmed with polished wood. An electric light glowed above her, the globe an opaque tulip shape. Harrison's haversack, filled with the things she'd borrowed from him,—sat at her feet. From inside the sack, Harrison's revolver seemed to wink menacingly at her. She was having second thoughts about bringing the darn thing. She was more likely to accidentally shoot herself than she was to use it against a Boer. What had she been thinking? She was no heroine, no adventuress. She was a grocery checker.

Her heart continued to race. Instinctively, she turned to the window beside her, but it provided neither fresh air nor a clear view. The entire train had been boarded up and steel-plated to protect against Boer attack. Always prone to claustrophobia, she felt as if she were hurtling through space in a sardine can.

Hurtling was, of course, an exaggeration. The train

crawled at best, making the thousand-foot climb from the Low Veldt to the High Veldt with a nauseating number of twists and turns. She could not see this, of course, but she felt it as the train lurched and grumbled. She took a deep breath, closed her eyes, and tried to calm down.

When she got to Jo'burg, as the locals called it, she could simply get on the next train back to Pretoria. She didn't have to go through with this insane plan. But with her eyes closed, her mind filled with Harrison's image, and her heart overflowed with longing to save him, and with the guilt of being responsible for his life being in jeopardy.

Her brain told her she was not responsible, but her heart felt otherwise. She knew this was how Harrison felt about his brother. Last night, when they were alone in his room, she suggested he jump through the lights with her the next time they appeared, and go with her to the future. She'd still been tipsy, and very sleepy, and they'd sat snuggled on the couch before the hearth. He'd said he couldn't leave Africa because of Jeffrey. And then he told her what had happened.

"My brother was on a scouting patrol up near the game reserves with three others, all of them young, inexperienced." He'd paused, as if gathering the courage to go on. His voice became gravelly with emotion. "They were picked off, one by one. Jeffrey was the last. He was very clever, my little brother, always has been." He paused again, inhaling deeply, shakily. "They didn't just kill him. There's a group of Boers up north who've gone demonic. They don't fight; they hunt. And when they capture their prey, they torture them."

In the firelight, tears had glistened on his hands where

they fell, unchecked. He'd said, "I can't leave Africa. until I find the man who hurt my brother."

And she must find Private Carter to be sure Harrison lived to fulfill his destiny, whatever that might be. So when this morning he'd gone out to meet with his attorney, she told him she would remain behind to take a bath. Instead, she'd systematically gone through every drawer in his room—every cupboard and even his trunk—looking for things she might need. Above the wardrobe, she found his empty khaki haversack. Into it, she stashed several maps of South Africa, a brass pocket compass, an unlabeled tin can of what she hoped was salted beef (bully beef, Harrison had called it), a water flask that she filled with purified water from the dresser pitcher. She also took a one-pound box of chocolate, a small pocket knife, and—though she had absolutely no idea how to use it—his revolver and a small cardboard box that rattled with heavy bullets.

To buy herself more time, she'd filled the tub in the adjoining bathroom with hot steamy water, adding a generous dollop of scented oil to help with the deception. Then she wrote Harrison a note, making it intentionally misleading:

I'm sorry I had to leave again. But I'll be back just as soon as I can. Watch for the lights. My Aunt Daisy is going to try to help.

Now here she was, on her way alone to Johannesburg to find Private Carter, feeling ridiculous and unprepared. And queasy. Just when she thought she couldn't handle another stomach-shifting lurch, the train found level ground. She took a deep breath as they began to pick up smooth speed.

And then the smooth ride ended.

"Whoooooaa!" she involuntarily cried, her eyes flying open as she tumbled forward, the iron wheels of the train screeching painfully in her ears. The entire car shuddered violently, then there was a side-to-side jolt, then another, and then all motion ended completely.

The fluted electric lights flickered, then steadied, and Ivy climbed back into her seat, as did the handful of other passengers—a few farmers and businessmen, and three very young British soldiers.

The end car door opened, and the conductor, in a navy blue uniform and cap, stepped gingerly inside, asking if anyone were injured.

Luckily, nobody was, except for minor bumps and bruises.

"The track has been sabotaged," the conductor explained in a vague sort of accent, a blend of many nations. "A twenty-foot section has been completely removed. We're off the line now. It'll take a whole crew and several teams of oxen to get us on again. Best make yourselves comfortable. It will be a long night."

"But we've got to get to Johannesburg," complained the three young soldiers who rode up front. "We're to report for duty in a few hours."

The conductor, a lean and stern-looking man in his dark uniform, pushed his cap back on his nearly bald head. He'd apparently had enough of England's finest. "It's just another fifteen miles. There's the door."

The three soldiers looked at one another, then as a team got to their feet.

"Wait," Ivy said, springing up. "Take me with you."

All eyes were on her now.

"All right, love," said one of the soldiers, an adorable blond boy so young-looking she would have carded him for cigarettes had he come through her checkout line. She grabbed her haversack and hurried off the train with the three of them.

Outside, darkness lurked, but fresh cool air filled Ivy's lungs and cleared her mind. Night insects sang as steam hissed from the engine. The conductor had followed them, and now told them to wait a moment. He tromped off, reappearing a minute later from the back of the engine with two brightly lit lanterns.

In the small spots of golden lantern light, Ivy and the soldiers stood on the sandy right-of-way, gearing up, putting on hats and coats. Ivy pulled the wrist bands of her trekking costume snug and made sure the tops of her boots had no gaps at all for anything to slither into. She then wrapped herself in the long trekking coat and tugged on the Stetson hat.

"Keen outfit you got there. You look like a regular Livingston, ready to explore the great interior," the cute blond said. The color of his hair, the shape of his nose and jaw, even his mannerisms, reminded Ivy of Harrison, and she thought Harrison's brother Jeffrey must have looked much like this young man. And now he was dead. She shivered with a sudden chill of apprehension.

"I'm Tom," the blond said, "and this is George." He pointed to the short chubby one. "And that's Harold." The third young soldier was tall and painfully thin with the double curse of bad acne.

"Hello. I'm Ivy."

"Hello, Ivy," they greeted her in chorus.

"Well," Tom said, hefting his bag. "We've got a long walk ahead of us. What say we begin?"

Ivy hesitated, and the three of them looked at her inquisitively.

"You sure you want to come along? They're bound to get the train going by morning."

Morning might be too late. It might be too late now. She didn't know the date or time of Carter's death.

"I'm coming," she said before she could change her mind. Private Tom reached for her haversack, but she politely refused his help. She hooked the haversack over her shoulder, feeling the revolver bump against her hip unnervingly. George and Harold slipped on their haversacks, and they headed out, the nearly full moon guiding them.

They walked, not along the tracks as she'd expected, but across a dry, clumpy grass field to a dusty rutted clay road. The logic being, according to Tom, that somebody might come along in a wagon or ox cart and give them a lift part of the way, if they were lucky. They were somewhat secure along the road, too, at least from Boers. Every mile or so, hired natives signaled to them that all was clear.

Johannesburg was visible ahead as a fringe of factory chimneys standing out against the blue-black sky. A dim yellow glow hovered over the horizon, like a blanket of nuclear fog.

The train's engine now a faint hiss, the constant eerie singing of insects filled the air.

Ivy was grateful for Tom's jovial prattle. As they

stomped along the red clay road at a steady pace toward the factory chimneys, she learned that Tom and George and Harold had been the best of friends since childhood, they'd all three turned eighteen two months ago, had left school in London against their parents' wishes, finding it terribly dull, and signed on to fight in Africa and have an adventure. They'd read every newspaper report printed since war broke out, had studied every book written about Africa, and had waited most impatiently to become of age so they could join the war.

By the time Tom finished how they'd come to be in Pretoria, they'd trudged for at least an hour, yet the chimneys of Johannesburg appeared no closer.

"Well, then, Miss, you know about us. Tell us about you. Are you an American?" asked Tom.

"Yes."

"What are you doing in Africa?"

"It's a long story."

"Good. We've still a long walk ahead of us. Begin at the beginning."

With three faithful companions ready to listen, and the black night full of eerie night-singing creatures, including the possibility of snakes with every step, so she told them the tale Harrison had created for them. She made up a childhood for herself with Aunt Daisy that was nearly the truth if one didn't consider the modern details she'd left out. She told them about being orphaned when her parents had been killed in a road accident (they'd been killed by a drunk driver on Interstate 5). She told them she worked at a grocer's market, and that last April she had taken the holiday she'd always dreamed of when she went to Paris and met the Earl of Wyndham. “They met near the Eiffel Tower,” she said, elaborating romantically. She'd been reading an illustrated book of children's classic tales. They fell in love, and they married.

She found the telling amazingly easy, like repeating a favorite fairy tale. None of this seemed real. It couldn't be real.

But it was real, and as if to drive home the fact, from a nearby hill came a shrieking animal cry and then a growling, scrambling sound of something being killed, something being eaten.

The four of them froze. Nobody mentioned the sound, yet they were all morbidly mesmerized by it. Ivy doubted the soldiers knew what it was they heard any more than she did. A lion? A cheetah? A wild dog?

Tom was the first to shake off his fear. The sound of his footsteps snapped Ivy out of her alert listening stance, and she scrambled with George and Harold to catch up to him.

"You came all the way to Africa to be with your husband?" Tom exclaimed, as if the pause had never happened. "To help him get his memory back?"

"It's all I could think of to do," she said truthfully.

"We heard about Lord Wyndham's paintings at the Cape when we arrived. He's famous."

Harold bent low, for he was very tall, and asked from under his shining new helmet, "Where are you going now?"

"To Johannesburg to look for Private Carter."

Tom countered politely, "You just said he was taken prisoner by the Boers."

"He was, but I have a feeling he's near Johannesburg, near a gold mine. Call it women's intuition."

"And why is it that Lord Wyndham isn't with you?"

"He's not allowed to leave Pretoria until after the hearing."

Tom gave her a sly, sideways smile, and she thought again that Harrison's brother must have been just like him. "Does he know what you're doing?"

"Not exactly."

The soldiers all whistled, and told her she was a brave girl; then they very delicately told her she was a foolish girl, and tried to talk her out of searching on her own.

"I have to do this," she said firmly, "but I could use your help with one thing." She dug into the haversack as they walked along and very carefully pulled out the revolver, holding it upside down by the handle. The shiny muzzle winked in the moonlight.

Tom whistled softly. "What have you got there, Lady Wyndham?"

"I was hoping one of you'd know. I've got a box of bullets. Could you show me how to load and fire it?"

For the better part of the next half hour, as they continued on their way toward the hazy skyline of Johannesburg, Ivy learned about the gun. She learned that the spinning thing where the bullets went was called a cylinder. She learned that the bullets were really cartridges and that only the lead bit at the end was called the bullet. The rest of the cartridge—the case or shell—remained in the cylinder when the gun was fired.

She learned how to open the revolver's cylinder, insert

cartridges, close the cylinder, cock the hammer, and aim by lining up the front and rear bumpy things called sights, located on top of the barrel.

"Best not fire it now, though," Tom said. "We can do without that sort of attention. The sentries don't care for unnecessary fire."

Ivy removed the cartridges, and carefully stowed the gun away again, feeling more sure than ever that she would never fire the thing at a living person.

They walked the next few miles silently. The stars twinkled with less vibrancy as they neared the city. The moon passed over them. The two glowing lanterns, held by George and Harold, sent undulating arcs of light over the barren rutted road.

They passed two guards, dozing at their sentry posts.

Ivy's feet were numb with the unaccustomed walking, which she realized was for the best because she most likely had blisters on every inch of skin.

"What's over there?" Ivy asked, pointing to electric lights that appeared as they crested a small rise. Off to the east, at a distance of perhaps a quarter mile, six dots of light illuminated what looked like a huge white hill.

"That's what you've come to see. A gold mine. Those hills," Tom explained, proudly revealing his studied knowledge, "are the dirt they excavate. Waste rock, they call it, or tailings."

Soon, six more hills of mining debris came into view. A half-dozen cement chimneys spewed gritty steam from humming engine houses, providing the energy for the lights and the ugly network of machinery, conveyors and cranes that pulled the earth out of the ground.

Night it might be, but work was in progress. The conveyors all moved with loads of earth, and tiny figures of men moved busily about.

She understood now why the sky over Johannesburg seemed to glow. All the dust and smoke hovered in this rainless winter season, and the electric lights of the industries sent the tiny particles glowing. She had not thought electricity so widely used at the turn of the century. She certainly had not expected it of Africa.

"Amazing what gold and diamonds can do to even the remotest of civilizations," Tom pondered aloud, his thoughts apparently in line with Ivy's.

They came to a sign outside a barbed wire fence, and Ivy stepped closer to read. *Amalgamated Mines. Keep Out.*

She gave a low moan of dismay. Crud! She'd wanted to get here, yes, but not so soon, not yet. She wasn't ready yet.

She studied the mine operation with a growing sense of dread. Now what?

"If the Boers have your man in there," Tom said quietly, indicating the many acres and buildings encompassed by the barbed wire, "it could take a long time to find him. And you really can't do it on your own; it'd be foolish to try. You must get help."

"I don't suppose you three would like to volunteer."

"We can't, Lady Ivy. And that's the honest truth. We're due on duty in a few hours. If we don't report in, it's the lockup. Tell you what, though. Come into camp with us, and we'll get the army to help you search. How's that for assistance, eh?"

Ivy shook her head. "The army is searching for Carter somewhere else. They'd never believe he's here, and I can't risk getting Harrison into any more trouble."

They stood for a moment, resting, thinking, staring through the fence at the gold mine, listening to the grumble of the machines. She remembered what she'd heard last night, that Fleming had hired Chinese laborers.

"The company doesn't seem bothered by the war," Ivy commented. So many lives had been taken, damaged, changed, but industry seemed to be flourishing.

"That's the thing of it," said Tom. "Here we are, fighting for the Empire, and yet the resources of Africa are going to private business. The war won't change a thing for them, either way."

George spoke up excitedly. "This is nothing. Have you heard of that hole they've got in Kimberly? The diamond mine, the Big Hole they call it. Four hundred feet deep, half a mile across, I've heard. Ten thousand men down it at once." He whistled, and added, "Jiminy Christmas, it must be a sight."

"I'll thank'ee not to take the Lord's name in vain," said a strange, deep voice above and behind them. Ivy's skin crawled. "A curse is still a curse, no matter how disguised. Turn around slowly, *asseblief*."

The final word uttered was definitely not English, and had the ring of Dutch she'd been hearing in Pretoria. The voice seemed to come from the air. It was friendly enough in tone—gravelly, mature—and yet somehow sinister.

All four of them looked over their shoulders at the source of the voice. Then all four slowly turned as requested, lifting their hands in the air, surrendering without question.

The voice had come from a man on horseback. He was either very stealthy or they had been very unobservant, for none of them had noticed the rider's approach. He sat easily upon his mount, his thin body loose. A full, bushy brown beard hid most of his face and trailed halfway down his chest. He wasn't in uniform, but in ragged farmer's clothing—trousers, a long patched jacket, leather knee-high boots. A wide belt of ammunition hung heavily across his chest, and a rifle sat gingerly in his hands, lowered and aimed in their general direction, a dirty finger looped before the trigger.

"Dankie," the man said when they had turned, which Ivy figured meant thank you. It was too dark to see the man's eyes clearly under the broad-brimmed hat, but his voice remained fairly pleasant. Only the rifle and his trigger finger told Ivy they were in big trouble.

"That's a Boer commando, isn't it," asked George.

Ivy said in disbelief, "Haven't you ever seen one?"

To which Tom replied, "We only just arrived in Africa a fortnight ago. We haven't actually seen any action yet."

"Ai," said the Boer commando from atop his horse, the long barrel of his rifle now pointed directly at Tom. "I am honored to be your first."

George whispered, "What do we do?"

Harold whispered, "I haven't a clue."

Ivy whispered, "Do whatever he says."

And the Boer leaned down from his horse and whispered, "Listen to the *meisie.* She is wise."

17

A giant snore woke Harrison.

He found himself slouched on the couch, the electric lamps on, the fire in the small hearth barely smoldering. The air was filled with the misty scent of lavender.

The door to the bathroom stood closed.

Had she heard him? That was his first thought. Had she heard that horrible noise and how long had he been making it? He'd hardly slept last night, laying so close to Ivy, he atop the covers, she beneath them.

He hadn't realized how tired he was until he'd sat down to wait while Ivy bathed. In a matter of minutes, he'd not been able to keep his eyelids open.

He sat back again now, eying the plaster ceiling, pondering Ivy O'Neal and the strange hold she had on him. Questions assaulted him. Why was she here? Who was she? Where had she come from? More importantly, why had her arrival in his life brought him such relief?

Gone were his nightmares, his mental torment. Gone were the physical compulsions to paint and draw her image. His appetite had returned, and his energy, now that he'd napped. Here he was, in deadly serious trouble with this court-martial business, his one eye-witness a prisoner of war, and still he'd never felt better in his life. He didn't feel mad any longer either. His main concern now was how to prove to the world that he was sane, prove to the court that he was not guilty. He was even beginning to think about tomorrow, about what he would do once the war was over.

He was beginning to think once again of Wyndham.

But why? That's what he didn't understand. No reasons had been offered to explain what he'd seen on the battlefield. No explanation of how Ivy O'Neal had come to be here except her tale of time travel.

Did he believe her?

How could he not? What other explanation could there possibly be?

And how long had she been in that blasted bath? He didn't like being apart from her, not for a single minute. He got up, crossed the room, and pressed his ear to the bathroom door. He heard nothing.

"Ivy?" he called out softly. "Are you going to bathe all day?"

She didn't reply.

"Ivy?" he called, louder this time. Still no answer. He knocked.

He tried the door, but the handle was locked from the inside. He jiggled it, but this didn't get a response from her either.

Damn! How long had he been asleep?

The bath had two entry doors. He went out into the hall and tried the other door. It opened easily. He sent his voice in first.

"Ivy? Are you still in there?" He threw open the door. The tub was still full. The water, cold. Cold and fragrant.

There were no wet towels. Propped on the sink was a penciled note telling him she'd gone.

He returned to the bedroom and dropped onto the bed.

Gone. Back through those swirling lights. Back to her own time to leave him making up excuses for her absence. What the hell did she hope to find in that future land of hers? And who was Aunt Daisy? The banana-tossing woman?

He realized belatedly that he'd not asked her a thing about her personal life. She'd known all about him, but he hadn't asked anything about her. Aunt Daisy. And Ivy. Was her whole family named after the plant kingdom?

And why hadn't he thought to ask? Because, he knew, he'd been too busy worrying about himself. Worrying about how she affected him and how she could help him, or harm him.

He sighed and rolled over, and his gaze met the top of his wardrobe. Its emptiness caught his attention. His haversack wasn't there. He sat up.

Why would she need his haversack to return to that Pig store of the future?

She wouldn't.

He sprang from the bed, ran into the little office and sure enough, she'd rifled through his trunk, taken maps and chocolate and his flask. And his revolver.

"The silly little fool!" he cursed as he imagined her alone out there in the dark, searching for Private Carter. He envisioned her lost in the mountains between here and Johannesburg, being hunted by a Boer commando. Logically, he knew this to be impossible. She'd taken the train to

Johannesburg, surely. But what the bloody hell did she expect to do with a revolver once she got there?

Another very real image flashed into his mind. That of Jeffrey—alone, separated from his unit, being hunted like game, his ammunition gone, his food gone, his water gone.

Not human, these savage commandos. This enemy was nothing like those Dutchmen who'd fought in the beginning of the war when both sides played by rules, a gentleman's war. The respectable enemy had been killed or captured, these hold-outs were of another caliber, an entirely different animal altogether, with no sense of honor, or decency, or respect.

Jeffrey had been nearly dead of exhaustion and starvation when the commandos finally caught him.

They had no need to kill him.

He shuddered violently now, raking his hair, willing the image to go away. The sound that emerged from his throat was an animal sound, part grief, part horror, part boiling anger.

He had to go after her. He recalled his attorney's parting words. *You understand you are to remain in Pretoria for the hearing, Lord Wyndham? I promised the court we needn't take measures to secure your presence.*

"Bloody hell and bilge water." Orders disguised as friendly advice were orders all the same.

He returned to the hall and summoned Jasper.

"Yes, Captain?"

"A favor, Jasper. Will you see that my wife and I are not disturbed? We won't be needing your services for the next few days while I'm on leave."

Jasper smiled broadly, his young face blushing profusely. "Yes, sir. Nobody to disturb you."

"Thank you, Jasper."

"Enjoy yourself, sir. I mean—"

"I know what you mean, Jasper."

Five minutes later, he slipped unseen down the back stairs and out of the house. Wearing his greatcoat, for the night was cold, he looked for a bicycle, but couldn't find one, so he set off on foot toward town.

After a frustrating trip to the depot, he found his way to the former dormitory of a boarding school, where a dozen court officials and military solicitors were being housed. He found his assigned attorney, Major Walton, still awake, and thankfully, alone in his room.

"I need a horse."

"Wyndham, are you insane? You can't leave Pretoria." Major Walton hastily shut the door, and then cinched the tie of his scarlet robe more securely about his thick middle as he scowled at Harrison.

"I'll be back before anybody knows I've gone, with any luck."

"Back from where, for God's sake?"

"Major, my wife is at this minute on her way to Johannesburg on a fool's errand. A train left a quarter hour ago, and was detained by damage to the rails twenty-some miles out. I'm sure she was on it. There's not another tonight, so I must have a horse."

"No," Major Walton said, even as he opened the drawer of a child's size desk and drew out a note pad. He wrote hastily, signing his name with a flourish. "No," he repeated, handing the note to Harrison. "You put this idea past me, I refused to help, and now I'm assuming that you're returning to the Recovery House as I strongly suggested."

Harrison nodded silently as he read the note. It was an order allowing him to take a horse from the stables.

"That is a forgery," Major Walton said, pointing at the note in Harrison's hands.

"I understand."

"And Wyndham, if your adventurous bride hasn't found Carter—"

Harrison met the major's eye and saw pity before the major looked quickly away. "Well," he continued, "it's not too far to Portuguese territory. There are places a man and wife could go."

Harrison shook his head. "This war has taken my brother from me, Major. I will not let it take my honor. Nor the one woman who has rekindled in me the desire to live."

Major Walton stared at him intensely, then nodded. "God pity a man in love. Go on. Get out of here. Find your bride, and get your arse back here."

18

With a surge of hope, Harrison spotted the jogging figures in the road ahead. The night was now at its darkest, but in the swinging lantern light he could easily make out three figures—a tall thin one, a short round one, and one of average build. He urged his mount into a gallop and came upon the soldiers, reigning to a halt before them, forcing them to stop. The three of them panted heavily as if they'd been running for some distance.

"Are you the three soldiers who left the train with an American woman?"

He hoped for a yes; he expected at least a straightforward response. What he received were three pairs of dropped eyes, and three pairs of shuffling feet, as they continued trying to catch their breath.

"What the hell has she gone and done now?"

When the three pathetically young soldiers still did not respond, their faces gleaming eerily in the lantern light, Harrison fairly growled, "You are in the presence of a superior officer. I suggest you respond appropriately!"

All three snapped to attention with sharp salutes.

"We tried to stop her, sir. Honest, we did."

"He had a rifle, and he caught us unawares, sir."

"Who?"

"The Boer commando, sir."

"The commando? One? Against the three of you?"

"Well, sir, we haven't actually had much field experience yet. And he did take us unawares as we stood, back there, before the mines. We were just now going to report the incident. As fast as we could."

Harrison looked across the dark expanse toward the electric lights of the Amalgamated Mines he had passed just ten minutes ago. Fleming's mines.

He would be calm, he would not yell, he would not beat the cowardice from these poor boys. Jeffrey had been not much older than these three when he'd arrived in Africa. In fact, the one of average build rather reminded him of Jeffrey. So young. So eager. So unprepared.

One of them, the short round one, began to cry. Harrison looked to the stars for strength.

"Tell me exactly what happened."

The one who reminded him of Jeffrey spoke up. "Well, sir, he had that rifle aimed directly at us. Lady Wyndham, the American girl, said we should do as he says, and the Boer said we ought to listen to her. Then he asked if we had any food or medical supplies. And so we gave him what we had. Then he told us to lie down on the road with our hands on our heads and not to move until he was gone."

"He didn't try to take you prisoner along with the girl?"

"No, sir. He didn't even want the girl."

"Didn't want—then why did he take her?"

"She insisted he take her."

He stared into their nodding, agreeing faces in disbelief.

"Pardon?" he finally asked.

"She asked the commando if he knew of a Private Carter who'd been taken prisoner yesterday morning near Pretoria, and he said he did. So she demanded he take her to him."

"Of all the idiotic—" he began, then continued cursing in silence, scanning the darkness, wondering where in hell she could be, and what was happening to her. He prayed the Boer commando she'd linked her fate with was of the old Bible-toting, God-fearing sort who wouldn't dare touch a woman that wasn't his wife.

"What direction did they go?"

The three pointed down the road, toward the mines. It was as if their pointed hands conjured Ivy's magic lights, for suddenly there they were, swirling and sparkling, an upright oval of possessed fireflies. In their center was the void, black and deep, from which objects, and Ivy, had fallen.

The soldiers appeared not to see it, and Harrison was curious how the swirling lights managed not to illuminate the road.

Then came the flash, so bright in the night that Harrison threw his arm to his eyes, sending the three young soldiers to the dusty road, heads buried under their hands.

"Oh, get up you three!" Harrison demanded. With his lantern, he dismounted, marched past them, and found, lying in the dust, a small brown manila envelope. He set the lantern down, and squatting, opened the envelope. Inside, he found a brochure of the Seattle Art Museum, such as the one to which Ivy constantly referred. And a sheet of slick paper that was a cleverly copied page of a book, titled "Carter is found." And a handwritten note, signed by one Aunt Daisy.

The soldiers stood silent and obedient while he read of Carter being found, not here near Johannesburg, but to the north, at the Tuli crossing of the Limpopo River. Found dead—half of him anyway. He'd been bitten in two by a crocodile.

Up north was Boer country, the rugged and desolate and still wild Transvaal. It was true the Tuli crossing was north and just a bit west of here, but that was far from Boer territory. The search party had gone after Carter toward the northeast.

Wasn't it possible they'd lost track of the raiders? Hadn't Ivy's predictions about Fleming's mines been accurate?

He read further, and found his heart nearly stopping.

Lady Wyndham was also found dead at the Tuli crossing, her throat slit and several fingers severed completely.

A white wave of panic washed over Harrison, blinding him, sucking the breath from his lungs. Anger reared up to overwhelm his panic with red and pulsing rage. With unsteady clammy hands, he read Aunt Daisy's letter, almost unable to focus with his heart now beating like a native drum.

My dear Ivy,

I pray this finds you. When I turn on the scanners, I can't see those lights of yours. Did you get the banana? It disappeared, so I'm going to throw this letter through as soon as I can. I do believe you are somewhere other than here, but I'm finding it hard to accept that this is all real.

I hope you know what you're doing. Are you all right? When are you coming home?

I've told that horrible Bob you have the flu and he's cov-

ered your shifts for the week. He had the nerve to ask for a note from your doctor, and I gave him a piece of my mind. He now believes both of us to be mad, and he may be right.

I see that the witness, Private Carter, is no longer found near those gold mines but up in some crocodile infested river. Does this information help? And did you know there was a Lady Wyndham? I don't remember you telling me Harrison was married. Is it his wife? Or sister, perhaps? She seems to be in trouble too, so do what you can to save her and your Harrison, and do be careful! Don't do anything foolish! Then come straight home!

My hopes and prayers are with you.

Love, Aunt Daisy

Harrison stuffed the items back into the manila envelope, then stuffed the envelope under his greatcoat. He turned to the three soldiers.

They weren't much, but they were soldiers, and they had youth and energy—not to mention guilt—to fire them on.

"Come along," Harrison said. "You are under my command now. Do as I say, and I'll take full responsibility for your actions."

To hell with requests to remain in Pretoria. To hell with regulations and official channels and proper authority. He'd put himself on active duty, as of this minute. He was already up for court-martial. How much more trouble could he get himself into?

19

An eerie series of rapid high-pitched barks jerked Ivy awake, and she nearly fell off the horse. The barks continued to echo into the faint grayness of predawn. She clutched more tightly to her filthy host, her nose numb to his scent after two full days of riding behind him.

"Baboon," the Boer explained, tossing the word over his shoulder. She'd introduced herself to him as Lady Wyndham, hoping the name would give her some protection. He'd not believed her until she showed him the ring she wore, and then his crinkled eyes had opened wide with respect and seeming recognition.

He told her to call him Oom Peter, a ridiculous sounding title, but it did soften her view of him. She recalled from her research that *oom* meant uncle, and *tante* meant aunt, and that these titles were used in the same manner as mister and miss in English. Even the Dutch leader, Paul Kruger, liked to be called Oom Paul.

She yawned noisily, stretching as best she could in her precarious position. Every bit of her backside ached.

When through her blurry, tired eyes she saw a dozen pairs of glowing eyes looking back at her through the dark outlines of deformed trees and long snake-like vines, her mouth snapped shut mid-yawn. Noticing the dark shadows of baboons running along the dark tree limbs, their tails arched over their backs, she blinked, suddenly wide awake.

Sometime in the night they'd descended from rolling rocky hills to eerie jungle, which was coming alive now with the call of yet another baboon, and another, until it seemed a hundred of them were crying at once. And then every bird in existence cried out, joining in the chorus to greet a new day. The sounds exploded in Ivy's brain.

She felt much worse than she had yesterday—no, the day before yesterday—after drinking too much at the officer's dinner. Aching, exhausted, so thirsty she was fantasizing about water, Perrier, Calistoga, mountain spring. Distilled. Tap.

The baboons barked crazily, taunting her, bragging that they knew where water could be found and she did not. Harrison's flask was empty. Oom Peter had offered her a drink from his flask, but she hadn't yet gotten to the point where she could put her lips where his filthy mouth had been.

Soon, they should come to a river, a stream, a water hole. *Please,* she prayed silently. *Soon.*

The path through the jungle was short. Before the sun breached the horizon in a blaze of golden-red, they emerged and were riding once more across the open misty veldt.

The sky was huge, clear, and cloudless blue, already promising heat. There was still a touch of green in the grassland here under the quickly evaporating mist. She'd never seen grass in such abundance and variety. Some patches were tall and coarse, some soft and fine, rippling in the morning golden-pink glow like a sea, shifting and swaying in undulating waves. The waves made her think of the ocean, of water. Of aisle sixteen and its shelves of liquid heaven. Tahoma, Seattle Springs, Crystal Clear.

They rode at a steady, fast pace. Oom Peter navigated by natural landmarks during daylight, and by the dome of a billion stars in the blue-black sky at night. They'd changed horses four times already. Oom Peter had known just where to find the isolated mud and thatch huts of sympathetic settlers, and the exchanges had taken place rapidly, with little conversation.

Oom Peter had so far acted a gentleman toward her. Silent and stern behind that long beard, unresponsive to her attempts at conversation, he had nonetheless given her privacy to see to her physical needs.

Her chocolate was gone (it had been delicious), as was her tin of bully beef (nasty stuff, salty and gloppy). She craved fruit. Apples, grapes, oranges. Anything sweet and wet and cool.

"Are we almost there?" she asked Oom Peter again, like a child from the backseat of the family car.

He nodded and said with solemn authority, "Yaw. Yaw."

But they continued to race northward across the open grassland, seeing not another human soul.

Occasionally, a long-eared brown hare darted across the grass, as did small brown plovers and fat startled partridges. From a greater distance, grazing beasts gave them wary glances.

Ivy thrilled with recognition. Herds of striped zebra grazed in the yellow grass, seeming to prefer the seedy heads and hay-like blades. Their thick manes were also striped, the hair coarse, standing up on their heads and sliding down the ridge of their necks and backs like broom bristles. Occasionally one would give an odd barking sound in apparent warning of some impending danger, and they would all scatter, regroup, then begin feeding again.

There were small herds of kudu, silent, at least while she observed them, the males with their massive spiraled horns and vertical white stripes.

Birds constantly dotted the sky. Great solitary birds of prey cried out in high-pitched screams, and small chirpy things sang sweetly as they danced and darted with colorful butterflies.

Most exciting was the lion, startled from its resting place in the tall grass at their approach on this, the morning of their second day out. She was a female—she had no mane—a sleek golden creature, lean through the ribs. She took a few half-hearted loping steps away and then opened her mouth in a jaw-splitting yawn that revealed sharp deadly teeth. The sound of her roaring yawn carried to them even as they rode steadily away.

As the cold morning became a warm dusty afternoon, Ivy began to sweat through the thick twill of her clothing, and her salty sweat attracted gnats. If it weren't for the netting attached to her wide-brimmed Stetson hat and tucked tightly into her collar, she would have been bitten to death.

On and on they rode.

It seemed for the length of an hour that they were approaching a small grove in the midst of the grassy but otherwise barren savanna. A lovely sight it was, just like a postcard. In the silhouette of the dark twisted trunks and reaching limbs, and especially the unique flatness of the canopy in sharp relief against the blazing blue sky, she could see the very essence of Africa.

When they at last arrived, Ivy saw that instead of many trees, there was just one impossibly huge fig tree whose branches towered a hundred feet high and spread nearly twice that distance wide. The upper reaches were filled with birds—rooks and kestrels, Oom Peter called them—and a family of small monkeys that chattered amiably.

He shot his rifle several times to be sure no lion or leopard lay sleeping up there or guarding its kill. The monkeys quieted, but no cat emerged. He marched about, searching for snakes, before he declared it safe for Ivy to dismount.

She could barely move. Oom Peter lifted her down from the back of the horse, smiling up at her and revealing straight though yellowed teeth, pleasant gray eyes, and a youthfulness she hadn't before noticed. She was shocked to realize he might be her own age. If not for that full bushy beard and need of a haircut, Oom Peter would be a fair-looking man. He smiled at her so gently, she couldn't think of him as the enemy, but as simply a soldier who happened to be on the other side of Harrison's war.

She staggered, bent over, hands on her knees, to the massive trunk of the tree and the deepest shade where the grass had been flattened and molded into soft beds by other mammals, perhaps even lions. There, she simply folded herself over Harrison's haversack and fell instantly asleep.

She woke to the scent of roasting meat, the midday sun still warm. Her mouth felt like it was stuffed with smoldering cotton. If Peter offered his water again, she would accept.

She sat up painfully. Under the outer edge of the fig tree's shady reach, a small fire burned within a circle of protective rocks, and the carcass of a small skewered animal hung above the coals.

Oom Peter stood at the edge of the shade, scanning the grassland. He turned, and his gray eyes settled on her.

"Goeiemiddag," he said with a nod, returning to his grill. "Are you hungry?"

"Starved," she croaked, lifting the netting from her face and removing her hat. The warm breeze felt good on her head. She thought of untying her braid, because her skull hurt from wearing it so long. But with no shower or shampoo in sight, she decided it would be best to leave it braided.

Oom Peter rotated the meat over the fire a quarter turn. The animal was small, pink, stretched on a stick like a tortured thing, its long back legs and front paws still furry.

"Rabbit," he told her simply.

She swallowed a dry knot of disgust. Since she doubted there was a Pig Palace anywhere nearby, she didn't ask where he'd gotten it. She was just glad she'd been asleep when it had happened.

"Here," Oom Peter said, tossing something round to her. She didn't react quickly enough, and it dropped to the grass at her knees. An orange. Small, hard, slightly green, but an orange all the same.

She attacked it, digging her thumb into the peel and tearing it open. She sucked the sour-sweet juice, her eyes closed in ecstasy. Nothing had ever tasted so good. She devoured the fruit, down to the thinnest outer peel.

"Thank you," she said gratefully. "Thank you."

Oom Peter nodded and turned the rabbit again.

She stretched her aching muscles, and gave a terrific yawn. The monkeys were being quiet. So were the birds, with the heat of day full on. She squinted up into the darkness of the branches, but could see nothing.

"Have you ever seen an elephant, Lady Wyndham?"

"Only at the zoo," she said, smothering yet another yawn with a sticky sweet hand. "And in Pretoria. There's a guy there that has a private zoo." She climbed to her feet, unable to straighten completely, and shuffled to Oom Peter's side.

There, she lifted squinting eyes to the bright sunshine, and her mouth fell open in pure astonishment.

Oom Peter pointed unnecessarily across the rolling grass.

Standing just the length of a football field away was a full-grown bull elephant. Ivy's weariness vanished. It was as big as a dinosaur. Standing so very near it, without a fence between them, was like being in the movie *Jurassic Park.*

The massive creature was, from the top of his humped, leathery back to the tips of his round flat feet, at least thirteen feet tall. He was nearly twice that in length, and his great ears were as tall as she was. She could hear them flapping as they moved lazily, like sheets on a clothesline.

Two scarred ivory tusks, the color of marbled pewter, jutted from the base of his trunk. Not a matched set, one tusk was straight, the other curved inward, but both ended in rounded points and looked quite capable of making a shish kebab of two foolish humans.

"Are we safe?" she whispered.

"If we don't threaten him in any way," Oom Peter replied in low voice. "He is happy with his grass."

"He's so beautiful," she whispered.

"Mmm," Oom Peter agreed. "One of God's finest creatures."

The elephant stood very still, watching them. A small dark hole winked near the tip of his flapping left ear.

"He's been hunted," Oom Peter said. "He's leery. He wants us to sit so he can go on with his eating."

They sat, keeping their movements slow and easy, and the bull gave a snort of appreciation through his long trunk. Then he began to graze. He was an old fellow, Ivy realized. His wrinkled, dirt encrusted skin sagged on his frame, especially around his knees and under his belly. His face, too, sagged. The thick skin, caked with dried mud and dust, draped over his skull, showing the detail of his cranial bones.

For the better part of a quarter hour, Ivy's mind was filled with nothing but the glory of the grazing beast. But eventually, thoughts of Harrison and her mission began to trickle in.

"Oom Peter," she began, unable to resist asking yet again, "You are taking me to Private Carter, aren't you?"

Gray eyes regarded her through a haze of smoke. The rabbit was browning nicely. He nodded once.

"And he's still alive, isn't he?"

Oom Peter turned the rabbit a quarter turn, and juices hissed on the flames. The smell was like roasting chicken, and Ivy's mouth watered.

He stared so long into the distance, she thought he wasn't going to answer. He turned the rabbit again.

"A few days ago," he said slowly, "Carter was in Johannesburg. Very near to where I came upon you on the road. It was decided he would serve our needs better elsewhere, alive."

"You had planned to kill him?"

"Lady Wyndham, we are a God-fearing people. We are fighting this war to save our honor and our land. We are not murderers. We are soldiers."

"I didn't mean it like that," Ivy said quickly. She pressed aside thoughts of Harrison's brother and how he'd been tortured alive. She knew she shouldn't judge all the Boers by the sick actions of a few of their members. "You're at war, and he's your prisoner."

"He is now."

"Why? Why did you take him, I mean? How will having him serve your needs, as you said?"

"There are those who wish Private Carter not to testify for your husband."

Ivy gasped with surprise. "You know about the court-martial?"

Oom Peter nodded.

"Are you saying Carter was captured on purpose? It wasn't just an accident?"

"His identity was known. He was shown to us."

"Who showed you?"

"He did not give his name, only gold."

"What did the man look like? Was he English?"

"I was not there. But I am told he was English."

"An Englishman paid you, the enemy, to capture Carter and take him prisoner to keep him from testifying?"

"Yaw, only he was to be killed in battle, not captured."

"But something went wrong," she prompted.

"It was decided that it would be unjust to kill the man for such a purpose. Instead, he was taken and questioned about the death of our missionary. We knew of this shooting, of course. Reverend Schmidt was a beloved man in our church. Peace talks were abandoned when it was learned his death had been ordered."

"But that's not true. Harrison never gave such an order. His order was to take the missionary into protective custody; I swear it."

Oom Peter shrugged as if the testimony of the accused's wife mattered little. "We had only the unnamed Englishman's explanation. We wanted to ask questions of our own. But more gold was offered if we would hand over the prisoner. Enough gold to purchase much needed food and weapons. One small sin for a greater good. We didn't like it, but it was agreed upon. The soldier was to be handed over, in Johannesburg, near the mine before which you stood."

"What happened?"

"You, Lady Wyndham. It was you who saved his life."

"Me?"

"We have friends in Pretoria. It is still our city, despite British occupation. We learned of the portraits your husband painted, and we learned of your arrival. We learned your husband was no longer being accused of insanity and that still he insisted he gave no order to shoot the good missionary. Our unknown Englishman became nervous. For some reason, this Englishman wants your husband proved guilty of giving the order. It occurred to us that perhaps Private Carter would be worth more to this Englishman in a few days' time."

"So he was taken somewhere else. Where you're taking me now. Are we almost there?"

Oom Peter nodded.

"Why were you still there? Near Johannesburg, I mean. Wasn't it dangerous for you?"

"Yaw. I stayed behind to make the appointment with the Englishman and tell him our new terms."

"Did you see him?"

"No. He did not come. But then I found you on the road, and you begged me to take you. You have doubled the value of our trade."

"Me? Why would anyone pay to get me back?"

"Not gold, Lady Wyndham, though I am sure your husband would pay dearly to have you returned to him safely. I am speaking of more than money. You, I believe, are worth several of our imprisoned leaders."

The elephant's grazing brought him closer, so close his shadow moved over Ivy. The breath in his trunk sounded like a child blowing through an empty paper towel tube, only the sound vibrated the very air and tickled Ivy's skin. On the end of his trunk, two fat finger-like digits twined around clumps of grass, gripping them, and then a huge flat-bottomed and very wrinkled foot swung across the base of the grass so that the sharp toenails neatly sliced away the pale green tops. Then the trunk curved under and stuffed the grass into the long droopy mouth. The ears, each about the size of Ivy's Honda but thin as cloth, flapped at constantly buzzing gnats, and the tail, which was like a giant rubbery straw broom, swatted at the ever-present flies.

Ivy was grateful the predominant wind was sending the elephant's scent away, for suddenly a great deep rumbling echoed in the massive creature, and the ground shook like a faint earthquake, and then a most undignified sound exploded from the elephant, sending the flies dashing away in a cloud.

Ivy blushed to the roots of her hair. But Oom Peter, apparently used to this habit of the elephant, paid no attention at all. Or maybe he was trying to spare her further embarrassment by not mentioning it.

"When my father first came to Africa," Oom Peter said very quietly, "the veldt was thick with such huge beasts of God. Then the English came with their rich hunters, who killed for sport. Now they wish to slaughter us, as they have slaughtered the elephant, until we are extinct."

Ivy couldn't speak. The elephant came so close, the breath of his trunk whistled over her as he felt for the tender grasses. His slowly flapping ears produced a hay-scented breeze. He seemed to notice her then, ceasing his eating to stare at her from a small dark eye that was covered with long thick black lashes. He then made a sound, very much like Audrey purring, only so much deeper that she felt the vibration in her stomach. It seemed a friendly yet terrifying noise experienced at such close quarters, and she exhaled with tremendous relief when the great creature turned and lumbered with surprising quietness toward a thick layer of tall grass fifty yards away.

"It has not been a merciful quick killing," Oom Peter said, his voice still soft. The tone of it made the hair on her arms raise. She'd forgotten what it was they were talking about. He sat on his haunches, tending the roasting rabbit. His kind gray eyes had taken on a glazed intensity.

"Piece by piece the English have taken us apart, killing us one at a time."

Her breath caught in her chest again, not because of the elephant this time, but because she had recognized Peter's words as those used by Harrison just a few days ago. Despite the heat, a cold clamminess seeped over her. Piece by piece.

Oom Peter removed the rabbit from the fire. He held the small body on the skewer, letting it cool in the breeze. The little charred corpse looked as if it were praying.

"An eye for an eye, a tooth for a tooth. Each man shall know the suffering England has inflicted upon my people." He sliced off a hunk of the rabbit, a furry hind foot attached, and extended it to Ivy.

He'd removed his gloves to do the cooking. His hand was bare, black with dirt under the fingernails, the skin rough and calloused and dark with sun.

She saw it then, as he held the rabbit out to her—the ring on his little finger. Its sapphire glowed in the reflection of the hot sun. The gold of the Wyndham crest was smeared with rabbit blood.

Ivy slowly cupped her hand over her mouth, not wanting to believe, but knowing with every fiber of her being, that she was staring at Jeffrey's murderer.

Oom Peter glanced from the ring to her face and repeated soberly, "One piece at a time."

20

Anything could be happening to her. He had to get to her in time. If the future predictions were correct, then she was still alive, still crossing the bush. But he didn't know that for a fact. So much lurked out there just waiting to strike: malaria-carrying mosquitoes, bubonic plague-carrying fleas—hadn't plague been reported at the Cape? Typhoid, fever trees, venomous spiders and snakes, the scorching heat of day and the numbing cold of night. Not to mention being at the mercy of her captor. And Ivy so naive and unprepared to deal with any of it.

"Tea, Captain?"

Harrison tore his gaze from the train window to glare at Tom. The boy held out a dainty tea cup, a service cart at his elbow loaded with a silver tea set and scones, manned by a smiling ebony-skinned native. The other two, George and Harold, sat across from him, drinking their tea, their khaki uniforms so new they still smelled of starch.

He wanted to refuse the tea, but his mouth was parched, and a strong sweetened cup would help calm his nerves and settle his churning guts.

"Yes, but get me a proper mug, will you? I'll be damned if I'll drink tea as if I'm at a garden party."

George and Harold exchanged a glance, then cleared

their throats and thrust out their chins, adjusting the china cups in their hands to a more masculine hold.

They'd ridden uninterrupted from Johannesburg to Mafeking, dropping from the High Veldt country with its vast gold deposits, into the Middle Veldt with its vast deposits of grass. While switching to the Bulawayo line in Mafeking, they'd avoided all but necessary interaction with the military presence, and Harrison had been relieved he was not yet being sought. And the young soldiers he'd commandeered were not yet late enough to their assignments to warrant any call for action.

They'd managed to secure a compartment in a passenger car, and while it was not so well outfitted as the Johannesburg line, it was more comfortable than the alternative, which was walking. Seated on a padded wooden bench, the window open for cross ventilation, screened to keep out unwanted pests, a man could, almost, imagine himself on his way to a recreational safari, and not out to save the life of a young woman who had somehow become everything in the world to him.

The tracks maneuvered them through twisting mountainous country, thick with brush, horn trees, and acacia. They plunged through a series of teetering turns down off the Middle Veldt and into the southwestern edge of the Limpopo River Valley.

What should have been a few hours train journey had taken half a day, with line repair delays. Even so, within an hour they would reach Mmamabula in the Bechuanaland Protectorate, and from there it would be another twenty-five miles to the Tuli crossing of the Limpopo. And though they had taken the long way around, they should arrive a full day ahead of anybody making the journey on horseback.

He'd had two options. Pursue the Boer and Ivy alone, on horseback, one hundred and fifty miles across the veldt and bush in territory unfamiliar to him but known intimately to the Boer. Or recruit these three youngsters, trust the information that had come through the magic lights, and ride in comfort and speed to a place of interception.

"There you are, Captain," said Tom, handing Harrison the mug, adopting a jovial accent disturbingly like Jeffrey's. "Nice mugga England's finest. Sweetened and creamed, just the way you like it."

Harrison took the mug with a grunt of thanks. This was perhaps the most embarrassingly unheroic rescue attempt in history. However, the tea was delicious.

"Get me the map, Tom. We'll have another go at the location. There are several crossings from the Transvaal into the Tuli Block in the region we're heading, and all are called Tuli-something."

Tom had given up asking why it was Harrison believed that's where they would find the Boer soldier and his American bride.

The map was not army issue, but native, purchased in Mafeking from a Zulu who swore it was drawn by a Bangwato hunter, who knew the Tuli Block well as it was his home. The general layout matched other official maps. A narrow strip of land, perhaps 350 kilometers long, bordered the western shore of the Limpopo River, which itself marked the border between the Transvaal and the British Protectorate. The detail revealed on the Bangwato's map, however, was so much greater than the others that Harrison hoped and prayed he could trust it. There were no names or words on this map, but the river markings, gullies and kopjes were obvious, as were the stick animal figures drawn in to indicate native inhabitants. Lions, elephants, antelope, snakes, hyenas, crocodiles—all were represented.

"We'll have to disembark here," Harrison said pointing to the map, "and scout each of these drifts. Damn, but I wish we had mounts."

He thought a moment of the problem of getting about once they left the train. Going by foot wasn't even thinkable. It would take far too long.

"George and Harold, I want you to find the conductor and tell him I'll give him one hundred pounds if he can locate four suitable rides—horses or mules—anything trained to the saddle."

Tom's brows lifted, and he whistled softly. George and Harold scurried off as ordered.

Ten minutes later they returned to the car with the conductor in tow.

"Lord Wyndham," the conductor began in a thick Scottish brogue, "I can't be seein' my way to deliverin' you any horses. They are scarce these days. Still, I might be able to find you something suitable."

21

Bile rose in Ivy's throat. She shook her head, refusing the rabbit, and Oom Peter cocked his head like a friendly dog. Surely he realized by her reaction that she knew about Jeffrey. That she knew the ring he wore matched the one she wore. And yet his manners remained friendly, his gray eyes, focused now, were gentle.

"You must eat. We have another full day of riding until we reach my compatriots and your Private Carter."

When she still didn't move, his expression abruptly hardened. "You are angry now because you think me cruel. Where were you when the Uitlanders came and raped the earth of its treasures? When they slaughtered the wild creatures living here, and drove my people ever northward into ever harsher country? Where were you when they burned our farms and locked our women and children in disease-filled camps?"

She didn't know what sort of answer to give him, to calm him. She simply shook her head.

"The English deliver destruction and expect gratitude. But we've shown them we are not so easily obliterated. Here we are, a few hundred remaining Dutchmen against the entire British Empire." He laughed much like the zebra, in a sharp bark, and his voice grew loud and angry. "We will show them, one Englishman at a time, what it is to be slaughtered. We will teach them to leave us alone!" He thrust the rabbit leg at Ivy with such force, she was afraid to refuse. She was at his mercy. She would die without his help crossing this desolate stretch of Africa. She would die if he decided she didn't deserve to live.

She took the small blackened leg, her hand trembling.

"Eat it!" he demanded in that zebra bark.

After the first few choking bites, she found her appetite returning in full. She devoured the meat in minutes.

A quarter hour later, she crawled to the far side of the tree and was sick. She covered the mess with handfuls of dirt and sweet grass, then cleaned her mouth by chewing the bits of orange rind. In her jacket pocket, she found her breath mints. The taste helped, but her thirst grew.

They spoke not at all for the next two hours. Oom Peter carefully put out the fire; then he lay down beneath the giant shady fig tree. He stretched out on his back, gripping his rifle across his chest.

The grassland was very quiet except for the constant buzz of insects. Everything slept through the heat; even the monkeys lazed, curled up in the crooks of branches, their small light faces burrowed in fur.

Ivy, wide awake, sat with her knees drawn up, watching Oom Peter. When his breathing slowed and deepened, she carefully crawled over the grass to Harrison's haversack, lifted the flap, and ever so slowly reached into the farthest corner. Her fingers met the warm curve of the empty bully beef can, the rough canvas covering of the water flask, the empty chocolate box.

But the revolver was gone. He must have taken it in the night while she relieved herself in the bushes. Or while she slept. She shuddered at the thought of him digging through her belongings. And where was the revolver now? On him?

Slowly, quietly, she crawled toward him over the shady flattened grass. A delicate long-legged spider skittered out of her path. A few of the monkeys above lifted their small white faces to look down at her curiously. She crawled as close as she dared to Peter, listening to his steady breathing. He lay very still but for the rise and fall of his chest. His faded leather ammo belt held nothing but rifle cartridges. In his holster was a pistol with a black grip—not Harrison's. His pockets hung slack. He hadn't put his gloves back on yet. Jeffrey's ring, as filthy as Peter's hands, was temptingly close where it lay across the rifle. But she dared not reach for it.

Carefully, she backed away from him.

The horse, a mottled gray skinny thing, was grazing in the shade on the far side of the tree. The saddle and saddle bags sat balanced on a gnarled tree root a few feet away.

Ivy got to her feet and hurried to the bags, constantly turning her eyes back to glance at Peter. Her heart hammered wildly in her ears.

She found the gun in the first pocket she checked, along with the box of cartridges.

With nervous fingers, she opened the cylinder and loaded the chambers as the young soldiers had taught her. She closed the cylinder, and it clicked into place. The monkeys above her chattered noisily, as if asking her just what she thought she was doing.

"Shhh," she whispered up at them. They hushed obediently, their small faces cocked like curious puppies.

She returned to within three yards of Peter.

She lifted the gun, grateful the monkeys remained silent, aligned the gun sights onto the filthy folds of fabric over Peter's chest, just above the place his ammo belt crossed him.

Do it! she mentally screamed. *Shoot!*

The sights danced as her hands trembled, from his chest to his face, to the tree, back to his chest, where she finally managed to steady herself again.

She swallowed hard, sweat pouring down her face, stinging her eyes.

He'd killed Jeffrey. Tortured him alive. He would do the same to her, if given the chance, if he believed it would help his cause.

Her finger moved toward the trigger, felt the warm metal.

And then what? If she pulled the trigger and actually managed to kill him and not just piss him off, then what? How would she find Carter? How would she find her way out of the bush and back to Harrison, back to the lights and Daisy and Audrey?

For some reason, it was the thought of Audrey—her purring meows and her kneading paws—that made Ivy all at once feel immensely homesick.

She could not find her way back home without Peter's help. More than she wanted him dead, she needed him alive. She slowly eased her finger away from the trigger, and breathed a quiet sigh of relief. She might not be able to shoot in cold blood, but she prayed she'd find the courage to shoot in self-defense. Before she could lower the revolver and hide it away, Oom Peter's eyes sprang open.

Ivy opened her mouth to explain, but no words would emerge. She stood frozen, afraid to move, knowing she should do something.

It wasn't until Oom Peter slowly lifted his rifle and pointed it upwards into the branches of the gigantic fig tree that she realized he had not seen her at all. His eyes were fixed steadily upwards.

A second later, his rifle exploded, and the monkeys screamed, a thousand birds took flight, and the elephant's immense weight thundered underfoot.

Peter rolled away, burying his head protectively in his arms as a twelve foot snake dropped like a coil of rope to the soft bed of grass he'd just vacated.

For another full second, Ivy didn't move. She still held the revolver straight out from her. And then it dawned on her she must move now or surely be caught, and she shoved the revolver into the generous pocket of her jacket, praying the thing wouldn't go off.

Her hand was still inside her pocket when Oom Peter twisted around and looked at her.

"Good shot," she said, forcing her mouth into a smile.

"Dankie," he said. His eyes lowered down the length of her, stopping, she feared, at the bulge her hand and gun made in her pocket.

He climbed to his feet and approached her, a hand shading his eyes from the sun. She stood perfectly still, holding her breath.

At her side, he stopped, his eyes not on her but out there, at the rolling grass and bush.

"It'll be cooling soon. Time to go. We'll be there before nightfall."

* * *

A full moon rose as the golden light of twilight hovered, angling across the kloof, the ancient ravine carved by the Limpopo. Harrison lay on his belly on the rocky cliff, looking down upon the Boer encampment. Five massive waggons formed a laager, a sturdy circular fortress with conical tents sheltered in the center. The only egress to the encampment was by way of the Limpopo shore, wide enough now during the dry season for waggons to pass, if only in single file.

Where on God's earth was Ivy?

The oxen, over one hundred head, and horses, perhaps two dozen, grazed a small distance upriver in a field of wheat-colored grass. To approach the camp from the north or south, one would face the expanse of shoreline which, by day, was occupied by hungry crocodiles, some of them nearly twenty feet long, sunning themselves, great mouths gaping, revealing lethal teeth. Though not enjoyable, a route through the forest of fever trees and thorn trees and acacia was preferable to strolling amongst so many armor-plated jaws.

Approached from the east, one was aware only of the forest, and perhaps the sounds of the river—the noisy abundance of birds and animals drawn to the source of water. There was no hint of the kloof until one practically fell into it. Without his native map, Harrison might very well have done just that.

The donkeys procured by the train conductor had proved stubborn, slow, and uncomfortable, but faster than traveling by foot. They'd all—beasts and men—arrived tired and sore. And now the interminable watching and waiting.

The encampment could only be seen from the west side of the river, just north of where the oxen grazed, and only by standing directly across from the ravine. The vegetation on the west side was sparser, the riverbank open and vulnerable.

From his perch, it was possible for Harrison to see for many kilometers across the grasslands and bush of the Tuli Block. As the sun dipped yet lower, the baobab trees morphed into black gruesome silhouettes, as if a giant had angrily ripped ancient oaks from the earth and then thrust them upside down to embed them with their twisted roots rising toward the fading blue sky.

The caravan of Arabian camels was an even more chilling sight. The line of them, with their distinctive single humps and long necks and knobby-kneed legs, looked like a child's cutting pasted onto a window. Each of the forty camels carried a fully loaded pack, and a dozen natives were employed untying burdens and carrying heavy cases to the river's edge where yet another dozen natives plus a dozen Boers formed a relay, passing the cases hand to hand across the river and ultimately into the back of the waggon nearest the shore.

Harrison dug his field glasses from his haversack and

focused on the sluggish brown river. The day was cooling, and dozens of crocodiles were showing signs of waking. Mouths already open stretched further into yawns, then snapped shut with a click that Harrison heard all the way up to his perch.

The Boers had secured one small stretch of beach for themselves, and guards stood with rifles at the ready to halt any crocodile who might attempt to reclaim his warm perch or interrupt the flow of cases. Harrison brought the field glasses to focus onto a case. Constant movement kept the painted letters dancing illegibly, but at last a pause by a tired native allowed him to read.

Provisions Corp.

The words brought a coiling sort of dread to Harrison muscles, making him ache with helplessness. Another of Ivy's predictions come to pass? Hadn't she said Provisions Corp was somehow linked to everything else? And now, here was proof. The Boers had Carter in the very location they were receiving a shipment of weapons. And that bloody Turk, who'd already made a fortune off the English, was apparently now going to bleed every drop of gold he could from the Dutch.

No one in the British army had even suspected that this northwestern district was the point of entry for enemy weapons. The Tuli Block was comprised of privately owned land, freehold farms, and game parks, given by the British to English and Europeans wishing to settle. The settlers had been chosen carefully, their loyalties confirmed, deliberately establishing a western block to Boer migration.

The owner of the tract opposite either didn't realize his

land was being used to smuggle weapons to the Boers, or he knew and didn't care. Or was himself profiting. Oom Paul Kruger had fled Pretoria with a million pounds worth of gold. If access was available, he had the money to pay for it.

Harrison lifted the glasses a quarter inch and found Private Carter, waist deep in the Limpopo, dead-center of the relay. Still alive and well, and with his legs beneath him.

A movement on shore caught his eye, and he moved the glasses in time to see a gruesome armored creature slip silently into the muddy river. He gripped the glasses more tightly to steady his hands.

Shouts rang out and a dozen shots exploded, sending white jets spraying from the river. There was a tremendous thrashing as a rusty red stain bled into the sluggish brown river. When the river quieted, half a dozen natives dragged the great beast ashore.

The shore, however, was now completely free of crocodiles. At the sound of the first shot, they'd all snapped their jaws shut for a final time and slithered, with amazing speed, into the water and disappeared. There was not a snout nor eye nor tail to be seen.

For a little while longer at least, Carter would keep his legs. But the monsters were in the river now, and they would not abandon their home territory for long. Dinnertime was not far away, and there were many tasty meals moving about the monsters' dining hall. Even with many eyes watching and rifles at the ready, one especially hungry and bold crocodile could dash all his hopes.

Harrison could do nothing until help arrived. There were far too many of the enemy. He had expected to find a small encampment—one waggon at the most, a handful of commandos. Not this. Not a hundred armed men. Certainly not a weapons delivery.

He'd sent George and Harold back to the train station to alert British headquarters of the Boer encampment and the movement of weapons. That had been hours ago, when the arrival of the arms dealer, in his flowing robes, and the cloud of dust far across the border in Bechuanaland told him something big was on its way. George and Harold were back, but as of yet there were no British troops in sight. If they didn't arrive soon, the weapons delivery would be complete, the Boers fully armed, and the British army would ride into a bloodbath.

Another movement caught his attention, indeed the attention of nearly everyone down below. A horseman had arrived at full gallop from along the beach, having braved the blanket of crocodiles or perhaps arrived advantageously to see them all depart. Not one rider, but two. Harrison's sharp intake of breath brought Tom's attention.

"What is it, Captain? Do you see your wife?" whispered Tom.

"Yes. Be quiet."

He froze, every inch of him wanting to run to her but knowing such action would end in death for them both.

The Boer commando was greeted with much fanfare and shouts from his compatriots, though the exact words didn't carry up to Harrison.

The Boer dismounted, then lifted Ivy down with a gentleness that made Harrison's skin crawl. He had no wish to see her ill-treated, but such manners, such courtesy, struck fear into Harrison's heart that liberties had been taken, that perhaps Ivy had been violated.

He shook with the thought, gripping the glasses painfully, focusing on Ivy's face. She lifted the netting away as he watched. Even in the dim golden light, he could see that her skin had been browned by the sun, the tip of her nose burned pink. To see those eyes once more, the uneven brows, that stubborn chin, made him nearly giddy with joy and terror both. She did not look harmed nor violated. She looked as if she'd just completed an exhilarating excursion and was eager for more. Slung casually over her shoulder was his very own haversack. And now he noticed her clothing, a fine trekking costume, complete with a wide-brimmed Stetson and attached netting, which she had just lifted.

Where in the bloody bush had she found that?

And what was she now saying to her captors? The leader of this unit, the Commandant, had stepped forward. Harrison only knew he was the leader because of his mannerisms, the way he gave orders to the other men, for none of them wore uniforms. They were independent soldiers. The Boers behaved more like brothers against a common cause than an organized army, and it was this particular feature which was taking the British so long to overcome.

The bearded, ragged, fierce men, nodded politely at Ivy as if listening to a queen. Was she asking them to release Private Carter into her care? Did she honestly think they would grant her request simply because she asked?

Apparently so, for the Commandant shook his head and

gestured with his hands and pointed to the river.

But Ivy, stubborn and feisty as he knew her to be from personal experience, didn't seem to want to take no for an answer. She spoke again, and again the Boers listened, as Harrison watched, helplessly from above.

How the hell was he supposed to know what action would save her from the fate foretold by the magic lights? Theoretically, he supposed whatever he did would bring about the same end, since this information had come from the future and the future had recorded a tragic outcome.

But the future had changed once before, according to Ivy. And the information recorded in the brochure had also changed. So perhaps if he behaved differently than forecast, the future would once again change.

He was beginning to get a piercing headache. One step at a time, and to hell with the predictions.

He must get Ivy to safety, first and foremost. And secondly, he must reach Carter before a crocodile or Boer brought about his death. Thirdly, he had to get back to Pretoria in time for the court-martial hearing, or he would be charged with desertion.

So, what should he do?

Ivy was escorted to a tent and disappeared inside. The last of the twilight vanished, and Harrison's eyes adjusted to the bluish light of the full moon. He lay still for five minutes—that seemed an eternity—until at last he formed a plan.

"Tom," Harrison called softly. Tom and George and Harold moved closer to listen.

"Have you got matches in your kits?"

They nodded.

"Good. Here's what we're going to do."

A quarter hour later, they were all in position.

The three young soldiers had split up as ordered, climbed around the low ridge of the kloof, and lit a match to reveal their readiness. George was lookout, moving to a high position and keeping his field glasses trained to the south to watch for the approach of the army in order to lead them in. Harold was put on Private Carter, keeping him in sight at all times.

Also in that short amount of time, Harrison had done something he loathed, the most barbarous act of war he'd performed to date. He had killed, silently and stealthily, the nearest Boer sentry. A single slit to the throat had both silenced the man and ended his life.

Then Tom, who'd proved himself the most courageous and competent of the three youngsters, had stripped off his khaki and dressed in the dead Boer's dark and ragged clothing. He'd smeared his pale hair with handfuls of dirt, spit into his hands and grimed his face. The beard proved the trickiest. He must have one; there was not a single Boer below without whiskers.

Harrison cut a strip of dark cloth from the tail of the Boer's shirt. Onto this he smeared the sticky ooze of an aloe plant that grew in profusion amongst the rocks. He then trimmed the dead Boer's brown and gray beard and pressed handfuls against the aloe. This mess he tied to Tom's chin. The result was hideous, but from a distance Tom appeared to have the necessary beard. If he kept his face down and stayed silent, he might possibly slip by unnoticed.

When George signaled that he'd spotted friendly troops in the distance, Harrison turned to Tom. "Wait until you see me enter the tent, then make your way down. You know what to do?"

"Yes, Captain. You can count on me," Tom replied, as eager as Jeffrey had been to see action, to fight the enemy. Harrison experienced a sudden pang of fear for the young man, a strong sibling affection accompanied by troublesome worry. He didn't think he could bear being responsible for this one's death, too.

"Do be careful, Tom," Harrison said.

"I will, Captain. You do the same.

22

In the dry season, *there are always hungry lions watching.*

Those were the words echoing through Ivy's mind. She'd heard them repeated a hundred times over the past year on a cable channel commercial. Never before had the announcer's voice sounded so deep, nor so ominous. Never before had she understood the true meaning of those words. And she wasn't even hearing them now, only their echo, as she was marched into the center of the Boer camp, with the sluggish crocodile-infested Limpopo River behind her. Above, in the woods so different from home, ablaze in golden late day without a single Douglas fir or evergreen pine, a lion grumbled hungrily.

The conical tent in which Ivy found herself was small but clean, furnished with a cot draped in mosquito netting, and an overturned Provisions Corp case for a table. There was an unwashed smell to the space, mingled with the heavy dampness slipping in from the muddy river.

The floor was packed earth, swept clean and, she saw with relief, there was no place for a snake to hide, unless once again an overturned Provisions Corp case was serving as a reptile's home. There was no lamp in the tent, but there was enough light to see. The canvas walls glowed dimly with moonlight and the shifting reddish glow of the central fire blended to create what would be—in other circumstances—a romantic atmosphere. All in all, it was more than she expected.

Private Carter was here in camp, she'd been told, and that was something. The Boers had not agreed to release him. But they did say her arrival might alter their plans and so she was encouraged. Altered plans could mean altered history. There was hope. Harrison may live a long life after all.

She'd been in the tent just a few minutes when she heard a polite voice say, "Knock, knock," and in came a bearded Dutchman with a bowl of water, a washrag, and a sliver of lye soap. These he set down for her on the crate, hurried out, then returned, this time with a huge tin mug of very sweet and very hot coffee and a tin plate of some sort of cooked meat, cut in neat pink slices. She tried to ask what sort of meat it was, but "knock, knock" seemed to be the extent of his English.

He left her alone then, to eat and bathe. She wasted no time.

She longed for a tall iced tea. Her thirst all at once consumed her. But hot boiled coffee would at least be safe to drink, and it was wet. And it turned out to be delicious. After several burning sips, the flavor so familiar and missed she almost moaned with pleasure, she hastily stripped down to her cotton shift and bathed in the tepid water with the lye soap that removed dirt but added not a drop of pleasant scent. She brushed her teeth with her finger and her last crushed mint, then gargled with the piping hot coffee.

She tipped her head upside down to sweep any bugs or creatures from her hair. While in this position, she thought of the revolver in the haversack. During a tend-to-her-needs-behind-a-bush break, she'd managed to remove the revolver from her pocket, hastily shake the cartridges out of the cylinder, and stash it all safely away in the haversack without Oom Peter knowing. She'd been afraid of shooting herself if she left the thing loaded. But now, here in camp, she thought she probably should load it again.

She stood upright to rebraid her hair, and she was noisily shaking out her skirts when, out of nowhere, Harrison appeared.

She had to blink several times to be sure she wasn't hallucinating.

He stood before her in the diffused light, so alive, her heart flooded with joy.

He wore his field khaki, his slouch hat, his black riding boots. He was armed to the hilt, his ammo belt crossing his shoulder, circling his waist. There was a gun in his holster, a rifle on a strap at his shoulder, and he gripped a knife in his hand. He tucked the knife into his belt as she stared.

Though dusty from head to toe, he didn't look as if he'd spent the past two days chasing her across the bush, as surely he must have. He looked like a poster soldier for recruitment, ready for his picture to be taken. Picture perfect. Except for the dark red stain on his sleeve.

Blood.

His blue eyes told her two things. The blood was not his, and his soul had been wounded once again by what he'd seen. What he'd done.

She waited, but he said nothing.

"How did you find me?" she whispered, unable to keep the quaver from her voice.

She took his arm, but he still didn't move. She held him, looking up into his precious face, into those eyes so blue and so deep and so full of emotion. A fear for him—for herself if she lost this crazy attempt to save his life—gripped her. She cupped his face. She thought, in a flash, of all that had happened since she'd first seen him hovering over her checkstand.

She pressed her mouth to his ear and whispered ever-so-softly, "Private Carter is here, still alive."

He whispered back, "Are you hurt? Did they touch you?"

She shook her head.

He didn't move, though she felt his entire body coil like a spring. She pulled away to look at him, and he closed his eyes, as if with disgust.

Confused, she stepped back, dropping her hands. But he came to her so quickly that she gasped, and he took her face as she had taken his.

His eyes searched hers, hard and piercing, and then it was his turn to press his lips to her ear. "Don't leave me," he whispered. "Promise you won't ever disappear from me again."

"I can't promise that. When the lights come back, I'll have to go. I can't help you here. I'm just a grocery checker. I'm no expert on anything. I don't know how to save your life. If they don't release Carter, I'm afraid—."

He gripped her arms so savagely they hurt. "To hell with

Carter. Promise me you won't leave me again."

She wanted to say yes to please him. She wanted to erase the fear that had resurfaced in his eyes, was echoed in his harsh low whisper. But even here, now, surrounded by his enemy, with the wild dangers of Africa present in the very trembling air, she knew she would leave him again if she must. She would cross a desert, or travel another century—anything—to save him.

With a trembling voice she pleaded, "I can't."

In a lightning swift movement, his mouth descended on hers. He kissed her hungrily, and she returned the kiss, knowing it might be their last. It was hello and goodbye and whatever-happens-I-will-never-forget-you. He pulled away just enough to look into her eyes.

She became aware of noise, of voices and shouts. Gunshots. Harrison's body turned to steel.

He pressed his mouth to her ear. "That's the signal. I must go; you must stay. When a commando comes for you, go with him. Trust me, and do as you are told."

For a moment, she stood immobile, frozen by dread, by fear. Why did he want her to stay? Why had he come if not to rescue her and Carter?

"Get dressed," he mouthed silently. His words acted on her like a splash of cold water. She dressed as fast as she could. There were no more gunshots, but the shouts and noise from the river continued as Harrison disappeared through a flap cut into the back of the tent.

Barely buttoned into her skirt and jacket, she heard a Boer at the entry flap say, "Knock, knock." She swallowed, and took a deep breath.

"Come in," she said, her voice steadier than she'd thought possible.

The tent flap opened, but the commando outside did not enter. He demanded, "Come with me."

Trust me, Harrison had said. *Go with the commando.* She grabbed the haversack, stepped out into the moonlight, and saw what all the commotion had been about. Four dead crocodiles had been dragged ashore. Beside them lay their victims, unmoving, each of them missing a portion of a leg, or an entire leg. One poor man had no legs at all.

"Where are you taking me?" she asked the commando as he gently took her elbow.

"Come," he said simply.

She was led to the river's edge. The crocodile attack had not ceased the flow of Provisions Corp cases, though not a single black man was any longer in the river. Knowing the crocodile much more intimately than their employers, they had fled, all of them at once, drawing as much fire as the crocodiles. Several natives lay upon the ground, bleeding from gunshot wounds, but not a single Dutchman moved to help them.

Taking all this in, Ivy felt a deep, dark foreboding coil in her stomach. Every instinct told her to turn around, run away. But Harrison had said to go with the commando.

The commando shouted an order in Afrikaans, and a dozen uninjured natives surrounded Ivy. She felt their hands beneath her as she was scooped up, and handed over like a piece of luggage, her shoulders taken by the next man in line as her waist and legs were held up by the first. She clutched the haversack like a life preserver, too startled to even think. Below her, the brown sluggish river ran with trails of red, and her ears were full of many sounds—the grunts and calls of the men as they passed her along, the hoot of an owl, the thunderous growl of that lion again.

In the center of the river, her forward movement suddenly stopped, and she hovered there, suspended by four hands.

"Eina! Eina! Eina!" came a shout from directly beneath her, and she looked with panic for the crocodiles.

Upstream, shots were fired, and shouts rang out, and then amidst the noise and confusion, Ivy felt herself slipping down between the two men who held her.

"Nooo!" she screamed, desperately struggling to scramble up, away from the river, away from the mouth of the crocodile that surely waited.

A voice in one ear whispered harshly, "We're saving you; don't fight us!" And then a voice on the other side commanded, "Swim!"

She was yanked down under the brown and murky cool water. It was a shock to be so suddenly completely submerged, completely blinded. She was guided by hands that gripped her clothing, her heart pounding crazily, panic just at the edge of hysteria, knowing that any second she would feel the jaws of a crocodile snapping her in two.

But then she was being pulled to her feet, and the river was pouring in cascades from her sodden clothing. She could barely move as her saturated skirts clung to her, but scrambled all the same to get clear of the river. She saw through wet and blurry vision that she'd been returned to the shore she'd just left, and it seemed this rescue and swim had been a dangerous waste of time. Behind her, one of her would-be rescuers stumbled, and she turned to see the man, not a Boer, for he was beardless and in khaki, on his knees, his legs still submerged in the muddy shallows.

Carter. He must be Private Carter. Behind him, rising from the muddy water, a snout, and bulbous eyes, approached with the speed of a torpedo.

With a squeal of fear, she reached down and grasped Carter by his shirt collar, and with a burst of adrenaline, she pulled him completely ashore just as the crocodile surged forward in an open-mouthed lunge. The great jaws snapped shut, empty, and the monster slid backwards, disappearing into the murky deep.

More hands were helping her now, pulling Carter further ashore, and she blinked to find herself staring directly into Harrison's eyes.

How crazy of him to show himself, to come to the river's edge, expose himself to all these enemy soldiers. The moonlight revealed them all. What was he thinking? She could read only a fierce intensity in his eyes.

Stunned, she looked about her. Absolutely nobody was paying any attention to them. The Boers were leaving them completely alone. She looked from Harrison, to Carter, and then to the commando who had led her from the tent. His beard had dissolved in the river. No, wait, that was no Boer, that was—

"Tom!" she exclaimed. She had no time to say more. Harrison grabbed her hand, and they all began to run. Holding her wet skirts high, the haversack slung over her back, Ivy kept up as they raced through the circle of tents and waggons, scrambled onto a narrow, winding path, and climbed up out of the ravine.

She reached the top, breathless and sweating and shivering all at once.

"What happened?" she gasped. There was a growing cacophony of gunfire and explosions from down below.

Harrison turned her around to face the edge of the ravine. A wave of khaki swarmed below. The British army had arrived—hundreds of soldiers, on horseback, on foot—far outnumbering the enemy. The river was becoming a feast of Dutch blood for the crocodiles.

Across the river, the camels had panicked at the noise, and with their odd loping gait were fleeing in all directions. When a spray of dirt exploded beside Ivy, she didn't know what it was. She could hear nothing over the gunfire rising from down below. But Harrison seemed to know, and he threw himself over her, knocking her to the rocky ground. Carter and Tom both dropped flat.

"I'll kill her, if you don't heed my words."

She knew that voice. After two days and two nights, she knew that Dutchman's voice.

"Lay down your weapons and lift up your hands."

Harrison moved his body so that he blocked Ivy. He tossed his rifle a few feet away onto the grass. and slipped his gun from his holster, tossing it aside. His knife followed with a clang against the rifle barrel.

Oom Peter said, "Now you."

Private Carter had pilfered a Boer rifle on their uphill flight, and he, too, lay it down.

Tom was the last to obey, throwing his rifle on the pile

with youthful anger.

For a fleeting moment, Ivy thought Oom Peter meant to spare them. To let them go in exchange for her. But then she remembered him with the rabbit, with the glow in his eye as he sliced off the furry, blackened paw, with his firm belief in an eye for an eye. A limb for a limb.

"Now, crawl, just the three soldiers, over there," he said swinging his gun in an arc toward the forest of acacia and thorn trees that stood silhouetted in moonlight.

Ivy became aware of a faint plaintive mewing, like a kitten's hungry cry, followed by a low, sinister growling, but Oom Peter's leveled rifle was much more threatening.

Carter and Tom looked at Harrison.

"Go!" he hissed. They obeyed, crawling off slowly.

Harrison stayed put, raised up slightly on his knees, his broad shoulders between Ivy and Peter.

Ivy whispered in terror, "Harrison, go!" She pushed his shoulders, but he was a wall of granite and didn't budge.

"Don't be a hero," Peter warned. "I'll kill you if I must."

Ivy didn't give herself time to think.

Behind Harrison's protection, she ripped open the wet haversack, yanked out the damp gun, sprang to her feet, and over the top of Harrison's slouch hat, aimed the sights, cocked the hammer, and pulled the trigger.

Nothing happened. She heard only a click.

Oom Peter stood very still with his rifle aimed not at her, but at Harrison.

Oh, God.

She pulled the trigger again.

Click.

She hadn't loaded it.

Oom Peter cocked his head, his gray eyes narrowed.

She tried again.

Click.

Oom Peter took a step forward, smiling behind his thick beard.

Please, let there be one cartridge left! Please let her have missed one little cartridge! She pulled the trigger again.

Click.

And again.

Click.

She tried the final chamber. This time, there was an explosion, but not from the gun, from the woods. There came a great roaring yellow explosion that sent Ivy dropping to the ground, wrapped again in Harrison's protective embrace.

She didn't need nor want to look at what was happening.

She could hear all too well Peter's screams. She could hear all too well his flesh and clothing ripping and the guttural, bloodthirsty growls of the lion.

Harrison held her tightly, rocking her slightly, speaking soothing words into her ear.

"It's all right, just a mother lion protecting her young. It's all right . . ."

The rifle shot, when it came, rang in her ears, and she smelled the scent of hot gunpowder. When the ringing stopped, when she could hear nothing but the distant sounds of fighting down below, she cautiously lifted her head.

Harrison, as he held her, had managed to get hold of his rifle, and his one-handed shot, aimed at a tree, had frightened off the lion.

"Come along. Let's get away from here." Harrison urged her gently to her feet and began to lead her away.

"Wait." She looked toward Oom Peter. His bearded head rested at an impossibly crooked angle. Half a shoulder was gone, and a white bone jutted from a mass of bloody pulp. She tore her face away.

"Come along," Harrison urged her again.

She shook her head, her hand to her mouth, afraid she was going to be sick. She closed her eyes and took a deep breath. The air was thick with dust and smoky with gunfire and bitter with the scent of blood. She coughed.

Harrison bent to her. "What is it?" he asked gently.

She met his gentle eyes, and lowered her hand from her mouth. "Jeffrey's ring," she whispered.

Harrison frowned, his eyes searching hers.

"He's the one."

* * *

Three hours later, Ivy and Harrison and Private Carter were settled comfortably in a first class rail car, slowly winding its way back toward Pretoria. Tom, Harold, and George had returned to their company to belatedly report for duty and face the consequences. They carried with them a letter of explanation from Harrison and a personal promise he would see to any problems that arose.

The wheels clack-clack-clacked soothingly, and the engine kept time with a chug-chug-chug. The electric lights glowed whitely, reflecting off the dark glass of the boarded window.

Ivy, dry in borrowed khaki, and as clean as one can get with cold water and lye soap, rested her head against Harrison's shoulder as Private Carter told them how he came to be captured.

"Well, Cap'n," Carter began, taking a deep breath. "It's like this. You remember I was on leave? Well, I wasn't about to spend it idle, sir. Kyle Fleming is perhaps the biggest jackass what ever lived—pardon, milady—and I knew there had to be some way to prove him a liar. So I goes to his tent on account he wasn't there but staying in that fancy room in town. I had me a nice look 'round, and what should I find but a telegram. Before he come to you in hospital and confessed he might have shot that missionary, he'd wired his old man the grand baron, asking for advice. And the telegram I found was the reply. Just two words was on it. Saint Edward. Just them two little words.

"I was standing there," Carter went on, "red-handed as they say, reading the bloody telegram, when who should come storming in but that nosy Intelligence Officer, Captain Reed. He laughed when he saw what it was I'd found. Laughed his bloody head off like I was too daft to know about Edward the Confessor.

"Next thing I know, my leave is canceled, and I'm on patrol, and these three bloody Boers are draggin' me hither and yon across the bush to Jo'burg. They say it was an Englishman that put them to it, a small man with tiny mustache that leapt about like a furry mouse. Now who do you think they could've been describing? They were supposed to shoot me, but changed their minds. Thought I'd be worth more on trade. Thought I was their bleedin' leper!"

"Leper?" Ivy asked.

"Leper, leprechaun, pot o' gold, rainbow's end."

"Rainbow's end?" Harrison asked. "Why does that sound familiar?"

"Fleming, Cap'n. His favorite saying, innit? If he's said it once, he's said it a thousand times—Africa, she's the rainbow's end."

"Aah. Yes. And he always laughs after he says it."

"Like he's real clever. Just wait till he gets a load o' my mug back in Pretoria. And that Reed, too. Hah! We got 'em now, Cap'n. We got 'em now."

23

"Ivy?" Harrison knocked softly. "Are you decent?"

Ivy sunk lower into the milky bath. "Sort of," she said.

He opened the door and risked a peek. Apparently satisfied that she was obscured enough from his view, he opened the door fully and leaned against the jamb.

"You don't need to watch me. I won't run away again—not while I'm naked in the tub, anyway."

A sad smile flicked across his lips. "I'll watch you all the same."

He looked into her eyes for a long time as she lay immersed in the scented water, immersed in his blue gaze, immersed in sadness. A hot bath might be heaven, but it couldn't erase the fact that war was hell. She understood that in a way she never had before in her dull but safe life back home. War was hell. It was a horrible, soul-changing experience. And if what she'd gone through left her feeling this traumatized, how must Harrison feel? How did he go on? She told herself that men did go on after war. They focused on those they'd saved. On restoring peace. On returning home. And it was going to be all right now. Carter would testify. Harrison wouldn't be court-martialed. He'd leave South Africa soon, return to England, to his estate in

North Yorkshire where he was an earl. He'd save his mother and brother and sister from making bad decisions, and then he'd marry some lovely princess or baroness or someone else equally worthy, and have a dozen beautiful children.

Harrison cocked his head and frowned. He came to her and knelt down beside the tub. He reached out to her, gently wiping her cheek with a cold finger.

"Why are you crying?" he asked, his voice deep and gravelly with emotion.

"I didn't know I was."

He pressed the back of his hand to her forehead.

"Your skin is hot."

"I'm in a hot bath," she said, but couldn't muster a teasing smile. His eyes were far too serious.

"Who are you, Ivy O'Neal?"

She shook her head, taking a deep, unsteady breath, her eyes never leaving his. "I'm nobody. Just me."

He dipped the tips of his fingers into the milky lavender bath, then returned his fingers to her face, washing away the salt of her tears.

"Are you part American Indian?"

"Cherokee. How did you know?"

He traced her cheekbone with a wet finger. "Your bone structure. And the rest?"

"A bit of this, a bit of that, even some English."

"What's your favorite color?"

She was staring into his eyes and could only answer, "Blue."

"What sort of music do you like?"

"Old-fashioned and romantic. From the forties and fifties. The 1940s and 1950s."

He smiled wryly.

"What's your favorite pastime?"

"Soaking in lavender baths with an earl kneeling at my side."

"Have you done this before?"

"This is the first time. But I could get used to it."

He dipped his fingers again, then skimmed his wet fingertips over her face, along her jaw, as if he were finger painting her.

"Tell me about your Aunt Daisy."

"You're very curious about me all of a sudden."

He smiled. "Do you have any brothers or sisters?"

"Nope. There's just me and my Aunt Daisy."

"What about your parents?"

"They both died when I was young."

"I'm sorry."

"Well, it happens. Other than being orphaned young, I had a happy childhood."

"How old are you?"

"Twenty-seven."

"Are you? I thought you younger." His eyes narrowed, their blueness darkening. "You're not married?"

She laughed softly. "No."

He looked relieved, and his eyes turned bright, inviting. "But you've been in love?"

She looked away from him, unable to face those eyes with that question, afraid she might tell him she was in love, head over heels in love, at this very moment. She turned the question around on him. "Have you ever been in love?"

"Hundreds of times, but we're not talking about me just now. I want to know about you. And you still haven't answered my question. Were you ever in love, in your future world?"

She shrugged, and the feel of water rippling over her skin made her shiver. She sank a bit lower, suddenly cold. "I thought I was, once, another lifetime ago when I was just a lowly grocery checker and not a trekker on the great African veldt, nor the wife of an earl. What sort of title do I have as the wife of an earl? Besides lady, I mean. If the wife of a baron is a baroness, is the wife of an earl an earless?" She held up her left hand, braving another wave of chills, watching the gold and sapphire of Harrison's ring sparkle and glisten.

He laughed and said, "Heaven forbid. You are a countess." He laced his hand with hers. Jeffrey's ring on his hand glittered next to his ring on hers.

They both looked quietly at the rings, at their entwined hands, until the muted and distant sound of a lion's roar, followed by the trumpeting of an elephant, filtered to them.

"I don't know about you, Countess, but I much prefer the sound of those animals when I know they're safely enclosed."

"It was exciting though, being out there, in the wild. Did I tell you about the bull elephant? And how close he came?"

"Yes, you did. And how cleverly you evade my questions. Tell me about the time you were in love."

"It's very boring. You don't want to hear."

"You couldn't bore me if you recited train schedules from morning till night. I enjoy observing you; haven't you noticed? Now, tell me. Who was this undeserving fellow?"

She didn't want to talk about Bob; she didn't even want to think about Bob.

"Why are you angry? Did he hurt you?"

When she didn't answer, his eyes told her he took her silence for a yes.

He said, "I fail to understand how any man could ever choose to let you go."

"You see me through eyes of shock and gratitude."

"I see you through eyes of great affection and admiration."

She shivered again, and a wave of wooziness washed over her.

He felt her forehead. "The doctor is downstairs."

"I'll be fine. I'm just tired." She mustered a smile, but couldn't maintain it. She felt awful.

"Ivy, just who are we—you and I?"

"What do you mean?" she whispered. His face blurred; her head spun.

"I mean why are we being brought together? Is there a reason for it all, do you suppose? A reason why those machines of yours brought you here to me and not anywhere else, to anybody else?"

She shook her head very slowly. It felt like her brain was loose inside her skull.

She felt his fingertips on her wrist, as if checking her pulse, as he said, "Perhaps my fate was to be with you. Perhaps something went wrong in the grand scheme of things, and you were born too late or I was born too early, and now fate is trying to unite us as we were meant to be."

She wanted to speak, to tell him she felt the same way. But she didn't have the strength, and then blackness descended.

24

Dee, checking in lane nine, was telling her current customer how her son had just yesterday learned how to blow adorable spit bubbles when Ivy O'Neal fell onto the conveyor belt of express lane four.

The glass half-gallon jar of specialty milk fell out of Dee's hand onto her scanner. The bottle shattered, the scanner glass shattered, and milk ran freely through every crack, down into the core of the scanner itself, until the sizzle of hot machinery and then the frazzle of shorting-out wires sent up a trickle of smoke.

Dee was only partly aware of this. She was too shocked to see Ivy crumpled on the conveyor belt. Ivy's face was suntanned, her nose burned. She was wearing her uniform, but she wasn't scheduled to work. She clutched a grungy-looking backpack. And her aunt was there, Daisy, the eccentric old woman who'd been hanging around the store for the past few days.

The milk penetrated Dee's apron and shirt, and she looked down in time to see sparking deep down beneath the shattered scanner glass, and then the green light that indicated the scanner was up and operational blinked out. The little spinning thing down there quit spinning, and the display screen flashed an error message.

"Oh, no," Dee moaned, thinking that crying over spilt milk might not be useful but it was certainly what she wanted to do. But then her attention was again torn away by Ivy O'Neal.

For Ivy had collapsed onto the floor, and Daisy was shouting, "Help me, please. Call 911. Call 911!"

* * *

"I have what?"

"I can't pronounce it," explained Aunt Daisy. "Its name is about a hundred letters long. It's some sort of rare fever that no one has seen in a hundred years. Harrison called it typhoid, but the doctor's said it wasn't."

"Harrison?"

"There was a note in the pocket of your apron that said you'd come down with typhoid and needed a doctor."

Ivy blinked, still fighting through a thick fog of sleep. Every inch of her ached, as if she'd been beaten up. Even her hair hurt. She vaguely remembered being in the tub, feeling dizzy.

"My apron? Was I wearing it? Did I come through the lights?"

"You were wearing your uniform, and you fell onto Dee's checkstand. Don't you remember coming through the lights?"

"I don't remember anything." Harrison must have lifted her from the bath and dressed her in her uniform. A foggy memory returned of Harrison draping his haversack over her shoulder, holding her up, urging her to take a few steps.

She sank into the pillows, her head aching. "Am I going to live?"

"Indeed you are. After I told the medics you'd just gotten back from Africa, you were given the highest priority, not to mention a hazmat team and full isolation. I got the same treatment, mind you, until the tests for Ebola came back negative. But you do have some sort of wicked bug. They've given you the antidote, and say you're well on your way to recovery."

"Huh," Ivy replied, for she was attempting to sit up now in bed and look around at the stark and unfamiliar room with its metal closet and ceiling-mounted TV. Floral baskets and bouquets were piled on the metal dresser.

"Those are from Fai and Marina, and your friends at the Pig, and a couple from customers who say you're their favorite checker."

"Really?" She felt a pang of gratitude. "How long have I been here?"

"Four days."

"Wow." She released a long breath.

"Where's the haversack?"

"The backpack, you mean? At home, completely sterilized. They said to bleach anything that may have picked up a microbe."

"So you looked inside?"

"I couldn't help it. I don't even want to know why you had a gun."

"Me either. What about the thimbles? Did you find those?"

"Lovely, lovely things."

"They're yours. Harrison bought them for you."

Daisy's eyes lit with joy. "Thank you, dear. I can't believe you went all the way to Africa," and then she whispered, as if cameras lurked in the walls, "all the way back in time, and still remembered my silly thimbles."

"I could never forget you. And they're a small way of saying thanks. So, thank you, dear Aunt Daisy. For believing me, for helping me. We saved Harrison, you know. We found Carter, and the charges were dropped." She searched her Aunt's face. "Did Harrison's fate change? Tell me, please, did he live?"

"I hadn't thought to check! I am sorry. I've just been so worried about you." Daisy reached into her sweater pocket, but her hand came out with nothing but a shopping list. "Oh, bother. I left all the brochures in my coat pocket, and it's down in the car. I'll just go and get it."

But Ivy didn't want Daisy to make the trip out to the hospital parking lot. She looked exhausted, as if she'd spent the past four days sitting right there in that chair. And though she tried to hide it, she looked to be in a lot of pain.

"Never mind. We can just call the museum. I'm sure everything turned out wonderful, but it won't hurt to have it confirmed."

Daisy whipped out her trusty smart phone, and a few seconds later, handed it to Ivy.

"Hello. Could you tell me if Harrison Darby's works are being exhibited?"

The chipper voice quickly answered, "Yes, we have several Edwardian painters on display, including the works of Lord Wyndham."

"Would it be possible for you to read to me the brochure you have on his life? Just the bit about when he, uh, died."

"Sure, just a minute." There was a musical pause, during which Ivy's heart rate soared and her palms became clammy.

"Should I get the doctor?" Daisy asked, alarm showing on her face.

"No," Ivy said. "I'm fine." But she gripped Daisy's hand fiercely, silently praying until at last the friendly voice returned.

"Here I am. Now then, let's see." The friendly voice paraphrased as she read. "Lord Wyndham. Born January 27, 1870. Third Earl to Wyndham in North Yorkshire County, England. Served two years as Captain in the British army, his final months with the Bushveldt Carbineers in South Africa. Wounded in May 1901 in the Transvaal. The entire works of Lord Wyndham were produced between May and June of 1901, while suffering from amnesia. His memory returned upon the arrival of his wife, formerly Ivy O'Neal, American. No records of his marriage or of Ivy O'Neal exist, but her existence is verified by personal testimony of Lord Pepper, Major Walton, and many other officers then serving in Pretoria."

Ivy shivered with an eerie chill. She had to clamp her jaw tight to keep her teeth from chattering.

"Lady Wyndham disappeared on June 18th, the same day that Private Carter, the single witness in a court-martial hearing, was found dead by his own hand. He left a note recanting his testimony, and the court-martial was resumed.

Lord Wyndham was found guilty of ordering the death of a Boer missionary, and was executed on July the 5th, 1901. His—"

As the phone fell from Ivy's slippery palm, Daisy shouted for the doctor.

25

Harrison leaned against the cold cement wall, staring through the iron bars of the window. A desolate valley stretched into the distance.

The prison compound had once been a thriving ostrich farm with acres of grain reaching to the edge of the Middle Veldt. But the fields had been burned a year ago, before the capture of Pretoria, and the few ostriches that had not been slaughtered for food now struggled through the winter, shivering and spitting, scouring the earth for whatever bits of grain and grass they could find.

Harrison pitied the birds, who didn't belong here any more than he did. They were Sahara desert natives, brought here to be farmed for their valuable feathers. Now, their caretakers interned in Pretoria, their food burned, their concrete shelters inhabited by the British army, the ostriches had been left on their own to survive.

Little was left of the original homestead. The farmhouse had been converted to quarters for officers and the Highland Guards. The ostrich coops, large sunken concrete cubicles, were converted to jail cells, the windows barred, the doorways closed and padlocked. Low and dank and depressing, each cell contained a narrow cot on its earthen floor, a crate for a writing desk, and a bucket for a chair.

Harrison blew on his fingers to warm them, then sat at the makeshift desk. He dipped the pen into the ink jar.

My Dearest Ivy,

I will not mail this letter. Indeed, I have no address to which to send it had I been able to find sufficient postage to convey a letter such a great distance. A very great distance. But I must write to you. I must somehow communicate to you all that I feel.

I have no way of knowing if you recovered from fever. Did you? Is there some way you could let me know? Sending you away was the hardest thing I've ever done. The doctor at Recovery House told me to prepare for the worst. I chose instead to place my faith in the ingenuity of Americans. If you've sent a man to the moon, I'm hoping, praying, you've also done wonders in medicine.

There is so much I wish to say, but I fear my pen is not as poetic as my heart. Please know this~you are the reason I live and breathe. I don't know how that came to be, but it is so. I must have faith that someday we will meet again. Here in my world, there in your world, or in heaven.

My love to you, always,

Harrison.

* * *

Ivy could no longer see clearly. She wiped the tears from her eyes with the back of her sleeve, and read again the transcript of Harrison's letter. She sat on the braided rug of the living room, surrounded by books on the Boer War and Africa and England. Also books on time travel, with their warnings against paradoxes, their dire predictions of calamity if one were to meet oneself somewhere in time. Magazine articles, faxes, and photocopies formed a small mountain on the green recliner, and that was where Audrey now perched herself like a small black sphinx.

Since no specific answers had revealed themselves to her, Ivy had begun to study. She knew she would have to find the answer to Harrison's dilemma herself, and to do that she needed to understand everything. She'd read until her eyes ached, until she felt she understood the Boer War, the politics and economics driving the battles, and the real reasons for fighting, which of course were power and money.

But this new book she now held was different, and she harbored a secret pride that she had played a part in its existence.

The Wyndham Mystery was written by Jason Pepper, Joshua's grandson. She'd found the book on the Internet, on the publisher's publicity pages. The advance copy of the book had arrived just a few minutes ago, via Federal Express. The delivery man had only smiled as she'd signed for the package with a trembling hand.

The pages had fallen open to Harrison's final letter to her, and so far, she'd gotten no farther. Four hours later, she'd read the book cover to cover, and scoured every photograph.

"I grew up hearing my grandfather's tale of Lord Wyndham and his American bride," Jason wrote. *"The beginning of the end of the Wyndham legacy, my grandfather said. Wyndham had told my grandfather that he must encourage*

his grandson—meaning me, and I'd not yet been born—to find Private Tom Carter's diary. This odd request was prompted by Harrison's wife, the American called Ivy O'Neal, who claimed she had special psychic powers."

"I did not," Ivy exclaimed, recalling the brief conversation verbatim. But she supposed nearly a hundred years and all that champagne could alter the story. Anyway, Jason had found the great tragic love of Lord Wyndham and his American pauper beyond romantic, and his interest into why it had ended became an obsession.

Ivy couldn't read fast enough, but she slowed when she came to an excerpt from Tom Carter's diary, which Jason Pepper had found hidden under the floorboards of a boarding school dormitory where Carter stayed while awaiting his turn to give testimony.

Carter wrote: *"His Lordship was enamored of the vision of the girl in the lights. She was real to him, an angel of loveliness and grace. I believe she was real, though I did not see her myself."*

He told of his capture by the Boers, his suspicions of Major Reed and Kyle Fleming, his lack of clear understanding regarding their motives.

This much she had read before, in the SAM brochure. But there was more now. He'd written of his capture by the Boers, of his rescue, and of meeting Ivy. His final entry was dated just after the hearing, right before he was found dead of an apparent suicide.

Hastily scrawled, barely legible, the meaning was still a mystery to the book's author. The only words at all decipherable were: *I'm good as dead! Rotten Kipper! The Leper!*

Was he writing about killing himself? The words didn't sound like those of somebody despondent and about to shoot himself, but of somebody who was angry, and who feared death was coming. Kipper? Carter must have been referring to Kyle Fleming. The enlisted men called him Kyle Kipper. And leper? What had Carter said he meant by that? Leprechaun. Pot of gold. End of the rainbow. No, he'd worded it a little differently. Kyle Fleming always liked the expression, *rainbow's end.*

Ivy scratched her head, reading the few words again, trying to calm her mind enough to figure out what Carter was trying to say in that last panicked entry. Why did she feel this was the clue she needed?

She untangled her legs and moved to the couch with her laptop.

Idly, she tapped the keys. Too many divergent thoughts hammered her mind, and she couldn't pull them together to form any pattern. The cursor blinked in the little search box, waiting for a new request.

She thought of the telegram Lord Fleming had sent Kyle, the telegram Carter had found and been caught reading. What if by sending the simple message *St. Edward*, Kyle's father was not telling him to confess to something he did, but to confess to something he didn't do? More importantly, what if he was setting the stage for Kyle to tell the inquiry court that he'd only shot the missionary when ordered by his commander, Lord Wyndham?

But why would he do this? What did he possibly have to gain from Harrison's conviction and death?

She typed *Rainbow's End* in quotes and hit enter. The

search engine claimed to find more than a half million results. She added the words *Fleming*, *Africa*, and *Provisions Corp*.

And the first hit was a Provisions Corporation historical document that had been scanned into Google Books. Rainbow's End was the name of Provisions Corp's parent company. Based in Switzerland, its owners were shielded by that country's convenient privacy laws.

Her pulse picked up. Could this mean anything? She scrolled and scrolled and clicked and ran more searches.

And then she clicked on one of the search results: *A Virtual Tour of England's Castles*. Embedded in the online tour was a mention of Lord Fleming's castle in England, built by wealth acquired from gold and diamonds in South Africa. There were pages of photographs—the Red Room, the Blue Room, the Gold Room.

And Rainbow's End.

Ivy clicked the thumbnail image, and a high resolution image appeared of a carved stone fountain that was a tribute to Africa. Beneath a spray of erupting water were a carved lion, a crocodile, an elephant, and a giraffe.

The fountain was called Rainbow's End.

Ivy stared at the fountain.

She recalled Major Walton's words at dinner, "Nobody knows how he's financing the operation, but there he is, digging away. And he suddenly has the money to travel, don't you know. Named himself honorary diplomat, claims he'll be the one to bring both sides to the table. He visits Whitehall, he visits South Africa. He dines with Kitchener one night; then a fortnight later he dines with Kruger!"

Was Fleming the true owner of Provisions Corp? Was Provisions Corp the source of the mysterious wealth that allowed the baron to begin mining? And if so, wouldn't it benefit Fleming to see the war continue as long as possible?

What if Kyle had been given instructions by his father to look for opportunities to extend the war, to delay peace talks. The death of that missionary at the alleged direct order of a British officer had made the Dutch walk away from the peace table. Oom Peter had told her that.

Ivy's hands dropped to her lap. What did she know of war or politics? Only what she'd read in those books. Could she have guessed right? Had Fleming gotten rich in the war by selling weapons to both sides? Was Harrison's court-martial a plot to extend the war so Fleming could become even richer?

She rose like a zombie, dropped again to the floor, and pulled Jason's book onto her lap, opening it to the copy of Harrison's last letter to her. She touched the page reverently.

What if it had all been one big conspiracy?

All the pieces fit together. She had to be right. Her pulse began to race, but her heart ached with a twisting pain, a fear, a dread. Had she found the truth at last? But what in heaven could she do about it? How could knowing the truth save Harrison before it was too late? Even today, the connection between the Flemings and Provisions Corp wasn't recorded, not anywhere she'd yet found. The details were shrouded in banking secrecy. She had no proof that her wild theory was even right.

Fear began to cloud her mind. Harrison's death was recorded as July the 5th. Four days from now. Time was closing in on her. She had to find evidence to prove this conspiracy and return with it to the past.

"Oh, crap!" she growled, startling Audrey, who leapt from her perch, sending the papers tumbling to the floor.

The scanner in checkstand nine was still not fixed! There was no whine, no surge, no swirling window of lights. Every day she'd gone into the store; every day she was met with the same bad news.

"Parts are on order," she said now aloud, mimicking Bob. "What are you so worried about? What's it to you?"

Audrey replied with a snippy little meow, picked up her tailless behind, then sauntered into the kitchen in search of food.

The front door lock rattled, and Ivy, startled, looked up.

Aunt Daisy stepped in, the keys jangling in her hand. She was dressed in purple sweats and Reebok high-tops, and was returning from the mall where she and "the girls" walked the circuit.

"I found it," Ivy said, her voice amazingly calm.

"Are you still there on the floor where I left you?" Daisy asked, though it was obvious she was.

"Aunt Daisy, listen to me. I found it. I found out why Fleming lied."

Daisy stepped around the scattered books and eased down onto the red couch. Ivy scrambled up beside her and laid the open book on her lap, pointing to a small black-and-white photograph.

"It's you," Daisy whispered. It was Ivy and Harrison in the photograph, their backs to a piano. The caption read: *Only known photograph of Lady Wyndham, taken by Lord*

Joshua Pepper with a Kodak Brownie camera, in Pretoria, South Africa.

"I'm going back," Ivy announced.

"Ivy, no—"

"I have to. I have to save him."

"Hold on, now, Ivy girl. Not so fast. We need to talk about this. Now, tell me what you learned and just how you think you can help."

Ivy explained her conspiracy theory.

"But how would Harrison's death prolong the war?"

"It's all politics and greed and retribution. Fleming was making tons of money selling weapons to both sides. He was using the money to finance his gold mine, Amalgamated, in Johannesburg. When the Boers thought a British officer had ordered the death of one of their missionaries, they were furious and peace talks came to a stop."

"I see," Daisy nodded wisely.

"You do?"

Daisy patted her hand. "I'm old, dear. When you've seen as many politicians running for office as I have, you'll be able to recognize the dirty tricks men play. But even if you're right, you've still a long way to go. How, dear? How on earth are you going to convince the British army that it's all a big mistake? That the baron and his son have set up your Harrison on purpose?"

"I don't know. I just know I have to try."

"Be sensible now. Think about it. What sort of proof do you have?"

"Daisy, I have to do something!"

"I know. But you need proof. Real proof. You'll just have

to look somewhere else."

"But there is nowhere else to look!"

Daisy took Ivy's hands. "Calm down, Ivy. You're tired. You haven't been sleeping. You're still weak from your fever. And when you're not reading, you're at the store working. It's too much. You never stop."

"I have to work. I have to keep close to the scanners." She rubbed her face wearily, then sighed heavily. She was exhausted and wound up. But she couldn't give up. She couldn't give in. She said, as calmly as she could manage, "Daisy, when the scanner gets fixed, and when the lights come back, you do understand, don't you? I have to go to him."

"I understand. I also understand you need to go lie down and get some sleep."

"But I can't! I have to find proof, I have to save Harrison!"

Daisy spoke softly, countering Ivy's outburst. "You've got time, dear. Nothing but time."

"No, no, no!" Ivy slammed her fists into the couch cushions. "You don't get it! It's parallel. Time is parallel between now and Harrison. It's July the first today, now, and on the other side of the time-window in 1901. They're going to execute him on July the fifth, at dawn! In less than four days, they're going to shoot him! The time-window doesn't go backwards, only forwards. I don't know why, I don't know anything! I only know that time is running out!"

Daisy put firm hands on Ivy's shoulders, steadying her. "Even if those lights were here right now, going through wouldn't help Harrison. You have no proof to save him."

"But I have to!"

"Let me finish, Ivy, and I want you to listen carefully, all right? Now then. Since you can't go there and save him, think about it. When the lights come back, then you're going to have to use them wisely. Ivy, your Harrison is just going to have to come here, to you."

26

"Yes, he gave me an order."

"And what was his order?"

"I was to approach the farmhouse and shoot the Dutch missionary when he came out the door."

"You're quite sure you heard your captain clearly?"

"Quite sure. That was his order."

"And did you question that order?"

"No, sir. I mean, yes, sir. I mean I questioned the order in my mind. It did seem wrong. Very wrong. But I thought perhaps that Lord Wyndham knew something I did not. That perhaps the missionary was passing on secrets or weapons to the enemy."

"So you obeyed the order?"

"I obeyed."

"And later regretted having obeyed?"

"Yes, sir. Later, after seeing Lord Wyndham in hospital, after the report, the false report, was filed, I felt the order had been malicious. The guilt wore on me. I found I must speak up lest some other innocent civilian die to satisfy Lord Wyndham's lust for vengeance."

"What do you mean, vengeance?"

"His brother was killed a fortnight before the incident. Very brutally. It was Lord Wyndham himself who found the mutilated body. He changed after that. He grew angry and hostile. He wanted vengeance."

Harrison continued to stare at young Fleming with silent and intense anger. But Kyle would not look his way. He sat upon the questioning chair, his thin back straight, his features schooled in a sad attempt to appear honest and forthright. His twitching cheek, his pink pallor, his thin fidgeting hands, however, revealed the depth of his lies.

The damned fool! If he wanted to prove his manhood to his father, he should do it by standing up for himself, by doing what he believed was right, not by swearing under oath to lies that would get an innocent man killed! What in God's name did Kyle hope to accomplish? Harrison had done nothing but protect Kyle, giving him the guidance of a brother. And this was the thanks he received!

Harrison felt Major Walton's steadying hand upon his forearm.

"Stay calm," Major Walton whispered.

"I am doing my best," Harrison replied as Kyle rose from the chair, bowed to the court, clicked his heels, and marched out of the courtroom.

Harrison was then called to the stand. Thunder grumbled as he walked the short distance, his footsteps echoing on the stones to join with the raging clouds.

As he sat, the room suddenly darkened as the storm clouds blocked out the sun. A minute later, the sky was falling.

"You will have to speak up!" the President of the Court shouted over the roar of rain drumming on the high timber roof. But Harrison didn't speak. He sat in the witness chair, in the center of the stone floor, lifted his eyes to the ceiling, and waited.

Sitting back in their seats, the members of the court followed his example, for it was truly impossible to hear anything above the din.

After five minutes, the rain thinned to a softer clamor, and Harrison was again requested to answer the prosecutor's nearly shouted question.

"Did you give First Lieutenant Fleming the order to shoot the Boer missionary?"

"No, I did not," Harrison said.

"Did you promise Fleming he would be protected from the implications of carrying out your order?"

"No. There was no order."

"Did you dictate the report that was filed with Head Office and a copy of which is here today in court"?

"Yes, I did."

"Let me refresh all our memories." The rain suddenly ceased, and a dripping quiet allowed their voices to return to normal. "The report states: 'The death of the Boer, Reverend Schmidt, a missionary of the Dutch Reformed Church, was accidental and the result of crossfire exchanged outside the farmhouse in which the missionary was residing.' Lord Wyndham, do you agree with that statement?"

"I do."

"Even though Fleming has given testimony that this report was submitted in order to cover up your order, which resulted in murder"?

"There was no order to shoot!" His rage echoed as loud and deep as the retreating thunder, colliding with the stone walls and finally fading into the damp floor.

Nobody looked at him. Collars were tugged. Throats were cleared.

Finally, the prosecutor very calmly posed another question. "Lord Wyndham, we have heard from several witnesses during the course of this trial as to the state of your mental health at the time of the incident. They all reported your continued mentioning of swirling, mystical lights, and then the appearance of a girl, an angel, you called her. Do you have any comment on these accusations?"

"No, sir."

"Are you denying these accusations?"

"No, sir."

"Then it is fair to say that, at the time of the shooting of Reverend Schmidt, you were not of sound mind? That you were delusional?"

"No, sir. I was not delusional."

"Then explain what it was you thought you saw."

"My wife, sir. A memory of my wife in the flash of artillery."

"But the witnesses have stated that you stood in the middle of the farm yard, staring like one seeing a ghost, before the attack. That you yourself claimed you saw the lights and the angel—pardon, your wife—before the first shots were even fired. How do you explain that?"

"I can't, sir."

"And is it true that you sent Private Scully to search for the girl? The girl you'd seen in the lights, who you now claim was a memory of your wife?"

"Yes, sir."

"So at the time, you believed she was truly there, in South Africa, at this Boer farm. Did you not find it odd that your wife would be in such a place?"

"I didn't know it was my wife I saw. Not at the time."

"So, at the time, this angel, this vision, this woman you saw, was for all intents and purposes, a stranger."

"Yes, sir."

"She could have been a Boer, for all you knew."

"I did not believe she was a Boer."

"And why not? What other sort of woman did you expect to find in the northern Transvaal on a Boer farm?"

"No other. I just didn't believe she was a Boer, that's all."

"You thought it was your wife bringing you tea?"

A murmur of laughter issued from the court members.

"I did not know who she was. I knew only that I cared for her safety."

"You were injured immediately following this vision of lights and this unknown woman, carried to the relative safety of an outbuilding, and it was there you sent Scully to find the girl. Is that a fair statement?"

"Yes."

"Thereafter, Lieutenant Fleming arrived, and you ordered him to shoot the occupants of the farmhouse."

"No. I was told by my scouts that a missionary and a child were inside the farmhouse. I saw them as we approached. I ordered Fleming to take them into protective custody. They were to be taken to the refugee camp in Pretoria."

"And why not leave them in the farmhouse? What harm could an old missionary and small child do?"

"It was for their safety they were to be moved. We had orders, from Kitchener, to burn the Boer farmhouses, to burn the Boer crops. It's what we'd been doing for the past month."

"Tell me, Captain. How long had it been since your last meal when this incident occurred?"

"Nearly twenty-four hours."

"You'd been without horses for a week, without shelter for days. And now a full day without food. How were you going to care for the good reverend and child? How were you planning to feed them, shelter them?"

"We would have improvised, sir."

"Improvised. Yes. There is an interesting word. Isn't it true that because you had no hope of feeding the reverend and the child, that because you knew their chances for survival in Pretoria were slim because of disease and pestilence, that you thought it best to simply put them out of their misery?"

"No, sir. I did not think that. My order was to take them into protective custody. We were to send them to Pretoria. We did safely deliver the child."

"And the young woman, the girl in the lights—what did you propose to do with her, once you found her?"

Harrison remained silent, glaring at Major Kirby.

"Answer the question, Captain."

"I had not thought beyond finding her and seeing to her safety. Sir."

"I see. Thank you. That will be all."

The court president turned his attention to the defense attorney "Major Walton, have you any questions?"

"Yes, sir." Walton rose, striding to Harrison, his boot steps echoing on the stones. "Lord Wyndham, do you know from personal knowledge that it was a bullet from Lieutenant Fleming's rifle that actually killed Reverend Schmidt? Can you, or anyone, say with absolute certainty that Fleming killed the missionary?"

"No. As my report stated, I was behind an outbuilding. I did not observe the exchange of fire; I only heard it."

"So, is it possible that Reverend Schmidt was not killed by a soldier under your command at all? It is possible that he was shot by his own side—by the Boers themselves, is it not?"

"Yes, it's possible."

"Objection, Mr. President," interrupted the prosecutor. "This line of questioning is unfounded. The court of inquiry clearly established that Fleming shot Reverend Schmidt where he stood in the doorway, and that Fleming was under Lord Wyndham's command at the time of the shooting. This trial is not about who shot Reverend Schmidt, but about whether or not Lord Wyndham issued the order to shoot a civilian."

"We are all aware of the nature of this trial, Major Kirby. Now, Major Walton, have you any more questions?"

"Just one, sir. Lord Wyndham, were you of sound mind on the day in question?"

"I was."

"Did you issue the order as Fleming's written testimony states?"

"I did not."

"Thank you, Captain. That will be all."

"Lord Wyndham, you may stand down."

Harrison returned to his seat beside Major Walton just as the skies opened up and began to pour again. Under the cloaking din of the rain, he asked, "What was that all about?"

"A dribble of doubt," Walton muttered.

"Court is adjourned!" the President bellowed. He slammed down his gavel, but the sound was lost in the din.

Harrison rose mechanically from the rough wooden table. Major Walton, not meeting his eyes, gave him a hesitant pat on the shoulder.

"We ought to get word by three, then, all right?"

Harrison nodded. He slipped into his greatcoat, burying his hands in his pockets. The rare dry-season rain pounding on the roof above sounded as if it wanted to drown the world.

Three kilted Highland Guards came to escort him from the courtroom out into the deluge. Harrison's boots sunk an inch in the mud as he crossed the compound.

"Lord Wyndham," one of the Highland Guards shouted to him, his head bent against the pelting drops. The sound of his title being expressed with such respect came as a surprise, as if from the ancient past. "A letter's come for you today, my lord."

Harrison took the envelope and quickly shoved it inside his greatcoat. Once inside his cell, he shrugged out of the sodden coat, stomped the mud from his boots, and dried his hands and face with a rough towel. Only then did he examine the damp envelope.

Joshua Pepper's untidy handwriting greeted him. He felt a sinking of his heart. He'd been so hoping to hear from Ivy.

He'd not mailed his letter to her, of course, but tucked it among his personal belongings. But she, in her future world, might have read it, somehow, and sent some sort of response. If she had survived the fever. Her silence and the absence of those magic lights were more painful than waiting for the verdict. He exhaled another long weary breath.

At three this afternoon, he would know. At three, the waiting would end. At three, the final wait would begin.

A quick read of the letter told him his good friend was still by his side. Lord Joshua Pepper. A friend until death.

How the hell had things come to this?

A stormy wet gust bellowed through the barred window. Harrison moved toward it, gripping the iron, crushing the letter. He let his head fall. The rain washed over him, trickled down his neck and wrists, then soaked the crushed letter under his palm, its ink trickling away with his hope.

27

Ivy ran an unsteady finger down the checker schedule. No, no, no, yes. Four to midnight. Dee. Ivy checked her watch. Ten after one. She opened her simple cell phone and dialed.

"Hi, Dee, it's Ivy . . . ." she began, and a few minutes later had secured the late checking shift in exchange for another shift, later in the week.

She hung up, slumped, relieved, yet not surprised Dee had agreed so easily. It was the Fourth of July, and Dee was thrilled she'd now be able to see the fireworks with her little boy. Or shield him from them if he found them terrifying.

But this was only the beginning of Ivy's hopes for to-night. Her hands were already trembling. She hadn't eaten since yesterday. She couldn't.

She went to the window that looked down on the store floor and the line of checkstands.

He was there, again, the repairman from CRC, the Cash Register Company, in gray slacks, a white shirt, a black tie. His oversized briefcase full of electronic tools and parts was open on the belt. The ordered part had arrived at last, and the repairman was taking his own sweet time about in-stalling it.

She had tried to talk to him, casually, when she came in.

But since she was off the clock, she couldn't just hang around the checkstands. Bob had walked by twice and asked her what she was doing, why she was hanging around.

Finally, she had just asked the repairman when he would be done.

"Soon," he had said. "Soon."

She didn't trust the gleam in his eye, the gleam that said, "Hey, this is a holiday, double-time pay, and I'm paid by the hour."

She checked her new watch, a digital set for South Africa time, which now showed ten o'clock in the evening. Tomorrow at dawn, his execution was set. And dawn in South Africa tomorrow would come at 6:54 a.m. Less than nine hours from now.

There was absolutely nothing she could do until that scanner was fixed. She felt utterly useless.

* * *

Darkness held its breath.

Harrison lay on his bunk, dressed simply in khaki, suspenders, and dusty black boots. No officer insignia. No jacket. No weapons. Not even a tie.

He stared at the ceiling without seeing it. He'd shut down. Turned off all his senses and focused on just one image. Ivy.

Ivy and her warm, angelic eyes. Ivy and her sweet, wine-blushed lips. Ivy and her Cherokee cheekbones. Ivy and her hold on his heart.

He heard the rhythmic marching steps of the guards

outside, heard the final stomp and order—halt! He heard the rattle of the lock on the door; he heard the heavy wooden door open.

He got up without command, and stepped out into the cold semi-dark compound where morning and death prepared to meet him. Ten Highland Guards in full dress kilts stood waiting with their rifles. The court members were there in full field dress. An Anglican priest in clerical black came up beside him, and, as their slow march began out of the compound and across the flat veldt toward the chair waiting beneath the glorious huge predawn sky, the priest read to Harrison from the Bible.

"The Lord is my shepherd, I shall not want . . . ."

* * *

As the sun's light reached hungrily for the African horizon, it dipped below the Olympic Mountains, plunging Seattle into fiery darkness. The Pig Palace time clock said 10:00 p.m.; Ivy's watch, set to Harrison's time, said 7:00 a.m.

Dawn had come and gone in South Africa, and the scanner was not yet fixed.

Ivy sat in the bathroom stall, doubled over. Rocking. Trembling. Chanting, *no, no, no!* She'd vomited what little liquid was in her, then dry-heaved until the spasms at last ended. Now, she dug her fingers into her hair and gripped tightly, trying to hold in her screams.

After a few minutes, she forced herself to think, to search for any possibility of hope. Dawn. What did dawn mean to executioners? Did it mean they pulled the trigger at precisely dawn? Or was that when it all began, when the prisoner began his march to the field? She didn't know.

She jumped to her feet, ran out of the employee restroom to the break room window that looked down on the checkstands.

With the Fourth of July crowds, it had been easy to keep all the scanners on, all but the one in checkstand nine that was being fixed. But now, with full darkness outside, bursts of fireworks were beginning to appear, and the customers had dribbled down to a few unpatriotic souls.

She'd asked the CRC repairman a dozen times in the past hour, *how much longer? How much longer*? He'd been working on it for over nine hours! Even Bob was getting anxious as repair costs escalated.

His response was always *soon.* He must have thought she was nuts, but she didn't care. She needed the thing up and running!

She'd spent her break standing at the upstairs window, staring down at the repairman's wide flat behind, which stuck out from the side panel of the checkstand.

"Hurry, hurry, hurry," had been her chant. She'd twisted her numb hands into white putty as her watch ticked toward Harrison's death. And then she'd fled to the restroom.

Now as Ivy looked down at the repairman, he got to his feet, closed the side panel, then set the scanner glass gently in place over the scanner.

He closed his briefcase.

Ivy ran.

Without caution, she flew down the stairs, skipping steps, raced through the door, and out onto the black-and-white floor where she forced her steps to slow. The scanners were whining again, like mosquitoes, and she felt a tremendous surge of adrenaline. It was back.

The squeal was back!

Please let there still be time. Please, please, please, let there be time!

Her plan was simple. As soon as the lights appeared, she would climb up on top of express lane four, and when the center void flashed open, she would shout *Jump!* as many times as she could before Bob and the others hauled her away.

The lights always went to Harrison. She knew that.

They always appeared within twelve feet of him. She knew that, too.

But what if the repairman's tinkering had altered something? What if the lights went somewhere else, somewhere far away from Harrison?

She felt sick again. She slapped her hand across her mouth. What if she failed? What if Harrison didn't see the lights? What if he didn't jump when she shouted? What if he didn't believe they were a window through time and his only chance of escape?

She kept walking, slightly dizzy, her feet feeling disconnected from her body, the Muzak humming, the scanners screeching.

She passed checkstand eleven, then checkstand ten. A few customers moved past her; the Fourth-of-July crepe paper fluttered. A call for a price check thundered over the intercom into the vacuous space of the nearly deserted store.

Then she was at checkstand nine. The repairman was

still there, putting his tools away. He looked at her, and she at him. Her hand was still over her mouth.

He said, "It's up—"

Ivy didn't hear the rest of his sarcastic comment, for suddenly the whining began to diminish. Somebody had shut off a scanner.

28

"Would you like a blindfold, Wyndham?"

"No, thank you."

Harrison was directed to a Windsor chair. It rested primly, incongruously, upon the hard ground. Harrison sat upon the polished wood seat. Ten yards away, the ten kilted Highland Guards stood with their rifles, while a sergeant moved up the line, dispensing bullets.

Harrison thought it peculiar, considering he was about to be executed, that the sight of them in their dress uniforms of khaki and kilt brought a feeling of patriotism to his breast. The sky behind them, so very vast in this country that was larger than life, slipped from the dark blue of predawn to the pink and gold hesitation of a new day. The charred scent of the fields filled his nostrils, and the sad notes of the bagpipes sang across the veldt.

He focused on the horizon, feeling his humble existence to be unimportant compared to the vastness of Africa, the enormity of the entire planet.

From Pretoria drifted the plaintive tolling of the tower clock. Seven desolate, echoing bells.

The Highland Guards lifted their rifles, and lowered their heads to the sleek barrels. Harrison thought of Ivy, only of Ivy.

As he stared at the first rays to burst over the horizon, he tried to imagine those magic lights, and her, in the midst of them, his angel come to escort him to the next life, to the great beyond.

"Take aim!"

* * *

Feeling as if she were moving in slow motion, as in a nightmare, Ivy turned, looking down the line of checkstands behind her.

There, in lane eleven, Gail was calmly cleaning her scale with glass cleaner, her read-out display blank. She'd shut off her scanner!

Ivy ran, her legs like rubber, the air seeming thick as sea water pressing against her efforts to move. She could hear her watch—or was it her heart?—tick-tick-ticking like a bomb.

She pushed aside a customer and crawled up onto Gail's belt on her hands and knees, reaching down over the scanner at such a steep angle that she nearly fell over.

She flipped the switch.

The squeal returned, wound up, grew louder, swirling and piercing—such a lovely sound! Ivy got to her feet on the conveyor. She shot a glance down the line of empty checkstands, ready to race, but she had run out of time. The lights were there already—exploding, swirling—and the void was flashing.

"Harrison!" she shouted. "Jump!"

29

Mary Alice, in express lane four, wasn't paying any attention to her lone customer, another beer buyer. She was buzzing Gail's checkstand to find out what was going on, why Ivy was standing on the conveyor belt of lane eleven, screaming. Then, out of the corner of her eye she saw her belt begin to move forward. She braced the phone against her ear with her shoulder and turned, her mouth open to greet the beer customer.

"What the hell—" she mumbled, not sure she could believe her eyes. "There's a guy on my belt," she said into the phone to Gail. "Is there a full moon tonight, or what? I'll call you back."

The guy was actually very cute with a buzz cut and big blue eyes, dressed in khaki and boots and suspenders.

"Can I help you?" she asked, nervously. He might be good-looking, but Ted Bundy had been good-looking. Was he an escaped convict? Some whacko playing war games?

"Hallo," he said in dreamy Sean Connery sort of accent. "No, no. I can manage, thank you very much." He tried to crawl off the belt, triggering the light beam, and it began to move, throwing him again onto his behind.

"Do you mind terribly turning off this thing for just a moment? It's awfully difficult maneuvering with it moving."

Mary Alice mechanically reached down and flipped off the belt switch. The guy climbed down; then he began patting his chest, his ribs, his stomach. He glanced down at himself with a look of bewildered surprise. "I could have sworn I heard them go off."

Something small and shiny clattered to the floor. He bent and picked it up.

"Dear God," he said.

"Excuse me?"

He glanced up. "Sorry. Never mind." He pocketed whatever it was he'd dropped, smoothed his clothes, and looked around with his huge eyes glittering. He seemed unsteady on his feet. She figured he was either drunk or on drugs.

He asked, "Is Ivy here?"

"Ivy? Ivy O'Neal?"

Mary Alice glanced toward lane eleven, then further down the line toward the front office. She caught a glimpse of Bob dragging Ivy inside, and then the door slammed shut. "The manager just pulled her into his office."

The guy with the beer had set his half case on the belt with a thump, and stood glaring.

"Aah, well, never mind then. I'll just have a look round. Queer how it happened so fast. And this place is just like she described it. I'll have to eat my hat. Well." He waved to her, and Mary Alice waved back. He turned around, and with the stride of a zombie, wandered away.

* * *

"I'm waiting for an explanation, PJ."

"Ivy," she growled, before she could hold her tongue. "Ivy!"

"Explain," he demanded. He crossed his arms and leaned back in his squeaky office chair.

Why were all grocery offices stuffy and windowless and so ugly? Ivy wondered. She stood before Bob's paper-littered metal desk, clutching her hands to keep them from trembling.

"Well—" She couldn't think. He was out there. He'd made it! He was alive! He was here!

"I really don't have time for this. I want an explanation now or you can go home. Permanently. Take your pick."

"No, don't send me home. I'm sorry, really." *Forget about Harrison for a minute*, she told herself. *Concentrate on keeping your job, keeping your access to the scanners.* "It's my medication."

Bob's handsome features narrowed. His chair squeaked as he sat forward.

"From the fever I had," she hurried on. "The medication is supposed to help, the doctors said. There was pressure and swelling on my brain. That's what caused my odd behavior in the first place and why I thought I saw things. That's why I came in here that night, with my aunt. Remember I explained all that? *Lie on top of lie*, she thought, without a drop of guilt. "Well, this medication is supposed to help, but I guess tonight it didn't. It must not have kicked in yet. I'm feeling much better now. Honest. It won't happen again."

"What exactly happened?"

"Happened? Well, it's that buzzing sound from the

scanners, that's all. The, uh, pressure caused by the fever I had makes me hear things a normal person can't hear. Like a dog, sort of. And it's so loud it just drives me crazy, so I have to shut them off."

"But you were turning Gail's scanner on, not off."

"Well, yeah, because sometimes the sound is worse unless all the scanners are on, sort of like the noise of some of them cancels out the noise of the others. But hey, the medication has kicked in now and I don't hear a thing. I'm fine now, really."

"Ivy, I think maybe you should take a few days off."

"No. I want to work."

"We'll put you on medical leave. You'll get paid."

"No, please, don't make me go. Could I just take a break? Just ten minutes, and I'll be fine." She had to get back out there and find him, to tell him not to wander off, to kiss him and touch him and make sure he was really here and still alive! And she had to keep access to the scanners. If they put her on medical leave, her access to the scanners would be limited.

"Either you get back to work or you go home. I can't be letting you out for breaks all night." He leaned back in his chair again, regarding her as if he was sizing up her potential. As if he was wondering what sort of favors she would owe him if he let her keep her job.

He really was a son-of-a-bitch. "Never mind the break then, really. I'm fine." She swung her arms into the air, emphasizing her energy and health. She couldn't be sent home. "I'll just get back out there and check. Okay? Just let me finish this shift. Then I have the next three days off. I'm feeling much better now, really."

He studied her. She put on her best smile and prayed.

"You've changed," he said suddenly.

She lifted her brows. "Huh?"

"You never used to be so spunky. I don't think you used to be so pretty, either," he said. There wasn't a single note of sarcasm or flirtation in his voice. Then, as if sensing he was being slightly human, he smirked.

"I want a note from the doctor clearing you for work before your next shift."

"But I gave you one."

"I want another one clearing you to work while on this medication."

"No problem." She wasn't on any medication, but she'd worry about a note later. How hard would it be to fool Bob with a fake one? No one ever verified them. "Can I go back to work now?"

He nodded slowly, his eyes trailing her head to toe, lingering lastly on her face. Again, he seemed surprised. He said carefully, "Close Christine for her break. She's past due."

"Okay," Ivy said; then she shot out the door, closing it behind her with a gasp of relief. She walked as slowly as she dared, searching along the checkstands, looking down the aisles. Where was Harrison?

The other checkers and the courtesy clerks were eyeing her warily. She pasted on a smile, straightened her pink apron, and marched past them to Christine in lane eight.

There were two customers in Christine's line, one with a basket already unloaded onto the belt, another waiting.

"I can take you next door," she said to the customer still

waiting to unload. She pulled the chain across the end of Christine's lane, then opened up her own. She waved her hand in front of the infrared light and the conveyor belt began moving.

She let her gaze dash again—to the bakery, across front ends of the aisles, then a quick shot over her shoulder in the direction of Produce.

Automatically, she began to scan as items rolled to her.

"Does she want paper or plastic?" the courtesy clerk asked from the end of the bagging belt.

Ivy asked the customer, but didn't listen to the answer as she looked now toward the front doors, the floral department, Video.

"What did she say?"

"Huh? Oh. I don't know. Paper or plastic?"

"Plastic. I said plastic."

* * *

Harrison believed he was in shock. He'd seen men in battle wander about aimlessly, just as he was doing now, and he'd pitied the fellows. Now he was one of them. It was an odd sensation. He was keenly aware of absolutely everything—the bright lighting, the gleaming shelves and colorful boxes and cans and bags. The black-and-white tile floor reminded him of Darby House in London. He could hear the faint sound of strange music playing. The air smelled very clean, cool, yet drifting on the cleanness was the delicious scent of meat cooking. And then there were the people. A half dozen of them. Prancing about quite unashamedly in their underclothes. The men in colorful boxer shorts and undershirts. The women, more flagrantly, in men's boxers or cut-off trousers, in shirts too small to adequately cover them. Some even wore variations of the thing Ivy had called a bra.

He found himself stumbling before a huge water tank of live lobsters. A white cloud raced across his vision and a black veil began to fall, to engulf him. With his last hold on consciousness, he groped his way to a narrow hallway off the main aisle, and he dropped down to the floor, huddled in the corner, and completely blacked out.

After a bit, he came to. He took a deep breath, but didn't get up. His limbs felt weak. *Well*, he thought. *So that was what it felt like to faint. Not the least bit pleasant. Small wonder women loathed it.*

It wasn't the sudden thrust into the future that had overwhelmed him, not the bombshell that time travel really did exist, but the very fact that he was still alive that had got to him. He'd been resigned to death. He'd heard the gun shots. One usually felt the impact of the bullet before the sound of the guns even registered. Or so he'd been told. And yet, miraculously, he was still alive.

A fellow came down the narrow hall toward him. He was a dark-suited man with a badge that read *Bob, Manager, Pig Palace People Pleaser*.

"Are you feeling all right, sir?" Bob asked him.

Harrison got to his feet. He felt shaky, but his strength was returning. "Yes, thank you. I'm very well, actually."

Bob eyed him suspiciously. "Is there anything I can do for you?"

"No, thank you. I'm well enough."

"One of our checkers was concerned about you. She said you had climbed onto her checkstand. She thought you might need some help."

Harrison was no stranger to the managers of business establishments, at least in his own time. Looking at this Bob fellow, he didn't believe the nature of the men in such positions had much changed. He was a fair enough looking man, if one liked pale hair, an arrogant chin, and average height. But something in his manner grated on Harrison's nerves.

"Actually, I've just arrived from abroad. I'm a friend of Miss O'Neal."

Bob gave a sort of grunting snort.

"Are you implying something?" Harrison asked, his hands itching. His emotions were volatile, he knew, and so he resisted the urge to show anger.

"She meet you in the hospital?"

"Pardon?"

"You're on medication too, I suppose." Bob snorted again, rolling his eyes.

"I don't think I care for your manner, Mr. Bob. Good day." Harrison gave a curt nod, then strode away, his anger vanishing as he took in this amazing future-world of wonder.

30

Why were these people shopping? Didn't they have anything better to do on the Fourth of July? The handful of straggling customers had all come up front at once, as usual. Ivy had checked out three agonizingly long orders, smiling and nodding and asking, *Paper or plastic?* and *Debit or credit?;* Saying sweetly, *Did you find everything you needed?* and, *Have a nice evening.* She really didn't think she could stand another minute of it, and then she looked up, and there he was, in her line. Standing there, grinning at her like an idiot, and she nearly shouted with relief.

He wiggled his fingers at her in a little wave, and a smile burst onto her face.

"Is that my total? Miss?"

"Oh, yes, ma'am. Debit or credit?"

"I'm writing a check."

"Oh, yes, of course, a check." She was almost laughing. The customer looked at her as if she'd lost her mind, but she didn't care.

She looked again. He was still there, beaming at her. Wearing khaki, tieless, hatless. He'd lost a few pounds, and they'd cut his hair shorter than ever. His ears stuck out boyishly. His blue eyes sparkled. His dimple winked. Oh, heavens, it was Harrison. Here, in her time. In her store!

"Could I just get my receipt?"

"Oh, yes, of course. Sorry."

She checked out the next order, aware only of him, inching his way nearer. Her hands were trembling and clumsy; she kept dropping everything she picked up. She had to double-scan nearly everything, and the produce? The codes would not come to mind, and her fingers couldn't even manage to turn the pages of her code book, so she gave the customer bargain rates, making up prices as she went.

At long last, Harrison was next. He stepped up to the pay counter empty-handed The next customer behind him began to unload an overflowing cart onto the conveyor with the help of a two-year-old who flung items over his head up onto the belt.

"Hi," she said to Harrison, restraining herself from reaching over to kiss his face. His eyes held hers possessively, powerfully, consuming her right across the counter.

A box of Twinkies bounced on the belt, skipped across the scanner, and rang itself up. The two-year-old howled with delight.

"Hallo," Harrison said. "Am I really here?"

"I think so. Are you hurt?"

"A bit stunned, but other than that, I think I'll live. I've been having a look round. Thought I'd queue up so I could talk to you."

"I have to work until midnight."

"What time is it now?"

She tore her eyes away from his long enough to check her watch. "Almost eleven. Can you just sort of hang around until I'm off?"

"I haven't got anywhere else to go, have I?" He smiled and lowered his voice. "Are we in Seattle, and more importantly, in the future?"

"Yes."

"What's all the bunting for? Is it a holiday?"

"The Fourth of July. Independence Day. We're celebrating our freedom from the British crown."

"Are you now? What an uncivilized thing to do."

Their eyes were shouting so many things they could not say aloud. "Was it awful?" she whispered.

"Let's just say there were a few minutes when I thought this must be heaven. You've got impeccable timing."

"Thank God you jumped."

"I didn't jump," he said. "Those bloody wonderful lights grabbed me."

She had no time to contemplate his words. The two-year-old had emptied the basket of junk food, and now his mother glared at Ivy, then Harrison, obviously annoyed at the delay.

Harrison turned to the woman with a brilliant smile, and the woman's face flushed.

"I apologize for detaining the cashier. Aah, what a lovely child. And so clever. Good evening, madam." He turned to Ivy with a wink. "I'll be having another look round."

"Don't go far," she said. And he passed through the line, with not only Ivy's customer's flushed gaze following him, but many others of the female gender sending him appreciative glances.

Her phone buzzed. As she began to check, she answered it and heard, "It's Mary Alice. What's with the dreamboat?"

"He's a friend. I'll explain later." Which really meant she'd explain as soon as she came up with a plausible lie. That's all she seemed to do anymore—create lies. But right now, she didn't care. Harrison was here, he was safe, and if she had to lie to the Pope to keep him that way, she would.

And wasn't it wonderful to have all the other checkers looking at her with such envy?

* * *

The longest hour of Ivy's life followed. From her position trapped in her checkstand, she watched Harrison explore. He stood for fifteen minutes at the photo-processing counter, watching a customer upload photos from a thumb drive and the photos feed from the digital printer. He was at the magazine rack for another fifteen minutes, frowning mostly. He stood watching people at the cash machine for so long, Ivy had to get his attention and tell him to move on. He moved to the lottery machine, pressing buttons that did nothing because he hadn't fed in any money. He watched kids dump a coffee can of change into the Coin Machine, then followed them through the line to see what they did with the slip.

She lost sight of him several times when he wandered up and down the aisles, picking things up, reading their labels, putting them back again. He seemed to especially like the frozen food section, and kept opening and closing the doors so often that now the entire aisle was one long fogged-up window.

At 11:30, Ivy was the only checker still on duty. All the

managers had gone home, including a scowling Bob who hadn't said another word to her.

The night crew arrived. The Muzak changed to a rock-and-roll radio station. Harrison stood near the huge front windows, staring out at the parking lot and the headlights of cars passing on the highway, watching the occasional display of fireworks that still erupted into the dark sky.

Ivy, calmer now and able to think, filled the single pack cigarettes, her hands no longer trembling. Harrison shrugged an apology for not believing her earlier. Cigarettes really did cost a small fortune. Now only a few customers wandered through the store, but still Harrison respected that she was at work. He approached her just a few times when she wasn't checking. Once was to ask what that horrid sound was. He professed he'd thought the music they'd been playing earlier, while strange in melody, much more acceptable.

At last, Ivy punched out, and pulled off her bow tie and apron. She met Harrison where he stood gazing out the windows. A single white streak of fireworks touched the dark sky, then exploded into a puff, like a dandelion, then melted.

He turned to look at her, sending a great warmth sky-rocketing like fireworks inside her. His smile faded as he continued to gaze at her, and his blue eyes grew serious. She didn't know what the future held for them, but she was filled with a deep sense of relief. He was alive. He was here. She must be content with that.

She felt her stomach growl, and realized she hadn't eaten since yesterday. "Ever had pizza?"

He shook his head and turned to her with a crooked smile so adorable she felt ridiculously happy.

"All right then. Pizza it is." She chose a gourmet frozen pizza with feta cheese and Greek olives. Then she let him choose the wine. He selected an import from a Southeastern Australian winery that had been in existence, according to the label, since 1828, and which Harrison pronounced as excellent. Then on HABA, the health and beauty aisle, they chose a toothbrush, and a safety razor that intrigued him. He selected a can of shaving cream and he tested it right where he stood in the aisle, giggling at the dollop of fragrant foam the can produced. Ivy then chose for him a comb, a hairbrush, and deodorant.

"What do I do with this?" he asked, eyeing the deodorant stick. For once, the simplistic and obvious instructions on the back of the label were actually needed.

"Have you found me offensive?" he asked with a bit of alarm after reading.

"No, no, of course not. It's just what everybody uses now. Part of the modern *toilet,*" she explained, pronouncing the word as he usually did, with the emphasis on *let.*" Oh, and remember that here the word is pronounced *toilet,*" she now used the American pronunciation, "and sometimes it refers to scented water, but most often, it refers to the privy."

"Thanks for the warning."

The Pig Palace didn't sell much clothing, but there was a small selection of hosiery and underwear. Of these, Harrison chose a packaged pair of boxers, a muscle shirt, and a pair of black cotton socks.

The night checker, Danny, who'd been working both nights Ivy had leapt into the past, was a smiling freckle-faced college boy. Ivy stood at the end of the bagging belt as their order was checked. She asked Harrison, "Paper or plastic?"

"Plastic," he said, looking on curiously.

"Why?"

"Because I've never used it before."

Danny lifted a curious freckled brow.

She said, "It's not good for the environment, you know, and the store charges you for it." But she bagged in plastic anyway. She paid with the Pig Palace gift certificate she'd been given while in the hospital. She thanked Danny for his contribution, and he shrugged, embarrassed.

Harrison watched the process closely.

"How long were you in hospital?" he asked.

"Just for a few days. It wasn't bad."

Danny guffawed. "Not bad? You almost died. They had you in quarantine!"

Harrison took the bags, like the gentleman he was, asking no more personal questions until they were near the door and well out of the Danny's earshot.

"Are you sure you've fully recovered? You've lost weight."

"So have you," she said defensively.

"Was it typhoid?"

"No, it was a rare microbe nobody has seen for a century. I'm fine now. Really. Thank you for saving me."

“Thank *you* for saving *me*,” he replied

She looked up into his eyes and smiled mischievously.

"Well. Are you ready to go out there?"

His features became boyish with excitement. "Ready and eager."

"Come along, then." She headed out the automatic doors. They swished open before her. Harrison had been watching them do that all night, but still he hesitated. She continued walking out, and the doors closed behind her, leaving him on the other side. He took a step forward, and the doors swished open again. His boyish grin spread ear to ear; his dimple winked. He took another step, and then another. Then he was at her side.

"Well. That was fun. What's next?"

"Next, we drive home."

"I don't know how to drive a motor car."

"I didn't expect you to. Believe it or not, almost all women drive nowadays. Come on."

She led him across the black asphalt of the deserted parking lot to her little blue Honda Civic, which was parked under a light. She dug for her keys and unlocked the door on the passenger side, telling him to just put the groceries in the back seat; then she went around and got in on the driver's side.

He sat in the seat with his knees drawn up, ducking his head. She told him where to find the lever to adjust the seat. Even after he'd adjusted it as far back as it would go, his legs were still too long for her little car, but at least he wasn't scrunched.

She turned the key in the ignition and started the engine.

"Seat belt," she said. He looked at her blankly. She

reached across him, grabbed the shoulder strap, and pulled it across him, so close to him she could feel the heat of his body. She glanced into his face, and he kissed her, quickly, lightly, on the cheek. He was still grinning foolishly. She clicked the belt into place, then strapped on her own.

The feel of his kiss lingered on her cheek, sending tingling fingers down her spine. When she looked at him again, his eyes were on her, his excitement glowing in the blue depths. He was so utterly adorable that she could not resist leaning over to him again, pressing her lips to his. Very softly, she kissed him, and he returned the kiss with equal tenderness.

It was a kiss that said, *I've missed you, I need you, you are everything to me.*

His breath mingled with hers. She kissed him again, tasting his saltiness, feeling the roughness of his chapped lips, the silky softness of his mouth. She pulled away from him reluctantly, and shifted the car into first gear. The blood pounded in her veins, giving her a tremendous feeling of confidence, and harboring a healthy desire to show off now that she had him in her world, she zipped out of the parking lot onto the highway.

When she'd gotten up to fifty miles per hour, she glanced at him, and had to bite back a most inappropriate desire to laugh. His eyes were straight ahead, his mouth open in awe or terror or maybe both. She shifted down for the light ahead, then came to a stop at the red.

"Are you all right?" she asked guiltily.

He nodded dumbly.

She shifted into first as the light turned green, and off

they went again, but at a more sedate pace. It was a short drive home, and Harrison said nothing the entire way. He just gripped the arm rest and door handle and stared, growing paler and paler.

Turning onto the dead-end street, Ivy began to get nervous.

What would he think of her and Daisy's humble home in suburban Seattle? It certainly wasn't Wyndham Manor. It wasn't even as fancy as the Officers Recovery House. But it was home, and she loved the dear little place. She wanted him to love it, too.

She pulled into the driveway, and gravel crunched under the tires. She eased the car under the carport beside Daisy's Comet, pulled up the hand brake, and switched off the motor.

In the silence and near darkness, Harrison asked softly, "Are we through with this motor driving?"

"Yes."

He slumped into his seat. "Thank God," he breathed.

She did laugh then, and leaned over to give him a swift kiss on the cheek. "Come on," she said. "I'll show you my home."

31

The house was cottage-sized. Harrison liked it immediately. He'd always been partial to cottages, and Ivy's was painted white with a trim of green. The small cement stoop glowed in electric lamplight, as did enormous hydrangeas, fat with dewy flowers that looked violet in the artificial light. The lawn was neat and trim, the stoop swept, the brass-plate door handle polished.

The door swung open, and Ivy beckoned him in, taking the plastic grocery bags from him.

He found himself stepping directly into a parlor. There was no front hall. The floor was hardwood, gleaming but worn with age and use. A braided multi-colored oval rug reached underneath a plump rusty red couch, a leather chair, several small tables beneath crystal lamps, their white shades glowing softly.

Harrison met Ivy's eye. Her face was anxious, wanting his approval. He smiled, and let his gaze wander more, so curious was he about Ivy and her world. In the far corner of the room was a curio cabinet with glass panes. Inside, a display of sewing thimbles stood neatly arranged. Harrison recalled Ivy's request to purchase a half dozen thimbles for her Aunt Daisy, and there they were, front and center, proudly displayed.

"Daisy loves them," Ivy said. "Thanks for sending them home with me." She looked at him curiously. "Why did you send me back with your gun?"

"For protection," he said. He'd had no idea how rough this future-world of hers might be. She'd felt the need for his gun while in Africa, so he'd packed it in the haversack, along with the thimbles. It was one the hardest things he'd ever had to do. She had barely been able to stand, and he'd pushed her through those lights, toward the people he glimpsed, hoping and praying they would help her.

Through an open archway, he could see a round dining table, large enough to seat four, and directly before him against the wall stood a white painted bookshelf, full of colorful jacketed titles as well as pewter-framed photographs. He approached these, drawn to them as he was drawn to Ivy, wanting to see her as a child, a young girl.

The photographs did not disappoint him, but they did surprise him for they were in color. There was no mistaking Ivy in any of them. He'd know that face anywhere. Ivy as a toddler, smiling into the camera, holding a doll by its foot so that its spiky doll braids trailed on the floor. Ivy as a girl of maybe fifteen, caught off guard, her mouth open, her eyes wide, barely dressed in a bathing costume on some beach, her legs long and skinny, her curves not yet emerged He came then to a photograph of a man in cut-off denims wearing an undershirt on which were painted the words *Husky Football* in bold purple letters. Beside him stood a young woman in a denim skirt, her torso encased in a sleeveless, neckless thing. But there was something very familiar about the woman's brown eyes, the arch of her brow, the sweetness of her smile. The woman held an infant dressed in old-fashioned frills.

"Are those your parents? And is that you?"

He felt Ivy at his side. "Yes," she said affectionately.

"What are their names?"

"My mom was Rose, named after my great-grandmother. And my dad was Bill. William, really. But everybody called him Bill." She lifted her face to his. As always, when he looked into her eyes, he wanted to tell her how very much he loved her. But he hesitated, not knowing what was right. What would be proper when their future was so unsettled? When she'd kissed him, before the harrowing ride on the motorway, he'd seen her desire as clearly as he felt his own, but she was backing away from him now, as if also unsure.

"Aunt Daisy is asleep," she said softly, pointing down a narrow hall. "But I told her I'd let her know if I got you."

He captured her eyes again, wondering if all men rescued from the jaws of death felt this sort of overwhelming desire to ravish their women. "You have me, Ivy. Completely."

* * *

She wished he'd stop looking at her like that, with eyes so full of longing and questions. Resisting him was nearly impossible. If Aunt Daisy weren't home, she would have ripped off his clothes the minute they stepped inside the house. Shamelessly.

And then what? After hours and hours of passion—

could it really last hours, like in romance novels? Somehow, with Harrison, she felt it would—then what? Where would she be? Still having to send him home, to his life, his fate. To some other wonderful and worthy woman who surely was meant to be his wife and carry his children. She, Ivy O'Neal, modern grocery checker, was not supposed to have been in his life. She did not belong with him. He did not belong with her. So what if she felt complete happiness whenever she looked into his eyes? So what if she loved him more than life itself?

She knew that if she were really honest with herself she'd admit she was afraid. Afraid of having his love and then losing it. Afraid she would eventually bore him, and that he would begin to see her for what she truly was—plain and ordinary. She was terrified she could not possibly make him happy forever.

And she wanted him to be happy forever.

So, no. Making love, as heavenly as it would be, was out of the question. She forced herself to look away from him and to concentrate on something, anything, other than desire.

Hunger.

She felt suddenly dizzy from hunger. "Come on," she said, leading him into the kitchen. "We'll get the pizza going."

There followed a half hour of domesticity. Ivy crept into Daisy's room and told her the good news. Then, while the pizza began to waft its mouthwatering scent into the house, Ivy showered and changed into gray leggings and an oversized white T-shirt and tucked her feet into thick white socks. Comfortable clothing, true, but a far cry from slipping into a negligee. Not that she owned one. Her most glamorous sleeping wear was her *Sleepless in Seattle* nightshirt.

Next it was Harrison's turn to freshen up, though he only had his khakis to wear. He politely refused the offer of Ivy's fluffy pink robe.

They devoured the pizza like greedy children; she was all too aware that they were not children. As they drank the wine with sighs of appreciation, she wished the warm, sweet joy the wine produced would overpower her senses.

It did not.

Her desire for him continued to grow with each passing minute, each lift of his hand to his mouth, each lingering caress of his gaze. When the food and wine were gone, she sent him into the living room, and she floated into the kitchen to make tea.

She put the teapot under the faucet, and as the water splashed she thought how strange and wonderful it was that he was here, in her house, now in her living room and sitting comfortably on the russet couch. The water flowed, filling the pot, overflowing the pot, running coolly over her hands. She stared for a moment at the water, thinking in a vague jumbled way of kisses and touches and bodies entwined.

He was here, out there, on the couch.

She lifted her hands and splashed the cool water onto her face, pressed cold wet hands to her neck, to the pulse that throbbed just below her ear.

She half emptied the teapot before putting it on the

stove, took a deep breath, and joined Harrison in the living room.

He had buried his handsome nose in Jason Pepper's book. She carefully settled beside him, telling herself she was sitting this close only to read with him, and not because she wanted to feel the heat of his body, smell the clean spicy scent of his skin, or be near enough to brush his hand, his thigh, his lips.

"Have you seen this?" he asked hoarsely, tilting the pages toward her.

"Not since you arrived." She read the altered entry.

After the execution, rumors flew around Pretoria and England. Though under strict secrecy orders, the execution squad of the Highland Guards let it leak that, at the time of the shooting, Lord Wyndham vanished before their very eyes. An extensive search failed to produce any evidence as to his whereabouts. Headquarters decided to let the mystery drop. Lord Wyndham had been seen in the chair when the shots were fired. Therefore, he was dead. His casket was buried, and death certificate issued.

When I began this book, and learned of the rumors, I petitioned for an exhumation of Lord Wyndham's grave. After six months, permission was granted. When the casket was brought up from the ground and the lid opened, not a single bone was found inside.

Ivy looked up. Harrison shrugged and said, "I suppose that confirms I am truly here."

As if every awakened inch of her body was not proof enough.

"But how could they claim you're dead?"

"I don't see they had much choice. They could either admit I disappeared like a ghost, or pretend it never happened. The British army is not in the habit of reporting ghosts."

"I guess not. It will complicate matters when you go back, though. I mean, how will they explain you returning from the grave?"

He looked at her, shrugging again, and he seemed suddenly very tired. She wanted to pull him into her arms and rock him like a child. He'd had a very long day. So had she.

"Want to sleep?"

"I don't think I could. Not yet."

Neither could she, not with him so very near, his thigh next to her thigh, their hands almost touching. "Would you like some tea?"

"Tea sounds very familiar and comforting just now."

She leapt up just as the teapot began to whistle. A few minutes later she was again settled on the couch next to him; before them on the coffee table was a tea tray holding a little pitcher of milk, a bowl of sugar, and a plate of Daisy's homemade oatmeal raisin cookies.

With a steaming hot cup of tea in her hands, Ivy could not so readily touch Harrison as she longed to do. But in five minutes, her tea cup was empty, as was his. Their hands were free.

Daisy, she knew, would not get up. Daisy would not get out of bed and put on her robe and come out here to check on Ivy. In fact, Daisy had hinted before Ivy even left for work today that if she were successful and got her man here, that she would be the very essence of discretion.

Ivy had turned red as a radish and explained to Daisy that Harrison was not her man, and that there would be no need for discretion. Daisy had only smiled. It was a side to her aunt that Ivy had never seen before. It seemed as if Daisy were encouraging Ivy to pursue Harrison romantically. Physically. But hadn't she already decided that would be terribly wrong? For the life of her, as she sat resisting the desire to reach out to him, she could not think of a single reason why it would be wrong.

Harrison finally broke the silence "Does Jason Pepper's book tell us what will become of my family if I don't return?"

She gave a small gasp. She searched his eyes. "Really? You'd consider staying?"

His eyes steady, his voice pitched low, he said, "I'd consider remaining anywhere, anytime, as long as you were there."

Tears stung her eyes.

"Please don't cry. I'm afraid I might just do the same, and I've never cried in front of a woman before. Except my mother, of course. And my governess. And the upstairs maid when I was about seven. Cook, once or twice. I was always dashing though the kitchens. There was a young woman in London who once drove me to tears, but she had just stomped on my foot with her not-so-dainty heel. I might have deserved it. I don't now remember."

Ivy shook her head, laughing away her tears as she opened Jason Pepper's book, but her hopes of him staying crashed.

Under his youngest brother Stuart's care, the Wyndham

estate had fallen apart. He'd trusted the wrong people to help him, and ended up deep in debt. Maggie had married a wealthy businessman much older than herself, a man she did not love, in order to try to save the estate, but in the end the bulk of the property was sold to developers. Worst of all, Harrison's mother had died of heart failure in 1902, having never recovered from Jeffrey's and Harrison's deaths.

Harrison staying here, in his future, would mean locking his family into this particular fate. He wouldn't do that. He couldn't. And neither could she.

He said, "It all makes sense now, your odd requests."

"I thought that maybe if Stuart knew more about business and running an estate, he could save your family home, and save Maggie from sacrificing her happiness."

"And you hoped a diet of broccoli and beans would save my mother?"

Ivy nodded.

"Would she be allowed anything else? Or just those two? I'm not sure my mother could bear life without scones." His smile didn't quite mask his dismay at his mother's recorded fate.

She explained about heart disease, and the sort of diet that could help his mother not only be healthier but more able to withstand stress and trauma.

"Does everyone know such things nowadays, or just you?"

"It's common knowledge."

"I don't suppose there is a book which tells us what will happen if I return to South Africa."

"No, not until you actually do it. But isn't there some

law that says if the execution fails, they can't try again?"

"I believe if they hang you and you don't die, or if they actually manage to shoot you and you survive without medical intervention, then perhaps some law applies. But since I vanished inexplicably from my chair, I doubt they would hesitate putting me back in."

"Don't joke, Harrison."

He took a dull lead bullet from his pocket and held it in the soft lamplight.

"What's that?" she asked.

"That, my dear Ivy, is what was about to pierce my clothing, and then my flesh, at the very moment those lights of yours appeared."

He placed the small piece of lead in her palm. It was warm from being in his pocket, next to his warmth. So small. So deadly.

She was so stunned, she couldn't speak.

"I know," he said, acknowledging her shocked silence.

"I knew the timing was close," she said, her words coming in shallow gasps. "At first, I thought I'd miss you. I thought it was too late because it was past dawn." She swallowed hard as her body recalled the shock and anguish she'd felt. She explained about the broken scanner and the lazy repairman, and how she hadn't been able to activate the swirling lights until it was almost too late. "But then, finally, he was done, and the lights appeared, and you appeared. It was a half hour past dawn, but you're still alive."

He cocked his head. "I thought you said our years and times were parallel. We need only consider the nine-hour difference between here and Africa."

"That's right."

"But it was dawn when the lights snatched me, perhaps a few minutes past the very first rays. The sound of the Raadzaal bell still echoed across the valley ringing the hour. It was seven; I'm sure of it."

"No, it was twenty minutes after." She glanced at her new watch. She was sure it was right. She'd matched it with Greenwich Mean Time online. But she also knew that the handless Raadzaal clock in Pretoria had kept time perfectly when she'd been there. So why the twenty-minute discrepancy?

Harrison shook his head and grinned. "What matters is that it worked. The lights came, and here we are."

Ivy's heart twisted painfully. So close. So close! Harrison gently stroked her cheek.

"It shocked me, too. But I'm here, and we mustn't fill our minds with useless what-ifs."

Gazing into his eyes, her breathing slowly deepened, and her clenched heart calmed. He was here. She mustn't think of those twenty minutes, she mustn't think of how she'd so very nearly missed him. He was here. He was here.

"Tell me what you've learned. Is there anything I can take back with me to change my outcome?"

"Rainbow's End," she blurted out, before she could hate herself for being selfish and withholding what could possibly give him hope that returning home might change his fate, and his family's fate.

"Pardon me?"

"Rainbow's End. What does it mean to you?"

Harrison pondered this a moment. "Private Carter did

mention it, in the train. You remember, don't you?"

She nodded.

His eyes clouded with sadness. "You know about Carter?"

"Yes, but he didn't kill himself."

His eyes cleared and narrowed. "How do you know?"

"First please try to think more about Rainbow's End."

Harrison shrugged. "As Carter said, it was one of Kyle Fleming's expressions. He loved to say something about the glory of Africa being the rainbow's end, and then he'd laugh like he'd just made the most humorous and insightful of observations."

Ivy tucked Harrison's bullet into his shirt pocket, then got to her feet and found the computer printouts of the websites she'd accessed. She sat beside Harrison again, and showed him the fountain.

"The Rainbow's End," he read aloud. "Lord Fleming's tribute to Africa." He glanced up at Ivy. "Is this supposed to mean something, other than a concrete example of Kyle's attempt at wit?"

In reply, Ivy shuffled the papers and placed on top the financial report for Provisions Corp. Harrison again read aloud. "Provisions Corp is owned by the international corporation, Rainbow's End."

He turned to her, eyes wide, mouth open as hers had been. She pressed a finger under his chin and closed it.

He promptly thanked her with an energetic kiss. And then, as if consumed by a burst of energy, he got to his feet and began pacing.

She said, "I guess we made the same conclusion."

"It answers so many questions! Lord Fleming is, or was, stone broke. He has no means to buy property or purchase equipment or hire laborers. He needed great sums and quickly. That explains everything. Everything. He can't let the war end, not yet, not until his mine strikes a rich vein, one large enough to sustain the operation. The peace talks were going well until Kruger heard that lie about my giving Fleming an order to shoot the missionary. This whole court-martial business has meant perhaps tens of thousands of dollars to Fleming. We saw that huge shipment of supplies, didn't we?"

"We did," she said eagerly, drawing her legs up beneath her on the couch, pressing away any thoughts that his eagerness meant he would leave.

"And now that you know you were set up—" she began, but stopped when Harrison's excitement abruptly faded into frustration.

"I have no way of proving Fleming's ownership of Rainbow's End and Provisions Corp. He's much too clever for that. Those records of yours even today don't reveal the true owner's identity."

"Neither company exists anymore, and if any old records are still around, I don't know where to look. They could be in private storage somewhere in the world, or they might have been destroyed. What we need is someone from your time that knows the truth." And then it came to her. "Reed! Captain Reed knows. He's been helping Kyle all along. It was Reed who arranged for the Boers—"

"Ivy, Reed has been transferred to India."

"So they can un-transfer him. Make him testify."

"The trial is over. They will be calling no more witnesses on my behalf. It was a mock trial, yes, the whole thing rigged against me, but those in South Africa, the court members, all of them, they believed they were hearing truths and dispensing justice. The only ones who know the real truth are the Flemings, the bloody bastards!"

Though his anger grew, his voice remained just above a whisper. "Oh, I can see how it happened. Kyle would do anything to get in his father's good graces. He must have been thrilled to see that missionary shot; what an opportunity! He cables his father, and I'm as good as dead.

"And what the bloody hell am I supposed to do when I go back? How can I clear my name? If I start shouting that the mighty general Lord Fleming is making enormous profits selling weapons to the Boers, and I accuse him of using me as a scapegoat for his own bloody purposes, they'll shoot me all right, but not nice and clean and proper at sunrise, no. They'll take no chances this time, they'll get it right. Oh, Ivy. There is no choice! I stay here and condemn my family to ruin. I go back and condemn them to the same."

He began pacing again, back and forth across the braided rug.

"Harrison, wait. We know you were set up. There must be evidence that can prove it. Evidence that even the British army will have to acknowledge."

He stopped pacing and turned to her. "What sort of evidence could there possibly be?"

"What was it you said that lawyer of yours asked you at the end of the trial? Something about not being sure if Kyle actually killed that missionary?"

"He was only trying to stir up doubt."

"Didn't you say that there was a lot of gunfire, from a lot of different directions?"

"Yes, but the court of inquiry established that it was Fleming who shot Reverend Schmidt."

"What sort of evidence did they have?"

"Well, Fleming's admission."

"Is there any way to tell if a person was shot by an English soldier or a Boer soldier?"

"The difference isn't in the soldier, but in the weapon. And honestly, there isn't a weapon we used that they didn't. But I know on that day we were using Lee-Enfield rifles. They're .303 inch caliber with bolt-action breeches, and we were using smokeless cordite ammunition."

Ivy stared at him blankly. All she knew of guns was what Tom had taught her about Harrison's revolver.

"The point is," he continued, "the Boers that day had German Mausers. The caliber is different, and so is the ammunition."

Ivy asked, "Is the difference enough that you could tell by looking at the wound?"

"It wouldn't have taken an expert to tell what sort of bullet hit him. The Boer were using homemade dum-dums."

"Dum-dums?"

"They'd cut off the points of their bullets, then scored four slits down the sides of them."

"Why would they do that?"

"To make them expand. The bullet enters the body neatly enough, but then just sort of explodes once inside, and rips a gaping hole in the body on exit."

Ivy shuddered. "How horrible."

"It pretty well assures you kill what you shoot."

"Who saw the reverend after he was shot? Did anyone look to see what sort of wound he had?"

Harrison stared at her, his brow knit with intense thought.

"What is it? Harrison, you're remembering something. Tell me."

"We were under attack off and on fairly steadily until the next day. It was a bit of a mess. Boyle was the closest to the farmhouse, so he ran and grabbed the child and took him into the storage cellar of the barn."

"Did he see Reverend Schmidt? His wound?"

"No, at least not that he said, not then and not later. He was too concerned about the child, I think, to spare a glance at a dead man."

"Who did see him?"

"I was flat on my back, directing this affair from a stretcher, unable to move, fading in and out, and still worried about that angel I'd seen," he said, with a wry grin at Ivy. "But I had a few of the men dig a grave behind an outbuilding. It was McKruder, a Royal Dragoon who'd joined us just a fortnight past, who went into the farmhouse and carried out the reverend. McKruder was our strongest man, and the reverend was small."

Ivy's hope faded again. "And he would have mentioned if it looked as if the missionary had been hit by one of those dum-dum bullets, right?"

"He never got the chance to say anything. He was killed

a few minutes after he covered the grave."

"So nobody knows for sure?"

"I didn't say that."

"Harrison, you're driving me crazy. Do you know it was Kyle who shot the missionary, or could it have been a Boer?"

"I guess I'm saying I don't know. Kyle came to me, terrified, nearly frozen with guilt. We now know from Carter that this was after he received that cable from his father. The one that said *St. Edward.* Fleming seemed positive the missionary's death was his fault, but if he was setting me up intentionally, it's possible he didn't shoot the priest at all. He wasn't much of a shot, to be honest. Nor much of an actor, but his trembling might have been fear of letting his father down. Come to think of it, it does seem more reasonable to me that Fleming had not shot the reverend, but simply used his death to further his own end. Rainbow's End."

Ivy's hope soared. She grabbed her laptop computer, dropped back onto the couch, and started typing.

"What you doing?" he asked, sitting beside her and eyeing the computer.

"I'm searching," she said. "People all over the world put information on what's called the web, and to see that information, you just search for it by typing keywords. There," she said, pointing at the screen. "The Dutch Reformed Church."

"I don't understand," Harrison said.

Ivy's fingers flew, and in seconds the home page of the website appeared.

"We are now reading information being sent from a server in South Africa," Ivy explained. "This, Lord Wyndham, is the information highway."

"I still don't understand. What are we looking at, and what do you hope to find?"

"I hope to find proof. I've been here before—to this site, I mean."

She glanced at Harrison, and he shrugged, shaking his head.

"It doesn't matter. What's important is that I know that Reverend Schmidt's body was removed from your temporary grave, brought to Johannesburg, and buried in church ground. What I don't know is if there is any sort of death certificate or documentation. I'm going to try to find out."

It was too much to expect to find information about Reverend Schmidt's death accessible right there, and they didn't. But they did find the e-mail address of the Minister of Church Records, and Ivy sent an urgent e-mail requesting his assistance in locating Reverend Schmidt's death certificate. She also asked if it were known whether any records were destroyed or missing. As clever as Lord Fleming was, he wouldn't let evidence sit around waiting to be discovered.

Ivy then opened the online white pages. Telephoning the Minister of Records directly would probably be the fastest approach. It was mid-morning in South Africa, so somebody should be around, manning the phone.

She had to run a search to find an international phone listing; then she dived into several linked pages before she found South African church numbers. At this point, a friendly male voice announced over her computer, "You have mail."

"Mail," Harrison repeated. "Surely, your machine isn't

telling you that a reply has come already? In a matter of minutes? From Africa?"

"I don't know. Let's look and see."

Ivy felt the comforting warmth of Harrison's nearness as she clicked open her mail.

Dear Ms. O'Neal.

I would be happy to assist you in your search. Reverend Schmidt's records, if available, should be located in our archives. In May of 1901, an arson fire destroyed most of our depository. Fortunately, since it was during the war, record keepers had prepared for such an event. Most documents were sealed in fire boxes and hidden beneath the church. They suffered only minor browning.

I'd be glad to forward a copy of the document if located, in a day or two, I should think.

Sincerely, Reverend Haroldsmith

Heart pounding wildly, Ivy e-mailed her thanks to the Minister of Records.

"What does he mean? Forward? Copy? A day or two?" Harrison asked.

"There are machines that can look at a document, create an image that is digital—that can travel over the Internet, and show up in my email. Then I can print it here."

He looked doubtful, confused, and amazed. She smiled up at him, her heart full of hope. This had to save him. It just had to.

"If we get information that says the Reverend was killed by a Boer bullet, then when you go back, you will find a way to get the real document, the real proof, from the church in Johannesburg."

"That would prove Fleming did not shoot the reverend, but it would not prove he is lying about me giving him the order to do so. It's the order that got me court-martialed."

"But it would provide doubt. It would show that Fleming's account is flawed. They would have to set you free. They would have to," she repeated. If she said it enough, maybe it would become truth. The quietness of the house settled around them like a gentle cloak.

Her heart gave a painful twist that brought tears stinging her eyes. She closed her laptop and set it aside, then slipped into Harrison's arms, holding tight. So alive, so warm. God, how she loved him.

He pulled her into his arms, cupping her face in his palms, gazing into her, consuming her with his eyes. His lips claimed hers, tenderly, tasting, savoring, for a moment hesitant, and then with an increasing hunger that bordered on abandon. His breathing deepened, quickened, as his fingers dug into her hair, cradling her to him with a gentle fierceness.

Having given in to her need to touch and feel and caress, she found it impossible to stop. Tomorrow was so far away. Harrison was alive, and nothing else mattered. His heart pounded steadily against her breast, his warm strong hands stroked her with possession. She'd not known lovemaking could be so serious, so life-and-death. She'd not known her body could feel so on fire with desire while her heart cried with love and fear.

He must not die. He must not!

She vaguely heard a familiar sound—a click, and then voices. Harrison's kisses abruptly ended. She peeked, opening her eyes to see that he was no longer paying attention to her. His eyes were wide open, averted, and his face was bathed in the bluish hue of the television.

"What on earth—" he whispered.

"Oh, fudge," she muttered, and they both sat up.

"Ivy, what is this?"

"Television. That's a rerun of *Star Trek*. Here. This is yours." She dug the remote control out from under her shoulder and slapped it in his hand.

"And what's this?"

"Don't worry. You're a man. You'll figure it out."

She left him staring wide-eyed at the screen and went to take a very long, very cold shower.

32

Sunlight streamed dustily through the cracks of the Venetian blinds. Ivy blinked. The low coffee table came into focus. The teapot, two stained china cups, and Jason Pepper's book. She sat up stiffly in the recliner.

"Good morning," Harrison said from the couch, his voice emerging gravelly and deep and extremely formal. He was sitting up, Daisy's handmade afghan over his khaki lap with Audrey atop the afghan, purring contentedly as he stroked her with a broad bronze hand.

"Hi," she said softly.

The click of a doorknob erased the chance of any more private words.

Ivy carefully untangled herself from both the recliner and her fuzzy robe—which she'd used as a blanket—and was on her feet when her aunt, dressed in a cream-colored polyester pantsuit, came into the living room. Harrison eased both Audrey and blanket aside, stood, and nodded politely, his hands folded before him. An officer and a gentleman.

"Aunt Daisy, this is Harrison Darby, Lord of Wyndham," Ivy said, taking her aunt's hand and leading her forward. Daisy stared at him like he was a ghost.

"I'm very pleased to meet you, Aunt Daisy."

Daisy held out her hand, and Harrison grasped it firmly. Contact with him seemed to revive Daisy. "Oh my goodness. Nice to meet you. Oh, Ivy, what am I supposed to call him?"

"Just call him Harrison. Don't you dare call him my lord, or everyone will think you've gone crazy, too."

"I can't believe you're really here. I mean, seeing your picture in those history books, and at the museum, and then to have you here in the living room . . ." Her voice trailed off.

"I know. It's all rather difficult for me as well."

"Are you hungry?"

"Yes, in fact."

"How about a nice big breakfast? And coffee? Do you drink coffee?"

"I do."

"Good. Good," she said, still beaming. He released her hand, and she hurried into the kitchen. Ivy smiled at Harrison through a stifled yawn.

"You want the bathroom first?" she asked.

"After you, m'lady."

* * *

Harrison watched her pad down the short hall like a sleepy child. He stood staring after her long after she'd disappeared.

"Lord Wyndham?"

The sound of Aunt Daisy's voice startled him out of his reverie. He turned to her, smiling down into her gentle upturned face.

"Just Wyndham," he corrected her. "Or Harrison, if you prefer."

"Oh, pooh," she said, her eyes wrinkling with pleasure. "Grant an old woman the pleasure of using a title. I've never met an earl before."

He dipped his head in acquiescence.

"I know time is short, and I wanted to talk to you, without Ivy."

Curious, he lifted a brow.

Her thin, pale skin flushed slightly. "Oh, my. You are a handsome man."

"Thank you," he said with a chuckle.

"She's afraid," Daisy said firmly, clasping her hands across her bosom in a maternal way.

"Afraid? Of changing my fate again, you mean?"

"That's part of it, of course, but not the reason she slept in the chair and you slept on the couch."

He didn't know what to say. She couldn't be implying they should have shared Ivy's bed. Could she?

"She's afraid she won't make you happy."

"She will, she does, make me happy. She's everything to me."

Daisy's eyes, so like Ivy's, misted. "And I believe you are everything to her, but she can't get past the fact that you're a rich earl and she's a middle-class grocery checker."

"Such things don't matter to me."

"It's easy for you to say that, if you'll pardon my rudeness. You were born to compliments and privilege. Not Ivy. You see, her whole life she's been a plain and gentle girl. Happy with the simple things. She's smart, mind you. Got straight A's in school, but she never found anything to aim her smarts at. She's searched, but nothing ever appealed. I understood her, but her schoolmates didn't. She was teased for being quiet, teased for being content. Teased for being an orphan, for living with an old aunt. Teased because she would rather spend time with me out in the garden than go to some mall or go water-skiing. Do you understand what I mean?"

He understood, although he didn't know what a mall was nor how one skied on water. He loved Ivy for the very reasons her schoolmates had once rejected her. Her simple joyfulness filled him with happiness. She didn't need castles and diamonds to be happy, and for that reason he wanted to shower her with them. She would appreciate the beauty of Wyndham, down to the lowliest buttercup.

"But what should I do?

"Make love to her," Aunt Daisy said, quite seriously. "You must make love to her. I know my Ivy. She's stubborn when she's afraid. The only way you'll convince her that you're sincere, and that your love will last, is to show her."

Harrison didn't know what to say. A light sweat broke out on his forehead.

"I can see I've embarrassed you," she said. "And I'm sorry, but it can't be helped. I would never say this to anyone I didn't believe truly loved my child, for I do think of her as my very own. And she loves you."

The sound of running water ceased. Daisy lowered her voice. "She's a virgin. So mind you're gentle with her. Now, I've got breakfast to make."

Harrison was so shocked, he could find no reply.

She stretched up and placed a motherly kiss on his cheek. "You're a dear man. I trust you. Don't let me down."

Daisy abandoned him for the kitchen just as the bathroom door opened and Ivy emerged.

She wore a white cotton sleeveless dress patterned with pale green tendrils of ivy. The collar was high on her neck, the bodice snug about her waist and ribs and the softly-flowing skirt stopped mid-calf.

She looked pure, sweet, virginal.

And he'd just been granted permission—no, given the order—to seduce her.

33

"You two go out and play," Daisy said, shooing them out the door an hour later. "I've got a house to clean, and then I'm off to meet the girls. There's a new movie with that Sherlock actor we want to see."

Harrison followed Ivy out of the house uneasily. He'd been behaving strangely ever since she'd come out of the shower this morning.

It was a clear, warm, breezy day. The sky overhead was a pure summer blue. They stood for a moment on the cement porch, inhaling the fresh sweet morning, the scent of dewy grass. Birds chirped merrily in the maple, and the leaves rattled softly in the wind.

She looked up at Harrison. His tanned features had an undertone of pale worry. "What's wrong?" she asked.

"I just realized that we must again climb into your horrible little motor car."

She laughed, relieved, and took his hand in hers, pulling him off the porch toward the carport. "I'm sorry. I promise to drive as sedately as the speed limit allows."

"I saw those posted limits. Couldn't we walk?"

"Nobody walks anymore, not the distance we have to go."

Hesitantly, Harrison allowed himself to be led. But he

stopped again, halfway across the yard, turning his face up to the blue sky. Ivy followed his gaze. A jet was on approach to Sea-Tac airport.

"That," she said with a touch of gloat in her voice, "Is what had you in a fit of laughter. That is a jet airplane."

He gaped adorably. "How far up is it? What size is it?"

"Well, it looks like a Boeing 747. I'm not very good at telling them apart, but the 747s are easy because the nose is like a bulb. And it's going to land at Sea-Tac Airport, so it's not very high right now, a couple thousand feet up I guess."

"A couple thousand feet! And it's still visible?"

"It's pretty big. Probably a few hundred people on board."

"Two hundred? Up there? Way up there?"

She took his arm and pulled him toward her car, laughing, happy, wanting to show him everything of her world.

"No, more like four hundred. Tell you what, we'll go downtown shopping, get you something to wear, do a bit of sightseeing, and then I'll take you to the airport. How does that sound?"

* * *

A few hours later, they were on their way to the modern wonder Ivy called the airport. They'd shopped in gleaming stores of a dozen floors, dined on fish at the waterfront while watching sailboats and incredible seaplanes and enormous barges loaded with freight in the busy bay. He'd seen his artwork on display at the Seattle Art Museum, and been struck dumb at the praise it had been given.

He'd grown nauseous when, after driving the vehicle into a cavernous low-ceilinged cement garage, Ivy proceeded to spiral around and around, up and up, until at last she found a vacant slip between two white lines, and stopped the car. He believed he hated parking garages.

Now, once more on the road in the passenger seat of Ivy's little motor car, Harrison knew he might look like a man of a new millennium in new denim trousers and blue T-shirt that felt like an undergarment, but he didn't feel like one. His knuckles were white as he gripped the armrests, and his neck ached from constant bracing for what he was sure was an imminent crash.

"I'm quite all right," he said. It was becoming his mantra.

He was unprepared for the volume of traffic on the roadways. Everyone was in a motorcar. There wasn't a single horse or carriage or streetcar to be seen, and he spied only one bicycle with a helmeted rider in clothing so tight he might have been naked, weaving in and out amongst the speeding vehicles. Harrison couldn't watch.

It was like Oxford Street multiplied a thousandfold. Miles and miles of business establishments. He found them all rather ugly. There weren't even any false facades to give the square functional buildings any sense of beauty. And signs were everywhere—enormous and small, flashing and steady, the clear and the vague. And telephone and electric wires and colored lights at the intersections that controlled the flow of traffic—which was staggering—overwhelmed the senses. It was a wonder modern people kept their sanity.

The sizes and shapes of the cars were also staggering,

from two-wheeled motorized bikes to great huge things Ivy called eighteen-wheelers with enormous trailers behind their thunderous engines. And Ivy—daredevil or fool, he knew not which—slid in and out of tiny spaces between these monstrous vehicles, like a little bird darting between the legs of an elephant. When he saw her flip the lever and heard the click-click-click of what he now knew to be a lighted turn signal, he covered his eyes and waited for it to be over. She never slowed to perform this dangerous stunt, rather she usually sped up. In one horrifying moment, he'd seen the little gauge register sixty-five miles per hour.

She took him on a tour of the Museum of Flight, leading him by hand past futuristic craft that had flown around the world and even into outer space. He'd been amazed, and incredulous. *It couldn't be real*, he'd kept saying. The things he saw could not possibly fly. They could not carry people safely as far and as fast as their signs boasted.

To prove to him that it was true, she drove them southward, and he glimpsed distant rows of giant aircraft before entering another cavernous garage, and she led him into the airport that gleamed with polished floors and modern steel. He saw crowds of passengers, flashing electric signs, and automatic circular belts that moved luggage for convenient pickup. What he didn't see were the airplanes.

"We can't get to that part of the airport without a ticket," she said. "Not since—" She bit her lip, her brow knit.

"Not since?"

"I'd rather not explain. But there is a place I know. Come on."

They got back into her little vehicle and drove a short

distance to a back road with trees on one side and a grass berm on the other, topped by a barbed wire fence. She parked on a gravel strip, and then said, "Up here." She climbed atop her car and sat on the roof, her legs dangling down the windshield. "Come on," she said. He gingerly climbed up beside her, hoping his weight wasn't denting the metal.

Once there, he understood why. He could now see over the berm, beyond the barbed wire, to a long black pavement on which the giant aircraft sat in a row.

And there, her hand clamped securely in his, the full force of his time travel hit. The nearest aircraft was one of those 747s she'd described. The engines hanging off the wings, where enormous fans whirled, were big enough for a man to stand in. The noise of the machine increased, grew from a whine to a full-blown roar, and then the craft began to move, rolling down the pavement, then racing, and then, impossibly, lifting off the ground. How could anything so huge rise up into the air? It could not be, and yet there it was, soaring.

He shook his head, emitting a gasp of awe and disbelief every few seconds as, one after another, the great planes roared to life and lifted off. "Incredible," he said, his voice lost in jet thunder. "Incredible!"

They sat there for nearly an hour before climbing back into her auto, where the sound was low enough for them to hear each another speak.

She beamed at him, and he bent to place a single tender kiss on her lips.

"Where do you want to go?" she asked, gazing at him

with those fabulous brown eyes that held his heart. How mad were these future people? How could they see Ivy O'Neal as plain, as lacking in any way?

"It's your city; you choose."

"No, I mean where in the country? In the world?"

"In the world? You don't mean you and I—" he pointed in the direction of the huge jets. "Get on board, and—" He pointed upwards. "Fly?" he whispered.

"No, not really. I'm sorry, Harrison, I shouldn't have teased you. Even today, some people are afraid to fly. I do wish I could take you on a flight, but you don't have any identification, and you can't fly without it."

"Thank heavens for that."

"Would you have gone, if we could have?"

"I would have tried. It's not every man who gets a chance to travel to the future and fly in such a machine."

"That's true. As far as I know, you're the only one."

"Do you know where I'd like to be?"

She shook her head, smiling into his eyes. They had so little time left, and while he'd enjoyed the tour she'd given him, he didn't want to spend any more time exploring. He wanted to spend his time in the one place in this future time that truly meant something to him. The one place where he could fill his mind and heart with memories he could cherish the rest of his life, however long that might be.

"Your home," he said, tracing a finger along her jaw. "I'd like to go home."

34

Harrison felt a comforting sense of relief when Ivy maneuvered her little motor car down the now familiar dead-end street in the quiet neighborhood.

She pulled into the covered drive and switched off the engine. The other motor car, Aunt Daisy's, was missing. Just as she'd said she would do, she had gone out. Harrison knew this should make him happy, for now he and Ivy could truly be alone. But, as he climbed out of the little car and gratefully stretched his legs, tugging at the denim trousers that he found a bit too snug to be altogether comfortable, he could only think that somewhere out there in the city, perhaps at a moving picture, a white-haired woman sat wishing him luck.

In the full light of day, he saw that Ivy's little cottage was kept in ship-shape order, not an easy task for two women on their own in this modern world with no servants or gardeners.

Ivy came round to him and took his hand. A soft gentle breeze danced in her dark hair. A bird sang. A dog barked. A motor car in the distance roared its engine, then droned away.

"You want to see the rest of the place? And by "rest" I mean the backyard."

He squeezed her hand. "Lead the way."

"Let's check my email first."

In the parlor, she opened her laptop machine and tapped away. Her quick intake of breath told him a response had been sent early. She looked at him with eyes that danced with anticipation, and he heard a gentle mechanical humming across the room. Paper slid out of another machine, and she held it up for them both to see. It was a death certificate. Not the real thing, it was black writing on white paper, and it looked somehow flatter than a real certificate. So this was a copy. A careful, well-schooled hand had filled in the details—the missionary's full name, his date of death, and the cause of death. Fatal injury consistent with wound inflicted by altered ammunition fired from a German Mauser.

Ivy pointed at the date the certificate was signed. "May 15, 1901."

"The missionary's body was moved from the battlefield grave two weeks after he died, long before I was put on trial."

She said, "And his body examined by a doctor in Johannesburg. The signature looks like *A. Meer*. Altered ammunition from a German Mauser—that's got to be proof. Your men weren't using those weapons or that type of ammunition. Right? Why didn't A. Meer say something to the British officials? Your trial was commonly known, wasn't it?"

He met her gaze. "I will ask *A. Meer* when I find him."

They didn't discuss all that his words implied, including the challenge of a supposedly executed military officer traveling to Johannesburg and the unlikelihood of finding A. Meer willing to cooperate. This proof that Kyle Fleming had not killed Reverend Schmidt, if he could go back and get it, might change his own fate. Or it might not.

Ivy returned to her machine and began typing. They sat on the couch, and Harrison watched as the screen changed rapidly, delivering information and images at an incredible speed. So much knowledge available to anyone, so quickly, was a miracle of science. Besides those enormous flying machines, it was the best invention he'd seen since arriving.

"Is that a newspaper?" he asked, as a familiar image appeared.

"The May 18th edition of the *Johannesburg Daily*. There's a mention of the church fire."

She did something on the keyboard and the article grew in size and became easier to read. *Incredible*, he thought for perhaps the hundredth time since he'd arrived in this future-world.

The fire occurred on May 17, two days after Reverend Schmidt's death certificate had been signed. Reverend Dr. Andries Meer, who saw to the "physical and spiritual needs" of his church members, "escaped harm as he'd been away, touring Amalgamated Mines."

Ivy looked at him and voiced what he was thinking. "Bribery. Kyle's father learned somehow about Reverend Schmidt's body being moved and he convinced Meer to tell no one about the true cause of death."

Her fingers flew again, and the next newspaper to appear on the screen was dated July 9, 1901. Ivy worked her magic to enlarge a sailing notice from the Cape. Dr. Andries

Meer was listed among passengers bound for America.

"He's running away. Probably with a lot of money. And a lot of guilt. Harrison," she looked at him with grave concern. "That's just four days away. You don't have much time to find him and convince him to tell the truth. They could exhume the body, but it's been nearly three months, and it's likely highly decomposed. I'm not sure what sort of forensic evidence would be left. There could still be some evidence in the remaining flesh, and certainly in the damage to bones, but I don't know if any doctor in Pretoria in 1901 would have the knowledge needed to testify with authority."

He shook his head. "How do you know all that?"

"I'm a big mystery reader."

"I will find him," he said with more confidence than he felt. "But not today. Today I intend to forget Africa and just be here, now, in this wondrous modern time, in your cozy cottage, with you." He folded the death certificate copy and tucked it into his back pocket. "How about that tour?"

She led him out through the kitchen door. The backyard was less than a half acre in size, enclosed and made private by a six-foot weathered fence, the gray slats butted one against the other. Trees were spaced evenly long the fence—a birch, a pine, a maple—their leaves all flush with summer green. At the back corner of the yard was a small rise, and atop this squatted the stump of some ancient enormous tree near a child's swing set of white metal tubing, rusting at the joints.

Ivy led him up the hill, then leapt atop the stump and posed majestically. "This is where I would play queen of the castle. The neighborhood kids would come over, and I would give them commands."

He laughed. "What sort of commands?"

"I would say, 'Fetch me an apple from the Miltons' yard!' and off they would go to steal me an apple." She leapt down, agile and light, and raced to the swings.

"And here's where I nearly tore off my finger when one of these chains broke and Daisy had to drive me to the emergency room." She bounced onto a swing, gave her legs a kick, then jumped off again, taking his hand. Her energy was contagious, and he felt like a child again, in this place she knew and loved so well.

"And here," she said, pulling him down the small hill to a stone enclosure surrounding a square patch of cement the size of a small room. There was a peeling red picnic table and bench, and a metal stove on spindly legs. "This is where we barbecue. When I was little and it got really hot out, I would drag out the lining of my old swimming pool and drape it over the stone and make a little lake. I'd fill it with the hose, and the water would warm in the sun. I once tried to make an ice skating rink in the winter, but it didn't freeze."

Harrison could imagine it all, little Ivy, running about this enclosed yard, happily playing, content, gleeful, her brown eyes lit with imagination as they were now. His own childhood came flooding back, the moments happy, carefree play, the blissful ignorance of things to come, of war and loss.

"Have I told you yet about the sheets?"

"No, what about them?"

She led him to the parallel clotheslines, now empty, a

few wooden pegs clinging to the lines.

"My very favorite memory of my parents happened right here. I was four."

She directed him to stand at one end of the line, between the poles, and she went to the other end, then turned around. "My mom and dad had hung the sheets earlier in the day, and they were almost dry, and they smelled clean and fragrant like Tide, which is a brand of laundry detergent. They were like a magic kingdom to me, those sheets. Wonderful, and white, and scary, too. It was like walking through thunderclouds. My mom stood at the end you're at, and my dad stood here. I was afraid to go through, but I wanted to so badly. My dad put his hands on my shoulders and said, *Go on Ivy, go through!* And my mom said, *Come on, baby, you can do it!* And then finally, I did. I closed my eyes and ran."

"Well," Harrison said to her. "Go ahead then. Close your eyes and run."

"But there aren't any sheets up."

"Come through anyway. I'll catch you."

Ivy stood hesitantly for a moment, staring at him. She'd forgotten those last words that her mother had said. *I'll catch you.* But Harrison had said them anyway, with all the love and promise her mother had given so very long ago. A chill tingled up her spine, and she rubbed the goose bumps on her arms.

He smiled invitingly, wriggling his outstretched fingers.

She lined herself up, spread her arms wide, closed her eyes, and ran.

He caught her up in his arms and twirled her around,

and they laughed and whirled until he grew too dizzy to go on.

He set her down gently, then bent and kissed her upturned face. She sank into his arms. Her hair smelled fresh and flowery, like Perky Shine shampoo. He held her close, rocking slightly, glad to be for this moment safe, with her, with his Ivy. He kissed the delicate warm place just below her ear, and thought perhaps it was the sweetest spot on earth.

He had never felt so completely at home.

She snuggled more deeply into him, and over the top of her head, he examined the small patch of garden in the other back corner of the yard. In neat rows there were bushy carrot tops, tomatoes still green on the vine, lettuce greens of various shapes and colors. Onions, broccoli, summer squash. Marigolds of orange and yellow made a border, and a trellis of green beans grew lushly along the fence.

His stomach growled.

She laughed softly, taking his hand again, and they crossed the dry trim grass, passing the empty clotheslines, entering the small house through the back door into the kitchen.

The tailless black cat greeted them with meows of admonishment.

"Hasn't Daisy fed you? Poor thing," Ivy said soothingly. The cat began to purr. Ivy put a handful of dry pellets into a bowl, and the cat attacked them as if they were mouse-flavored.

"Daisy's gone," Ivy said. She was now looking at a note attached to the electric icebox by means of a magnet. Of course, they'd known her aunt was gone. She'd said she was to see a moving picture as well; her motor car was not in the drive. But Harrison sensed Ivy meant something more, and again his conversation with Aunt Daisy came to him. He read the note.

Dear Ivy and Harrison,

The girls and I have decided to try our luck at an Arts and Crafts Antique Fair this weekend. It's in Anacortes, so we're driving up today and we'll be spending the night. I won't be home until Sunday. I filled the fridge and freezer with groceries. There's salmon to barbecue. You two enjoy yourselves. Time is precious, don't waste a minute of it.

Love,

Aunt Daisy

"Isn't she the sly one," Ivy said.

"She's left us unchaperoned," he said.

"The Anacortes Antique Fair was last weekend."

He could see in Ivy's eyes that she was thinking what he knew to be fact. That Aunt Daisy wanted them to be alone for one very intimate purpose.

"Well," Harrison said simply. How did one respond to such a gift from a progressive-minded aunt? One didn't just disrobe and have at it. In a way, she'd sort of dampened the entire thing with her generous blessing. How could he relax, knowing the aunt was out there thinking of him? Wishing him success?

Besides, as much as he wanted what the dear old gal demanded, this was not the right time or place. His future with Ivy was so uncertain. She was not like the sophisticated women he'd had brief entanglements with, women who wanted nothing more than an afternoon of pleasure to distract them from boredom. No. Ivy was different. What he felt for Ivy was different. This was not a dalliance. Taking things between them too far, without the promise, or at least the hope, of a future together, would not be fair to her. She was not his for the taking, despite dear Aunt Daisy's blessing. He would not hurt her for the world.

There seemed just one thing to do. "Shall we barbecue that salmon, then?"

* * *

Ivy cooked, and Harrison watched. She enjoyed being domestic with him, for him. Each small task filled her with a womanly sense of nurturing.

She dotted the fish with butter, chopped leaves of fresh basil, sprinkled salt and pepper, and cooked over white-hot coals on the barbecue out back. She made a salad of tender baby greens, grated carrot, cucumber and raw zucchini, all from the garden. She sliced sourdough bread and took butter from the freezer to soften.

They ate outside at the picnic table, a bottle of Australian white wine standing between them.

The day remained warm and breezy. The gusts tugged playfully at Harrison's T-shirt, and Ivy's eyes kept going to him, to his bronze hands, his broad shoulders, his haunting blue eyes.

Finished with their meal, they pushed their plates aside, put their elbows on the table, and talked. Soon, their hands were entwined, and they were lost in each other's eyes.

The laughter of children carried on the wind. Ivy told Harrison tales of her childhood, of growing up without parents, without siblings. Happy, a bit lonely, always loved.

Harrison talked of Wyndham, of the days before his father had died in India when Harrison was just eighteen. He talked of family celebrations, Christmastime when the village below the manor house had been like a wonderland, full of frosty white snow and sparkling candles and boughs of holly.

Ivy sighed, wishing she could see his home. "I don't remember much about my parents," she said. "But the few memories I have are vivid and very happy. Playing here in the backyard. Hanging clothes on the line with my mom. Dad on the Slip 'N Slide, face first."

"A slip and slide?"

"A long sheet of plastic. You hose it down, then take a flying run, throw yourself on it and go sliding to the end. It's great fun. And the teepee. Wow. I haven't thought of that in ages."

He lifted his brows. "Teepee?"

She smiled broadly. "Come on."

The sun had dropped below the horizon, and the sky was ablaze with reddish pink when they finished putting up the teepee.

Not a toy or kit, it was a genuine Native American teepee, though a relatively modern one, made of canvas not skins, which Ivy's mom had purchased at a reservation. It was kept in the carport, high up in the rafters. The poles were as long as the shed and difficult to get down. The canvas was rolled into a huge sausage. Together, they carried it to the backyard.

Once up, it was a beautiful familiar sight against the red sky. Her mom had set up the teepee every summer. Daisy had continued the tradition until her aching joints could no longer manage the poles, when Ivy had been about twelve. The sight of it standing once more in the backyard triggered all sorts of vague but deep warm emotions in Ivy.

Without actually discussing what they were doing, they began filling the teepee with comforts. They covered the rough grass floor with several surplus army blankets. Then came two sleeping bags, one a plush modern red nylon with warm plaid flannel lining, and the other, a thin faded yellow bag decorated with "Winnie the Pooh" and his pot of honey.

She produced his feather pillow, the one he'd tossed through the lights to see if they were really there, then found a battery-operated lantern, a flashlight, her mother's donut-shaped radio.

Standing in the kitchen, the only light coming from the small stove bulb, Ivy at last looked at Harrison.

His dimple deepened with the sexiest smile she'd ever seen.

Audrey sat on her haunches before the screen door.

"She prowls at night," Ivy explained. Harrison pressed open the door, and Audrey slipped outside.

He attempted to thrust his hands into his pockets, but the pockets of the jeans he wore could not be thrust into easily, so snugly did they hug his hips, so he crossed his arms and shrugged, smiling awkwardly. "Well, looks like we're all set."

Neither one of them moved.

"More wine?" she asked.

He seemed to consider this, then shook his head. "No. I don't want a cloudy mind, not tonight. I want to remember every single detail of every single minute I spend with you."

His words melted her. But still, she didn't move. They both knew why they were hesitating in the kitchen.

"We're being cowards," Ivy said.

"Nonsense," he said, but his eyes gleamed with agreement. "What say we look at that television again?"

"No," Ivy said firmly. She wasn't going to spend her precious moments watching him watch TV. "This is silly. Come on." She marched outside, and Harrison followed, closing the door behind him. The air was cool, the stars twinkled faintly, competing with the suburban lights and waning moon.

Ivy ducked under the teepee flap. It was almost pitch black inside. She switched on the lantern, which gave just enough light to keep them from tripping.

"Mind if I take off my shoes?" Harrison asked politely.

"Not at all, my lord," she answered with a bow. She kicked off her shoes, then switched on her donut-shaped radio. It was already tuned to her favorite oldies station.

She'd positioned the sleeping bags in the center of the teepee so that they could see the sky through the open flap at the top. They lay in each other's arms, staring up. As their eyes adjusted, and the night deepened, the stars grew brighter. They didn't speak at first, but the silence between them was comfortable.

He wondered aloud about the position of the stars on this side of the world, and more than a hundred years from his own home. They talked of stars and space, the wonderful things mankind was capable of, and they avoided mentioning the terrible, although they both wondered if lasting and universal peace on earth was possible. When "A String of Pearls" began to play on the little radio, the familiar and cherished melody was more than Ivy could bear.

Her tears came so suddenly, she couldn't fight them. Harrison held her close as visions of the movie about Glen Miller played in her mind. She heard the bombs of war explode amidst the notes, saw Mrs. Miller sitting by the radio, listening to her husband's music, the telegram announcing his death clutched in her hand. Oh, how had Mrs. Miller lived without her precious Glen? How had she carried on?

How would she go on without Harrison?

"Hush now," Harrison whispered. "It's all right. I'm here,. I'm here."

At last, the song ended and another melody began to play, a slow and romantic instrumental.

Harrison held her face in his palms, and then he traced her brows and placed a kiss there, and he traced the bridge of her nose and placed a kiss there. He moved to her wet cheeks, her lips.

"I've longed to do that from the very first moment I saw you," he whispered huskily. He pulled back and looked into her eyes. "We have to discuss what's to happen next."

It was like coming home. A filling up of her soul. Gazing into his eyes, an energy began to trickle through her veins. He was life, he was love, he was everything. Nothing else mattered. Nothing mattered but keeping him safe.

"I've been in love with you, Ivy, since the first time I ever saw your face."

Ivy's vision blurred with tears. "Ever I saw," she corrected him, her voice thick with emotion.

"Pardon?"

"It's *The First Time Ever I Saw Your Face*," she said slowly, reaching up to stroke his cheek. "It's one of my favorite songs. It's about that moment when you first see someone who takes your breath away, and you just know. Your heart knows."

"That they're the one."

"Yes." Her throat was so tight with tears, she could barely speak. She turned her face to the stars.

"Ivy, your aunt said you were afraid."

"Did she?" She sniffed and took an unsteady breath. "Afraid of what?"

"Of trusting us. Trusting that what we have is real. Forever. Trusting that I mean what I say and that I will never stop loving you."

She looked into his eyes. "Daisy said all that?"

"Yes, and more."

"Uh oh. What's the more?"

"I've been given orders to prove my love. Now. Tonight."

"She didn't," Ivy laughed, embarrassed and touched.

"She did." He was smiling, too, but his eyes were very serious.

"Are you going to carry out those orders?"

He kissed her tenderly, quickly. Then pulled away and said, "No."

Her heart twisted. "No? Why not?"

"Because we haven't discussed what is to happen next."

Her jaw was tight when she said, "Next, we get you back to your time so you can save yourself and your family."

"I mean what's next for us. Ivy, I want you with me forever."

She couldn't speak.

"Marry me."

Her heart leapt.

"Sorry. I didn't mean that to sound like a demand. Now it's me who's afraid. I'm afraid you will say no, but here goes. Will you? Will you do me the honor of becoming my wife, now and forever?"

Before she could answer, he hurried on, "I know it would mean leaving your aunt, and leaving this modern world and the home you love. I know you might find yourself a widow all too soon. I understand it may be too much to ask."

A gust of wind fluttered the canvas. It snapped and billowed, such a wonderful familiar sound, like the sheets on a clothesline, and Ivy felt a ghostly pair of strong hands on her shoulders, giving her a gentle push. She heard the echo of a loving voice whisper, *You can do it, Ivy. You can do it.*

She cleared her throat and found her voice. "Yes."

He smiled, and his eyes welled with tears. He stroked her face tenderly with trembling fingers. "Ivy, you will be giving up everything you've ever known."

"I won't be giving up you. I can manage without the rest."

"You don't need time to think about it?"

She bit her lip, shaking her head. Then she took a deep breath. "I love you."

He looked relieved. "That's the first time you've ever said so."

"I know. If you ruffle my hair, I'll hit you." She knew he didn't understand, but it didn't matter. What they had was forever. "I love you," she said again because it felt so wonderful to say. She wanted to say it again. A million times. But she decided that might be overdoing it.

"I don't suppose there is a way in this modern world of yours for us to get married right away? Tonight?"

"There are a few places, like Las Vegas, where people can get married on the spot, but not without some form of identification."

"Identification again? That is terribly disappointing."

"I agree. I would love to run off to Vegas and get married by an Elvis impersonator."

"You're talking nonsense, I believe."

"The modern world is full of nonsense. But what about your old-fashioned world? I won't have identification there."

"Not a problem. As far as I know, you simply claim to be yourself and no one asks for proof unless challenged. Pepper can vouch for you."

"How wonderfully simple and trusting. Now," she said, propping herself up on her elbow to look at him with more authority. "About that order."

"Dear Aunt Daisy's order?" he asked, his eyes teasing.

"Yes. Now that we've discussed what's to come next for us, is complying allowed?"

"The order was given with the understanding that compliance was the only way for you to overcome your fear. Now that we've established our love is mutual and eternal, it hardly seems necessary."

She rolled onto him and pinned his shoulders down. "It wouldn't be right for you to second guess an order, Captain."

"No, you're right. I'm duty sworn."

A long time passed before they gazed at the stars again.

35

On Sunday afternoon, they went into the house, hand in hand, beaming, to greet Daisy as she walked through the front door. Her eyes misted with tears, but her face was joyful and sly with complete understanding, except for one question. *Which world, his or hers?*

"His," Ivy said, and Daisy said, "Good," but she pulled Ivy into her arms and for a moment, they both gave in to tears. Daisy pulled herself together first. "Enough blubbering, my dear," she said. "We've got planning to do. When do you leave?"

Ivy and Harrison both answered, but with different replies.

"Tonight," Ivy said.

"In a few weeks," Harrison said.

Ivy turned to him. "What do you mean, a few weeks? We have to go as soon as possible."

"I must go tonight. You must not. We don't know where those lights will take me when I leap."

For a moment, Ivy's thoughts swirled with possibilities. The prison? The field where he was to be shot? Then a thought occurred to her, and she slapped her hand over her mouth with a gasp. He could leap through the lights directly into a closed, buried coffin.

"No," he said firmly as if reading her horrific thought. He took her shoulders. "No. I can't possibly be found where I never was. The history books say I disappeared. No bones, remember? I'll likely find myself where I last was, on the execution field outside the prison. Or nearby. It will surely be somewhere nearby, which means it will not be a suitable place for my wife to also appear. Even without those complications, between poisonous snakes, deadly tigers, and horrible fevers, South Africa is not a safe place. You'll join me in England as soon as I can get this mess straightened."

"Oh, Harrison, I promise not to touch any snakes, or leap in front of any tigers, and I won't go swimming ever again in the Limpopo River."

"No, you won't, because I won't give you a chance. Have you forgotten about Carter? Fleming has killed at least one innocent man in his attempt to stall the war. If he's discovered how much you know about his plans—no. We're going to do this right, and I'm taking no chances. You will wait here with your aunt and join me as soon as your history books say I'm safely back in England and not a minute sooner."

"But—" she began, but both Harrison and Daisy cut her off.

"No buts!" They said in unison.

With the two of them gazing at her with so much love and authority, how could she dare disagree? But the decision sat uncomfortably in her mind and tightened with an eerie cold around her heart.

36

"Climb up," Ivy whispered as she ducked into the checkstand and reached for the switch. The Pig Palace was empty except for the night crew, now out of sight down the aisles. Rock-n-roll blared, cans slammed onto shelves, the pallet jack's motor echoed.

Harrison, dressed in his khaki and boots, climbed onto the black conveyor belt, but before Ivy could flip the final switch, he bent over, grasped her face, and kissed her fiercely.

She inhaled his breath, felt his strength, his life force. He pulled away and stared into her eyes, as if memorizing her, and whispered, "I'll love you forever."

They'd already said their good-byes, and had agreed to do this as quickly, as painlessly, as possible.

"Oh, Harrison, this isn't good-bye. Can't I go with you now, please?"

"No, it's not safe. Come to me only when it's safe."

He straightened, and she flipped the switch. The squealing burst into a spray of swirling lights. The dark center void whisked aside, revealing a dark, gloomy space. For a flash she feared it was a coffin, but quickly she realized it was a room.

"It looks like my cell," he said.

The muscles in Ivy's neck and back tightened painfully with a wave of apprehension. "Maybe you should wait."

"No," he said firmly. "The sooner I do this, the sooner we can be together again. Wish me luck."

"Oh, Harrison," she began, reaching out to tug him back, but he'd already stepped into the lights. Without a backward glance, he vanished as the lights flashed blindingly.

Then the lights disappeared, and Ivy numbly shut off the scanner.

She stood cold and unmoving for a moment. Why his cell? Why darkness? It should be eleven in the morning in South Africa. She tried to picture Harrison dropping to the floor of that cell and lying still, feigning unconsciousness until he was found.

He'd planned to claim all ignorance of the passage of time. He planned to say he remembered hearing the shots, and then nothing. Would they believe him? What would happen now? Would they find Dr. Meer? If not, would they exhume Reverend Schmidt's body and try to determine what sort of bullet killed him?

Trembling, she dug her fingers into her pocket and pulled out a crumpled SAM brochure. Her hands were cold as ice, shaking uncontrollably, her heart beating in her throat.

"Please, please, please," she prayed in a whisper.

As she opened the brochure, the words leapt about in her unsteady hands, and she had to brace herself against the checkstand to hold them steady.

. . . Wyndham was executed on July 5, 1901 . . .Ivy

choked, a hand flying to her breast. No! It couldn't be. The brochure should have changed! Why hadn't it changed! She stared at the sentence, willing it to change. But the words stayed stubbornly solid and steady. July 5. She closed the brochure, counted to ten, then twenty.

She opened the brochure again.

Wyndham was executed on July 5, 1901.

"No," she hissed. "He returned on the seventh. He was alive on the seventh. He had the information to save his life. Tell them, Harrison! Tell them about Rainbow's End, about the Flemings' plot, Provisions Corp!"

She glared furiously at the brochure, but nothing changed.

What was the stupid brochure telling her? That he'd actually leapt back to July 5th? That he returned to his day of execution?

But that couldn't be! He'd left Africa on July 5th and come to her, here, which was the Fourth of July because of the nine-hour time difference. Two whole days had passed. He'd found the truth about his conviction. He'd returned to Africa on the morning of July 7, 1901. He must have. That's how the scanner lights worked between their worlds—that's how they had always worked before.

With the swiftness of a racing bullet, she knew. "No," she gasped. "No. No. No!" She slumped to the floor, hardly able to breathe.

The twenty minutes. Her watch, set to Pretoria time, had read 7:20 when he'd come forward. But Harrison said the clock tower in Pretoria had chimed seven. Which meant twenty minutes had been missing between their times.

They'd noticed it, but they hadn't seen the importance.

Backwards.

She should have seen it. The portal was going backwards! Whatever that greedy CRC repairman had done when he fixed the scanner, he'd altered the lights. He'd changed their nature. Time was no longer parallel with 1901 and going forward. Time was slipping backwards and Harrison was dead, gone. But how could that possibly be! If he'd leapt to a time in which he already existed, he would have met himself in that cell, and that was impossible! Or potentially catastrophic. All the time travel theory books said so. Meeting yourself in another time was the worst thing that could ever happen to you. But why?

Why?

She read the brochure thoroughly.

It seemed that Harrison had not argued with his guard when he returned and found himself in his prison cell. He'd not demanded to see his attorney or raised any sort of a fuss, but had meekly, dutifully, marched to the execution chair.

It was as if Harrison—the Harrison who had just left the Pig Palace—had never arrived in that cell. He'd stepped into a space in which he already existed, and there had been no explosion, no earth-shattering ripping of the time continuum. The meeting had been quiet and breathless and instantaneous. He'd stepped through the lights and vanished.

Ivy exhaled a long, fearful breath.

The Harrison who'd come to her, who had held her all night in the teepee, who had overwhelmed her with his deep, patient love—that Harrison had ceased to exist.

It was as if he'd never come forward at all.

And now he'd gone backwards. Too far backwards.

The thought swirled through her mind like a dust storm. Blurry and muddled and hopeless. And then a clear thought stepped out of the dust.

The lights were moving time backwards!

A burst of hope exploded through Ivy's veins.

She shot up from the floor, and ran.

* * *

"But Ivy, you promised Harrison you wouldn't go to South Africa." Daisy, in her thick purple robe, her white hair rolled into prickly curlers, poured Ivy a cup of steaming tea, then poured another for herself before settling down at the dining table.

Ivy, too, was in her bathrobe. The drapes were drawn against the night; the house was quiet. Audrey meowed from somewhere in the backyard, then was silent.

Ivy needed Daisy to understand, but she felt herself growing frantic. "I didn't know then that time was moving backwards, don't you see?"

"But must you go so soon? Tomorrow night, Ivy, dear? Can't you think about it?"

"No, Daisy. No. That first time Harrison jumped, there were just twenty minutes difference in our time lines. Tonight it was two whole days. It's not staying consistent. I've got to go before time backs up too far, don't you see? If I wait too long, I could—" Ivy stopped herself from saying stop existing. There was no reason to add more worry to Daisy's shoulders. The chance of her leaping to those few days she'd actually been in Africa—well, she wouldn't think about it.

But Daisy was not stupid. She understood what had happened to Harrison. "Ivy, honey, no."

"You're right. No. No, it will not happen. I was only there a few days. The odds are very good I won't meet myself. But don't you see that I must go as soon as I can? I don't know how quickly time is falling back. If I wait too long, I could end up anywhere, any time. What if I end up in a time before Harrison is even born? I have to go to him before too much time escapes, before I lose him forever."

Daisy nodded solemnly, her hands clasped so tightly her thick knuckles were a purplish white. Her pale blue eyes swam with tears, and they went to the paperwork before Ivy. "What are you doing?"

Ivy had spread the dining table with bank card receipts and statements. "I'm getting my things in order, insurance and all that."

"Ivy, I don't care about that."

"I'm not going to leave you with a bunch of paperwork. I just want to simplify my going."

"Oh, Ivy, this all sounds so final."

Ivy turned from the statements to take Daisy's hands, gently tugging them from their worried grip. They were cold, the skin papery soft. "You know I don't want to leave you. But I have to go to Harrison."

"I know. It just won't be the same without you."

"You've been the best mom in the world to me."

"And I couldn't have asked for a better daughter."

Daisy opened her arms, and Ivy got out of her chair,

knelt before Daisy and fell into her secure embrace. Daisy rocked her gently, pressing kisses to her hair.

"You will be all right, when I'm gone, won't you?"

"As long as I know you're with Harrison."

"I love him so much."

"I know you do, baby."

Daisy gave her a final squeeze, then released her, and Ivy climbed back into her chair.

"Here," she said, wiping her eyes. She handed over the signed will she'd downloaded from the Internet.

Daisy turned horribly pale. Her mouth trembled, and her stricken eyes flooded again.

"Eventually, you'll need it. At first you can just say that I've moved, but eventually you'll need this. There's a little money in my retirement. It's yours."

"But Ivy, what if you fail? Shouldn't I keep turning on the scanners for you, just in case?"

"I won't fail!" Ivy shouted, then instantly regretted her outburst. Daisy wiped at her eyes, pressing her lips into a tight, white, trembling line.

"I'm sorry. It's just that I can't fail."

"But you know I can't just sit here, afraid you want to come back. I'll go into the store every so often, and turn them on just in case."

Ivy nodded. "Read the museum brochures and the history books. They will tell you if I need you to keep the scanners on." But she couldn't fail, she couldn't. If only she didn't have to leave Daisy. "Oh, Daisy, I know! Come with me! Come with me and—"

Daisy shook her head. "Oh no, dear. I couldn't."

"Why not? It would be so much better if we could stay together."

"As much as I'll miss you, Ivy, I can't go with you. I'm too old and stuck in my ways. I belong here, in this time. You belong with Harrison, wherever and whenever he is. You go to him. I knew you'd leave the nest someday. I just never knew it would be to fly so far away."

Daisy was crying again, but she nodded firmly. "Go to him, Ivy. He needs you. But remember, you can always come back to me."

"Maaaaarow!" Audrey's plaintive howling made them both smile.

"How much you wanna bet she's on the door again?" Ivy said, wiping her eyes. "Come on."

They rose, stepped into the dim kitchen, and there was Audrey, clinging with sharp claws to the narrow window near the top of the door, her glowing eyes staring in at them.

"Silly cat," both Ivy and Daisy said. Ivy opened the door and rescued Audrey, and the cat sat purring in Ivy's cradled arms, tickling her chin with a wet nose. The night was cool and damp. The waning moon winked in and out of racing high clouds.

"A storm's brewing," Daisy said.

They stood in the doorway, smelling the air, feeling the night wind tug at their bathrobes, listening to Audrey's deep rumbling purr.

The empty clotheslines shivered in the wind, making a snapping sound as the lines tugged against the metal posts.

"Do you think this has something to do with them?" Ivy asked softly.

"I was just wondering the same thing myself. It is odd that only you and Harrison can see and hear those lights."

"They're real. I mean, they exist and not just inside our minds. The scanners make them, I'm sure of it. But it does seem like we're being guided, somehow. That we've been given this ability to see what others can't. Just Harrison and me. Just us."

"Your mom and dad loved you so much. It's a comfort to me to think they're looking after you. I don't feel so much like I'm sending you off all alone."

37

Ivy parked her little blue Honda in the Pig Palace parking lot under the glow of the neon pink pig. She climbed out, feeling slightly foolish, dressed in a turn-of-the century tailored suit with a flared skirt and fitted jacket. It was fashionable yet the fabric serviceable, vintage 1903. The most historically accurate she could find in such a short time. It had cost her a fortune on eBay, with overnight shipping, but she would appear grand enough, yet practical enough, to be the wife of an earl, recently arrived in South Africa.

She shut the car door, then ran her fingertips over the edge of the smooth metallic roof. A faithful friend the car had been. She locked the keys in the car. Daisy had the spare and would come by later to drive the car home.

She tied the strings of a wide-brimmed sun hat about her neck, and let the hat hang down her back. On her feet were black leather button boots, and in a tapestry satchel she carried a pair of new kid gloves, a white cotton nightgown, a change of cotton underthings (new, but as simple as she could find them), a handkerchief, a flask of water, a tin of sardines (minus the wrapper), and some dried fruit wrapped in a cloth. Along with Harrison's revolver, she carried a fresh box of .38 cartridges because she had no idea in what situation she might land. Money had proved the most difficult. She'd found online, in an 1899 issue of the *Ladies' Home Journal*, an article with tips for Americans traveling to England, but its suggestions for securing spending money proved impossible for her. She couldn't have her bank send a letter of credit to a bank in the past, and the cost of purchasing a quantity of old English or American coins and paper notes were far beyond her means as they were now collector items. She ended up purchasing a few precious old English coins to get her by when she first arrived, and she put the rest of her meager savings into five very worn American 1899 gold coins, each with a face value of twenty dollars. They had cost her nearly two thousand dollars each. The value of the gold in them was valued at around eleven hundred dollars apiece, but when she arrived in 1901, they would be worth only twenty, for that was the price per ounce of gold then. It had shocked her to learn how much their value would drop once she leapt through the lights, but when she googled the cost of living in 1901, she learned that their total value of one hundred American dollars was a respectable monthly wage. She felt good knowing she had money that wouldn't be questioned and should be fairly easily traded.

With a determined though unsteady breath, she marched across the parking lot, unable to keep a grin from spreading wide across her face. It was a grin of excitement, of nerves, of complete frazzled uncertainty.

The Pig Palace doors swished open and she strode in, ready to explain her strange outfit to the night-crew with a lie about going to a costume party.

But there was nobody there to question her. Rock-n-roll music played, and from the depths of the aisles she heard Danny singing along. There wasn't a customer in sight.

She ran from one checkstand to another, flipping on the scanners.

As she raced around the belt of checkstand eight, she came to a screeching halt.

There, open on the belt in checkstand nine, was a CRC briefcase. And in the customer lane, a shopping cart held assorted computer parts, bits of wire, nuts and screws. Footsteps clomped down the break room stairs as she stood gaping, and a CRC technician, the same tech who'd been here on the Fourth of July repairing lane nine, appeared and headed toward her, carrying a steaming mug of coffee.

Ivy's heart went to her throat. "What's wrong?" she asked.

He looked at her warily, as if remembering how weird she'd been on the Fourth, how she'd nagged him relentlessly, how she'd climbed onto a checkstand and screamed.

"Nothing's wrong," he said cautiously. His narrowed eyes scanned her outfit. "Costume party?"

"Then why are you here? Why are all those spare parts in that cart?"

"Calm down. It's just a power module."

"Is the scanner working?"

"The scanner's working. The power module's not. It keeps smoking."

"But you fixed it, right? It's working now?"

He took a step away from her, moving to his briefcase, before saying, "No. It's not fixed. I don't have the right part here. I'll have to order it."

"How long will that take?"

"A week. Maybe two."

"Two weeks!" By then the lights might send her back to the dinosaur age! "I don't believe you! Fix it now!"

He set down his coffee, slapped his briefcase closed, snatched it up in both hands, turned on his heel, and hurried off toward the doors.

"Wait," Ivy called, running after him.

He didn't wait. After one last look over his shoulder at her, he sprinted off and didn't stop until he was in his car, squealing out of the parking lot.

Ivy hurried back into the store to checkstand nine and flipped on the scanner switch. Nothing happened. The scanner remained perfectly still and silent.

She raced around to the customer lane, and shoved the part-laden cart out of her way, then unlatched the service panel, got down on her hands and knees, and peered inside.

She saw a large flat computer component, another box-shaped one, and dozens of wires. Dust balls and other nasty stuff littered the floor. A crusty cheese puff, two shriveled grapes. An unidentifiable fuzzy glob. Didn't they clean under here when they installed the new equipment?

She heard the front doors swish open, and she froze. She heard feet pass by and disappear down an aisle.

"Power module, power module," she muttered, sticking her head deep inside, trying to read the labels in the semi-darkness. A bit of color caught her eye—a bright orange switch, far in the back. Above it was a peeling label that said simply, *Power.*

She stretched, but couldn't reach it. The walls of the small space pressed around her, but she crawled inside anyway.

If that creepy repair guy could fit, so could she.

Straining, her fingertips met the switch. She flipped it up and felt a click. She heard the machinery just above her head surge with a whine, and the small space flooded with red scanner light.

Yes!

Hastily, she backed out, scraping her arms and head as she went. She shot to her feet and turned toward express lane four.

Nothing. No swirling lights. No high pitched whining.

She uttered a word she'd never said before, then dropped to her knees again and crawled back inside.

The red light reflected from the scanner above now revealed an innocent-looking knob with an arrow.

She turned the knob, and a small trickle of smoke lifted from a metal box near her palm. She cocked her head, listening. No whine yet.

Smoke trickled more thickly now, stinking like burnt rubber.

She twisted the knob as far as it would go, and sparks flew from the small metal box. She backed out so quickly, she tore her sleeve on an exposed screw.

But her ears were greeted with a wonderful painful squeal, and the magical lights were exploding and swirling above lane four, brighter and faster and more intense than ever before.

She ran, snatching up her satchel. She scrambled up onto the belt before the lights and waited breathlessly. The smoke was heavy now, and sparks sizzled from lane nine; the red scanner lights spun crazily, sending red beams dancing.

The flash and opening of the time-window came so brightly it temporarily blinded her. She couldn't see where or when the lights would take her.

A voice somewhere in the store shouted, "Fire!"

She was out of time. It was now or never.

She jumped.

38

Ivy fell to the ground, still blinded. Her palms hit wet grit. She smelled rain. She heard voices, foreign yet familiar, chattering and laughing. She heard the clip-clop of hooves on hard surfaces, the crunch and rattle of wheels, the hum of a busy city.

She blinked rapidly, stood too quickly, and became a little dizzy. She had to drop her head to steady herself.

When the dizziness passed, and her vision fully cleared, she saw first her vintage shoes looking up at her from stone pavement. The damp pavement damp sparkled in sunshine, and little clouds of steam rose. The shadows on the pavement formed huge curving arcs that looked like cathedral windows. Slowly, Ivy lifted her head until she was looking at a massive iron tower.

Not South Africa. Not England. She was in Paris, staring at the Eiffel Tower.

"Harrison!" she shouted, and his name lifted up and echoed on the rising steam.

Around her, voices hushed, movement paused.

Ivy dropped her gaze to the crowd, not really seeing them as she searched for just one beloved face. She followed the patterns of light on the damp pavement, calling Harrison's name, searching the faces, until she was in full sunshine. She turned and tilted her head far, far back, until she was looking nearly a thousand feet up to the top of the Tower.

Sunshine streamed through the wrought iron latticework of the enormous structure, shifting and blinking as huge puffy clouds raced across a lovely blue sky. What was the date? The year? Where was Harrison?

She lowered her gaze to eye level, and for the first time really looked at the crowd—Parisians and tourists, the men in fancy dress suits and silk top hats, the women in bustled dresses and flowery hats, carrying lacy parasols. Turn of the century, definitely. She put a hand to her racing heart and felt its *thud-thud-thud* under her palm.

She turned quickly in a full circle, calling, "Harrison? Harrison!" She was answered with wary glances, and people nearby hurried to pass.

If the scanners behaved as they always had, then Harrison could be no more than twelve feet away. "Harrison! Where are you?"

Her breath caught—a uniform! But no, the soldier turned; he was too young, too short. She turned full circle again, searching.

"Harrison!"

"*Mademoiselle? Pardon? Mademoiselle?*" The voice was elderly, thick. "Hallo, American lady!" Ivy turned in the direction of the voice. Along the leafy green edge of the wide boulevard she saw the vendor, a bookseller, beckoning to her.

She waited as a shiny omnibus passed along the broad avenue, the horses' hooves clacking on wet pavement stones, then she crossed to the awning-covered book stall. The vendor was a very small man. His bald head gleamed in the winking sun; his aged and wrinkled face smiled pleasantly.

"I don't speak French," she said. "Do you speak English?"

"Yes, *mademoiselle.* Can I help you? I hear you shouting. You are looking for someone, no?"

"I am looking for someone, yes. A soldier. A captain. Harrison? Lord Wyndham?"

The vendor's mouth pursed as he shook his head and shrugged his shoulders. "This man, I do not know. There are many soldiers in Paris. He will perhaps be here later? Everyone, they come to see the Eiffel Tower. You buy a book, yes? It will pass the time while you wait. What sort of book do you like? A love story, perhaps?"

Ivy looked around again, searching the faces. The wind was warm and sweet. Blustery and full of promise. The clouds seemed eager to run away and leave nothing but blue and sunshine.

The shadow of the Eiffel was patterned like lace over the swarming tourists and carriages. Along the wide avenues leading from the Tower, lush green trees waved freshly opened leaves, and the fragrance of white and pink blossoms sweetened the air. Where was he? He had to be here; he had to be!

She turned quickly to the vendor. "What day is it? I've been traveling, I've lost track."

"The day? It is Tuesday. April the 2nd. You are American, no?"

April? "Yes. I am. Do you sell newspapers?"

"Ah, *oui.*" He handed her a slim paper. It was, of course,

in French. But the year was printed numerically. 1901! Still, blessedly, 1901! April 2, 1901. One month before the battle in South Africa that would lead to Harrison's court-martial. Harrison was here, now, in Paris, on leave. From March 21st until April 3rd. Until tomorrow.

"I'll take this," she said, indicating the newspaper, "and a book," she added on a whim. "Do you have a children's book of fairy tales? One with illustrations?"

"Aah, *oui.* I have just the thing. Classic tales. Now, where did I—ah, here it is." He handed her the small leather-bound volume. "There is a tale in here I find especially delightful. It is all about three little pigs . . ."

She looked over her shoulder as he spoke, searching, so afraid she would miss him in the crowd. A uniform! British, khaki, the size, the shoulders, the gait, all familiar. But he was heading away from her.

"Oh, here," she said, digging into her satchel for the few English coins. "I'm sorry, that's all the money I have."

"No problem, Mademoiselle. English money is good in Paris." He adroitly palmed the coins and smiled at her, offering no change.

She spun around and ran. "Harrison! Wait!"

She pushed past sedately strolling couples, dodged a horse-drawn taxi, then raced under the dappled light of the Eiffel.

"Harrison!"

The soldier stopped and turned around, brows lifted, mouth tilted in a curious smile. Ivy's heart plummeted to her toes. Blond, yes. Tall and lean, yes. But Harrison? No. It wasn't him. She waved away the confused soldier, apologizing, "I'm sorry. Never mind. I thought you were somebody else."

"Pity I'm not," he answered with a nod, then turned from her and continued on his way.

Ivy took a deep breath, pressing the book of fairy tales to her heart. *Think*, she chanted to herself. *Think, think, think!* It was April 2, 1901. Harrison was on leave from Africa. He was here somewhere.

She must try to be calm. She had time now. Not much time, but some. The trial had not happened yet. Fleming hadn't filed any reports against Harrison yet. Reverend Schmidt hadn't been shot yet.

And Harrison had not yet seen Ivy hovering in magical sparkling lights.

Ivy's mouth slowly dropped open. She felt the fingers of her left hand. No ring. She wasn't wearing Harrison's ring. He'd not yet given it to her. Everything that had been his was still his. She opened the satchel. His gun was gone. Here, in April, the events which would put those things in her possession had not yet taken place. She had no idea why everything else hadn't vanished, but then it made no sense that she was here either. And this was not the time to ponder the paradoxical nature of time travel. She needed to find Harrison.

Think!

The air was so sweet, so full of steaming beams of sunshine. She needed to calm her mind to think, so she closed her eyes and tilted her face into a beam that pierced the lacy tower architecture. *Harrison, where are you? I'm here!*

Her eyes flew open, and for a moment sunlight danced

before her like the scanner lights. Harrison had no idea she even existed.

This was Harrison's world before everything.

Before everything.

Before the scanner lights, before he painted her portrait, before her trek across the African bush. Before the snake and the officer's dinner and the crocodiles and Oom Peter. She'd gone through all of that for nothing. For absolutely nothing.

None of it had happened anymore.

Suddenly, she felt sick. She stumbled out from under the Tower, down a broad tree-lined boulevard, and when she spied a black wrought iron park bench in a dappled patch of sun, she collapsed. The book of fairy tales fell open on her lap, and three pink pigs smiled up at her.

He didn't know her.

He didn't love her.

Tourists wandered by as she sat, staring forlornly. Americans, Germans, Italians. There were many English soldiers in their regimentals about town, on leave from South Africa and India. None of them were Harrison.

Why? Her brain shouted over and over. Why? Why had she been put through all of that? The hot and miserable days with Oom Peter, the torment of falling in love and being so afraid he wouldn't love her back, the fear she'd not be able to save Harrison. That horrible fever, the crocodiles, that elephant! All those hours of research, of worry, why?

She turned her eyes searchingly to the sky, to the white clouds that angered her with their cheerful puffiness. What if she didn't find him in time before he returned to Africa?

How would she save him? Would she have to follow him? In wartime? And if by some miracle she succeeded in getting there, in finding him, would she be in time to stop the chain of events that led to his court-martial? Would he listen to her? Would he care about her at all if she was just some ordinary American woman instead of a vision in swirling lights? Why had she gone through so much only to have to start all over again?

"Don't do it. Whoever he is, he's not worth it."

Startled, Ivy blinked, turning her head as a shiver ran up her spine. The sun was to his back, so only his shape was discernible. He was tall and broad-shouldered, and his familiar, beloved voice lingered in the air, skimming over her skin like a caress. Her heart skidded to a thumping stop.

Her question had been answered.

She knew instantly, in her heart and soul, why everything had happened. She'd had to live it, to know it, all of it, in order to prevent it from happening. She had to love Harrison now, fiercely and confidently, if she were to have any chance of changing his fate and changing history.

He stood before her, unsmiling. He looked completely confused. He pushed his slouch hat back from his forehead and narrowed his wonderful blue eyes, as if studying her. He opened his mouth as if about to speak, but then closed it, remaining silent, regarding her intently.

"Hi," she said simply, so happy she felt she would burst with joy.

"Hallo. You aren't contemplating throwing yourself off the Eiffel, are you?"

"Huh?" she asked stupidly, too dazed, too happy, to follow his teasing words.

"I'd never seen anguish on such a sweet face before."

He came around beside her, bringing his face out of shadow and into sunlight as he whisked off his slouch hat.

Her breath caught. It wasn't that he was handsome or that his dimple was sexy or his eyes so very blue. It was simply that he was Harrison. And she loved him so much she was afraid she would simply shout the words at him any minute. She tore her gaze away and looked to the Eiffel Tower, that wonderful, romantic tower, her pulse racing wildly. She must not frighten him away. He didn't know her. He didn't yet know her.

"Women certainly are changeable creatures. Now you look as if you've just been crowned queen of England. May I?" He waved his hat toward the bench, and she nodded.

He sat, bouncing his hat playfully by the brim. A smile now teased the corners of his mouth.

"Lovely day to be in Paris, isn't it?"

She nodded.

"Do you speak? Or are you about to do another about-face? Warn me if you're going to scream. It wouldn't do my reputation any good at all."

"Reputation," she scoffed, a laugh bursting from her.

"What, you doubt I have one? Well, let me assure you I've got quite a dandy reputation. Unfortunately, it's all good. You could help me change that," he said, lifting his brows seductively. She continued giggling. "No?" He shrugged. "Well, I tried. Say, then, what did have you looking daggers?"

"I've been searching for someone," she said carefully.

"Ah." After a long silent moment, he continued, "Well, it looks as if you've found me. Will I do?"

"Yes," she said after another long pause, during which their eyes never parted.

"You're American?"

She nodded.

"On holiday?"

"Sort of. Yes."

"Evasive creature, and unpredictable. I like that in a beautiful woman." He took a deep breath of the spring air, stretched his long legs, then sighed with pleasure. "Paris in the spring with pleasant company? Life does not get any better."

He was being so playful, so flirtatious. She'd never seen him this way.

He tilted his head and studied the book laying open on her lap. "What's that you've got? Those are three of the pinkest pigs I've ever seen. A pig lover, are you?"

"No," she laughed. "I just like fairy tales."

"I see. I like that in a beautiful woman, too." He gave her a seductive, playful wink that sent her heart soaring. He looked again at the three pigs.

"Funny, in a way, to find you reading that particular tale. I've recently had a recurring dream about pigs."

Ivy bit her lip. Could it be? Could he really have some memory of things that had not yet happened? That might never happen?

"Tell me about the dream," she said in a breathless rush.

He shook his head with a grunt of laughter. "It's too bizarre to tell. Besides, I remember little of it."

He toyed with his hat, and a pulse throbbed at the base of his suddenly tense jaw.

Ivy stared. He was uncomfortable with his dream. Was it possible? Could he, deep down, remember? What was time, after all? Hadn't she learned that time wasn't some straightforward path that could only be traveled once, in a single direction? Time was a stream, a whole wonderful river, deep and wide, full of back eddies and undercurrents. His mind might not know her, not yet, but their souls had met and fallen in love. That really and truly had happened. And it had happened before now, in some strange other dimension, in some little back eddy of time. Surely souls did not forget falling in love. Surely such a love is everlasting.

He shot her a glance, and their eyes met again, sending her heart pounding furiously against her breast. It was there in his eyes.

She mustn't move too quickly. She must not frighten him!

She struggled to get her breath. "Are you on leave from South Africa?"

He ceased bouncing his slouch hat, and his shoulders heaved with a heavy sigh. "Yes. In fact, tomorrow, my leave is up."

"Oh?" she breathed, her voice sounding husky as she tried to control her desire to beg him not to end his leave. "We've only just met. It's a shame you're leaving so soon. I don't even know your name."

"That's easy to remedy." He sat up straight. "Lord Wyndham. Harrison, to you. I'm an earl, but don't let that bother you. You needn't call me my lord, unless you'd like to, of course. As it's wartime, I don't think we need hold with formalities." He extended a hand, and his family crest ring winked. She slipped her hand into his, thrilling in the roughness of his skin, the warmth of his palm, the steady strength of his pulse.

"Harrison," she echoed. "Harrison."

"Your hand is like ice," he said, chafing her hand gently with both of his. He returned her hand, now pink and warm, to her. "Have you heard of Wyndham?"

"The name is familiar to me."

"Wyndham is my home—a lovely estate in North Yorkshire County. We've a manor house that looks down on the sweetest village, all nestled in rolling green moorland." He sighed, wistfully, as if homesick, as if longing to return. "Have you been to England?"

"I don't think so."

"You don't think so?" He laughed softly, tossing his head back. He'd let go of his troubled thoughts, his bizarre dream, with a deep, contented breath. He was carefree and lighthearted, and she'd never seen him like this before. He was younger somehow, much younger than he'd been in Africa, in Seattle even. A young man who still believed in tomorrow.

She realized with an audible gasp just why.

Jeffrey. Of all the things which had not yet happened, Jeffrey's tortured death was the worst. But now, in this new now, Jeffrey, his beloved little brother, was still alive in South Africa. Alive. He'd not yet been hunted by the Boers, and Harrison had not yet found his mutilated body.

Harrison was watching her, amused and confused.

"You haven't told me your name," he said with teasing accusation.

"Ivy," she whispered. "Ivy O'Neal."

It was he who gasped this time.

"Do you recognize my name?"

"If I told you I heard that name in the same dream about pigs, would you be offended?"

She laughed and shook her head, and he suddenly tossed his hat aside and reached out to her. He touched her face with trembling fingertips. He traced her cheekbones, her jaw, her chin.

"I beg your pardon," he said, drawing away and reclaiming his hat. "I don't know what's come over me." His words were spoken lightly, but she heard a telltale quaver in his voice.

"I do," she whispered happily. "I do."

A shrill whistle carried from across the wide green lawn. Three soldiers in khaki waved, and Harrison waved back. He seemed glad for the intrusion. He seemed eager to get away. His relaxed posture had tensed, and he wrung the rim of his hat with nervous fingers.

"I must beg your pardon yet again," he said, getting hastily to his feet. "My mates are waiting. It's our last day in Paris, you understand."

She nodded, her heart racing wildly. He took a step away.

She must stop him, but how? How to keep him here without sounding foolish, without sounding crazy? Without frightening him away forever?

He looked down at her, as if not wanting to look again

into her eyes but unable to help himself. He dropped his gaze to his hat before he spoke. "It was a pleasure meeting you, Miss O'Neal." He lifted his gaze quickly again, a polite, tender smile trembling at his mouth. "I hope you enjoy your sort-of holiday and that you find whoever it is you're searching for. *Au revoir.*" He turned from her, tapping on his slouch hat.

Frozen with fear and indecisiveness, she could only stare at his departing back as he hurried toward his friends. He was halfway across the green before she sprang to her feet, dropping the book, gasping for breath, for words to shout. Her heart silently screaming as she stood frozen, watching him walk away.

He stopped. His back stiffened. He turned around.

Very slowly, he came walking back toward her, his stride strong and steady. He crossed the cut green grass, stepped onto the stone pavement of the boulevard, and finally stood before her.

She couldn't see him clearly through the blur of her tears. Her teeth chattered.

He bent, picked up the book of fairy tales, handing it to her.

She swallowed hard and blinked away her tears.

As he stared at her with a burning intensity, her heart and soul shouted silently, *I love you, I love you, I love you!*

"Miss O'Neal," he said earnestly. "Ivy," he added softly, as if testing the weight of it, the sound of it, on his tongue. "I don't know how to explain. It's rather the oddest sensation. I can't seem to leave you."

"You can't?" she whispered.

"Would you," he drew a breath. "Would you consider spending the day with me?"

The day, the year, a lifetime.

He added, "Please. Say you will. I don't think I could bear it if you said no."

"Neither could I," she said, smiling, trembling.

He extended a hand to her in invitation, and with joy flooding her heart, she slipped her hand in his.

39

Daisy dialed the Pig Palace, and asked for the manager.

"This is Bob Evanston. How can I help you?"

"This is Daisy, Ivy's aunt."

"I'm sorry, who?"

"Ivy's aunt. Ivy O'Neal."

"I'm sorry, ma'am. I don't know anybody by that name."

"Don't be ridiculous, young man. Ivy O'Neal. The checker. PJ," she said, in such a way that she conveyed her hatred of the nickname. "I'm calling to let you know she won't be back to work for a while." *Most likely never*, she thought but didn't say, just in case.

"We have no checker named Ivy O'Neal here. I think you have the wrong store."

Daisy held the phone away from her ear and stared at it as Bob's voice continued on, denying any knowledge of Ivy, saying he must go now because the checkstands were all out of order. All the scanners had burned to a crisp. His checkers were ringing orders with calculators. Slowly, Daisy hung up.

Burned to a crisp. All of them. How long would that take to repair? She couldn't help Ivy. Not for a long time. What if Ivy needed her soon?

She went through the living room, down the hall, then stood on the threshold of Ivy's bedroom. Everything sat as Ivy had left it—her bed, her dresser, her Pig Palace apron, stuffed animals, and memory box. And yet everything looked wrong. Daisy couldn't quite put her finger on it, but it was as if the room was hesitating somehow. Waiting, lingering in a way. But for what?

Earlier today, Daisy had telephoned Sophie to say she wasn't feeling up to their usual mall walk, and Sophie hadn't known who Ivy was either. Nobody remembered Ivy, except Daisy. It was all too much for an old lady to take. She staggered into the living room, past the bookshelves and pewter frames whose photographs reflected the same odd hesitation. She sat heavily in her easy chair.

So what had happened to Ivy last night? Was she safe? Had she found her Harrison and prevented his execution? Oh, there was so much to worry about!

When the doorbell rang a few minutes later, Daisy was nearly too upset to heave herself out of her chair. She managed to get to the door on the third ring to find the mailman there with an enormous registered package. The box was very heavy and awkward, and the mailman had to carry it in for her. He set it on her coffee table.

Daisy signed for it and shut the door. She got a knife from the kitchen, slit open the packing tape, then opened the flaps. Inside was an old-fashioned trunk with leather straps.

She unbuckled the straps and lifted the lid, revealing thick manila envelopes, dozens of them, all of them dated. The earliest was dated 1901, the last, 1970. And there was a pretty wooden jewelry case, which she couldn't resist peeking into. Inside on scarlet velvet lining were thimbles, dozens of them, each an antique and so very pretty.

"Oh, my goodness," she whispered.

Then one of the manila envelopes caught her eye. In bold black letters, it was labeled *Open First.*

Daisy began to tremble. The envelope was old, slightly yellowed, and musty. The handwriting was eerily familiar, slightly childish with its fat letters.

She took the envelope, and dropped into her easy chair.

The brittle flap peeled open easily, and she pulled out the letter.

May 20th, 1901

Dear Aunt Daisy,

I'm safe! I'm alive and happy and healthy, and everything's perfect except that you're not here.

I found Harrison.

"Oh, my," Daisy exclaimed as she hurriedly read about Paris and the Eiffel Tower.

Harrison proposed to me that very first night in Paris, and he took an extended leave from active duty. We got married just two weeks ago. Now, I'm at Darby House in London—a huge Victorian mansion.

I met his mother—she's classy and polite and a bit shocked, but so kind I'm sure we'll get along. And his younger brother, Stuart, is shy and sweet and a poet. Little Maggie, just twelve, is a rambunctious and beautiful girl. She laughs at me all the time because I make so many silly mistakes (did you know one must remove one's gloves and rest them on one's lap while drinking tea?)

I'm eager to meet Jeffrey. That's one of the most wonderful things that has happened. Harrison wired Joshua Pepper in South Africa, and managed to get Jeffrey transferred temporarily to a non-combat post in Pretoria. Jeffrey's furious about the transfer—and going to take leave as soon as he can to come home and yell at Harrison. Isn't that great! He may never understand, but that doesn't matter at all.

Harrison is amused by my "fortune-telling" but he indulges my "whims" nearly every time. He says when he looks into my eyes, he sees something there, a connection, and he has shadowy memories of what he calls "our past life together." I haven't told him I came from the future. He knows only that I have an Aunt Daisy in Seattle whom I love and miss very much.

It's strange, though. While my memories of you remain vivid, my knowledge of general history, of the future, is fading. I can't remember the outcome of the Boer war, or details of any war since. It's a relief, in a way. I couldn't possibly change all that is coming and make a perfect future for the world. My experience with trying to save Harrison taught me how easily I could make things worse. I'll simply have to do what I can within my own scope, and trust the future will be what it's supposed to be.

Harrison has set private investigators on Lord Fleming's trail, and already evidence is turning up to prove the baron's connection to Provisions Corp. With luck, soon Kyle and his father will never get the chance to hurt anyone ever again.

There's so much to tell you, I don't know where to begin. My plan is to write you a letter once a week, for the rest of my life. And I'm going to leave instructions with Harrison's solicitors (that's the English way of saying lawyers) that the letters are to be mailed to you, by future members of the firm or their assigns, so that they arrive on the day I left.

There is just one thing that bothers me. I'm not sure what is going to happen next month, in June, when I'm not only here in England, but also in Africa. I can't be in both places at once. I don't know which one of me will continue existing.

Daisy gasped, which sent her coughing. She reached for a tissue and wiped her eyes. When her vision was again clear, her glance caught the bookshelves. There were no pewter framed photographs of Ivy any longer. Daisy felt quite certain that if she went into Ivy's bedroom, none of her things would be there either.

She knew which Ivy had continued on—the Ivy who had written her this letter.

Ivy had travelled—irrevocably—to Harrison. The destruction of the scanners had somehow sealed history. The arrival of her letters had been the final step in her departure. Daisy knew she should be feeling terribly upset that Ivy was so completely gone from her life, but she didn't. She was far too happy that Ivy was safe, that she had found her Harrison, and that she had found a way to talk to her across this strange separation.

With a smile, and a renewed energy, she turned again to Ivy's letter.

I feel deep down that it would be wrong to use my situation for personal financial gain, but, before I forget them, I've written down the names of a few companies I'll invest in when they go public. Not for me, but for you. I want to know that you're well provided for, and I'd love for you to be able to travel. Come see England, come visit Wyndham, in North Yorkshire. It's the most magical place on earth. When Harrison's duty is up, we'll move there and stay forever as lord and lady of the manor.

I'm going to get Harrison's mother on a good diet whether she likes it or not, and I'm going to do all I can to help Jeffrey and Stuart and Maggie live full and happy lives.

Oh, Daisy, thanks to those wonderful, crazy scanners—thanks to my mom and dad, who I'm sure played a guiding hand—and thanks to you!—I'm the happiest girl in the world. It's all so wonderful!

Daisy paused, frowning. She set the letter aside, got to her feet again, and returned to the trunk. She was never one to enjoy a book unless she knew the ending, and the same went for letters. She began looking for the newest envelopes, pausing for a moment to gape at the gilded green certificates of stock with the letters IBM. My heavens! She might very well be rich!

At last she chose—not the final envelope—but a thick one about three-quarters of the way into the lot. It was dated September 1945. She opened the flap, reached inside, and pulled out an eight-by-ten black-and-white photograph of about two dozen people of assorted ages, whom she didn't know. She recognized the place from Ivy's history books as the curved steps of Wyndham Manor.

The clothes, too, brought back pleasant memories, for Daisy had been a little girl in 1945. In her opinion, it was one of the best dress eras. The narrow waists and broad shoulders of women's clothing were so flattering. Those were the days when men still wore suits and women wore dresses that sufficiently covered the knees.

Everyone in the photograph was either waving, or making a silly face, or holding a square of paper with a letter on it. In the top center of the photograph was a tall silver-haired grandfatherly man, his face in profile as he gave an exaggerated kiss to a shorter white-haired woman in a pill box hat, who in turn was blowing a kiss toward the camera.

Daisy eyed the photo a bit more closely. Dear heavens, that was no grandmother; that was Ivy! Ivy—looking nearly the spitting image of her own great-grandma Rosie—which meant that handsome old man beside her must be Harrison.

Look how happy they were!

Daisy extended her arm, and eyed the photograph from a distance. Suddenly, the squares of paper with their letters formed words. They spelled *Hello Aunt Daisy*.

"Oh, my heavens!" Daisy exclaimed, a hand going to her breast. She turned the photograph over. On the back was written, in Ivy's handwriting, the following:

Forty-fourth annual "Wave to Aunt Daisy Photo," September 23, 1945.

An especially precious gathering as nearly everyone at last is home, WWII finally ended. Not pictured, Maggie's son Robert, still in France, but reported to be safe and hopefully home soon; and Mama Louisa, whom we lost this spring at the age of 93.

Top row, Jeffrey (69), his wife Hannah; Maggie (57), her husband Tyler; Harrison (74), me (70—can you believe it?); Stuart (63); and Joshua Pepper and his wife Linda

Second Row—our children: Walter (42), his wife Dee; Bill (40), his wife Penelope; Daisy (your namesake, now 36), her husband Julian; and our baby Rose (31) and her husband John.

Third and Fourth Rows—our grandchildren . . . .

Daisy sighed contentedly. She took the envelope back to her chair and settled herself comfortably.

She could read now, quite happily, and enjoy the ups and downs of Ivy's life, the joys and sorrows the letters would surely reveal. Because now she was assured that Ivy's life—all of their lives—had turned out just the way she'd been hoping and praying. It was very satisfying for an old woman. Life's mysteries were indeed wonderful, and it was a joy to discover such magic at this late stage. Life on Mars? Surely, there could be. But wasn't life on Earth just as incredible? Yes, indeed. Life anywhere was incredible. And love. Well, love knew no earthly bounds. Heaven seemed to have master control over that.

Daisy lifted her eyes to the ceiling. "Thank you," she whispered. "Thank you for taking care of our precious girl."

She pulled a letter from the envelope, blinking away tears of joy, believing more strongly than ever in happily ever after.

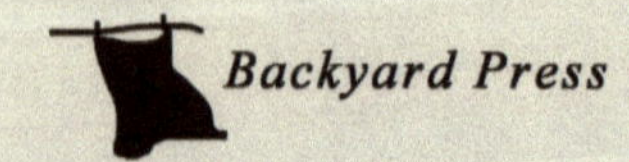
Backyard Press

www.ingramcontent.com/pod-product-compliance
Lightning Source LLC
Chambersburg PA
CBHW051938240626
47153CB00005B/1539

* 9 7 8 0 6 9 2 4 3 4 9 4 9 *